CVO
covert vampiric operations™

ROGUE STATE

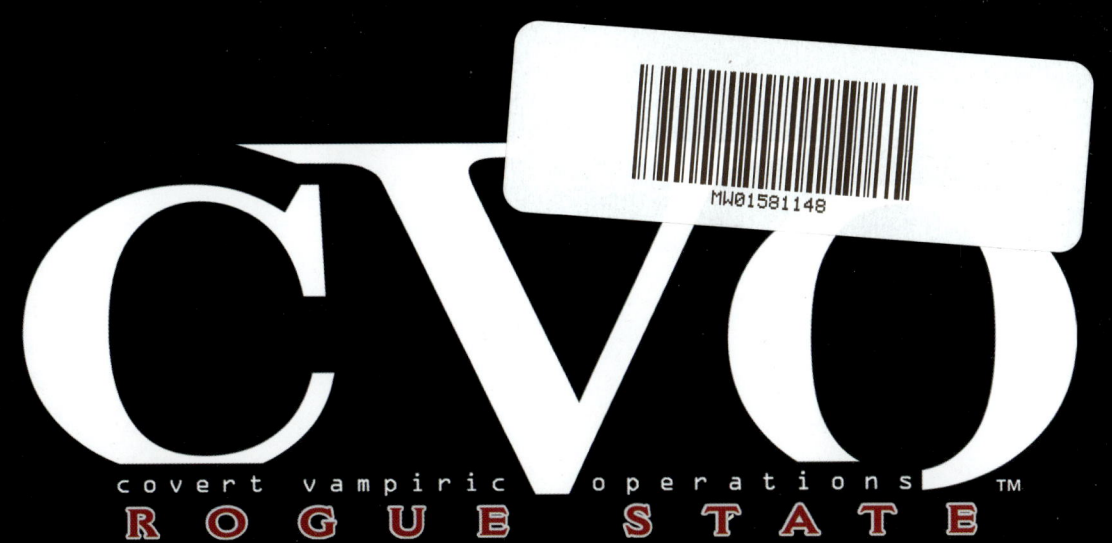

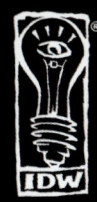

IDW Publishing
San Diego, CA

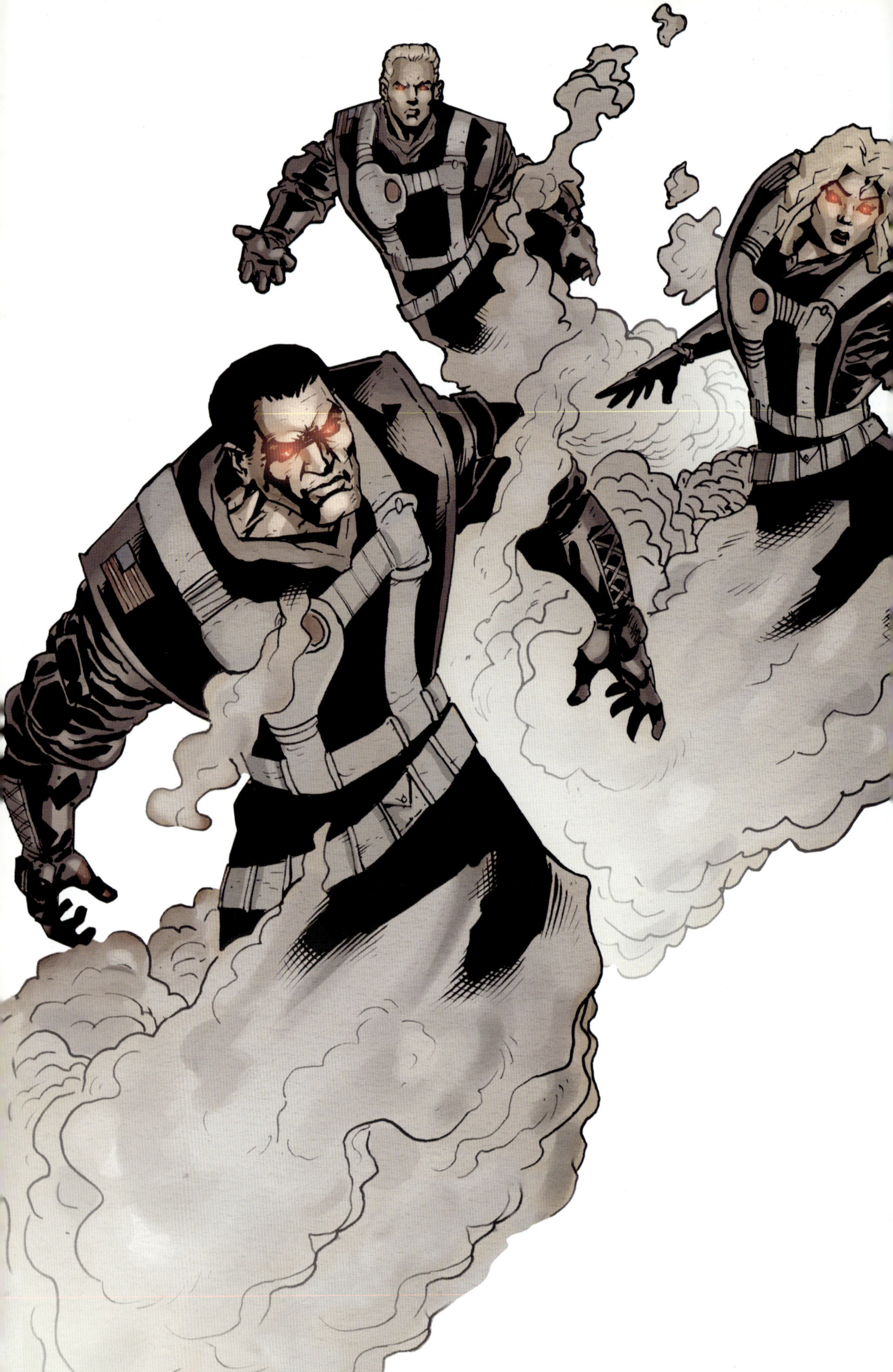

CVO
ROGUE STATE

CVO created by
Alex Garner

Written by
Jeff Mariotte

Pencils and Inks by
Antonio Vazquez, Sulaco Studios

Colors by
Fran Gamboa, Sulaco Studios

Lettered by
Tom B. Long

Original Series Edited by
Kris Oprisko

Edited by
Alex Garner

Designed by
Tom B. Long

www.idwpublishing.com
ISBN: 1-978-932382-93-8
10 09 08 07   2 3 4 5

IDW Publishing is:
Ted Adams, President
Robbie Robbins, EVP/Sr. Graphic Artist
Chris Ryall, Publisher/Editor-in-Chief
Clifford Meth, EVP of Strategies/Editorial
Alan Payne, VP of Sales
Neil Uyetake, Art Director
Justin Eisinger, Editor
Tom Waltz, Editor
Andrew Steven Harris, Editor
Chris Mowry, Graphic Artist
Amauri Osorio, Graphic Artist
Matthew Ruzicka, CPA, Controller
Alonzo Simon, Shipping Manager
Kris Oprisko, Editor/Foreign Lic. Rep.

CVO: COVERT VAMPIRIC OPERATIONS: ROGUE STATE. DECEMBER 2007. SECOND PRINTING. IDW Publishing, a division of Idea and Design Works, LLC. Editorial offices: 4411 Morena Blvd., Suite 106, San Diego, CA 92117. CVO is ™ and © 2007 IDW Publishing and Konami. KONAMI® is a registered trademark of KONAMI CORPORATION. All Rights Reserved. The IDW logo is registered in the U.S. Patent and Trademark Office. Originally published as CVO: Covert Vampiric Operations–Rogue State #1-5. Any similarities to persons living or dead are purely coincidental. With the exception of artwork used for review purposes, none of the contents of this publication may be reprinted without the permission of Idea and Design Works, LLC. Printed in Korea.

CHAPTER ONE

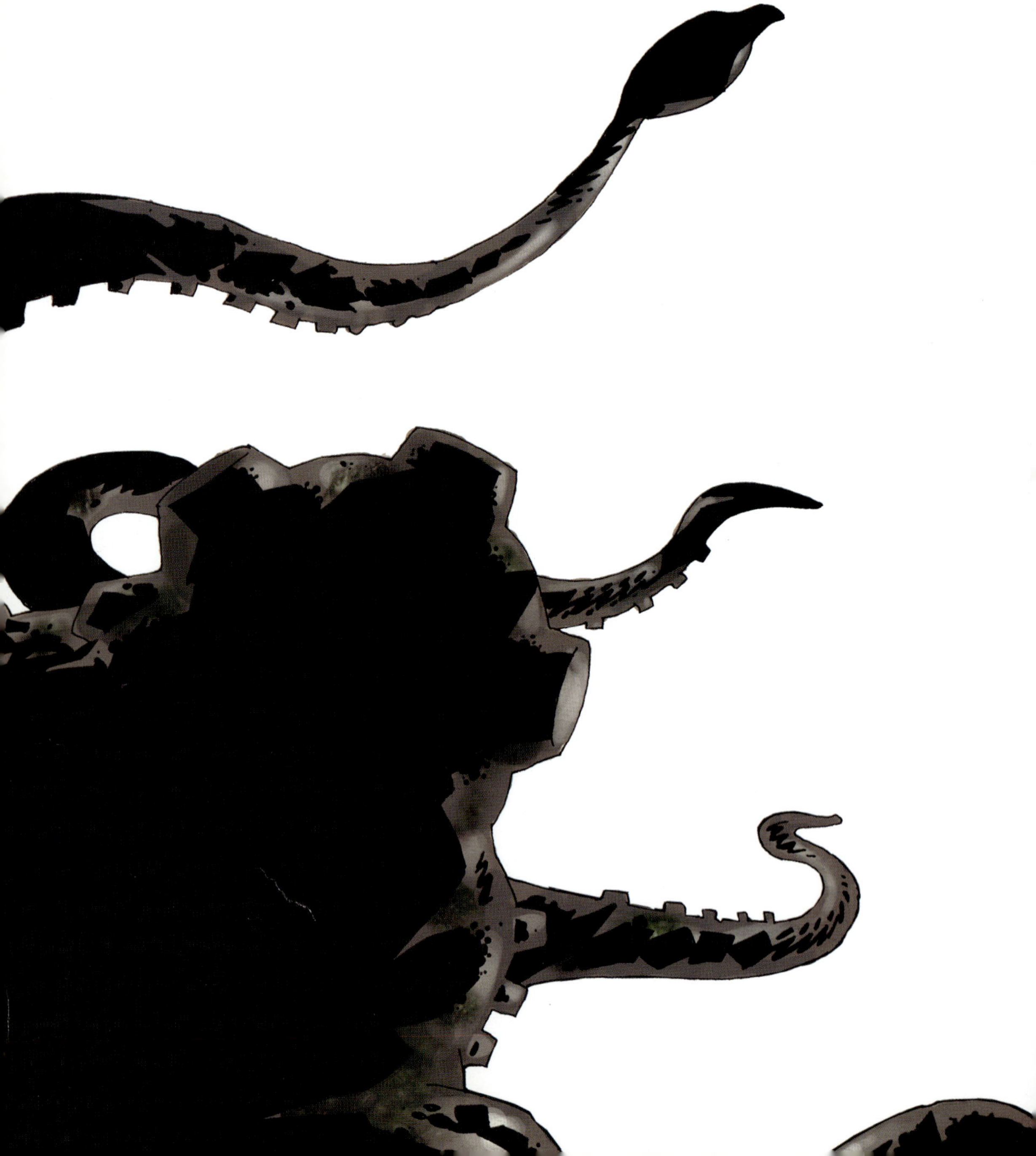

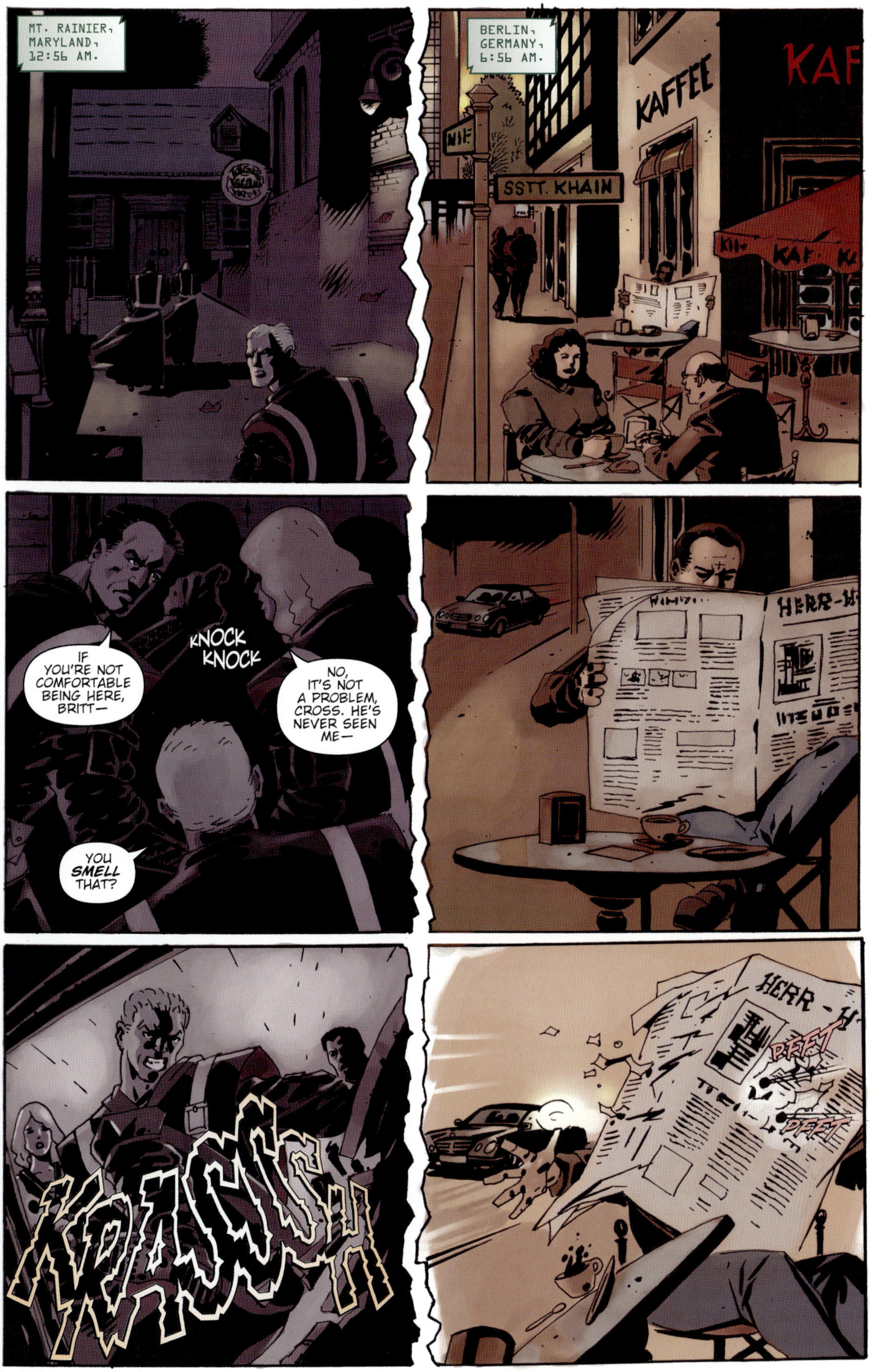
MT. RAINIER, MARYLAND, 12:56 AM.
BERLIN, GERMANY, 6:56 AM.
KAFFEE
SSTT. KHAIN
IF YOU'RE NOT COMFORTABLE BEING HERE, BRITT—
KNOCK KNOCK
NO, IT'S NOT A PROBLEM, CROSS. HE'S NEVER SEEN ME—
YOU **SMELL** THAT?

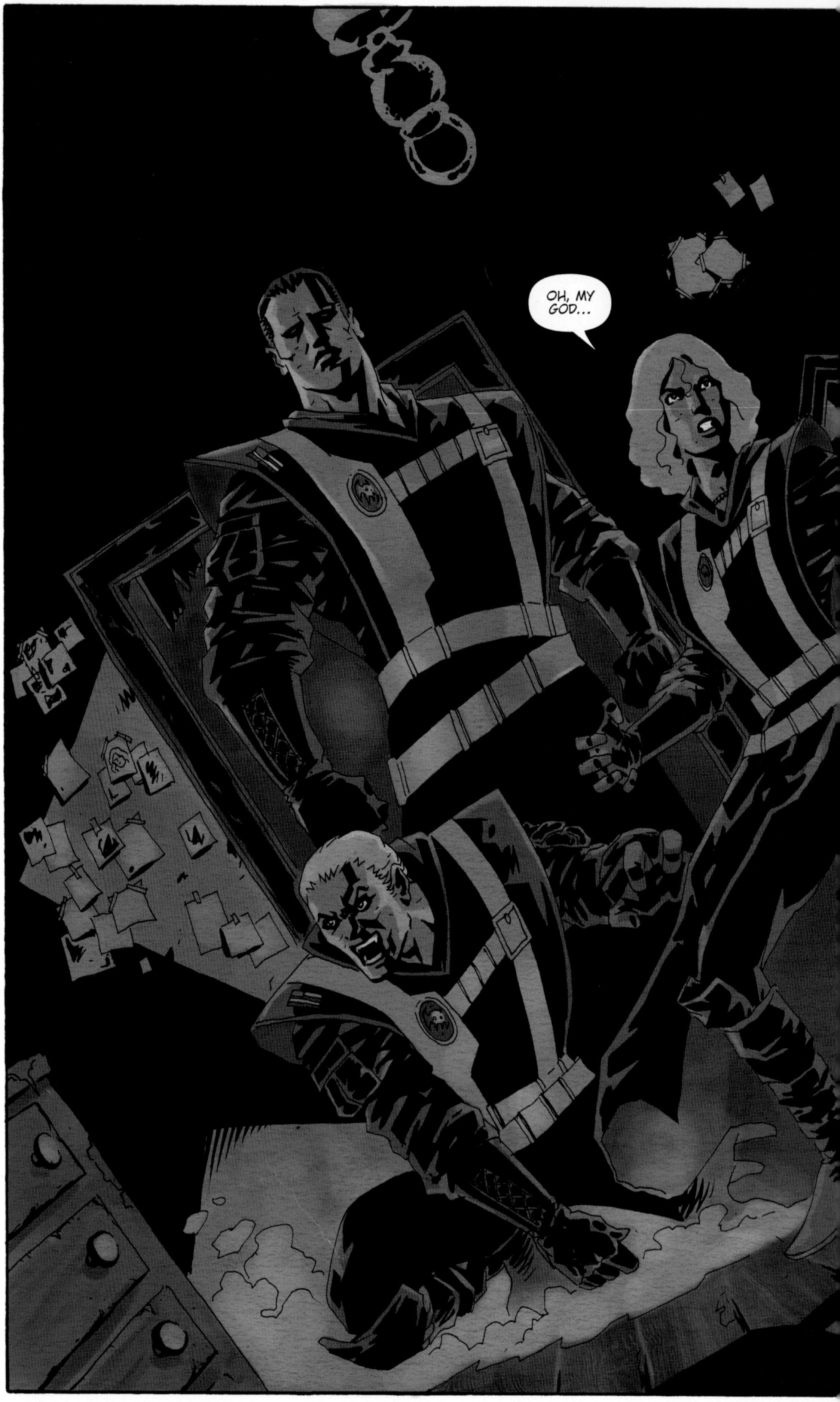
OH, MY GOD...

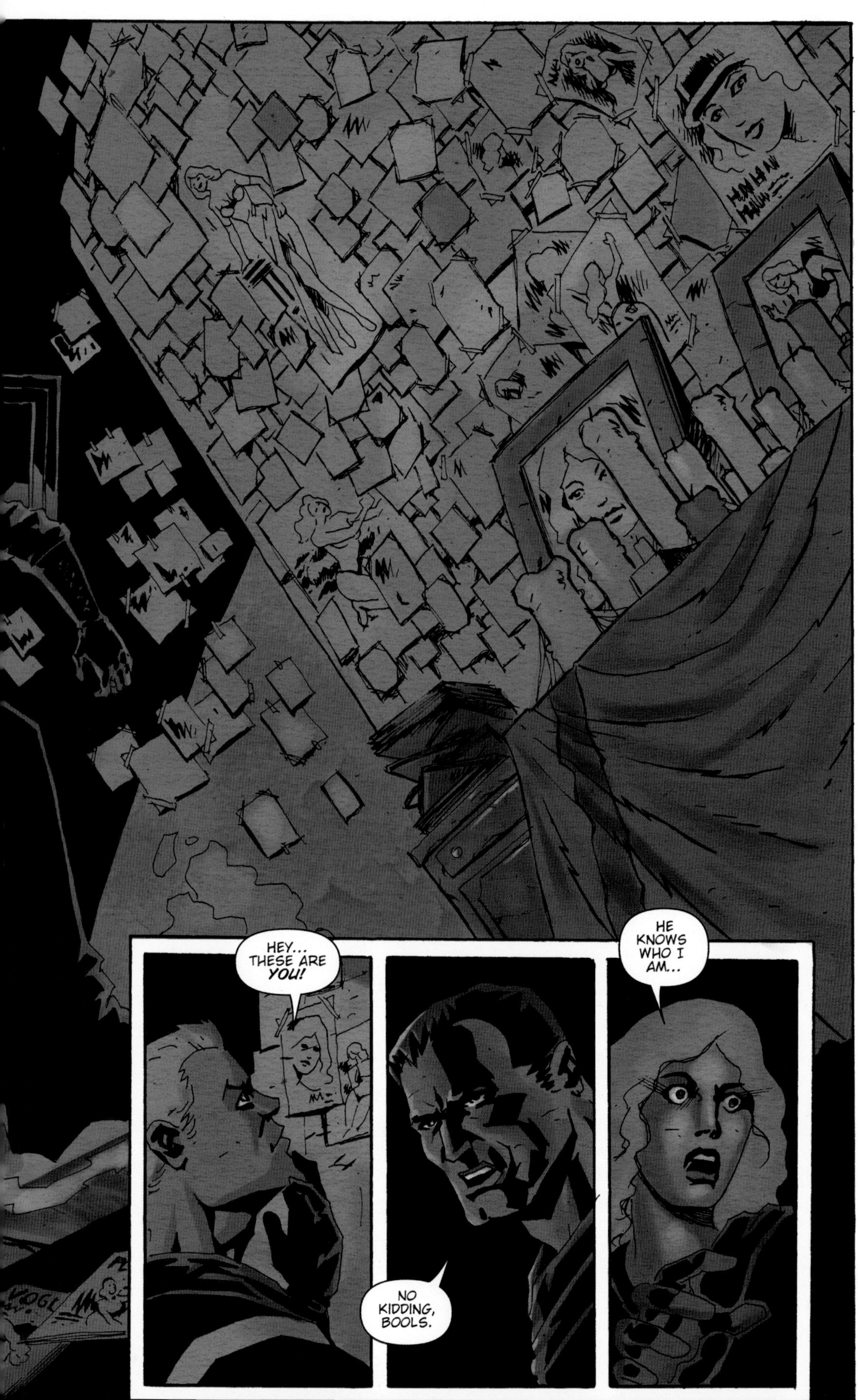
HEY... THESE ARE YOU!
NO KIDDING, BOOLS.
HE KNOWS WHO I AM...

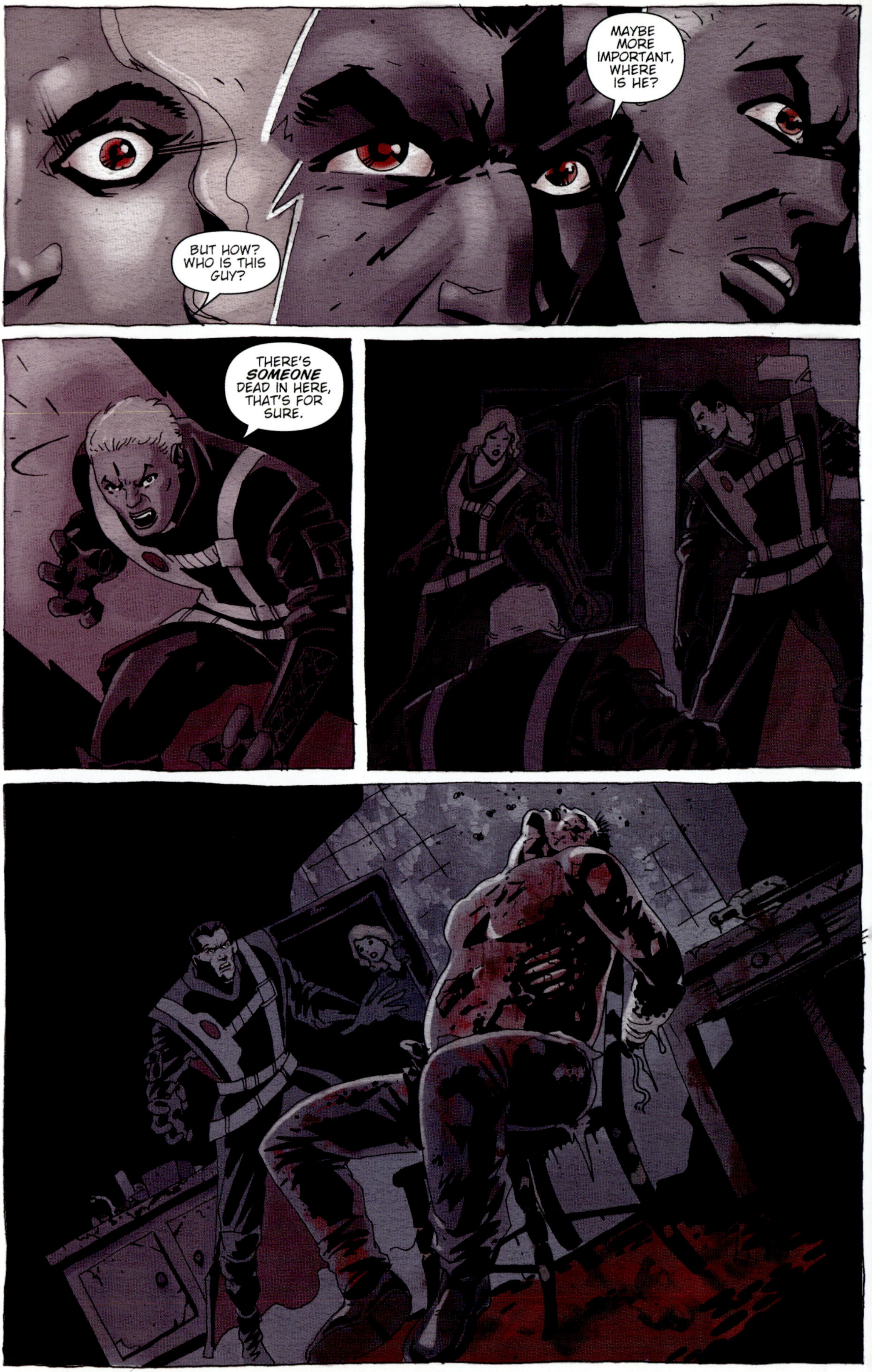
BUT HOW? WHO IS THIS GUY?
MAYBE MORE IMPORTANT, WHERE IS HE?
THERE'S *SOMEONE* DEAD IN HERE, THAT'S FOR SURE.

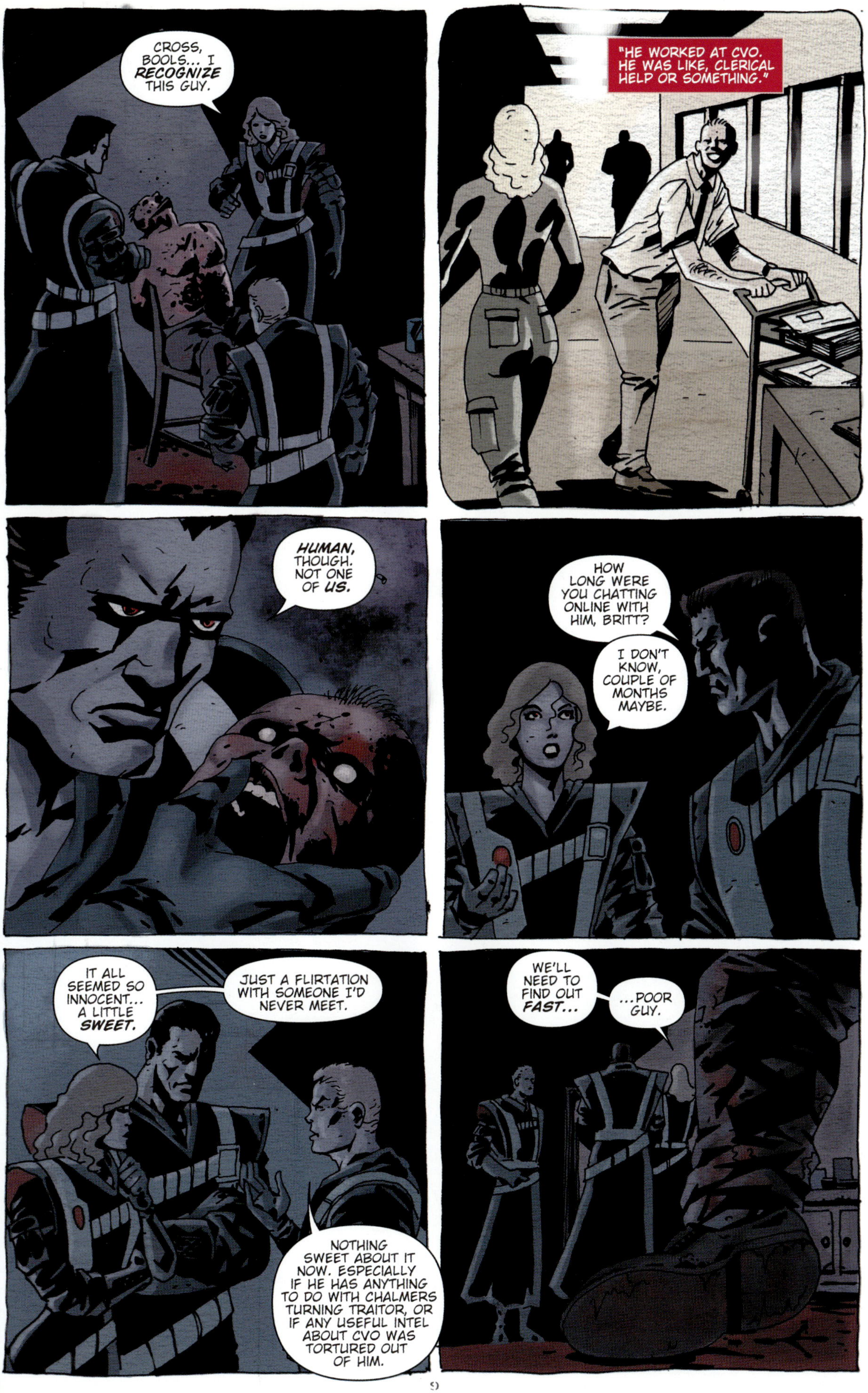

CROSS, BOOLS... I RECOGNIZE THIS GUY.
"HE WORKED AT CVO. HE WAS LIKE, CLERICAL HELP OR SOMETHING."
HUMAN, THOUGH. NOT ONE OF US.
HOW LONG WERE YOU CHATTING ONLINE WITH HIM, BRITT?
I DON'T KNOW, COUPLE OF MONTHS MAYBE.
IT ALL SEEMED SO INNOCENT... A LITTLE SWEET.
JUST A FLIRTATION WITH SOMEONE I'D NEVER MEET.
NOTHING SWEET ABOUT IT NOW. ESPECIALLY IF HE HAS ANYTHING TO DO WITH CHALMERS TURNING TRAITOR, OR IF ANY USEFUL INTEL ABOUT CVO WAS TORTURED OUT OF HIM.
WE'LL NEED TO FIND OUT FAST...
...POOR GUY.

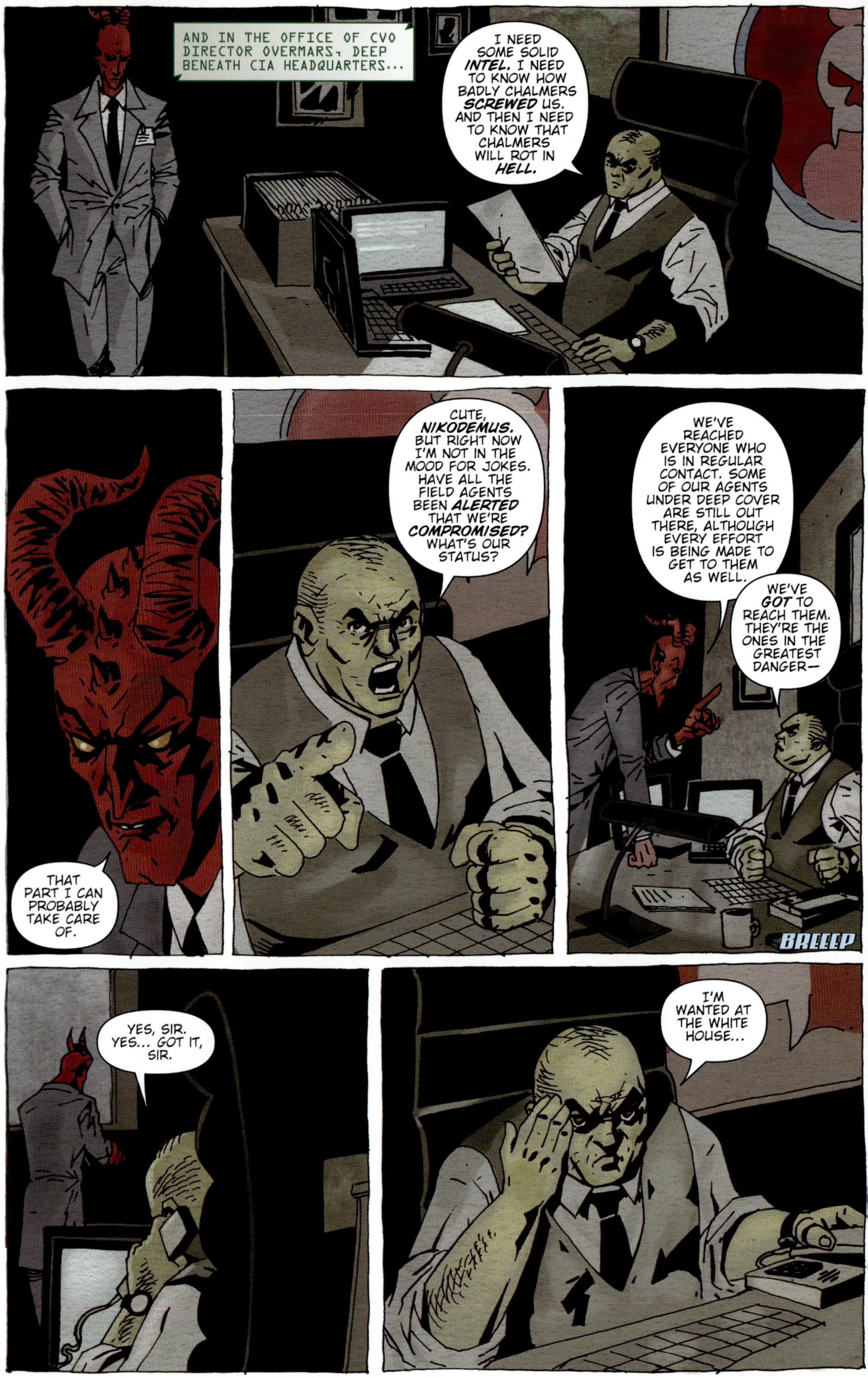

AND IN THE OFFICE OF CVO DIRECTOR OVERMARS, DEEP BENEATH CIA HEADQUARTERS...
I NEED SOME SOLID INTEL. I NEED TO KNOW HOW BADLY CHALMERS SCREWED US. AND THEN I NEED TO KNOW THAT CHALMERS WILL ROT IN HELL.
THAT PART I CAN PROBABLY TAKE CARE OF.
CUTE, NIKODEMUS. BUT RIGHT NOW I'M NOT IN THE MOOD FOR JOKES. HAVE ALL THE FIELD AGENTS BEEN ALERTED THAT WE'RE COMPROMISED? WHAT'S OUR STATUS?
WE'VE REACHED EVERYONE WHO IS IN REGULAR CONTACT. SOME OF OUR AGENTS UNDER DEEP COVER ARE STILL OUT THERE, ALTHOUGH EVERY EFFORT IS BEING MADE TO GET TO THEM AS WELL.
WE'VE GOT TO REACH THEM. THEY'RE THE ONES IN THE GREATEST DANGER—
BREEEP
YES, SIR. YES... GOT IT, SIR.
I'M WANTED AT THE WHITE HOUSE...

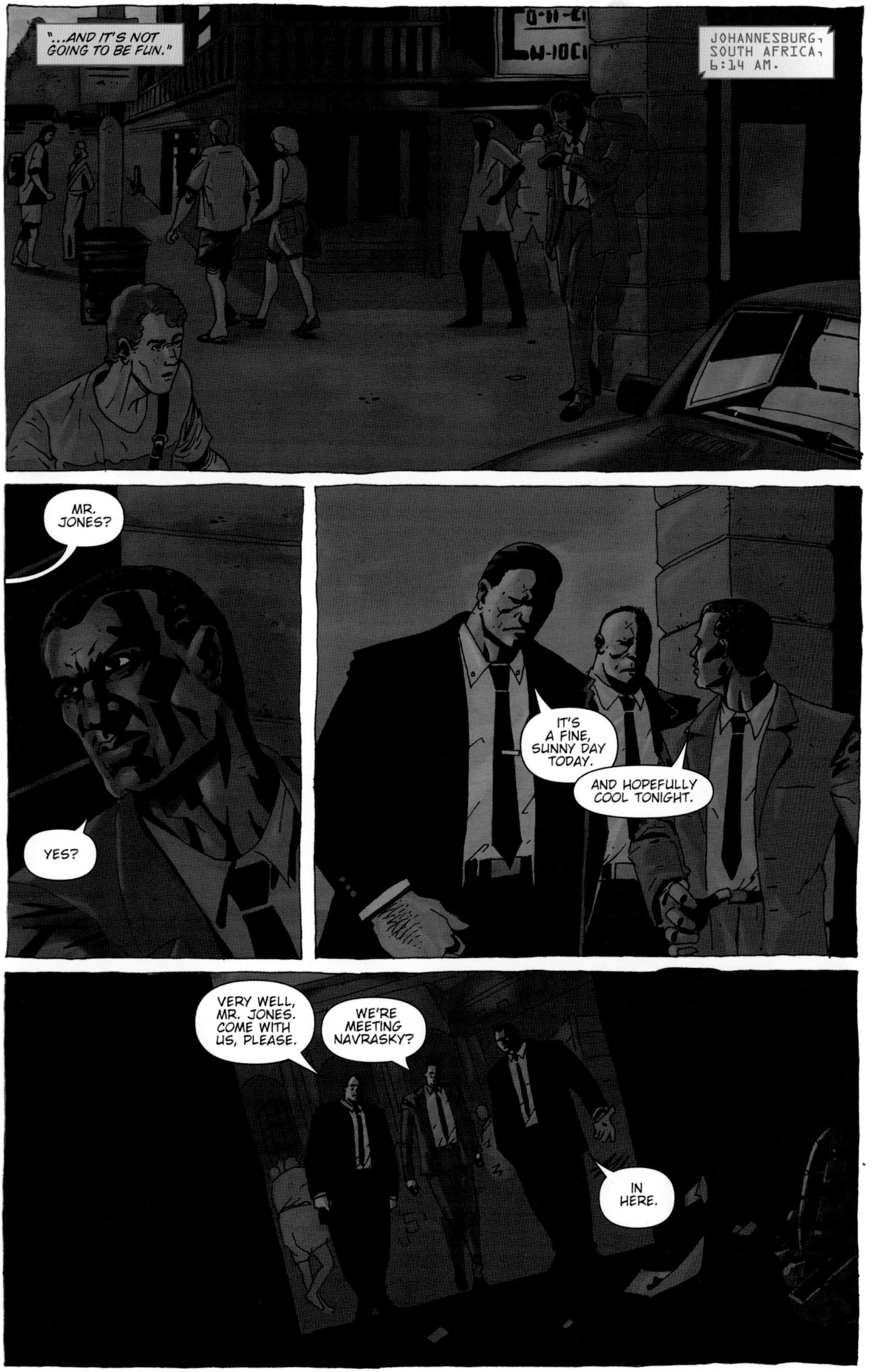
"...AND IT'S NOT GOING TO BE FUN."
JOHANNESBURG, SOUTH AFRICA, 6:14 AM.
MR. JONES?
YES?
IT'S A FINE, SUNNY DAY TODAY.
AND HOPEFULLY COOL TONIGHT.
VERY WELL, MR. JONES. COME WITH US, PLEASE.
WE'RE MEETING NAVRASKY?
IN HERE.

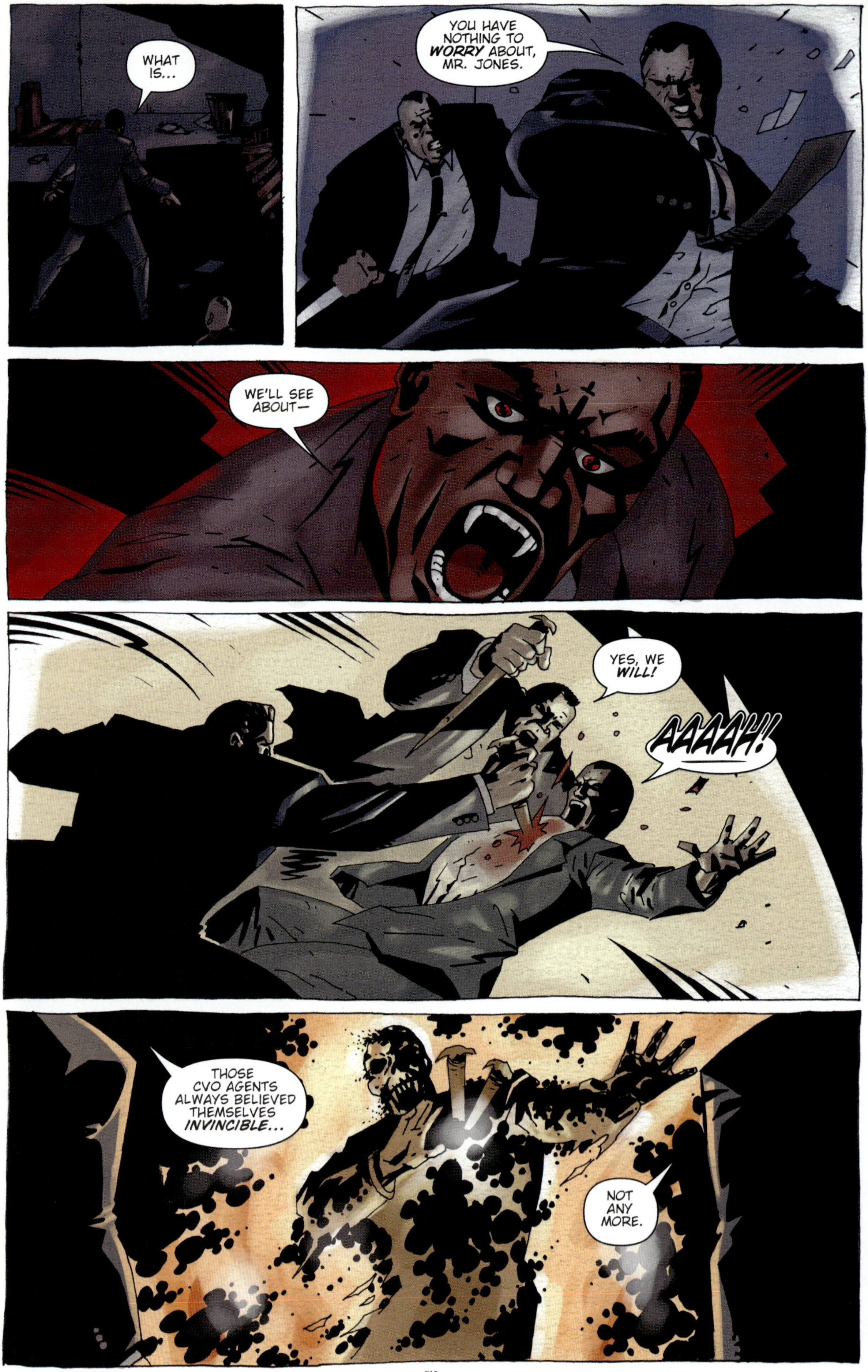
WHAT IS...
YOU HAVE NOTHING TO WORRY ABOUT, MR. JONES.
WE'LL SEE ABOUT—
YES, WE WILL!
AAAAH!
THOSE CVO AGENTS ALWAYS BELIEVED THEMSELVES INVINCIBLE...
NOT ANY MORE.

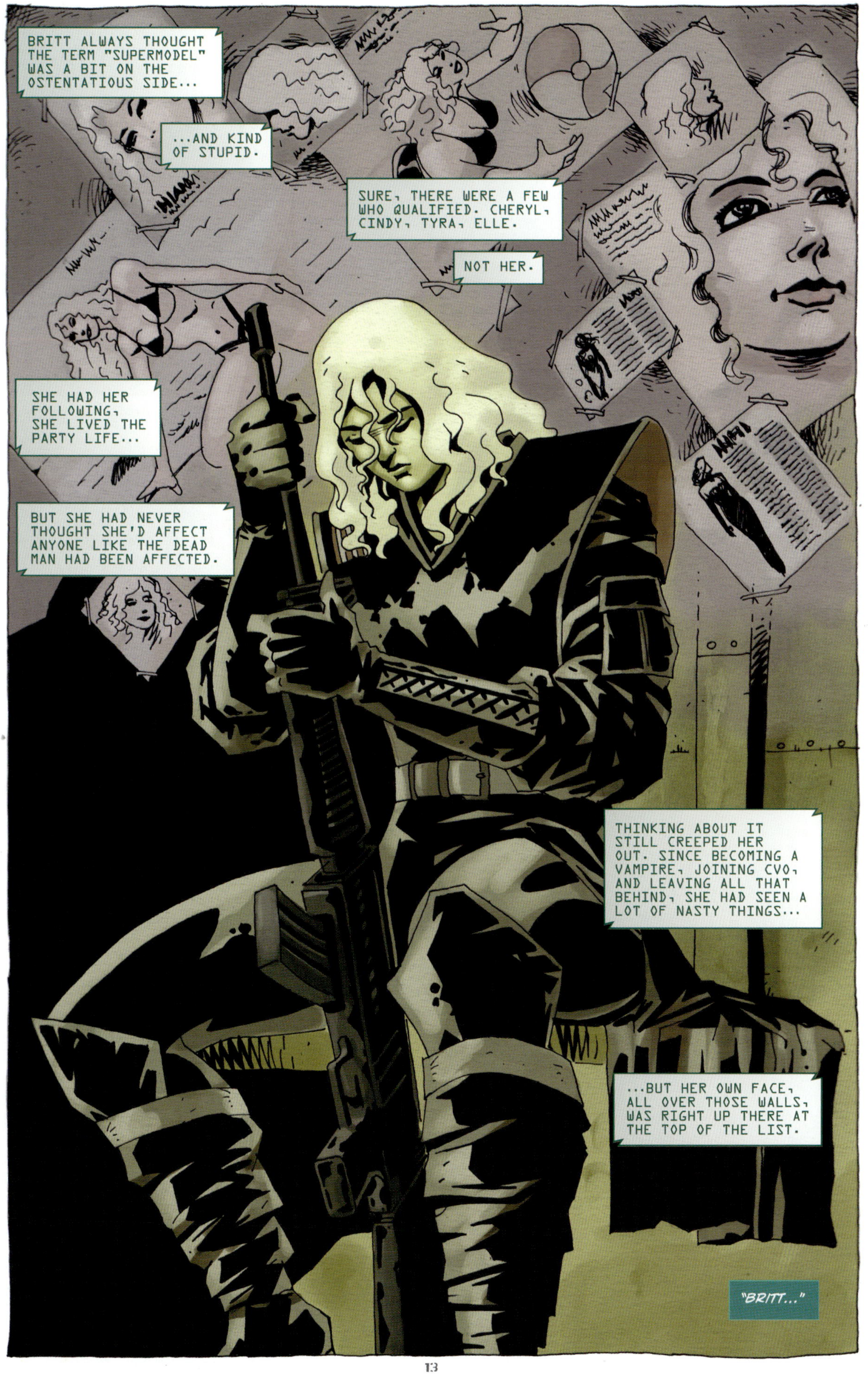
BRITT ALWAYS THOUGHT THE TERM "SUPERMODEL" WAS A BIT ON THE OSTENTATIOUS SIDE...
...AND KIND OF STUPID.
SURE, THERE WERE A FEW WHO QUALIFIED. CHERYL, CINDY, TYRA, ELLE.
NOT HER.
SHE HAD HER FOLLOWING, SHE LIVED THE PARTY LIFE...
BUT SHE HAD NEVER THOUGHT SHE'D AFFECT ANYONE LIKE THE DEAD MAN HAD BEEN AFFECTED.
THINKING ABOUT IT STILL CREEPED HER OUT. SINCE BECOMING A VAMPIRE, JOINING CVO, AND LEAVING ALL THAT BEHIND, SHE HAD SEEN A LOT OF NASTY THINGS...
...BUT HER OWN FACE, ALL OVER THOSE WALLS, WAS RIGHT UP THERE AT THE TOP OF THE LIST.
"BRITT..."

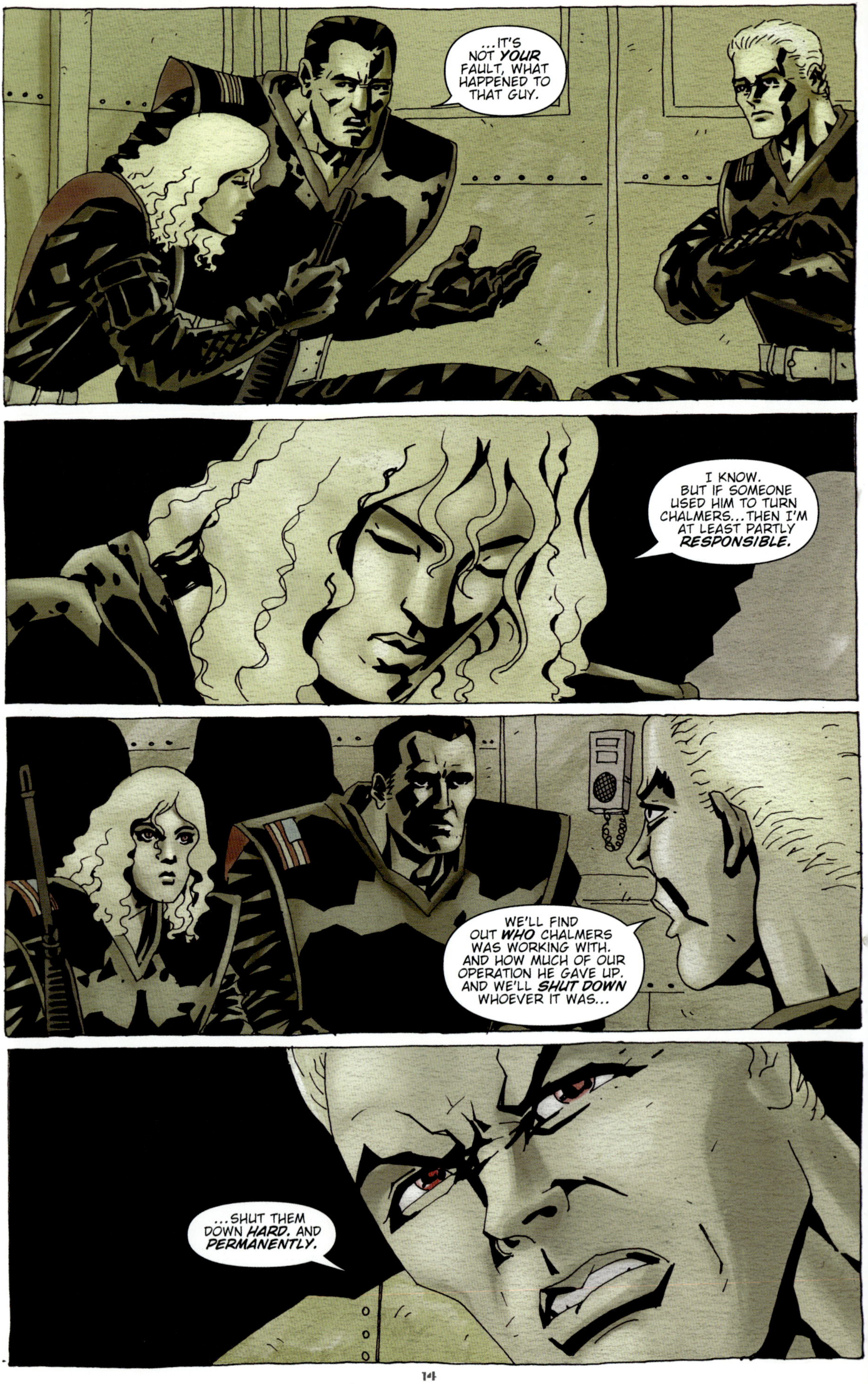
...IT'S NOT YOUR FAULT, WHAT HAPPENED TO THAT GUY.
I KNOW. BUT IF SOMEONE USED HIM TO TURN CHALMERS... THEN I'M AT LEAST PARTLY RESPONSIBLE.
WE'LL FIND OUT WHO CHALMERS WAS WORKING WITH. AND HOW MUCH OF OUR OPERATION HE GAVE UP. AND WE'LL SHUT DOWN WHOEVER IT WAS...
...SHUT THEM DOWN HARD. AND PERMANENTLY.

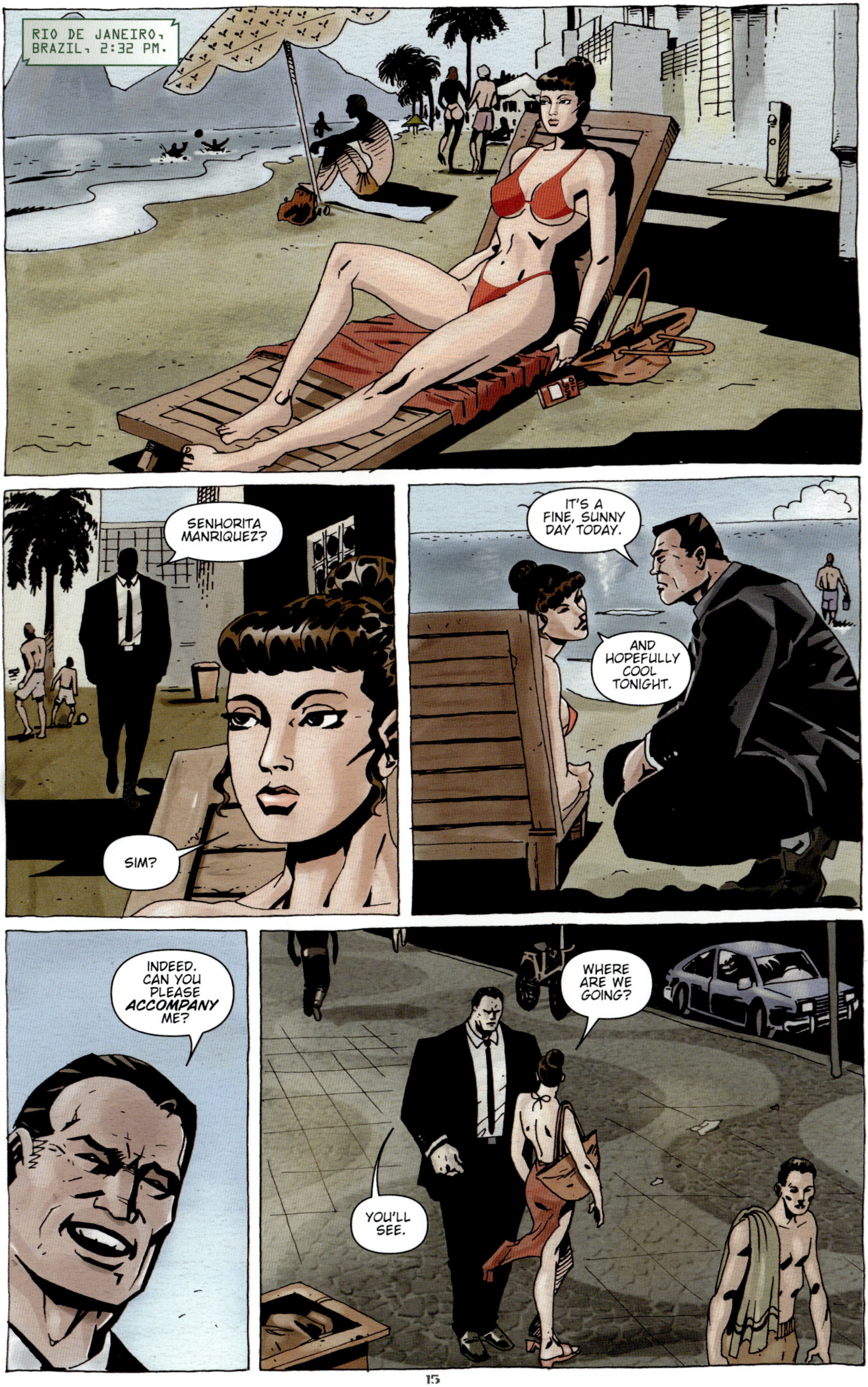
RIO DE JANEIRO, BRAZIL, 2:32 PM.
SENHORITA MANRIQUEZ?
SIM?
IT'S A FINE, SUNNY DAY TODAY.
AND HOPEFULLY COOL TONIGHT.
INDEED. CAN YOU PLEASE *ACCOMPANY* ME?
WHERE ARE WE GOING?
YOU'LL SEE.

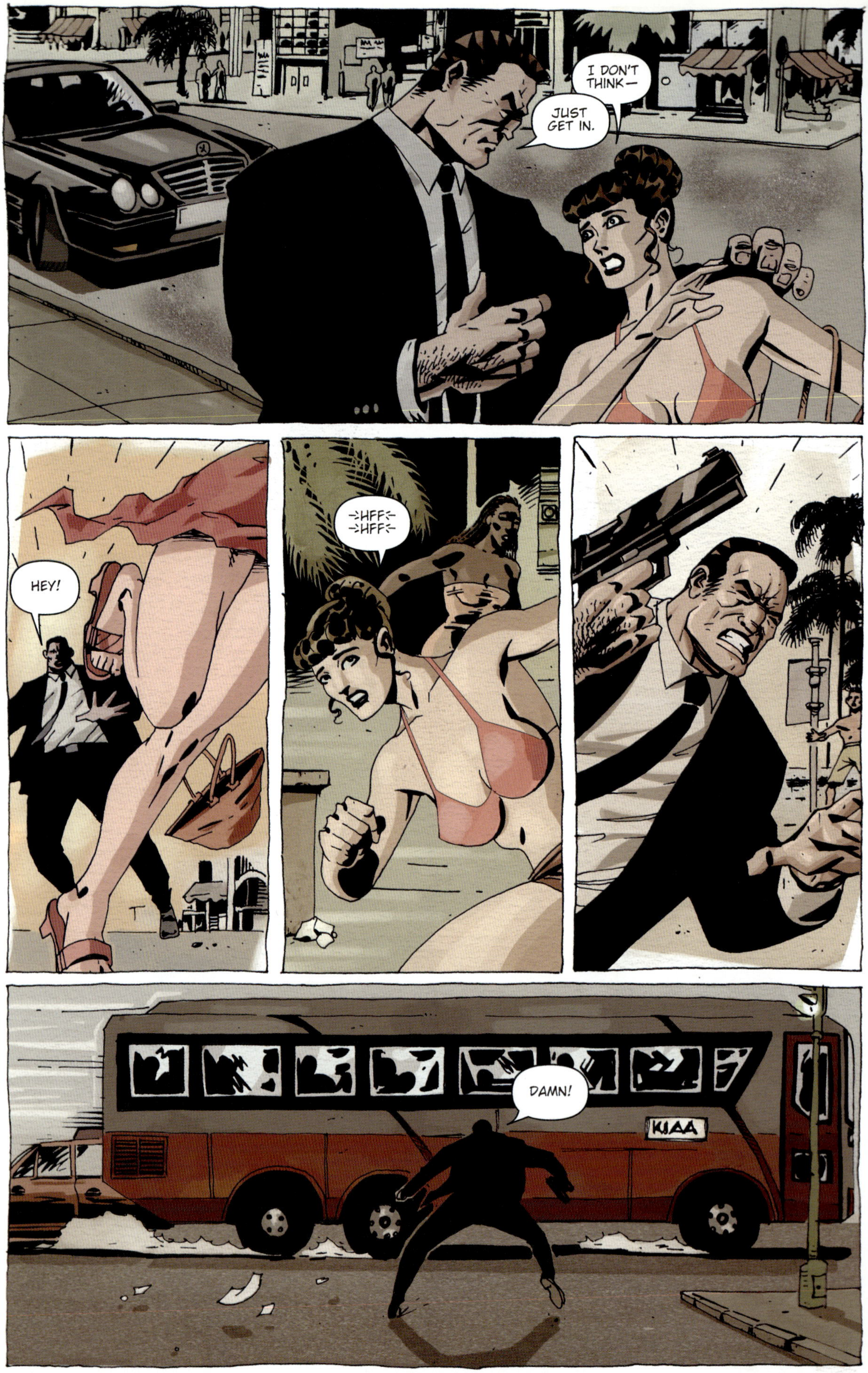
I DON'T THINK—
JUST GET IN.
HEY!
HFF HFF
DAMN!
KIAA

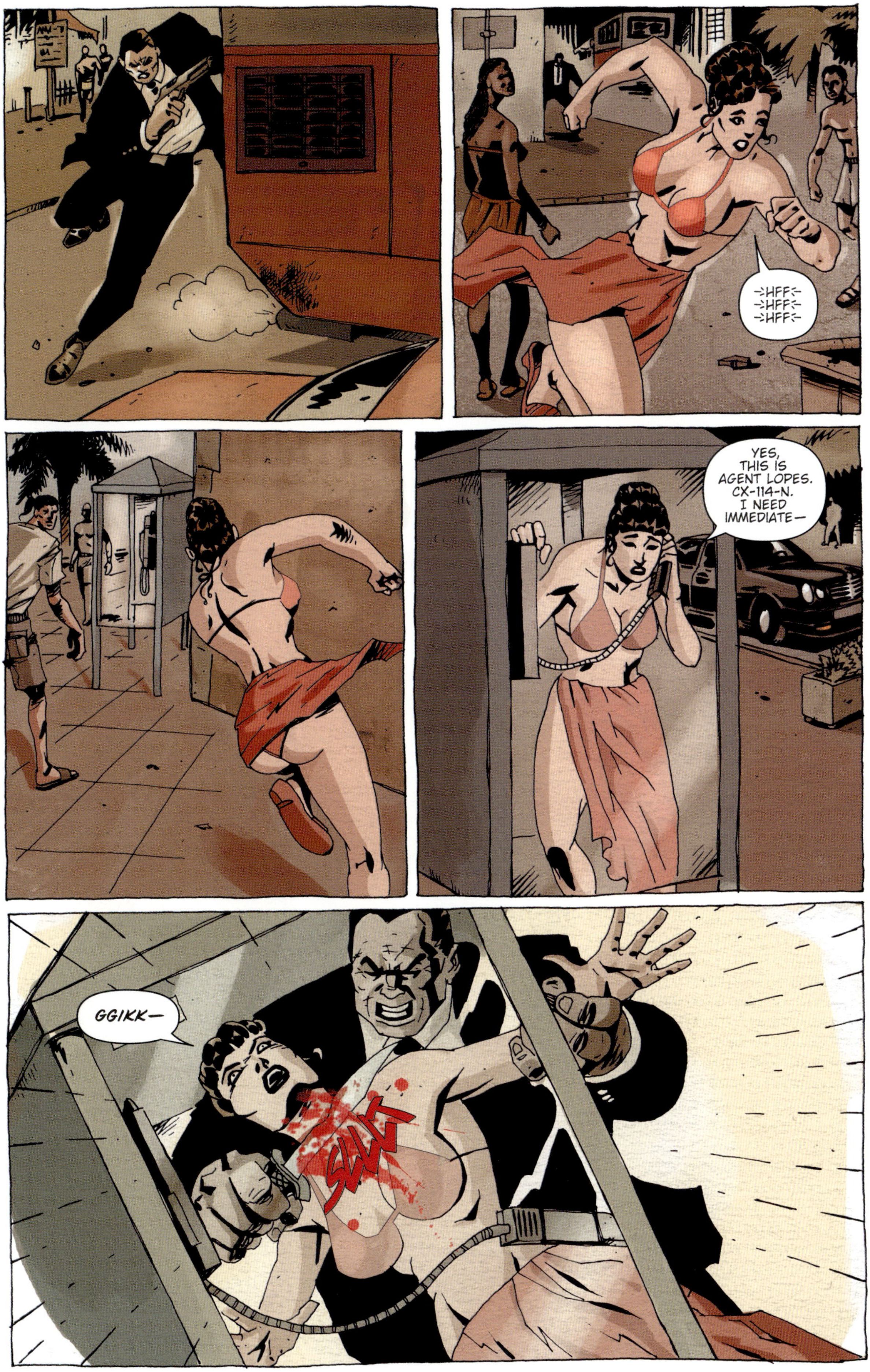

HFF
HFF
HFF
YES, THIS IS AGENT LOPES. CX-114-N. I NEED IMMEDIATE—
GGIKK—
SLUT

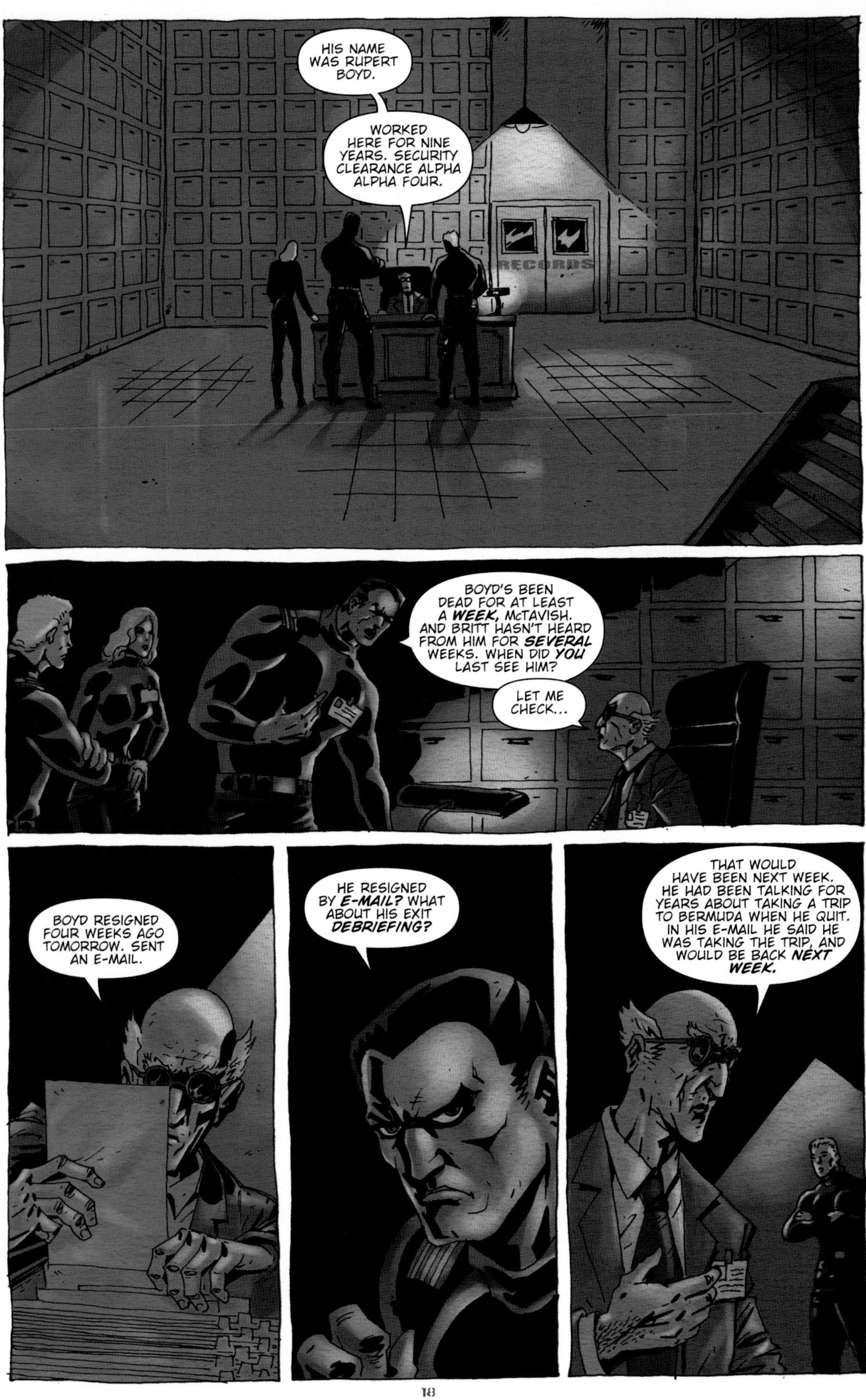
HIS NAME WAS RUPERT BOYD.
WORKED HERE FOR NINE YEARS. SECURITY CLEARANCE ALPHA ALPHA FOUR.
RECORDS
BOYD'S BEEN DEAD FOR AT LEAST A WEEK, McTAVISH. AND BRITT HASN'T HEARD FROM HIM FOR SEVERAL WEEKS. WHEN DID YOU LAST SEE HIM?
LET ME CHECK...
BOYD RESIGNED FOUR WEEKS AGO TOMORROW. SENT AN E-MAIL.
HE RESIGNED BY E-MAIL? WHAT ABOUT HIS EXIT DEBRIEFING?
THAT WOULD HAVE BEEN NEXT WEEK. HE HAD BEEN TALKING FOR YEARS ABOUT TAKING A TRIP TO BERMUDA WHEN HE QUIT. IN HIS E-MAIL HE SAID HE WAS TAKING THE TRIP, AND WOULD BE BACK NEXT WEEK.

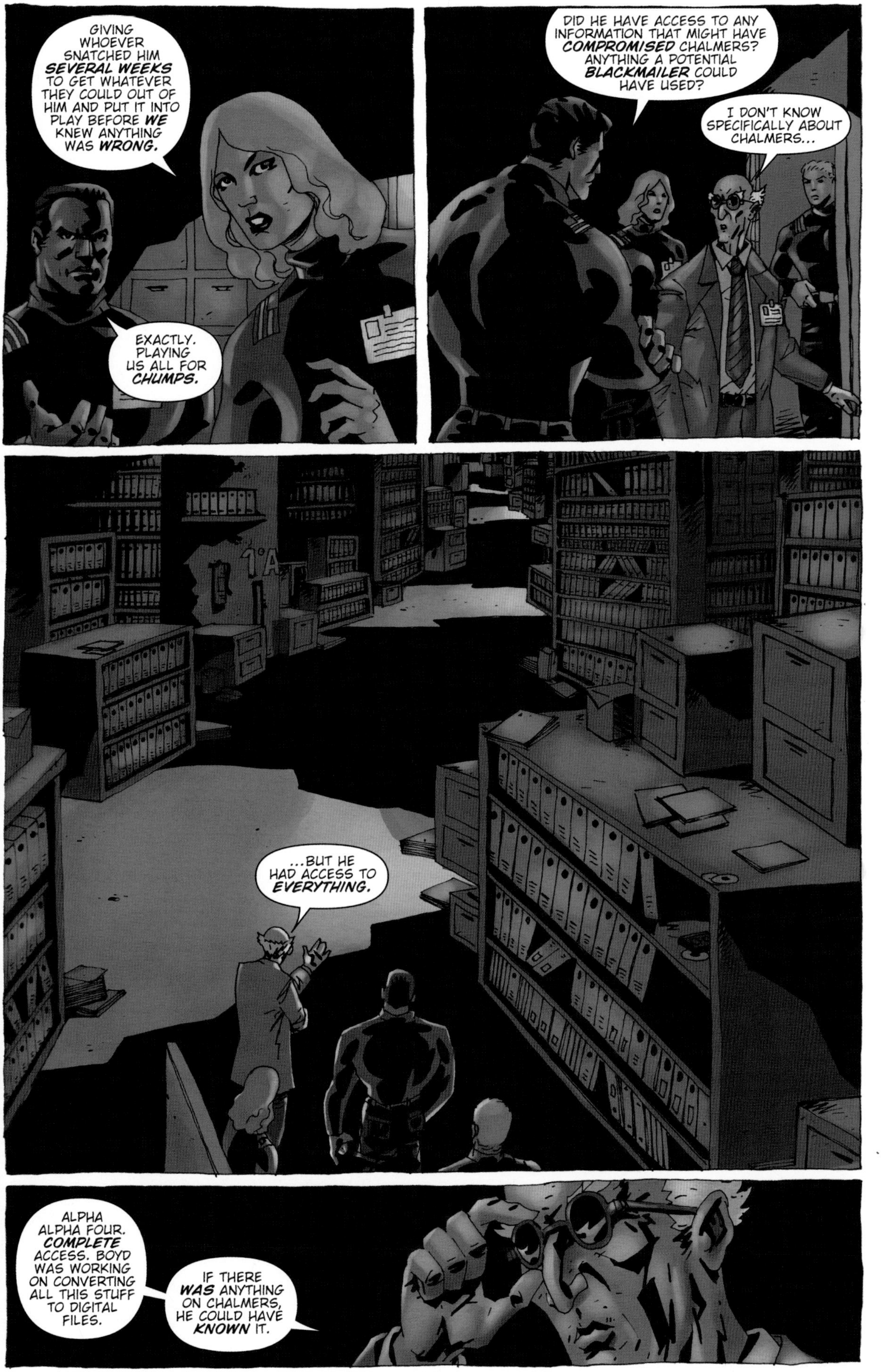
GIVING WHOEVER SNATCHED HIM **SEVERAL WEEKS** TO GET WHATEVER THEY COULD OUT OF HIM AND PUT IT INTO PLAY BEFORE **WE** KNEW ANYTHING WAS **WRONG.**
EXACTLY. PLAYING US ALL FOR **CHUMPS.**
DID HE HAVE ACCESS TO ANY INFORMATION THAT MIGHT HAVE **COMPROMISED** CHALMERS? ANYTHING A POTENTIAL **BLACKMAILER** COULD HAVE USED?
I DON'T KNOW SPECIFICALLY ABOUT CHALMERS...
1°A
...BUT HE HAD ACCESS TO **EVERYTHING.**
ALPHA ALPHA FOUR. **COMPLETE** ACCESS. BOYD WAS WORKING ON CONVERTING ALL THIS STUFF TO DIGITAL FILES.
IF THERE **WAS** ANYTHING ON CHALMERS, HE COULD HAVE **KNOWN** IT.

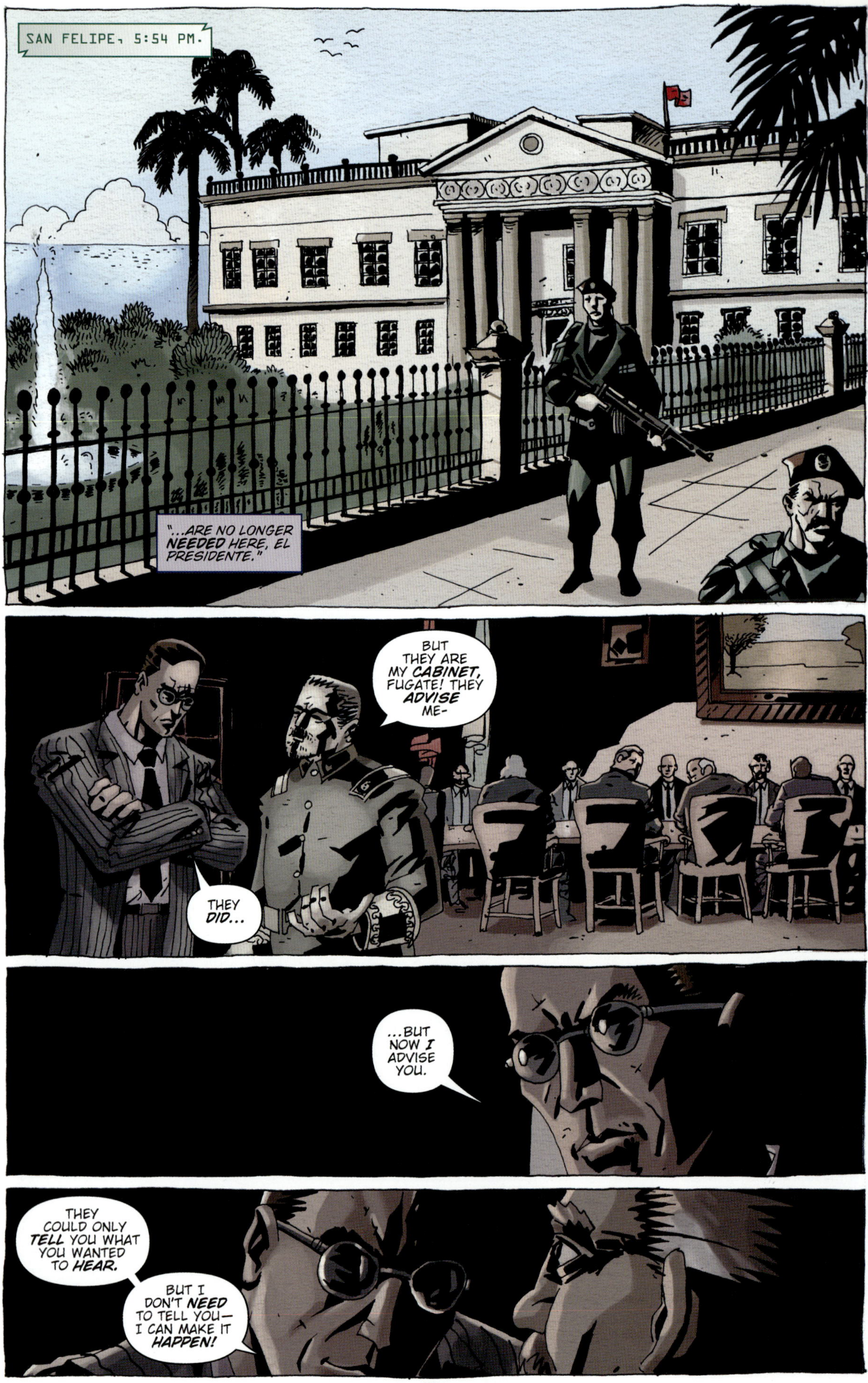
SAN FELIPE, 5:54 PM.
"...ARE NO LONGER NEEDED HERE, EL PRESIDENTE."
BUT THEY ARE MY CABINET, FUGATE! THEY ADVISE ME-
THEY DID...
...BUT NOW I ADVISE YOU.
THEY COULD ONLY TELL YOU WHAT YOU WANTED TO HEAR.
BUT I DON'T NEED TO TELL YOU— I CAN MAKE IT HAPPEN!

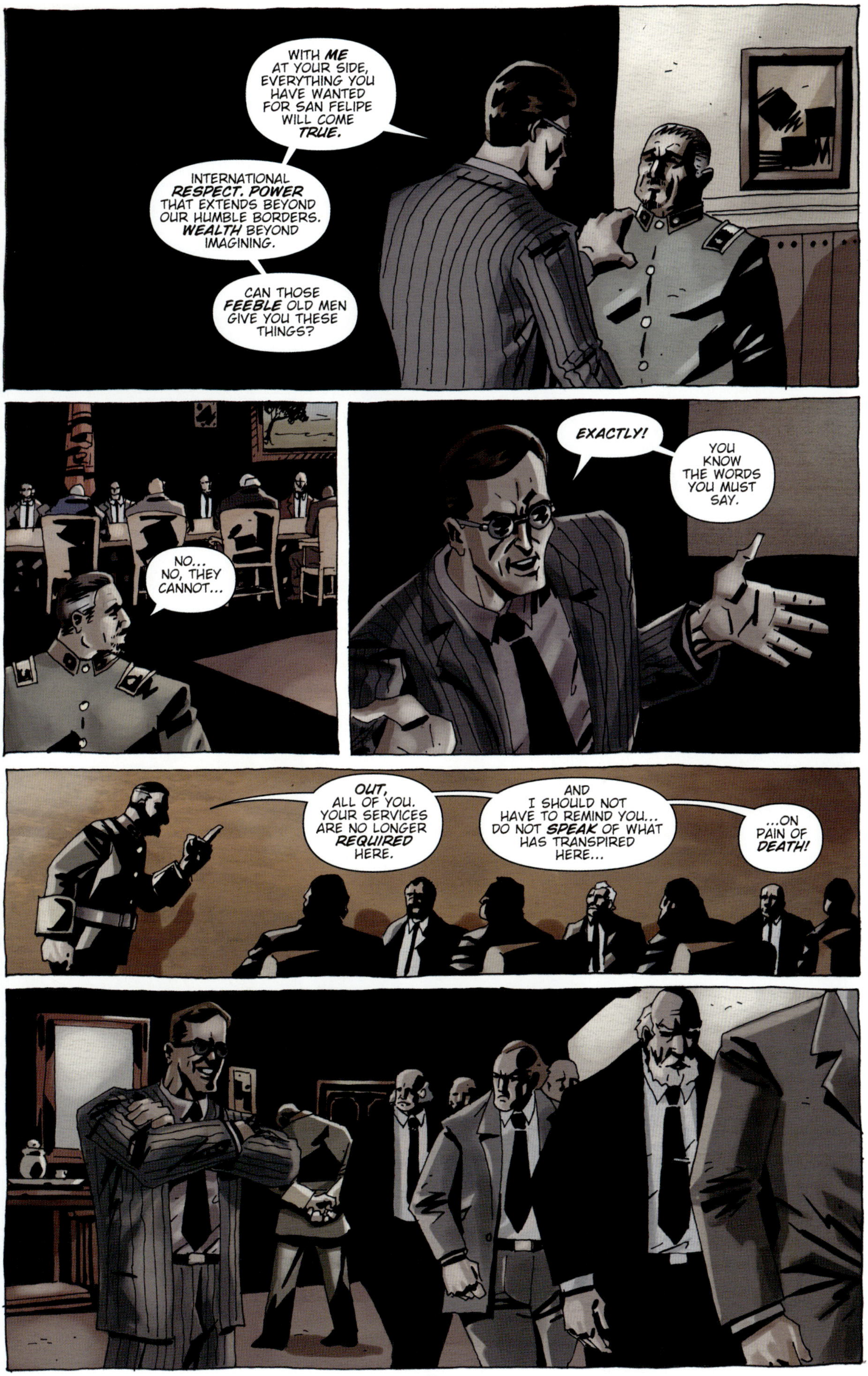
WITH ME AT YOUR SIDE, EVERYTHING YOU HAVE WANTED FOR SAN FELIPE WILL COME TRUE.
INTERNATIONAL RESPECT. POWER THAT EXTENDS BEYOND OUR HUMBLE BORDERS. WEALTH BEYOND IMAGINING.
CAN THOSE FEEBLE OLD MEN GIVE YOU THESE THINGS?
NO... NO, THEY CANNOT...
EXACTLY!
YOU KNOW THE WORDS YOU MUST SAY.
OUT, ALL OF YOU. YOUR SERVICES ARE NO LONGER REQUIRED HERE.
AND I SHOULD NOT HAVE TO REMIND YOU... DO NOT SPEAK OF WHAT HAS TRANSPIRED HERE...
...ON PAIN OF DEATH!

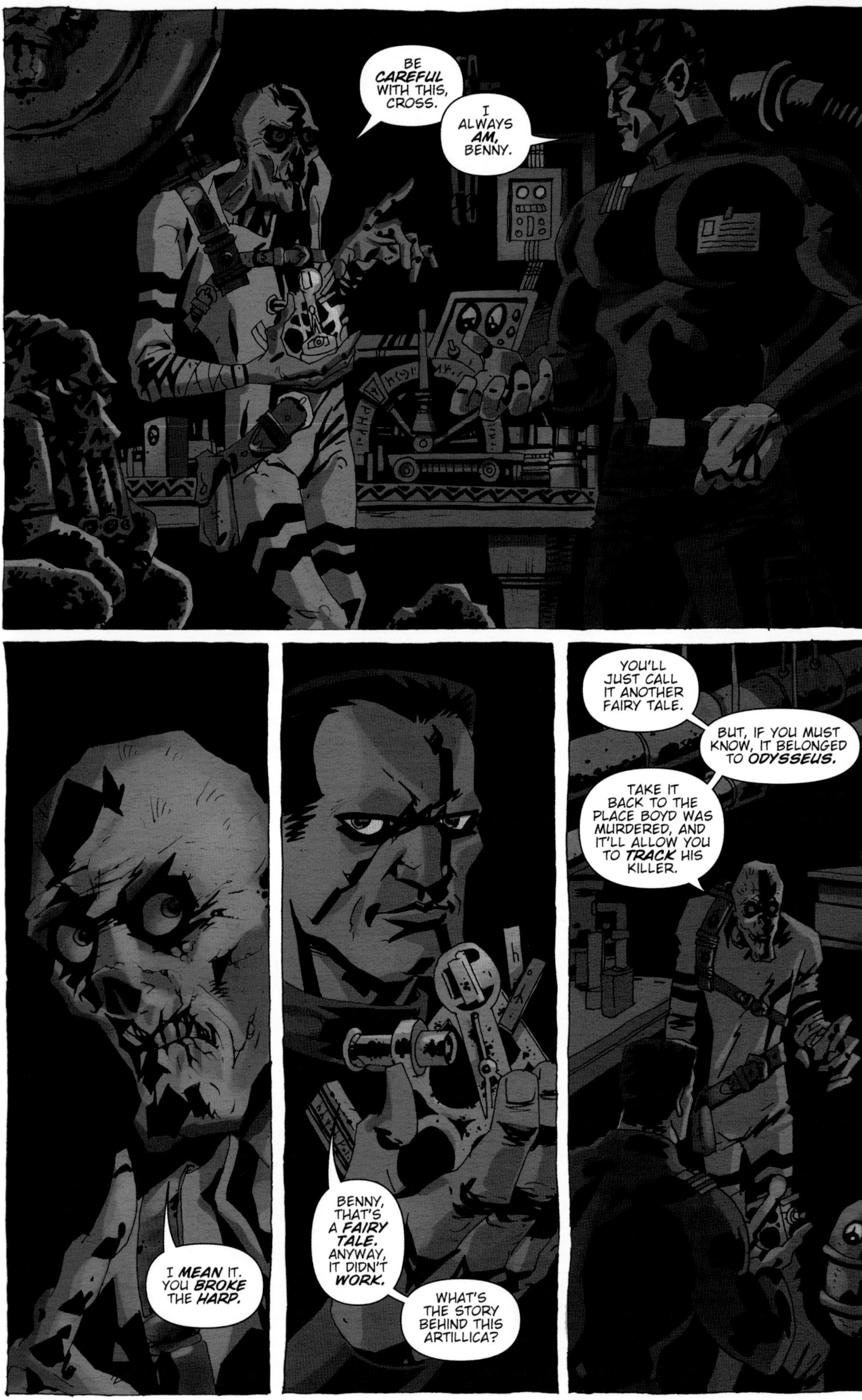
BE CAREFUL WITH THIS, CROSS.
I ALWAYS AM, BENNY.
I MEAN IT. YOU BROKE THE HARP.
BENNY, THAT'S A FAIRY TALE. ANYWAY, IT DIDN'T WORK.
WHAT'S THE STORY BEHIND THIS ARTILLICA?
YOU'LL JUST CALL IT ANOTHER FAIRY TALE.
BUT, IF YOU MUST KNOW, IT BELONGED TO ODYSSEUS.
TAKE IT BACK TO THE PLACE BOYD WAS MURDERED, AND IT'LL ALLOW YOU TO TRACK HIS KILLER.

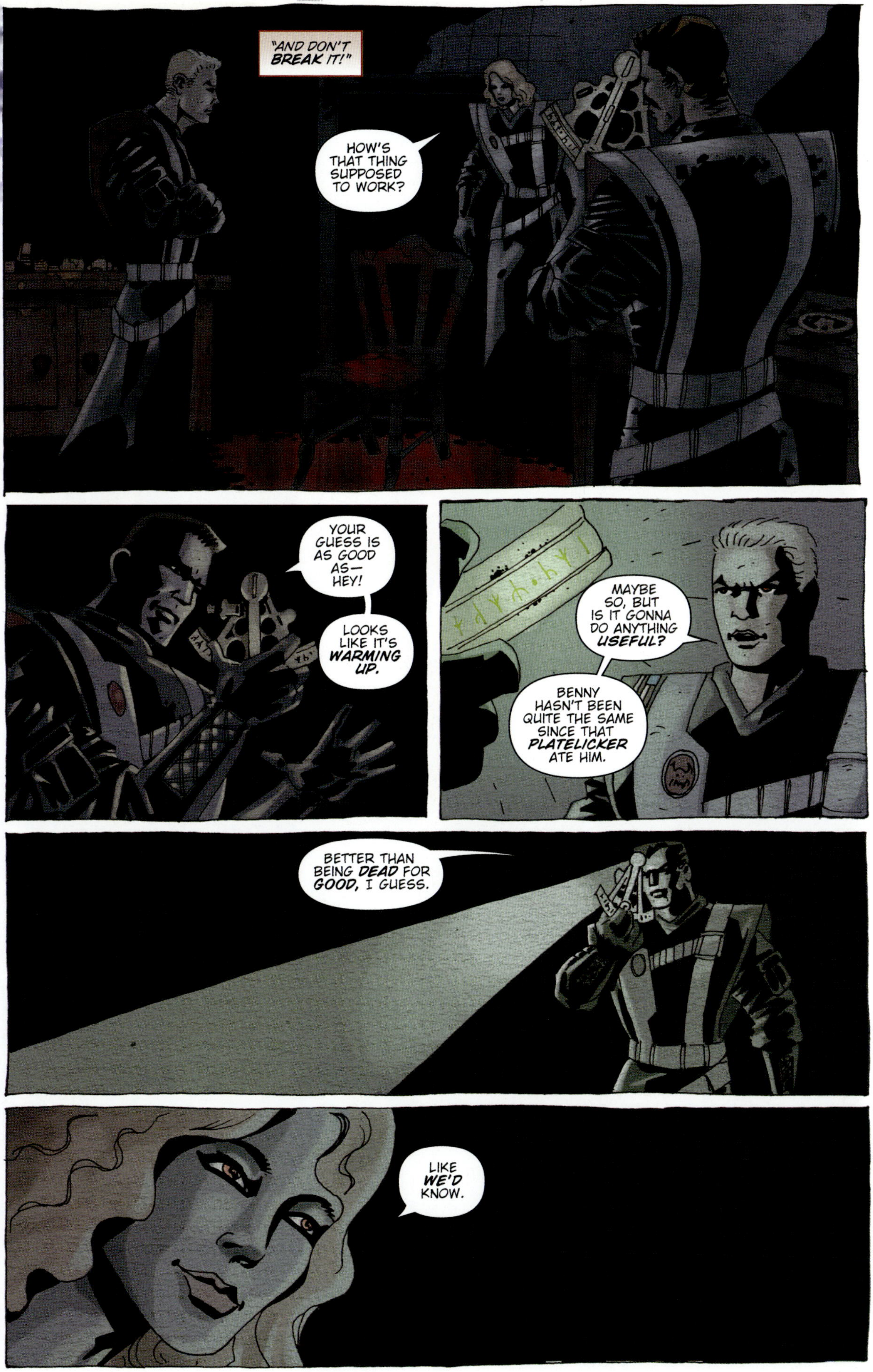
"AND DON'T BREAK IT!"
HOW'S THAT THING SUPPOSED TO WORK?
YOUR GUESS IS AS GOOD AS— HEY!
LOOKS LIKE IT'S WARMING UP.
MAYBE SO, BUT IS IT GONNA DO ANYTHING USEFUL?
BENNY HASN'T BEEN QUITE THE SAME SINCE THAT PLATELICKER ATE HIM.
BETTER THAN BEING DEAD FOR GOOD, I GUESS.
LIKE WE'D KNOW.

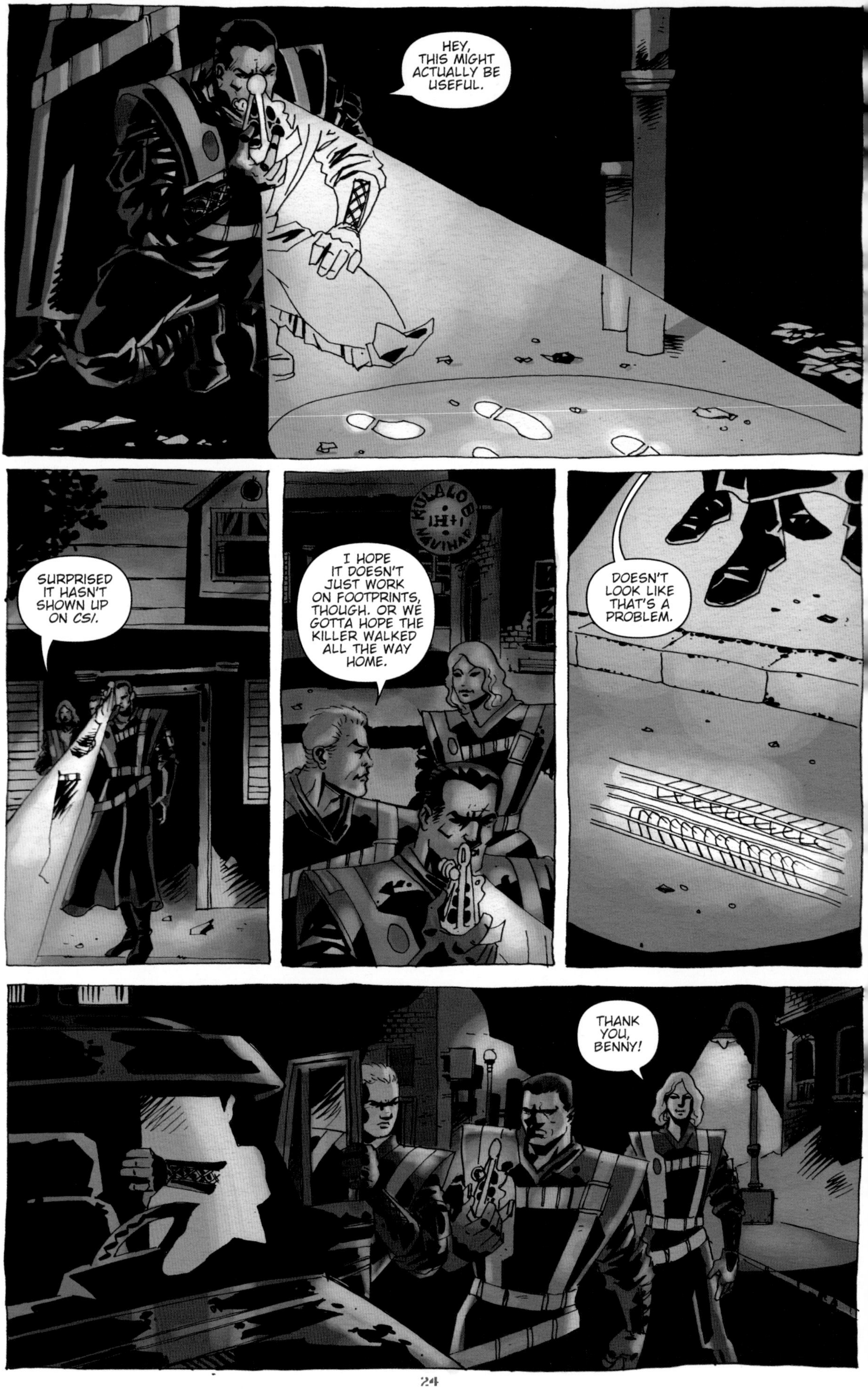
HEY, THIS MIGHT ACTUALLY BE USEFUL.
SURPRISED IT HASN'T SHOWN UP ON CSI.
I HOPE IT DOESN'T JUST WORK ON FOOTPRINTS, THOUGH. OR WE GOTTA HOPE THE KILLER WALKED ALL THE WAY HOME.
DOESN'T LOOK LIKE THAT'S A PROBLEM.
THANK YOU, BENNY!

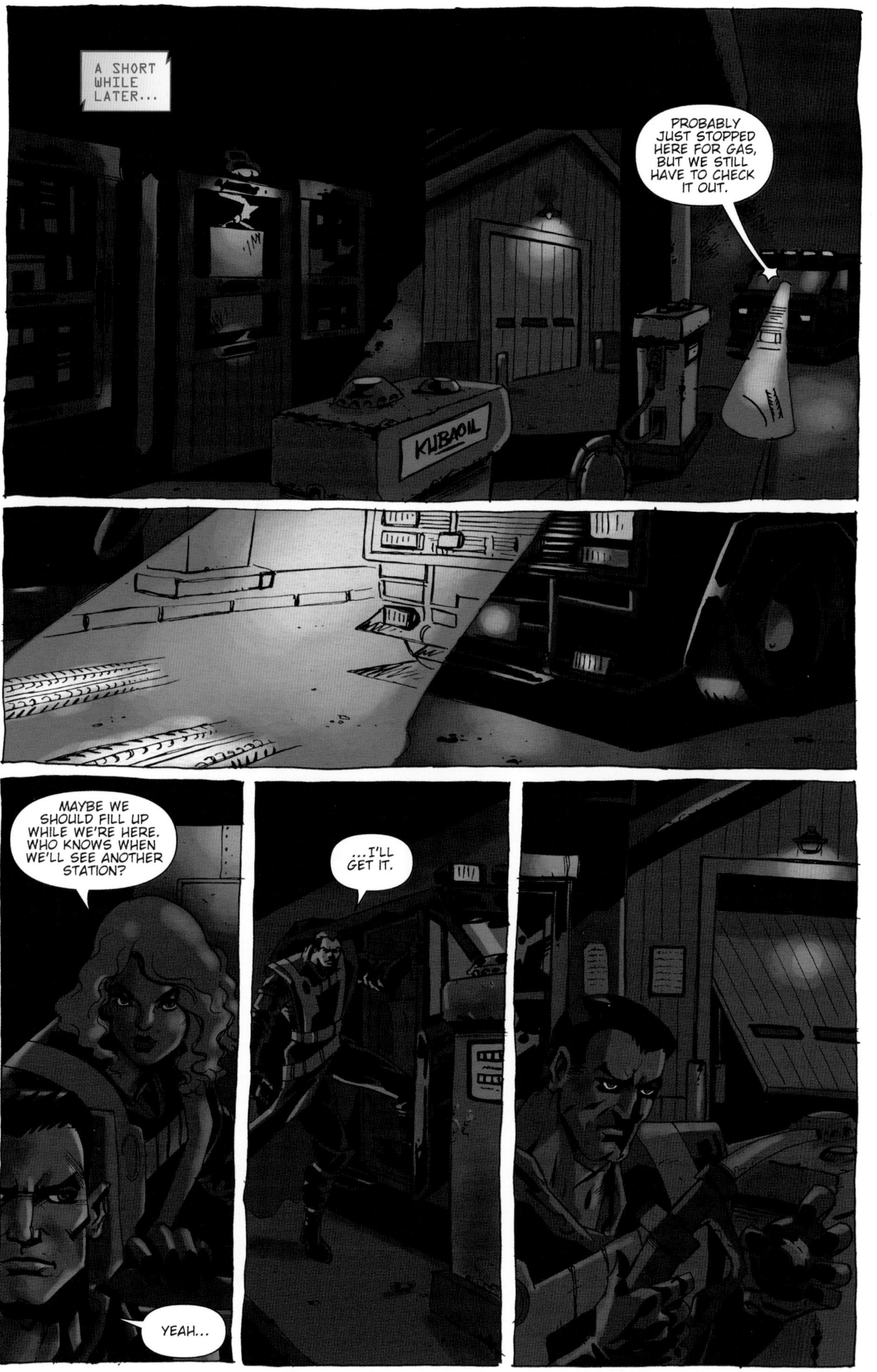
A SHORT WHILE LATER...
PROBABLY JUST STOPPED HERE FOR GAS, BUT WE STILL HAVE TO CHECK IT OUT.
KUBAOIL
MAYBE WE SHOULD FILL UP WHILE WE'RE HERE. WHO KNOWS WHEN WE'LL SEE ANOTHER STATION?
YEAH...
...I'LL GET IT.

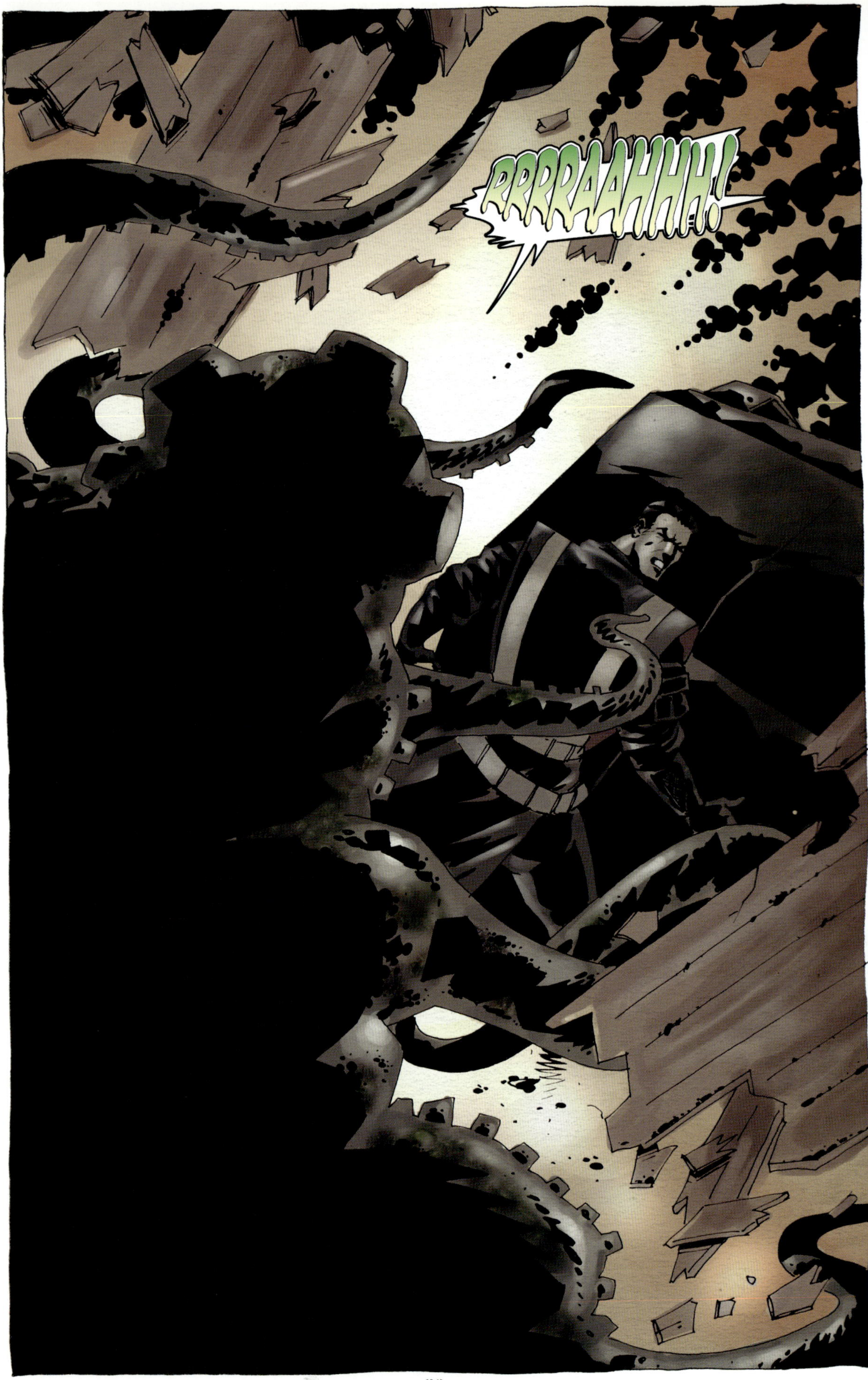
RRRRAAHHH!

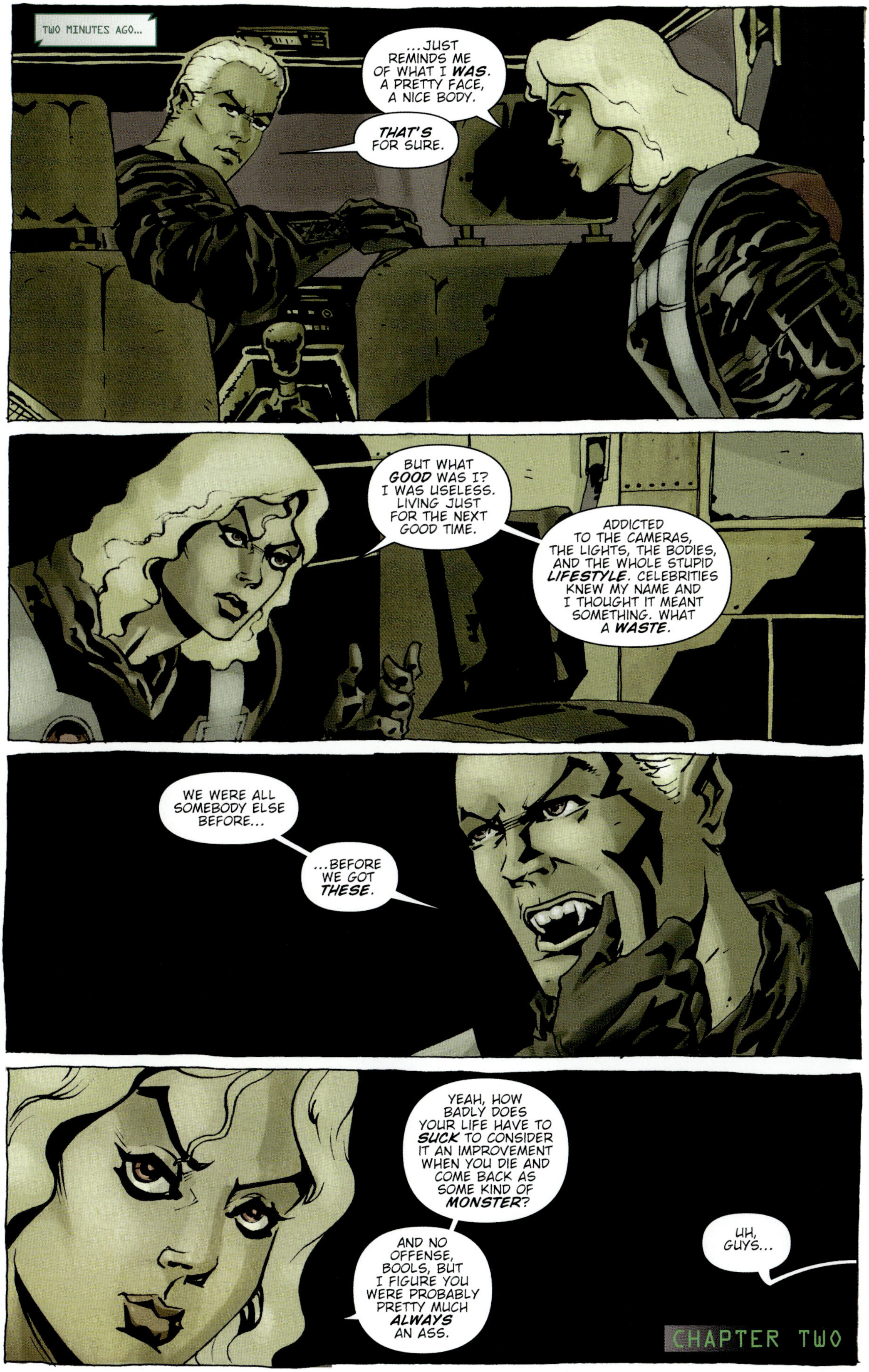
TWO MINUTES AGO...
...JUST REMINDS ME OF WHAT I WAS. A PRETTY FACE, A NICE BODY.
THAT'S FOR SURE.
BUT WHAT GOOD WAS I? I WAS USELESS. LIVING JUST FOR THE NEXT GOOD TIME.
ADDICTED TO THE CAMERAS, THE LIGHTS, THE BODIES, AND THE WHOLE STUPID LIFESTYLE. CELEBRITIES KNEW MY NAME AND I THOUGHT IT MEANT SOMETHING. WHAT A WASTE.
WE WERE ALL SOMEBODY ELSE BEFORE...
...BEFORE WE GOT THESE.
YEAH, HOW BADLY DOES YOUR LIFE HAVE TO SUCK TO CONSIDER IT AN IMPROVEMENT WHEN YOU DIE AND COME BACK AS SOME KIND OF MONSTER?
AND NO OFFENSE, BOOLS, BUT I FIGURE YOU WERE PROBABLY PRETTY MUCH ALWAYS AN ASS.
UH, GUYS...
CHAPTER TWO

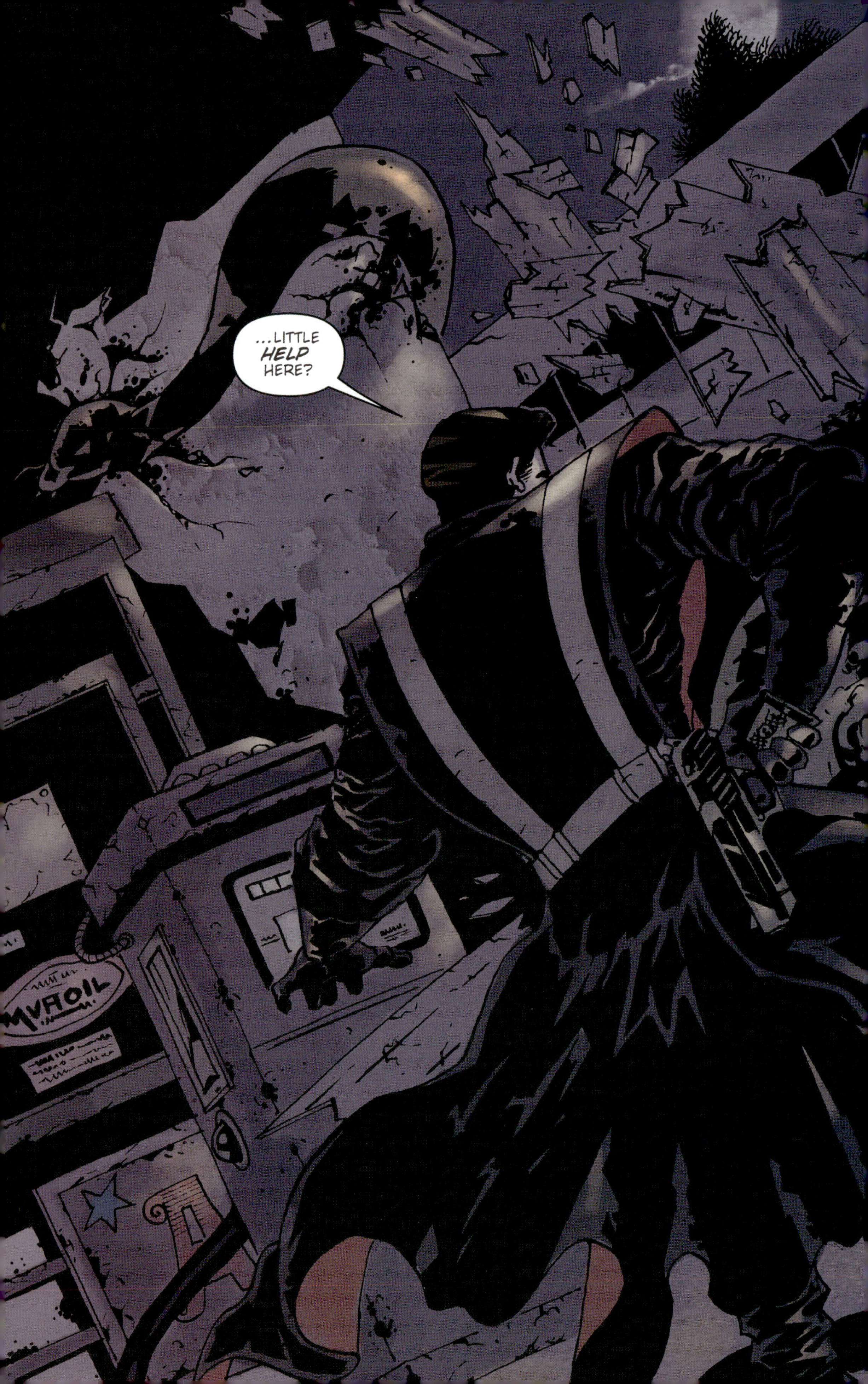
...LITTLE HELP HERE?
MVFOIL

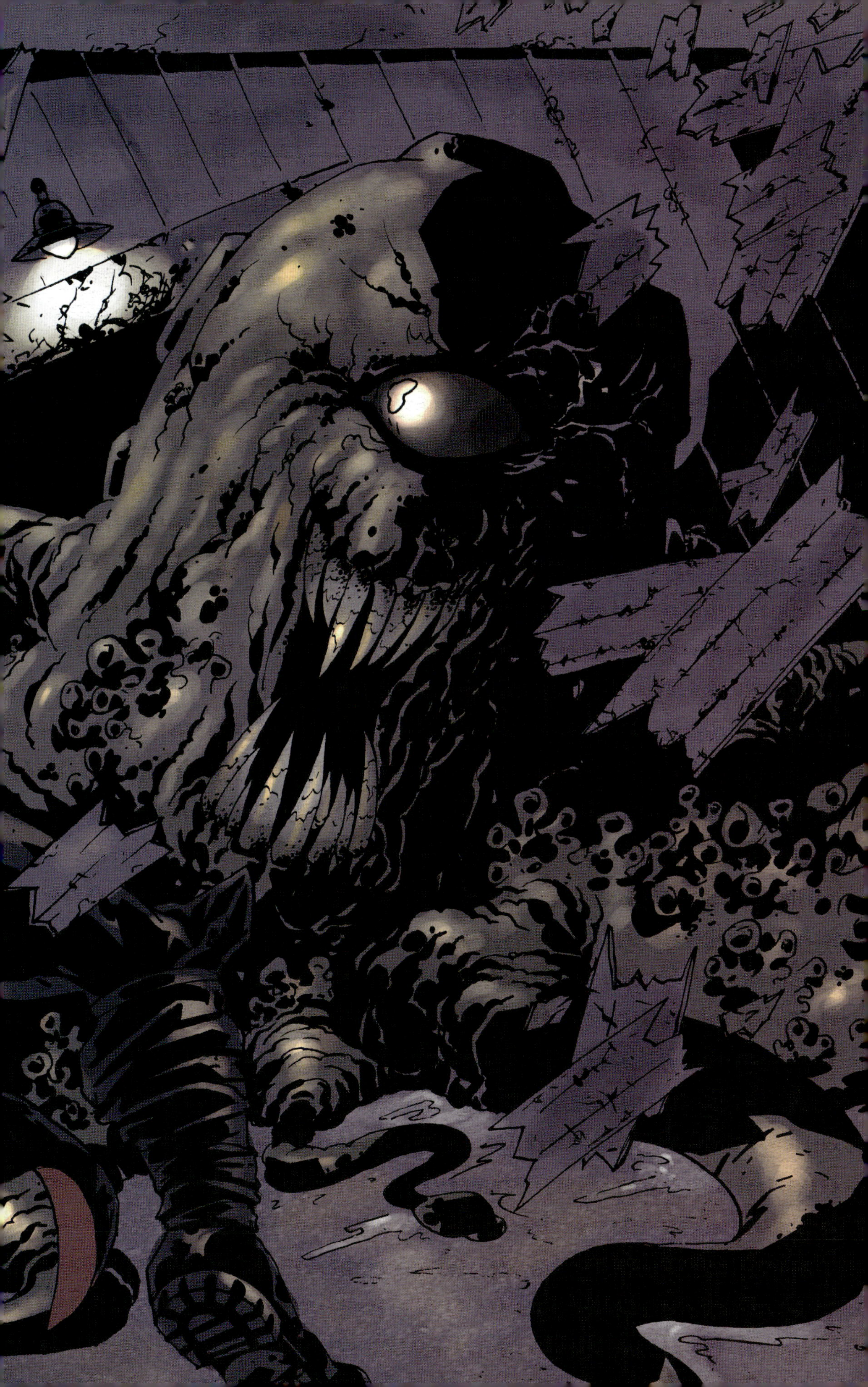

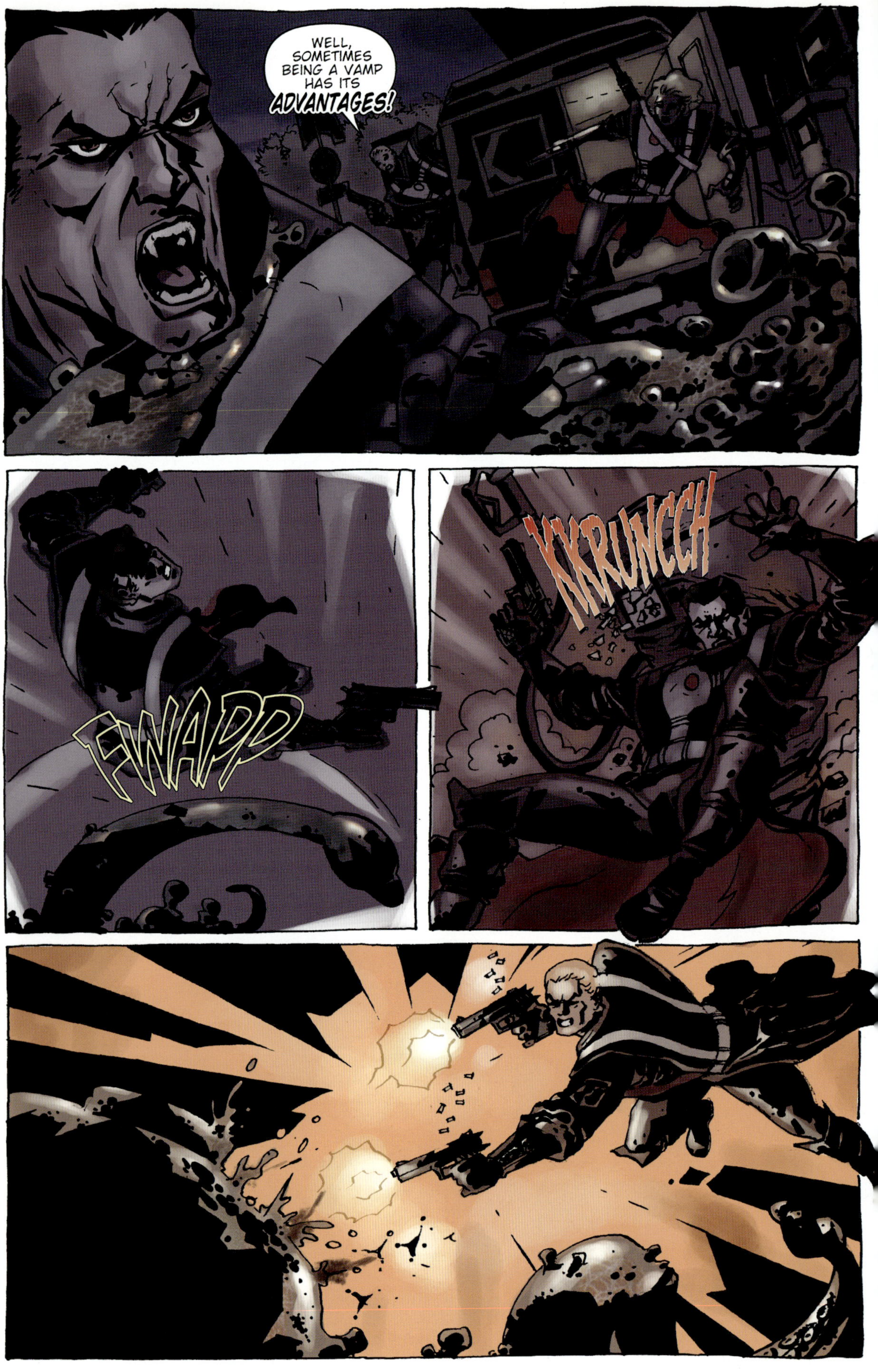
WELL, SOMETIMES BEING A VAMP HAS ITS ADVANTAGES!
FWAPP
KKRUNCCH

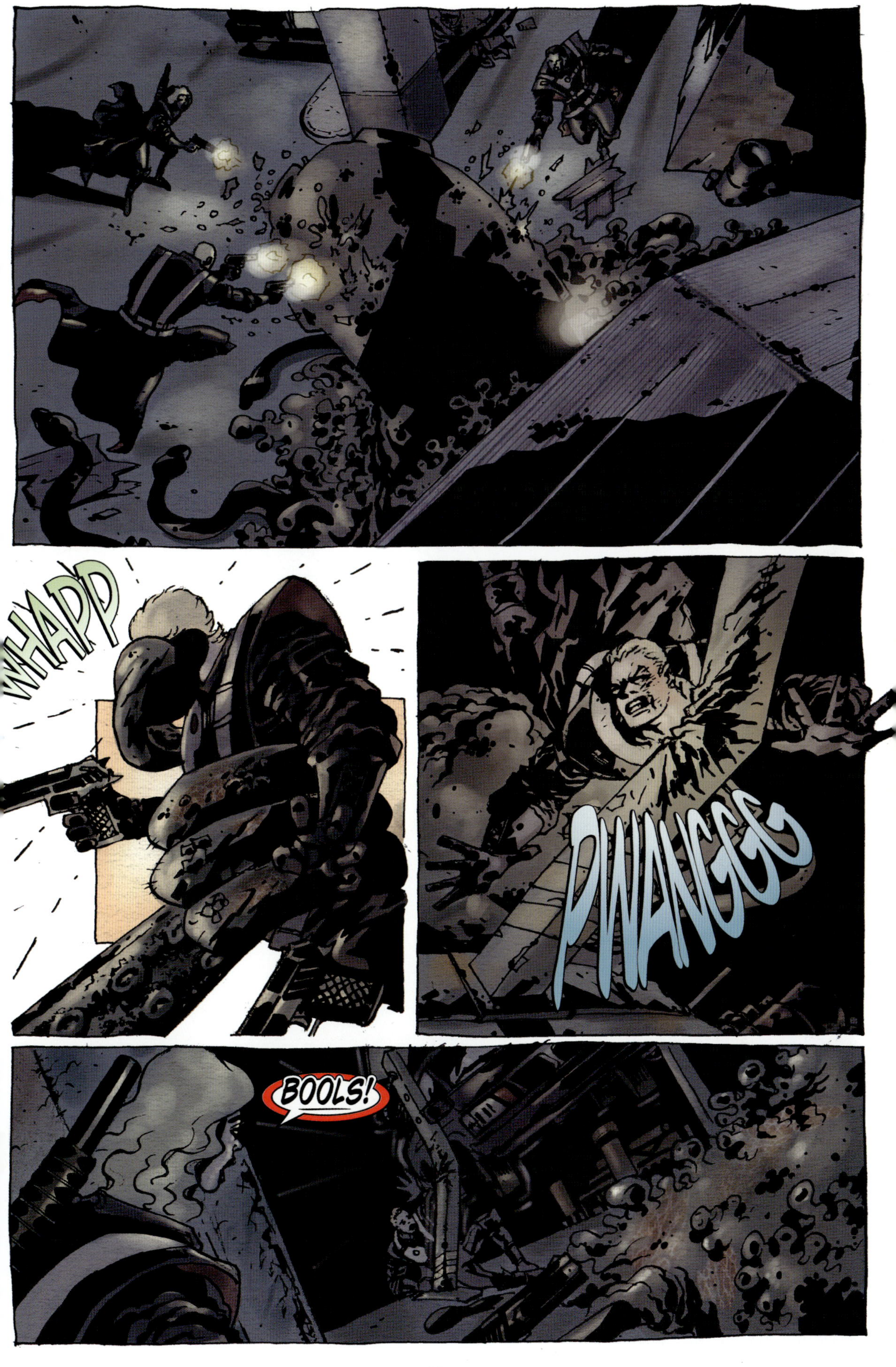
WHAPP
PWANGGG
BOOLS!

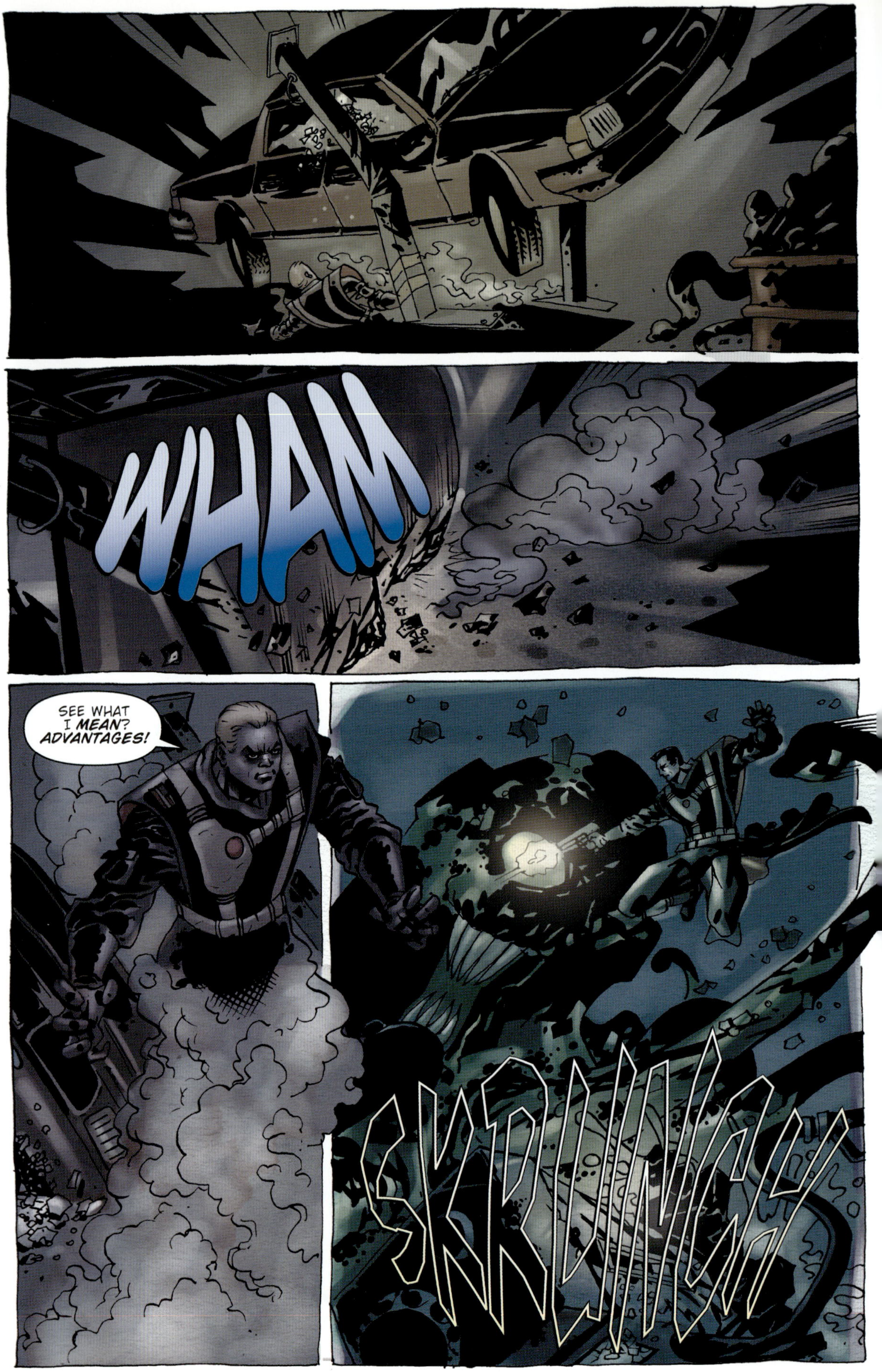
WHAM
SEE WHAT I MEAN? ADVANTAGES!
SKRUNCH

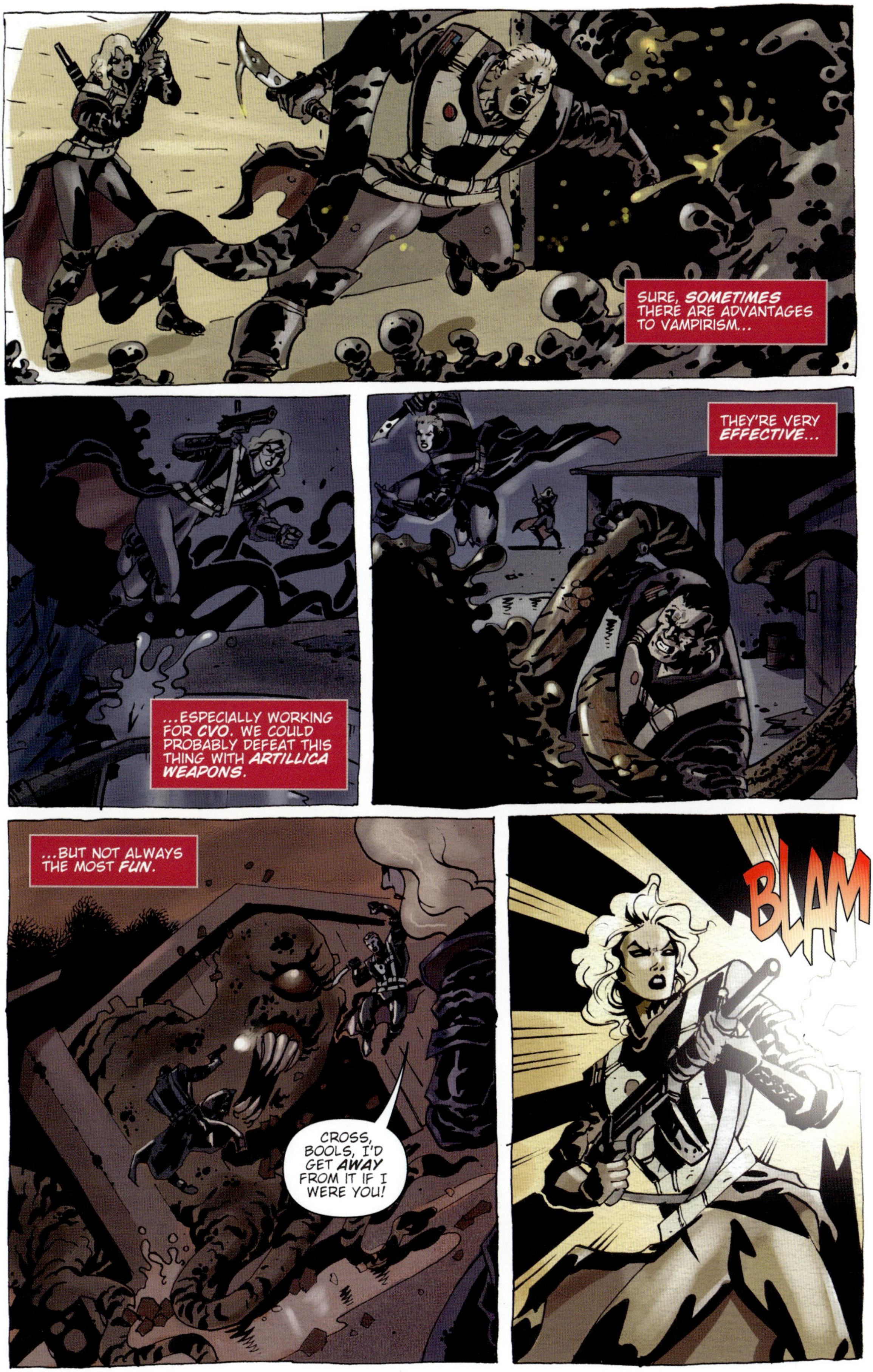
SURE, SOMETIMES THERE ARE ADVANTAGES TO VAMPIRISM...
THEY'RE VERY EFFECTIVE...
...ESPECIALLY WORKING FOR CVO. WE COULD PROBABLY DEFEAT THIS THING WITH ARTILLICA WEAPONS.
...BUT NOT ALWAYS THE MOST FUN.
CROSS, BOOLS, I'D GET AWAY FROM IT IF I WERE YOU!
BLAM

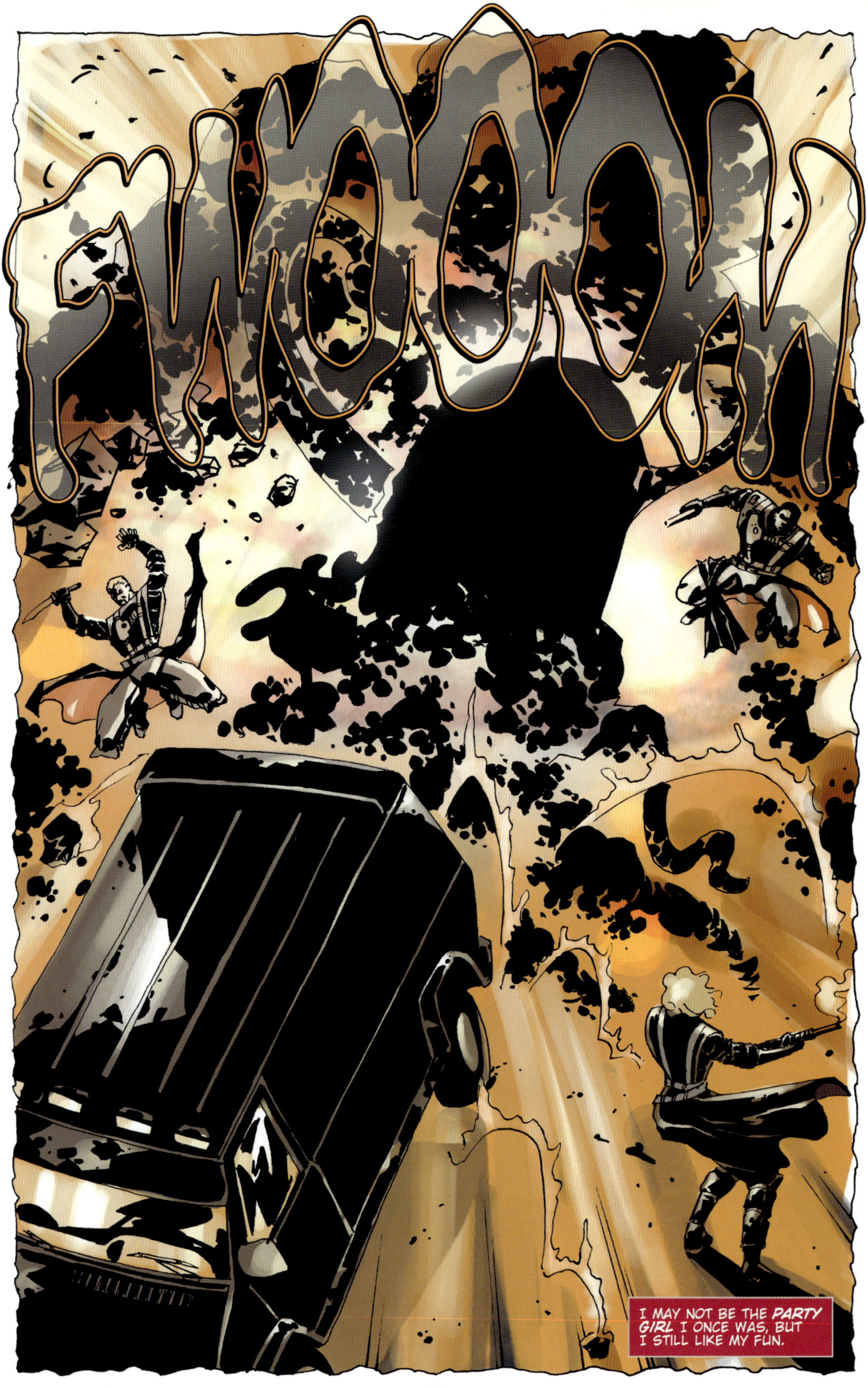
FWOOOOM
I MAY NOT BE THE PARTY GIRL I ONCE WAS, BUT I STILL LIKE MY FUN.

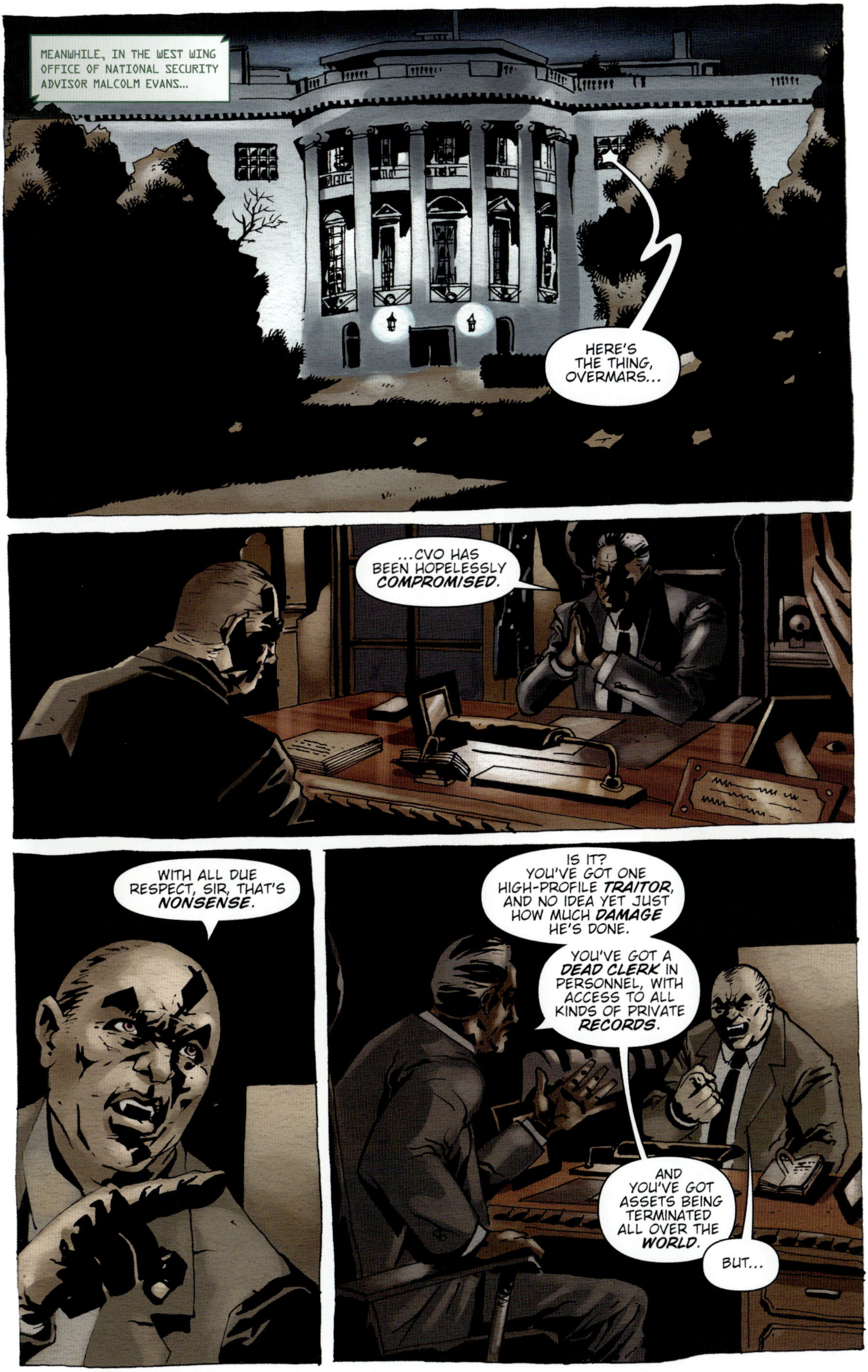
MEANWHILE, IN THE WEST WING OFFICE OF NATIONAL SECURITY ADVISOR MALCOLM EVANS...
HERE'S THE THING, OVERMARS...
...CVO HAS BEEN HOPELESSLY COMPROMISED.
WITH ALL DUE RESPECT, SIR, THAT'S NONSENSE.
IS IT? YOU'VE GOT ONE HIGH-PROFILE TRAITOR, AND NO IDEA YET JUST HOW MUCH DAMAGE HE'S DONE.
YOU'VE GOT A DEAD CLERK IN PERSONNEL, WITH ACCESS TO ALL KINDS OF PRIVATE RECORDS.
AND YOU'VE GOT ASSETS BEING TERMINATED ALL OVER THE WORLD.
BUT...

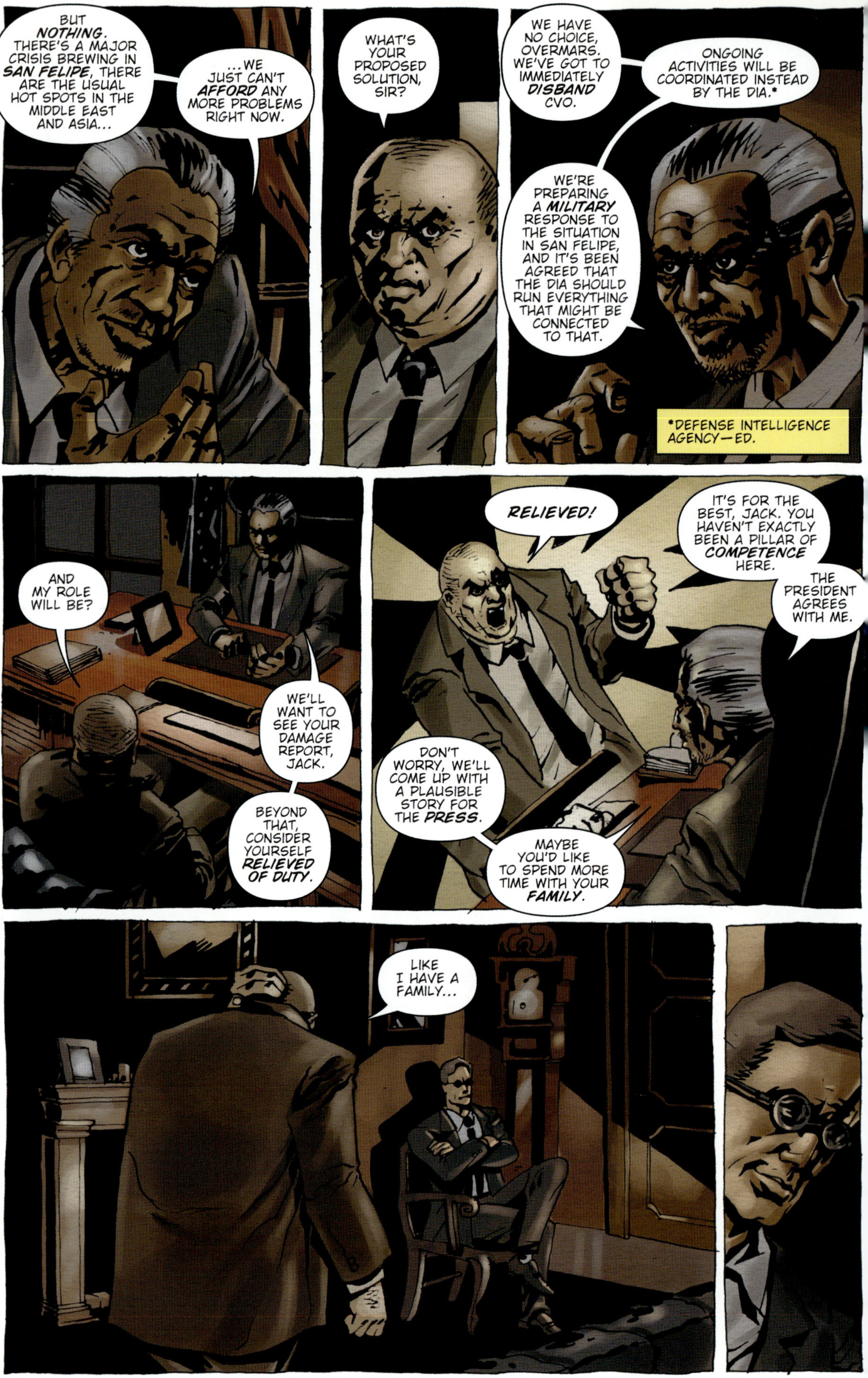
BUT NOTHING. THERE'S A MAJOR CRISIS BREWING IN SAN FELIPE, THERE ARE THE USUAL HOT SPOTS IN THE MIDDLE EAST AND ASIA...
...WE JUST CAN'T AFFORD ANY MORE PROBLEMS RIGHT NOW.
WHAT'S YOUR PROPOSED SOLUTION, SIR?
WE HAVE NO CHOICE, OVERMARS. WE'VE GOT TO IMMEDIATELY DISBAND CVO.
ONGOING ACTIVITIES WILL BE COORDINATED INSTEAD BY THE DIA.*
WE'RE PREPARING A MILITARY RESPONSE TO THE SITUATION IN SAN FELIPE, AND IT'S BEEN AGREED THAT THE DIA SHOULD RUN EVERYTHING THAT MIGHT BE CONNECTED TO THAT.
*DEFENSE INTELLIGENCE AGENCY—ED.
AND MY ROLE WILL BE?
WE'LL WANT TO SEE YOUR DAMAGE REPORT, JACK.
BEYOND THAT, CONSIDER YOURSELF RELIEVED OF DUTY.
RELIEVED!
IT'S FOR THE BEST, JACK. YOU HAVEN'T EXACTLY BEEN A PILLAR OF COMPETENCE HERE.
THE PRESIDENT AGREES WITH ME.
DON'T WORRY, WE'LL COME UP WITH A PLAUSIBLE STORY FOR THE PRESS.
MAYBE YOU'D LIKE TO SPEND MORE TIME WITH YOUR FAMILY.
LIKE I HAVE A FAMILY...

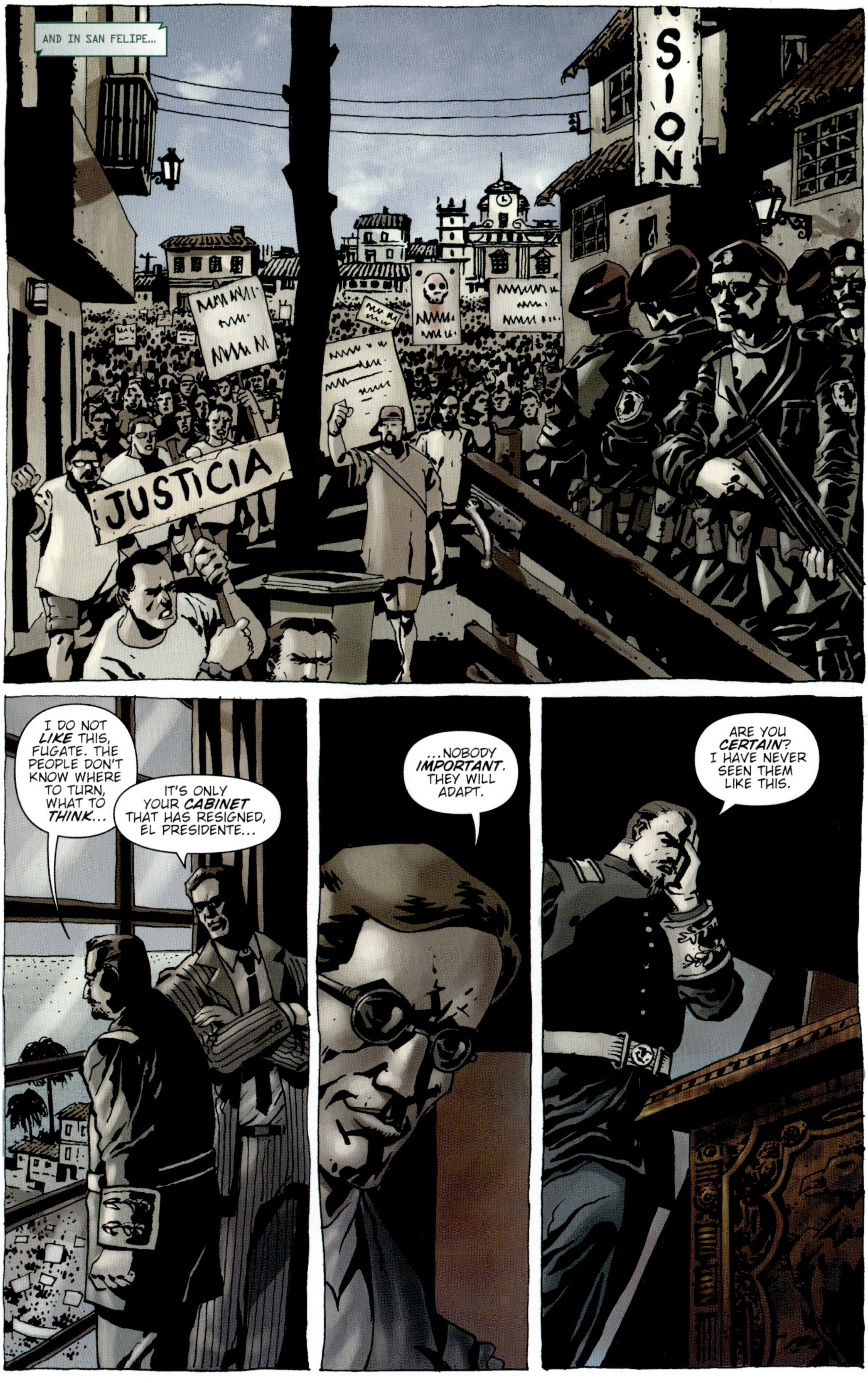
AND IN SAN FELIPE...
SION
JUSTICIA
I DO NOT LIKE THIS, FUGATE. THE PEOPLE DON'T KNOW WHERE TO TURN, WHAT TO THINK...
IT'S ONLY YOUR CABINET THAT HAS RESIGNED, EL PRESIDENTE...
...NOBODY IMPORTANT. THEY WILL ADAPT.
ARE YOU CERTAIN? I HAVE NEVER SEEN THEM LIKE THIS.

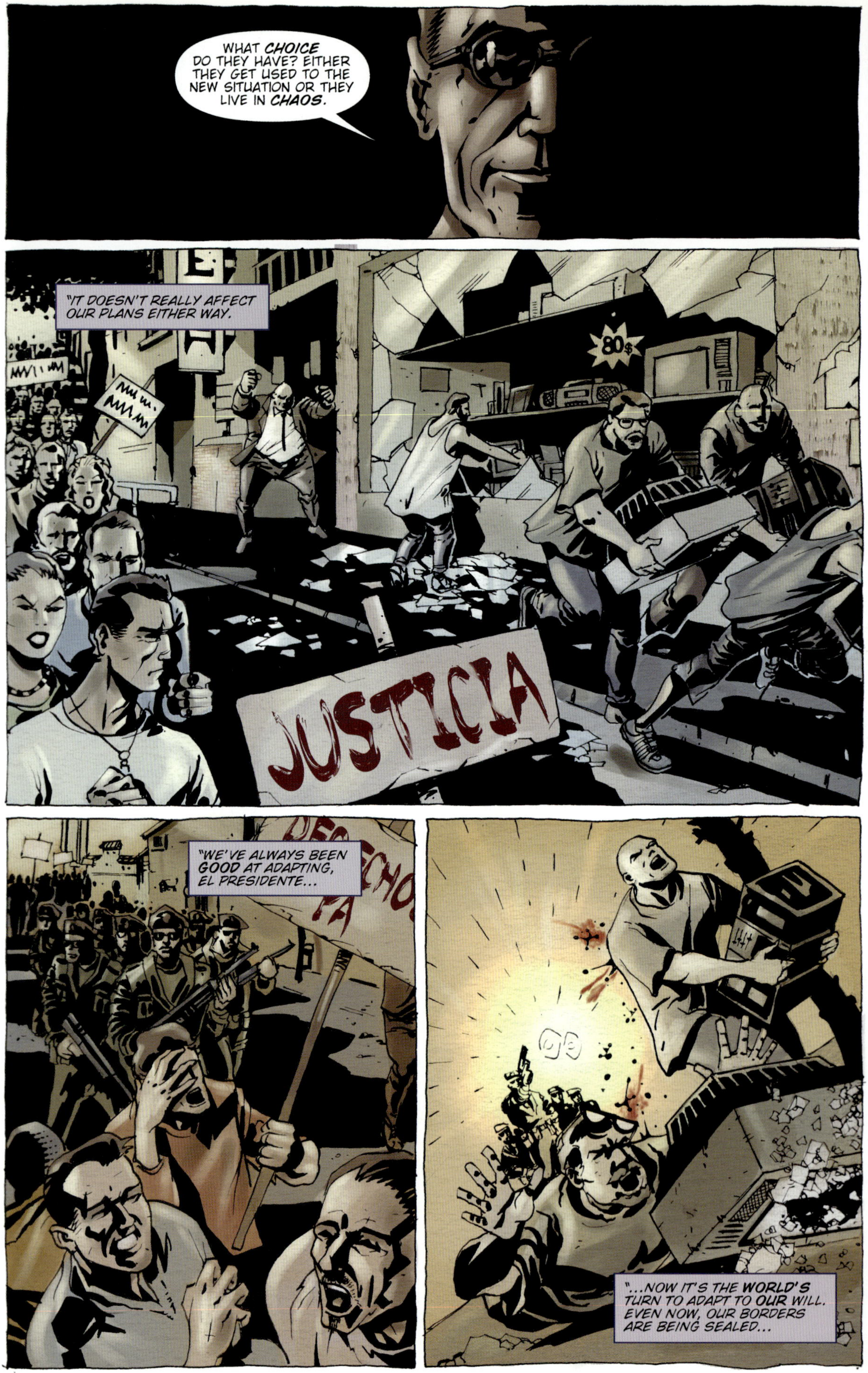
WHAT **CHOICE** DO THEY HAVE? EITHER THEY GET USED TO THE NEW SITUATION OR THEY LIVE IN **CHAOS**.
"IT DOESN'T REALLY AFFECT OUR PLANS EITHER WAY.
80$
JUSTICIA
"WE'VE ALWAYS BEEN **GOOD** AT ADAPTING, EL PRESIDENTE...
"...NOW IT'S THE **WORLD'S** TURN TO ADAPT TO **OUR** WILL. EVEN NOW, OUR BORDERS ARE BEING SEALED...

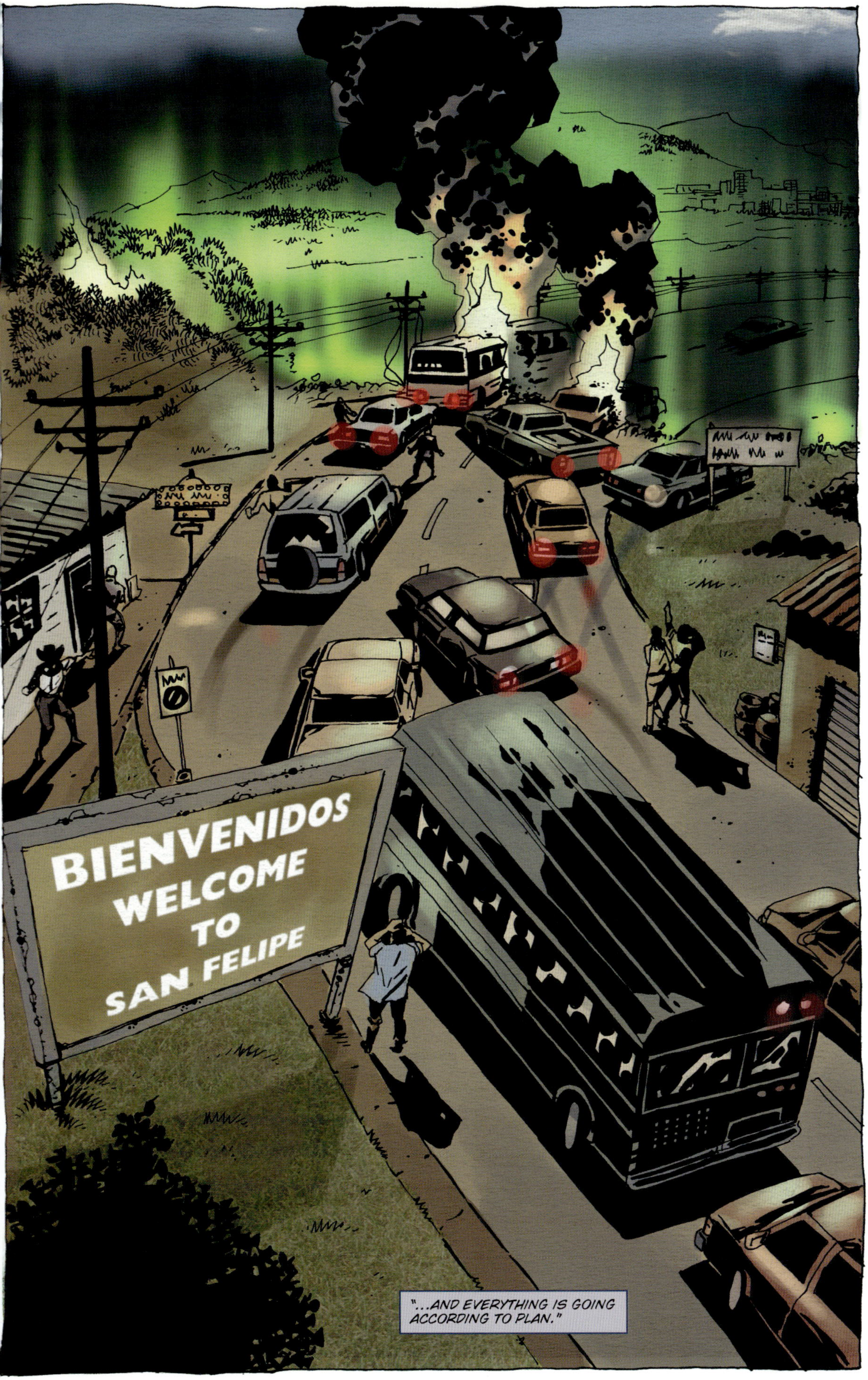
BIENVENIDOS
WELCOME
TO
SAN FELIPE
"...AND EVERYTHING IS GOING ACCORDING TO PLAN."

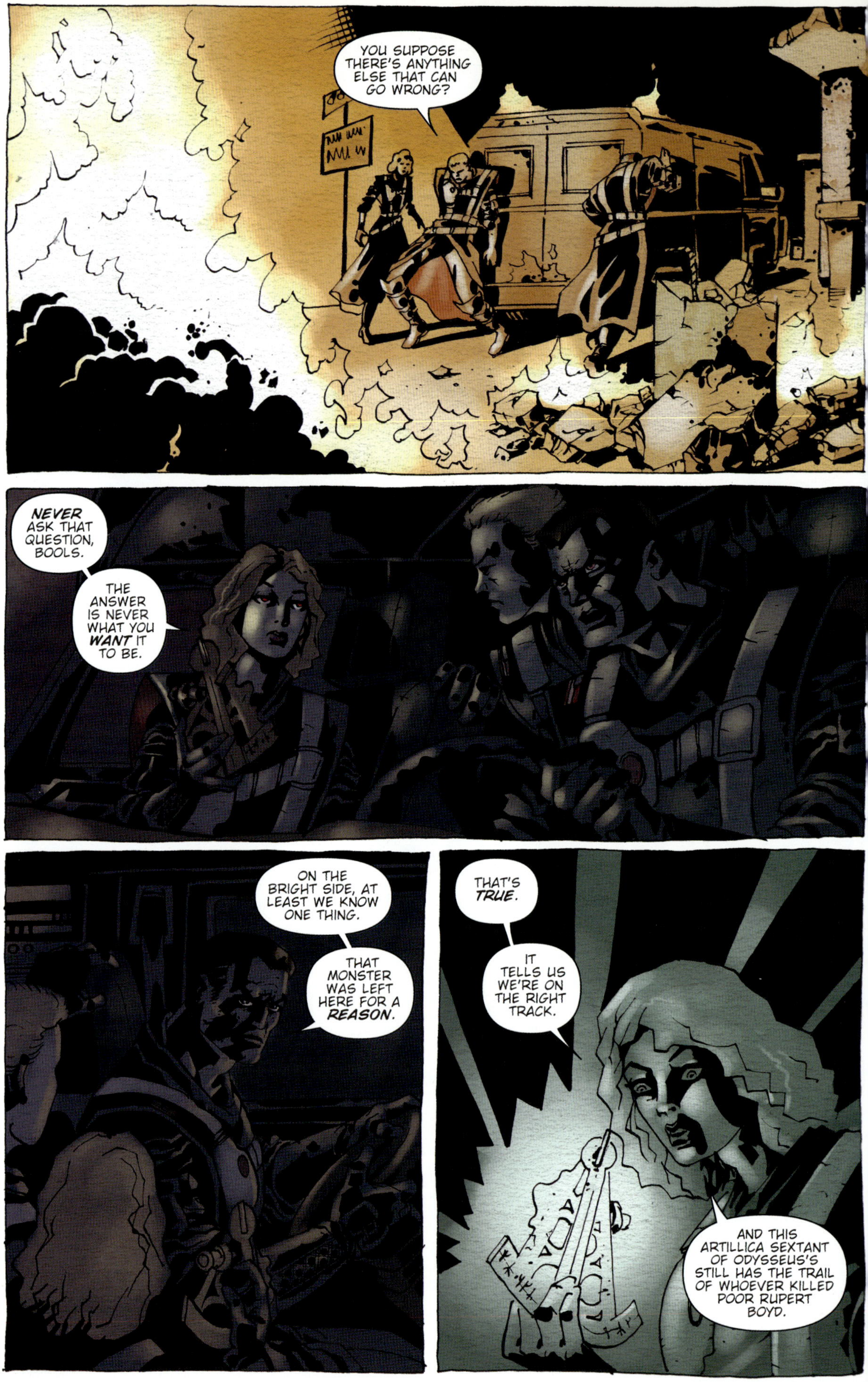
YOU SUPPOSE THERE'S ANYTHING ELSE THAT CAN GO WRONG?
NEVER ASK THAT QUESTION, BOOLS.
THE ANSWER IS NEVER WHAT YOU WANT IT TO BE.
ON THE BRIGHT SIDE, AT LEAST WE KNOW ONE THING.
THAT MONSTER WAS LEFT HERE FOR A REASON.
THAT'S TRUE.
IT TELLS US WE'RE ON THE RIGHT TRACK.
AND THIS ARTILLICA SEXTANT OF ODYSSEUS'S STILL HAS THE TRAIL OF WHOEVER KILLED POOR RUPERT BOYD.

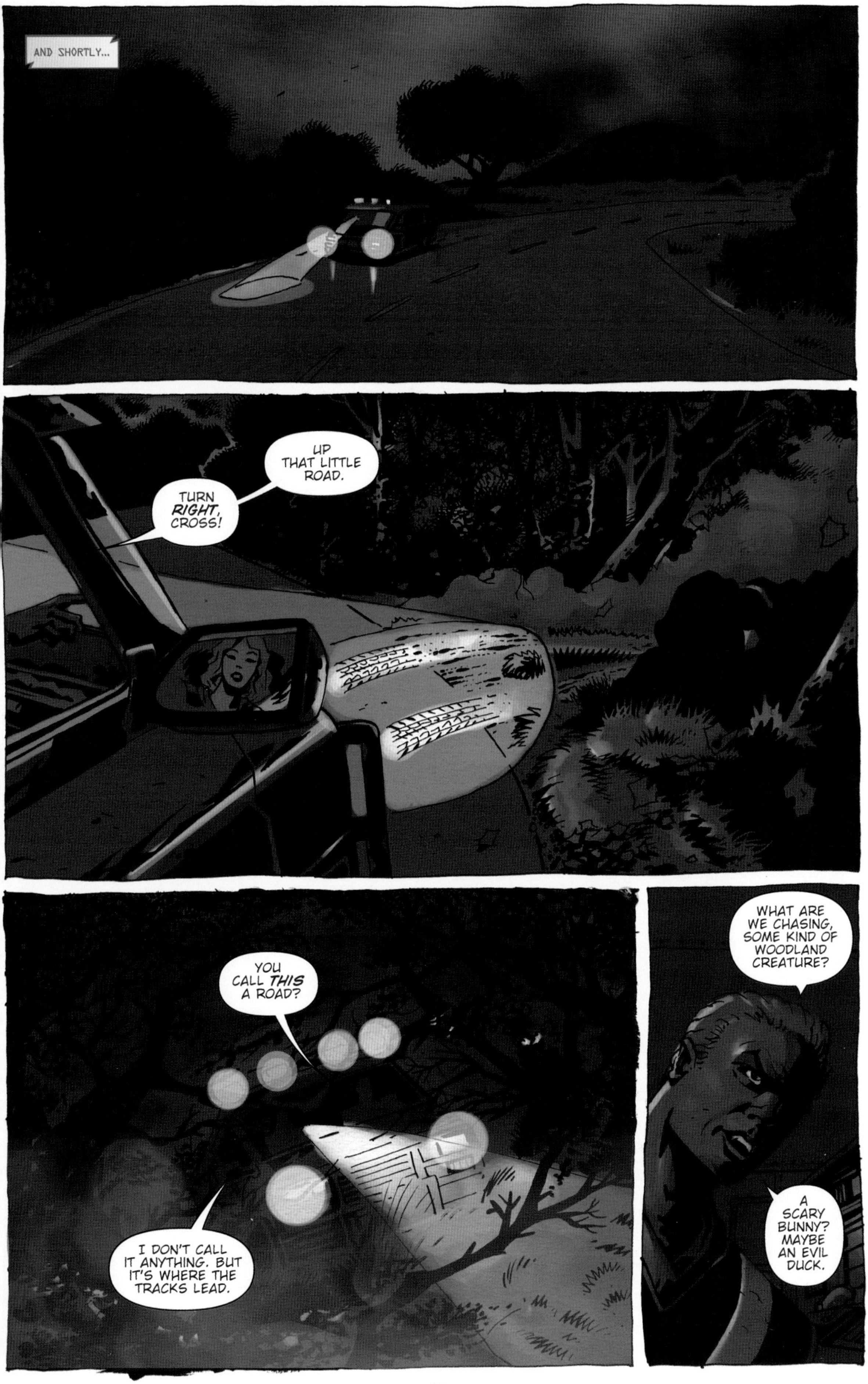
AND SHORTLY...
TURN RIGHT, CROSS!
UP THAT LITTLE ROAD.
YOU CALL THIS A ROAD?
I DON'T CALL IT ANYTHING. BUT IT'S WHERE THE TRACKS LEAD.
WHAT ARE WE CHASING, SOME KIND OF WOODLAND CREATURE?
A SCARY BUNNY? MAYBE AN EVIL DUCK.

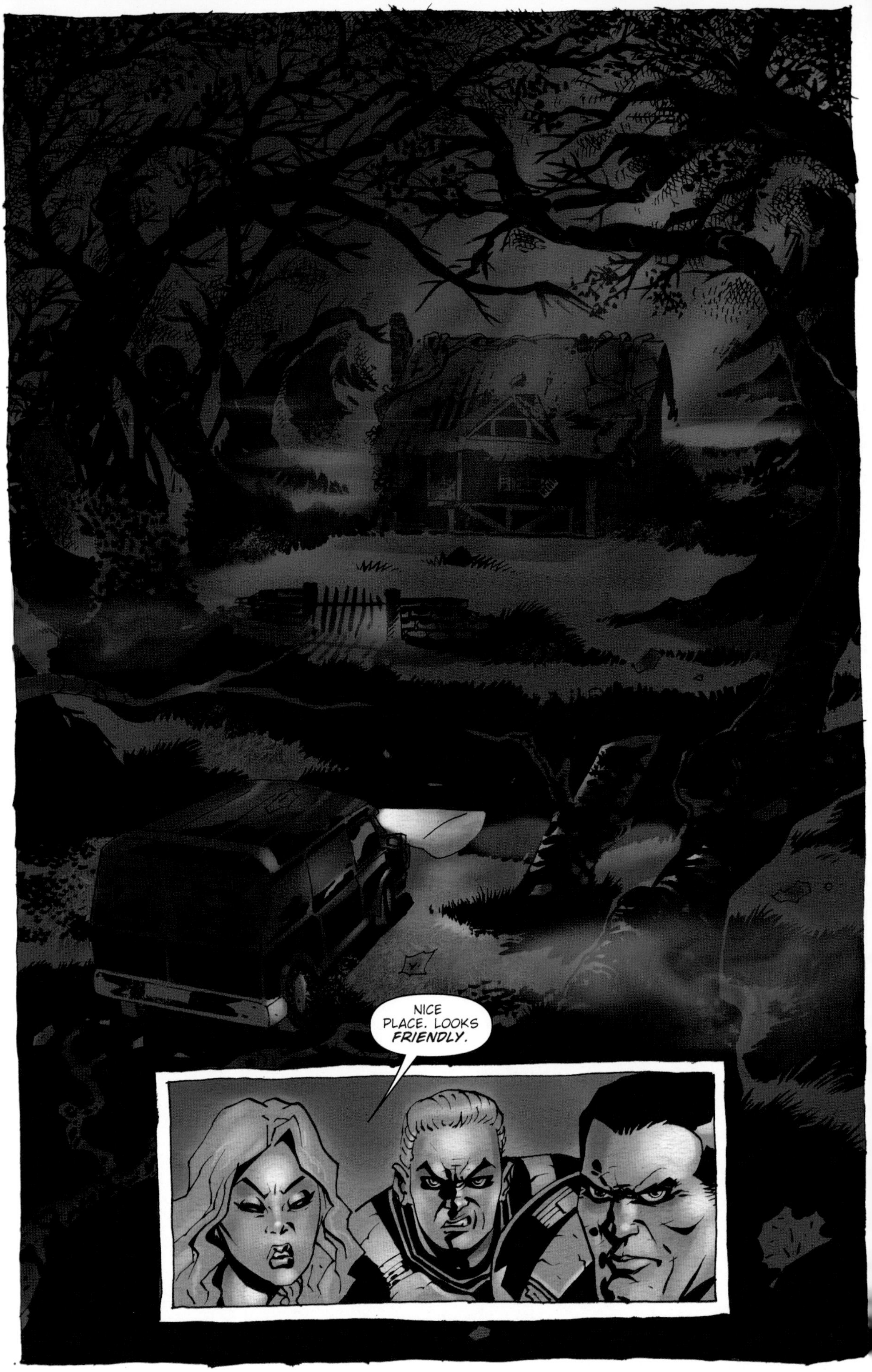
NICE PLACE. LOOKS FRIENDLY.

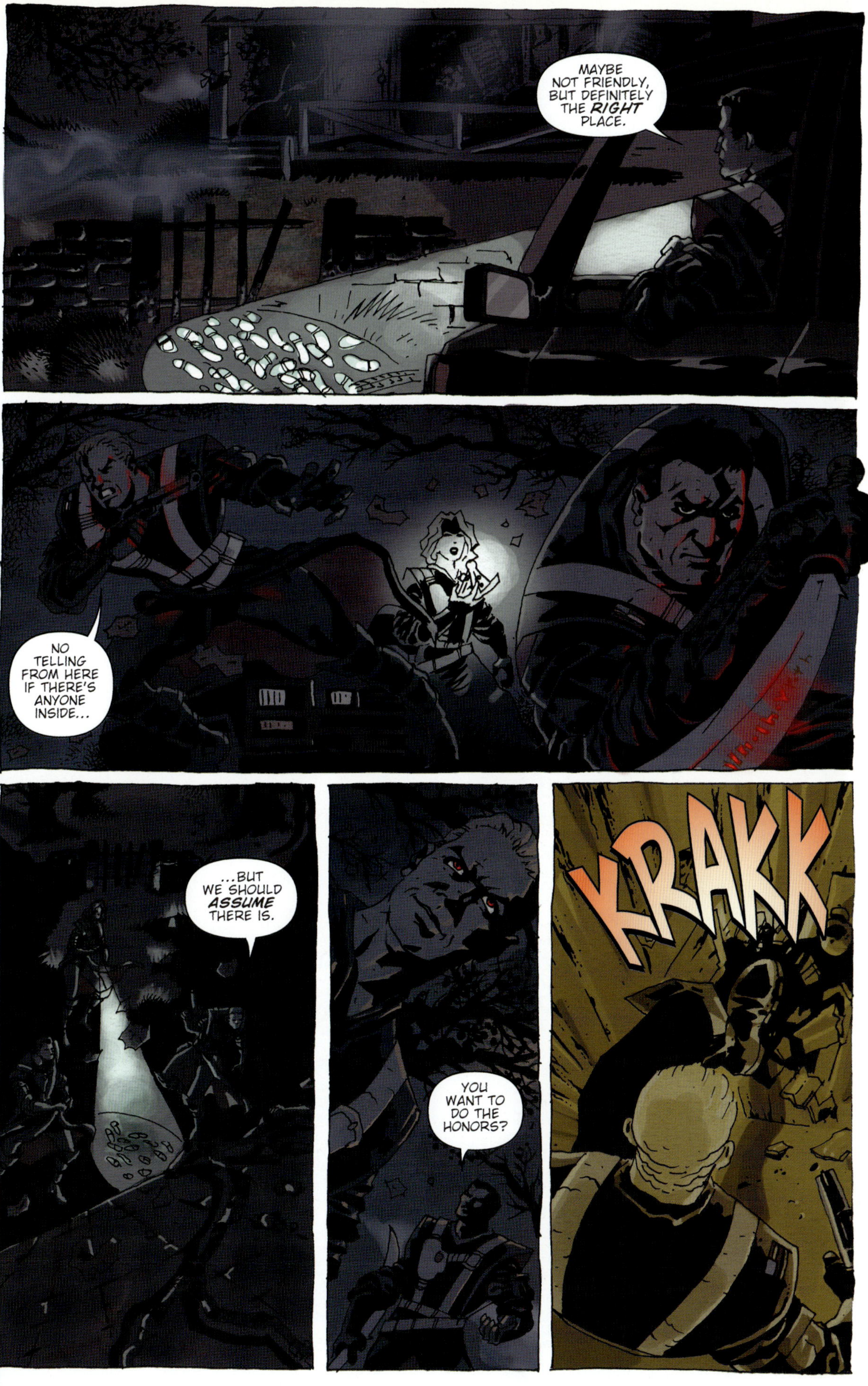
MAYBE NOT FRIENDLY, BUT DEFINITELY THE *RIGHT* PLACE.
NO TELLING FROM HERE IF THERE'S ANYONE INSIDE...
...BUT WE SHOULD *ASSUME* THERE IS.
YOU WANT TO DO THE HONORS?
KRAKK

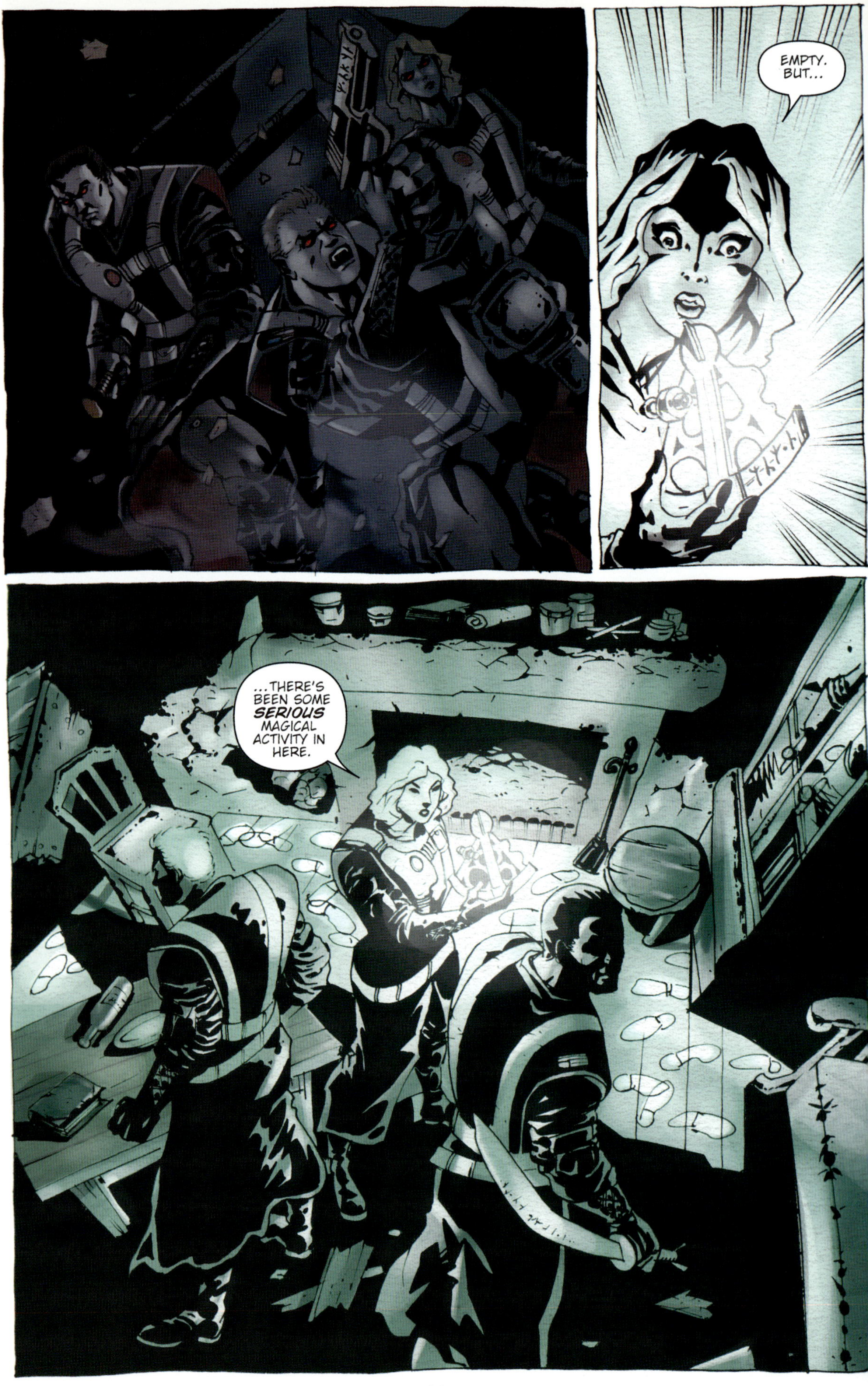
EMPTY. BUT...
...THERE'S BEEN SOME **SERIOUS** MAGICAL ACTIVITY IN HERE.

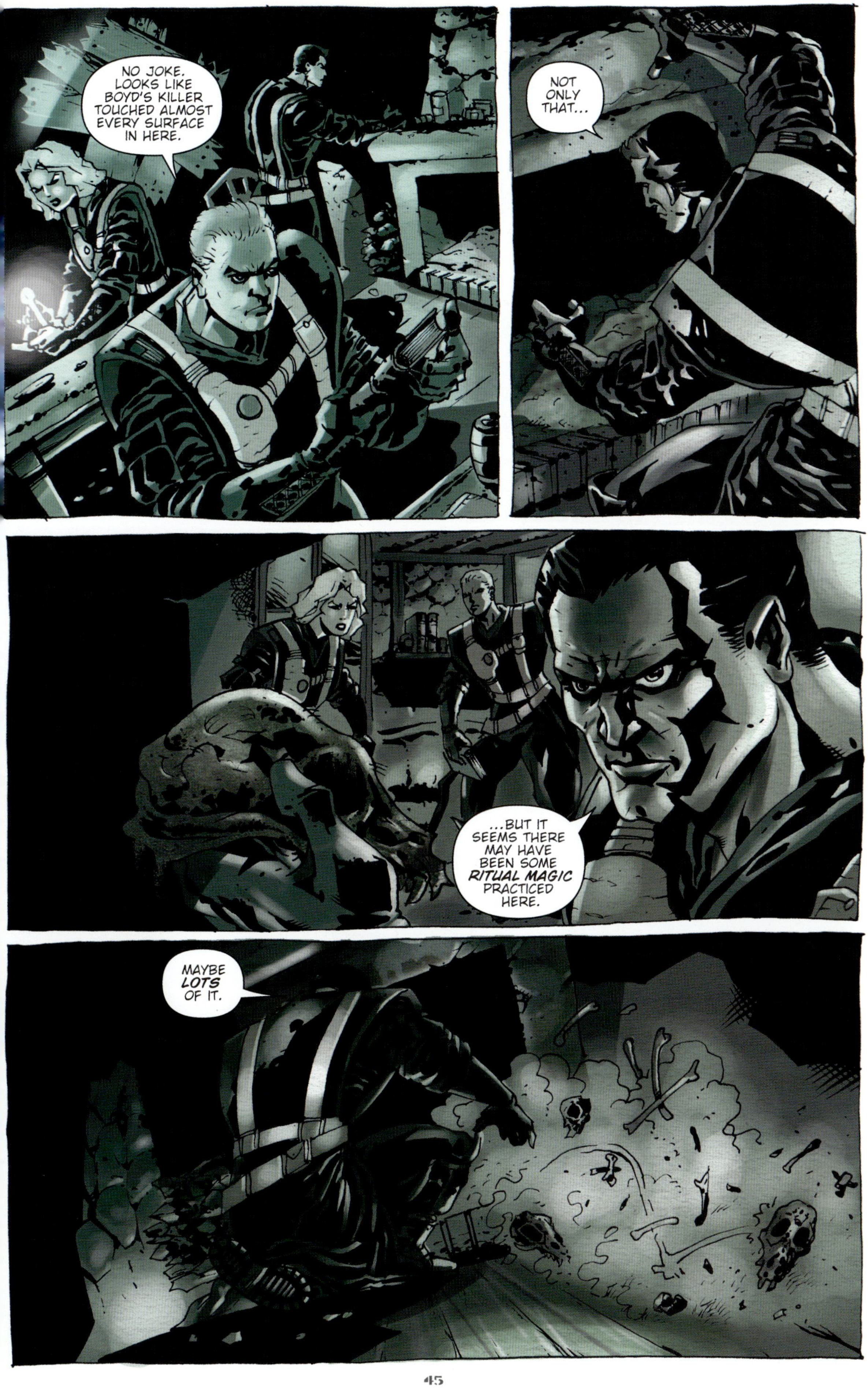
NO JOKE. LOOKS LIKE BOYD'S KILLER TOUCHED ALMOST EVERY SURFACE IN HERE.
NOT ONLY THAT...
...BUT IT SEEMS THERE MAY HAVE BEEN SOME *RITUAL MAGIC* PRACTICED HERE.
MAYBE *LOTS* OF IT.

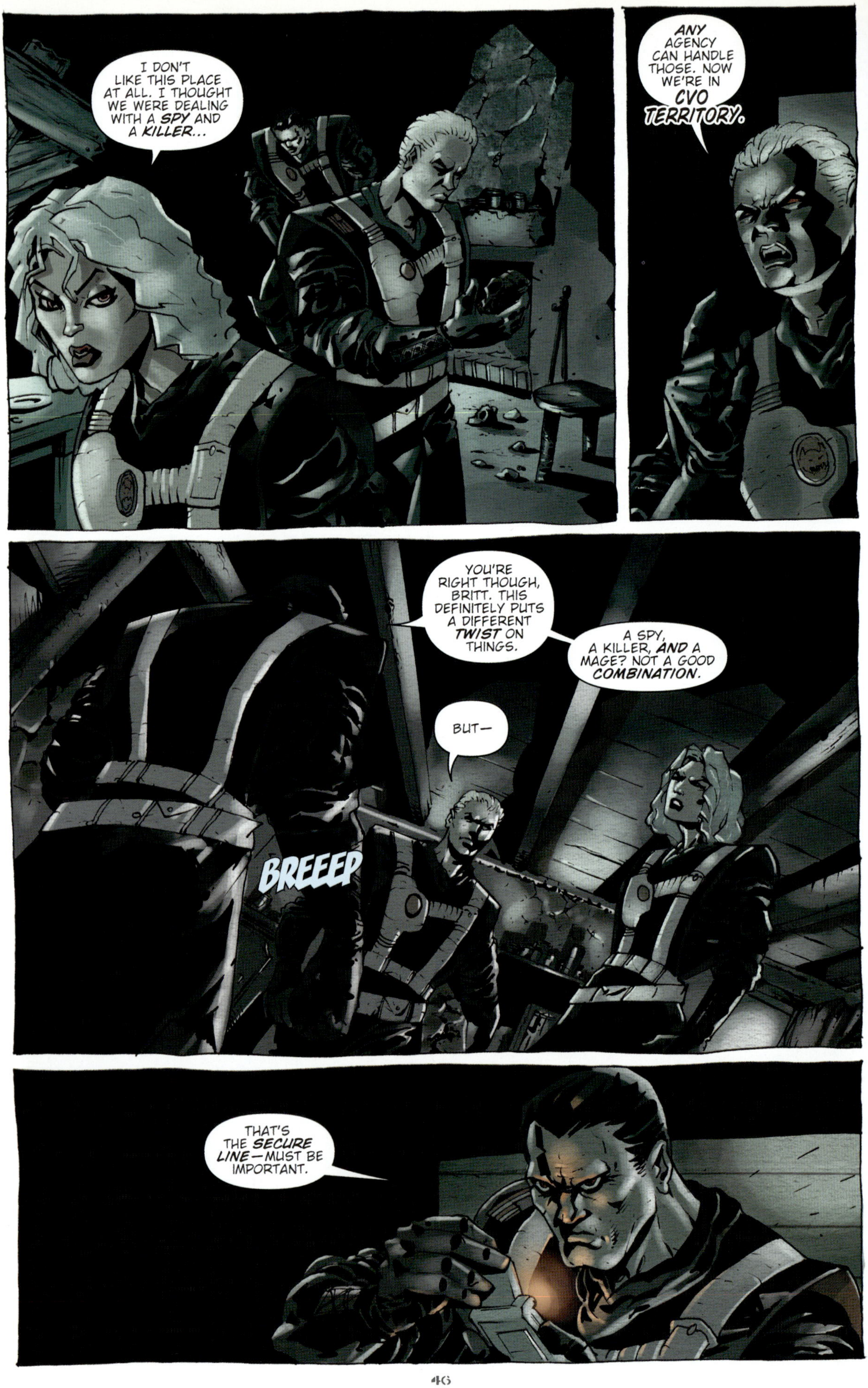
I DON'T LIKE THIS PLACE AT ALL. I THOUGHT WE WERE DEALING WITH A SPY AND A KILLER...
ANY AGENCY CAN HANDLE THOSE. NOW WE'RE IN CVO TERRITORY.
YOU'RE RIGHT THOUGH, BRITT. THIS DEFINITELY PUTS A DIFFERENT TWIST ON THINGS.
A SPY, A KILLER, AND A MAGE? NOT A GOOD COMBINATION.
BUT—
BREEEP
THAT'S THE SECURE LINE—MUST BE IMPORTANT.

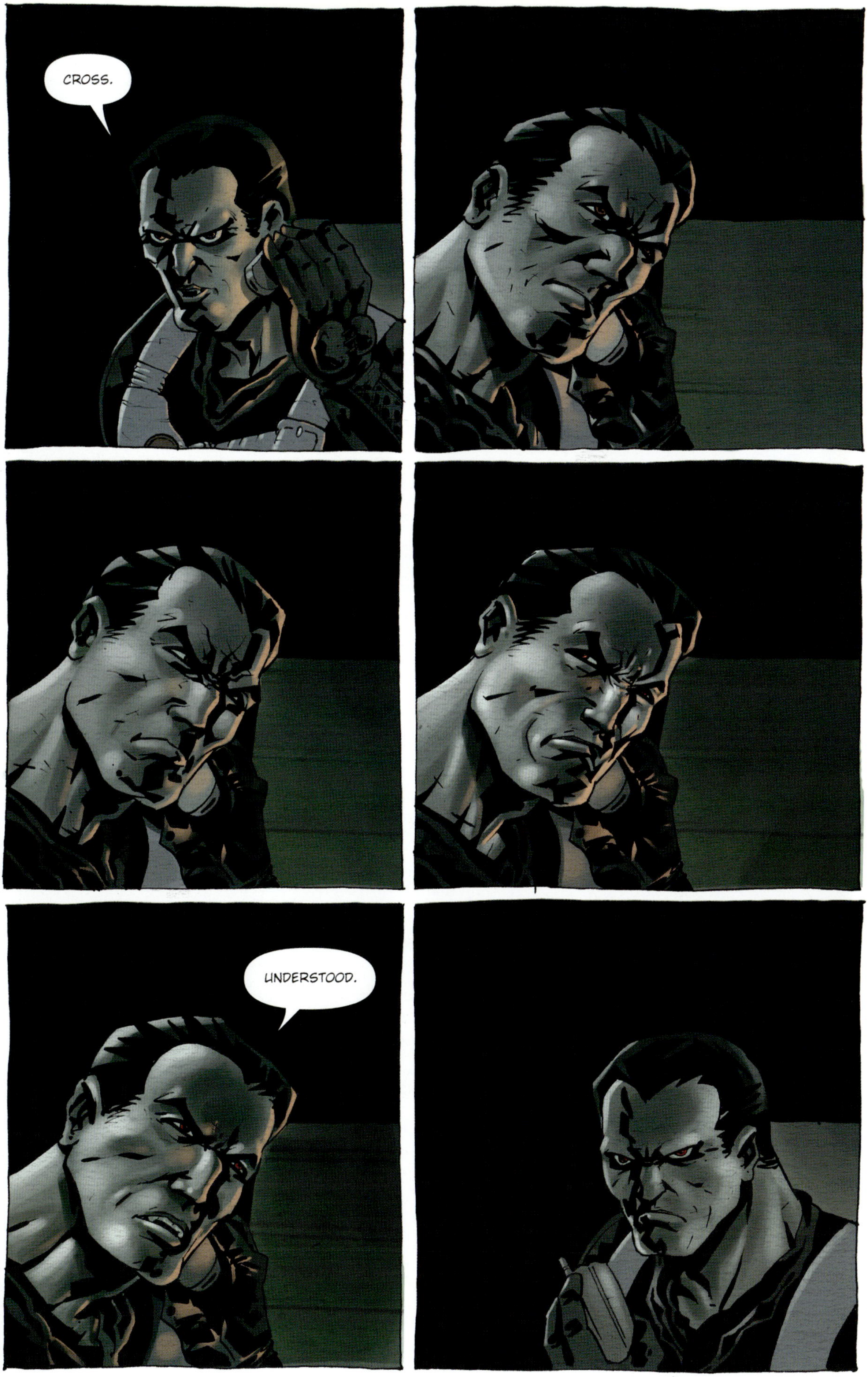
CROSS.
UNDERSTOOD.

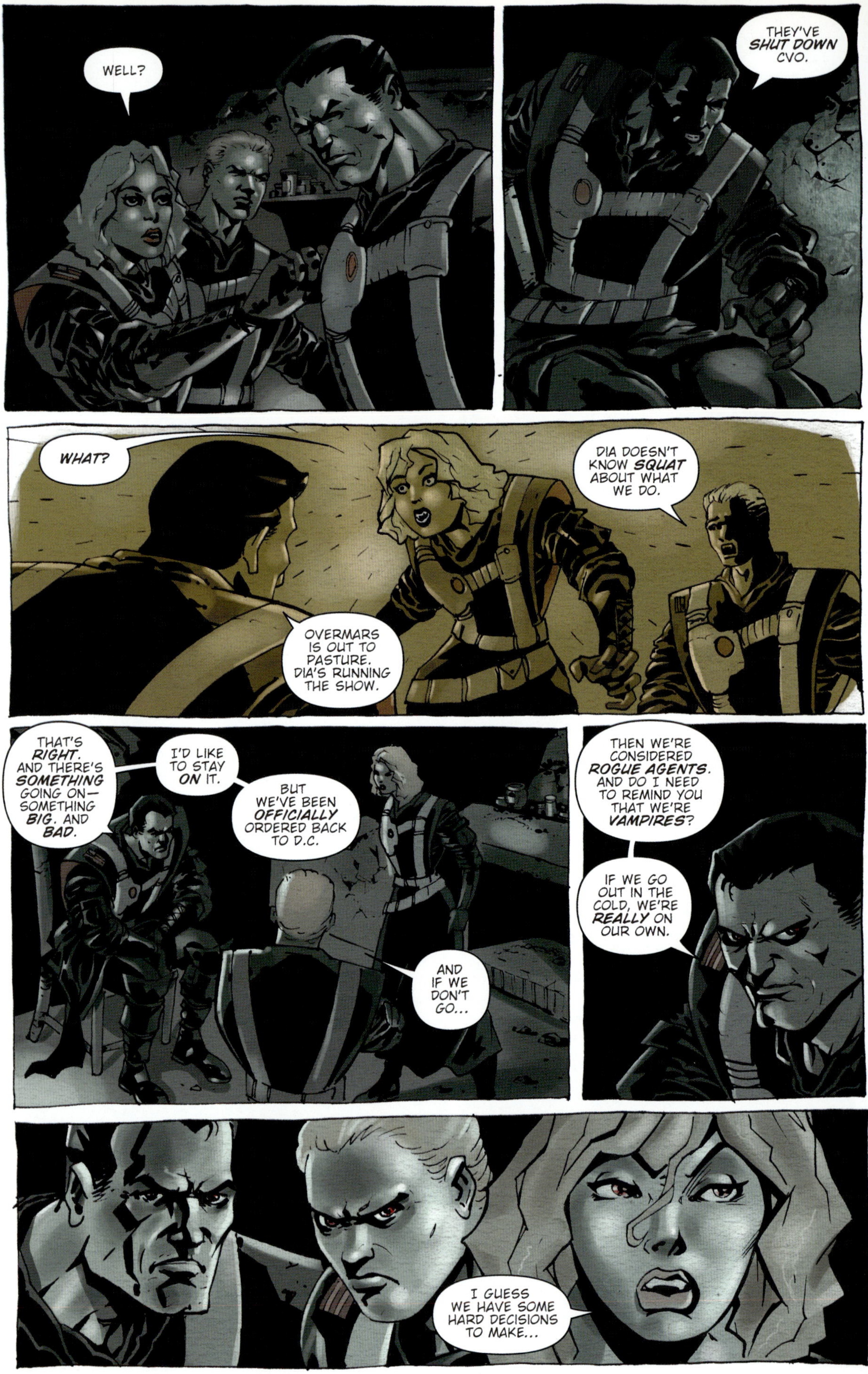
WELL?
THEY'VE SHUT DOWN CVO.
WHAT?
DIA DOESN'T KNOW SQUAT ABOUT WHAT WE DO.
OVERMARS IS OUT TO PASTURE. DIA'S RUNNING THE SHOW.
THAT'S RIGHT. AND THERE'S SOMETHING GOING ON— SOMETHING BIG. AND BAD.
I'D LIKE TO STAY ON IT.
BUT WE'VE BEEN OFFICIALLY ORDERED BACK TO D.C.
AND IF WE DON'T GO...
THEN WE'RE CONSIDERED ROGUE AGENTS. AND DO I NEED TO REMIND YOU THAT WE'RE VAMPIRES?
IF WE GO OUT IN THE COLD, WE'RE REALLY ON OUR OWN.
I GUESS WE HAVE SOME HARD DECISIONS TO MAKE...

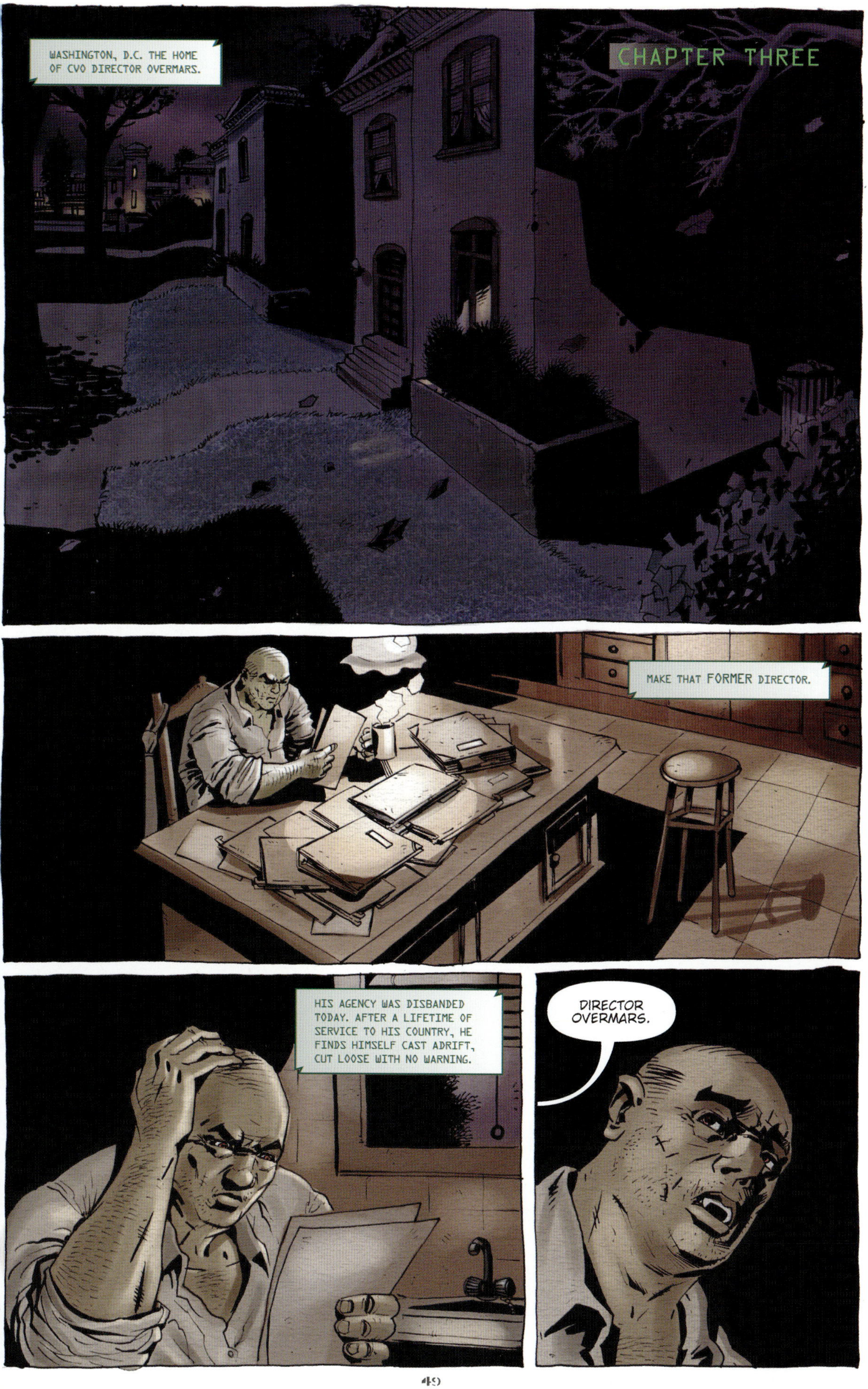
WASHINGTON, D.C. THE HOME OF CVO DIRECTOR OVERMARS.
CHAPTER THREE
MAKE THAT FORMER DIRECTOR.
HIS AGENCY WAS DISBANDED TODAY. AFTER A LIFETIME OF SERVICE TO HIS COUNTRY, HE FINDS HIMSELF CAST ADRIFT, CUT LOOSE WITH NO WARNING.
DIRECTOR OVERMARS.

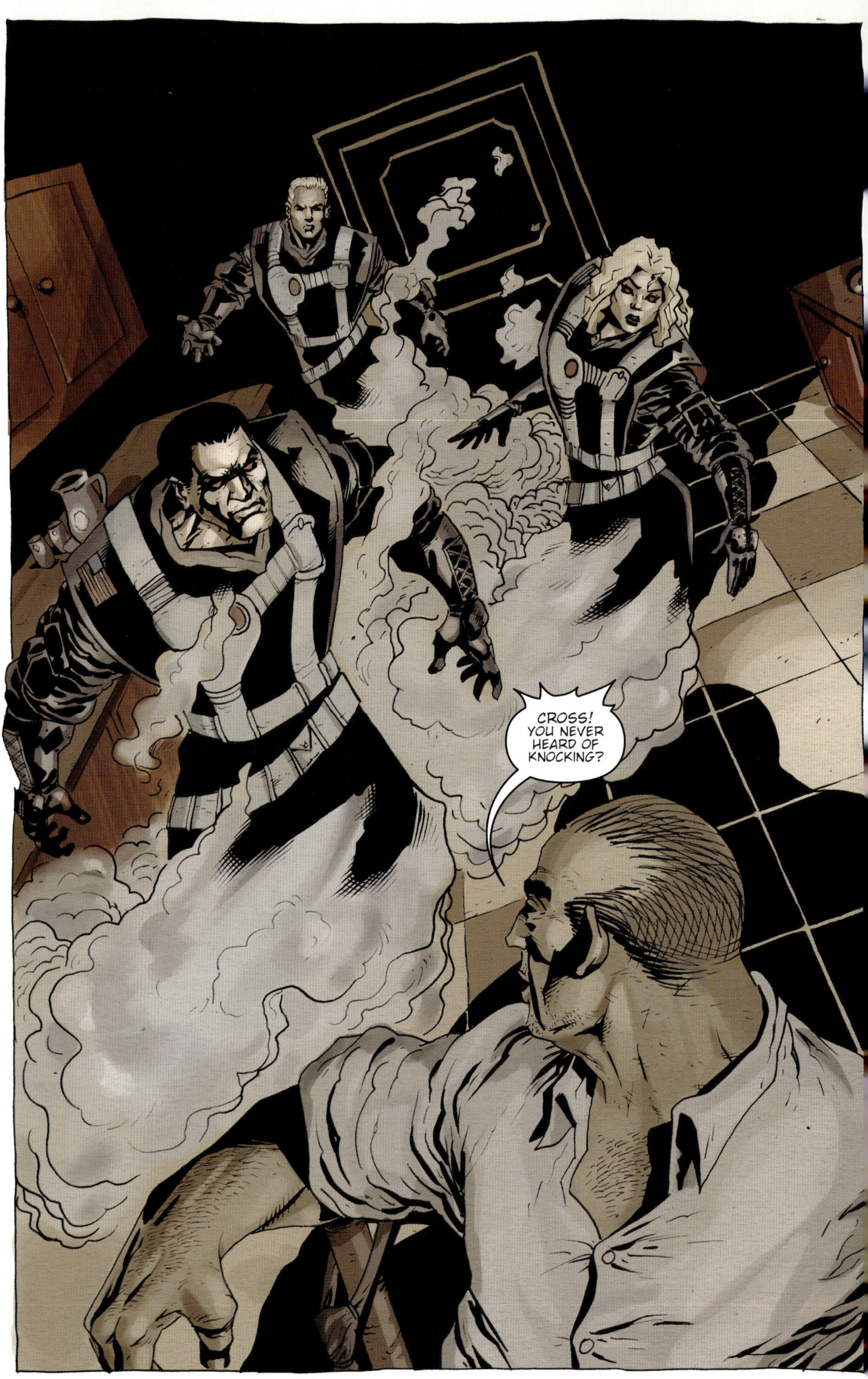
CROSS! YOU NEVER HEARD OF KNOCKING?

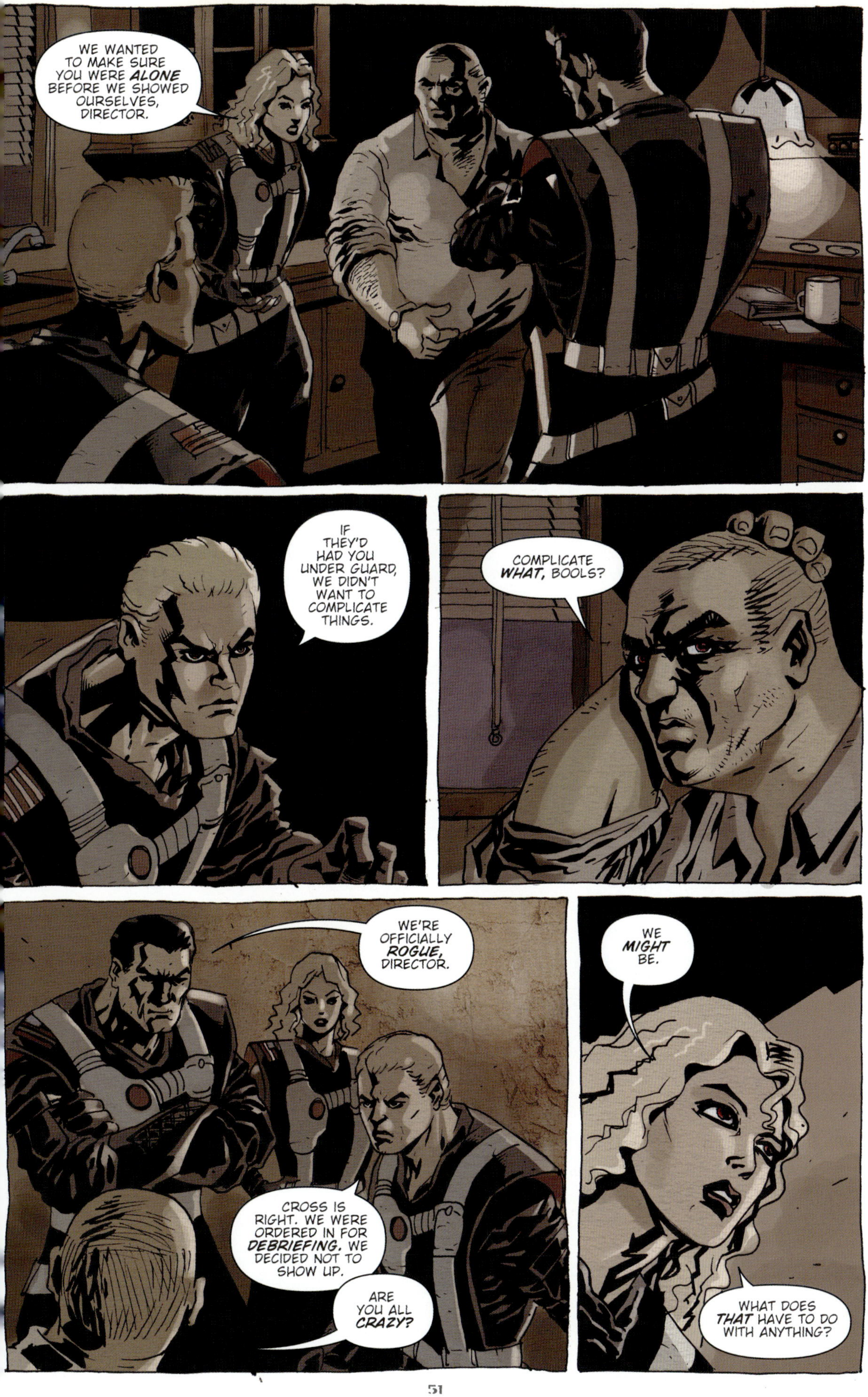
WE WANTED TO MAKE SURE YOU WERE ALONE BEFORE WE SHOWED OURSELVES, DIRECTOR.
IF THEY'D HAD YOU UNDER GUARD, WE DIDN'T WANT TO COMPLICATE THINGS.
COMPLICATE WHAT, BOOLS?
WE'RE OFFICIALLY ROGUE, DIRECTOR.
CROSS IS RIGHT. WE WERE ORDERED IN FOR DEBRIEFING. WE DECIDED NOT TO SHOW UP.
ARE YOU ALL CRAZY?
WE MIGHT BE.
WHAT DOES THAT HAVE TO DO WITH ANYTHING?

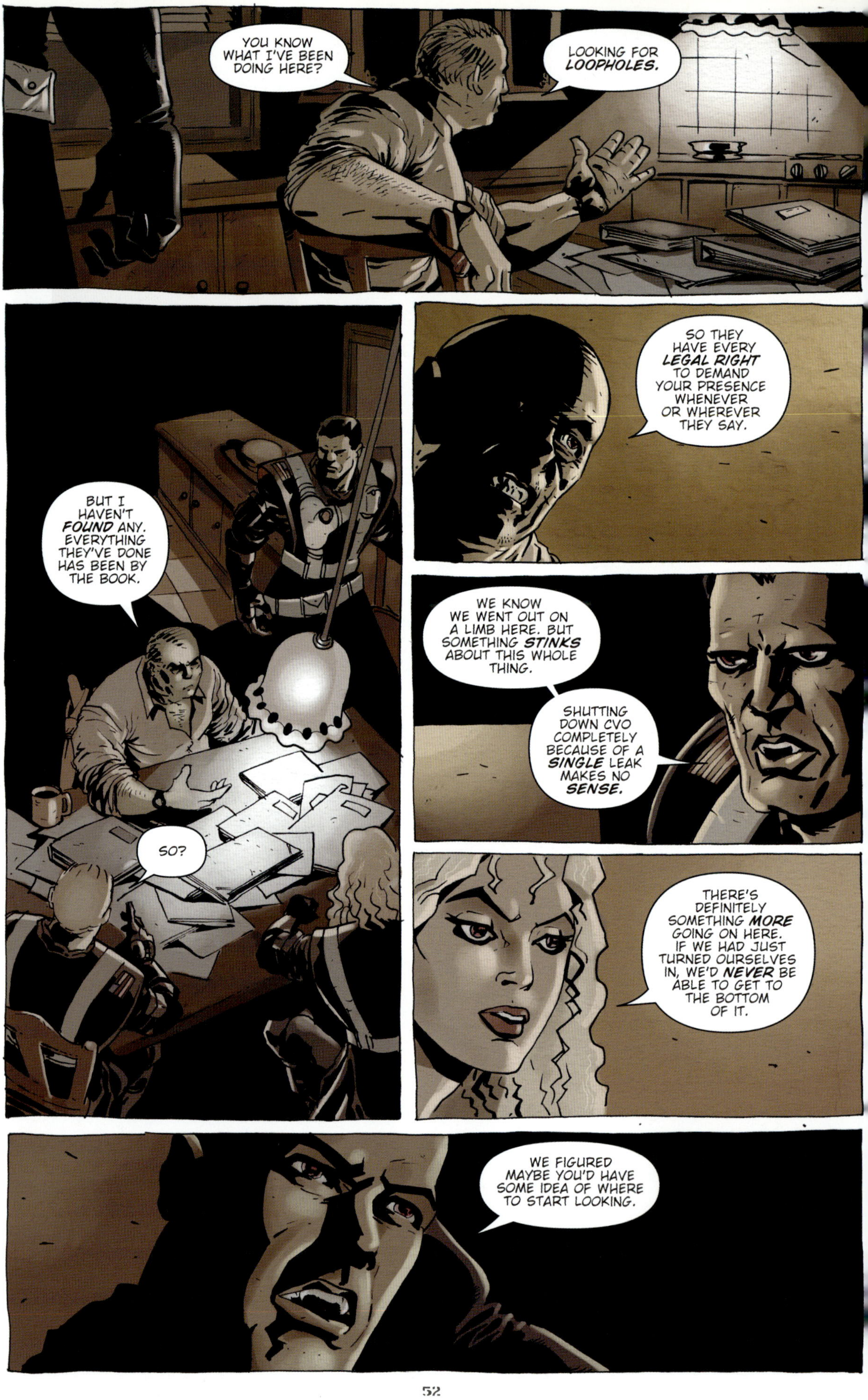
YOU KNOW WHAT I'VE BEEN DOING HERE?
LOOKING FOR LOOPHOLES.
BUT I HAVEN'T FOUND ANY. EVERYTHING THEY'VE DONE HAS BEEN BY THE BOOK.
SO?
SO THEY HAVE EVERY LEGAL RIGHT TO DEMAND YOUR PRESENCE WHENEVER OR WHEREVER THEY SAY.
WE KNOW WE WENT OUT ON A LIMB HERE. BUT SOMETHING STINKS ABOUT THIS WHOLE THING.
SHUTTING DOWN CVO COMPLETELY BECAUSE OF A SINGLE LEAK MAKES NO SENSE.
THERE'S DEFINITELY SOMETHING MORE GOING ON HERE. IF WE HAD JUST TURNED OURSELVES IN, WE'D NEVER BE ABLE TO GET TO THE BOTTOM OF IT.
WE FIGURED MAYBE YOU'D HAVE SOME IDEA OF WHERE TO START LOOKING.

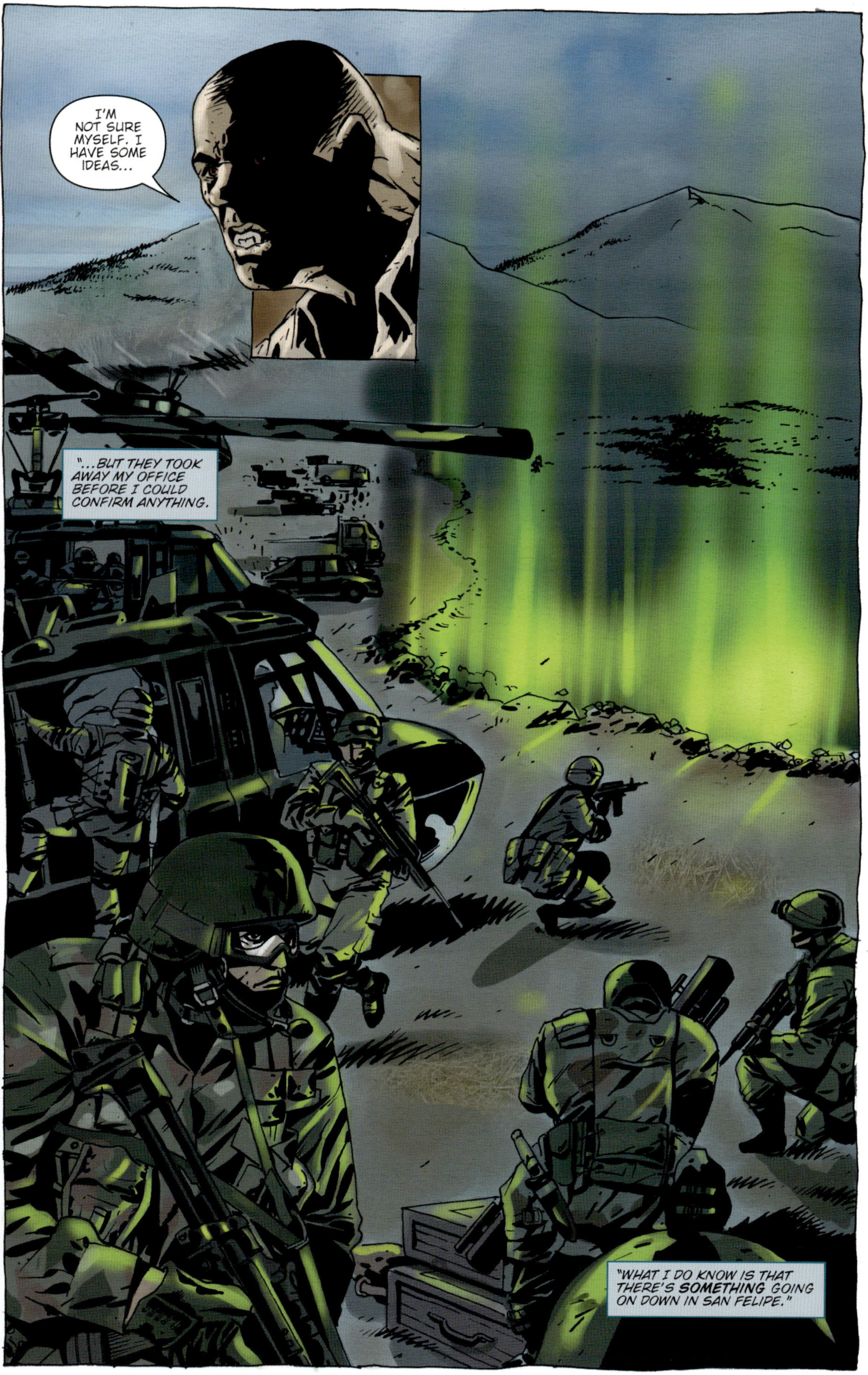
I'M NOT SURE MYSELF. I HAVE SOME IDEAS...
"...BUT THEY TOOK AWAY MY OFFICE BEFORE I COULD CONFIRM ANYTHING.
"WHAT I DO KNOW IS THAT THERE'S **SOMETHING** GOING ON DOWN IN SAN FELIPE."

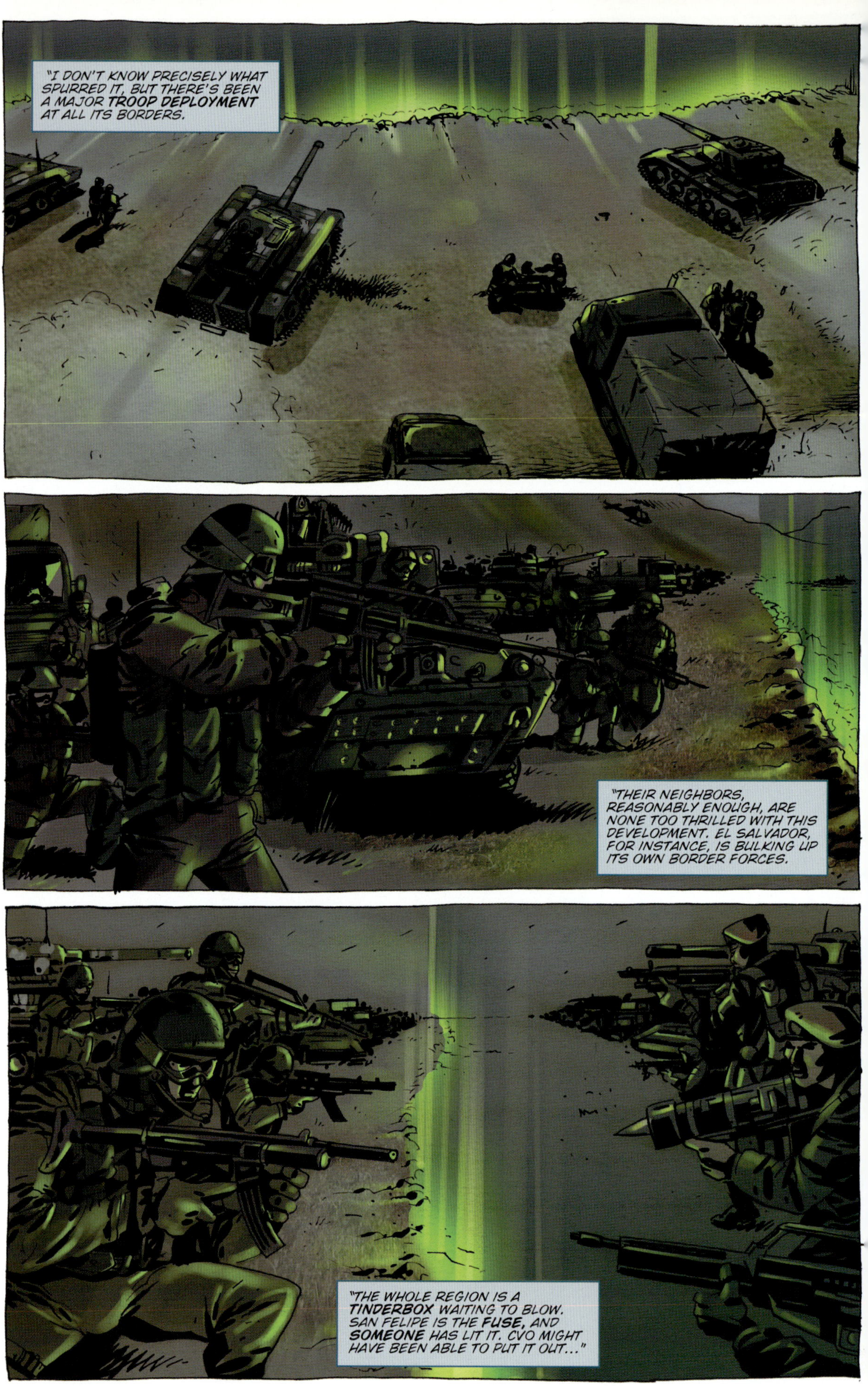
"I DON'T KNOW PRECISELY WHAT SPURRED IT, BUT THERE'S BEEN A MAJOR **TROOP DEPLOYMENT** AT ALL ITS BORDERS.
"THEIR NEIGHBORS, REASONABLY ENOUGH, ARE NONE TOO THRILLED WITH THIS DEVELOPMENT. EL SALVADOR, FOR INSTANCE, IS BULKING UP ITS OWN BORDER FORCES.
"THE WHOLE REGION IS A **TINDERBOX** WAITING TO BLOW. SAN FELIPE IS THE **FUSE,** AND **SOMEONE** HAS LIT IT. CVO MIGHT HAVE BEEN ABLE TO PUT IT OUT..."

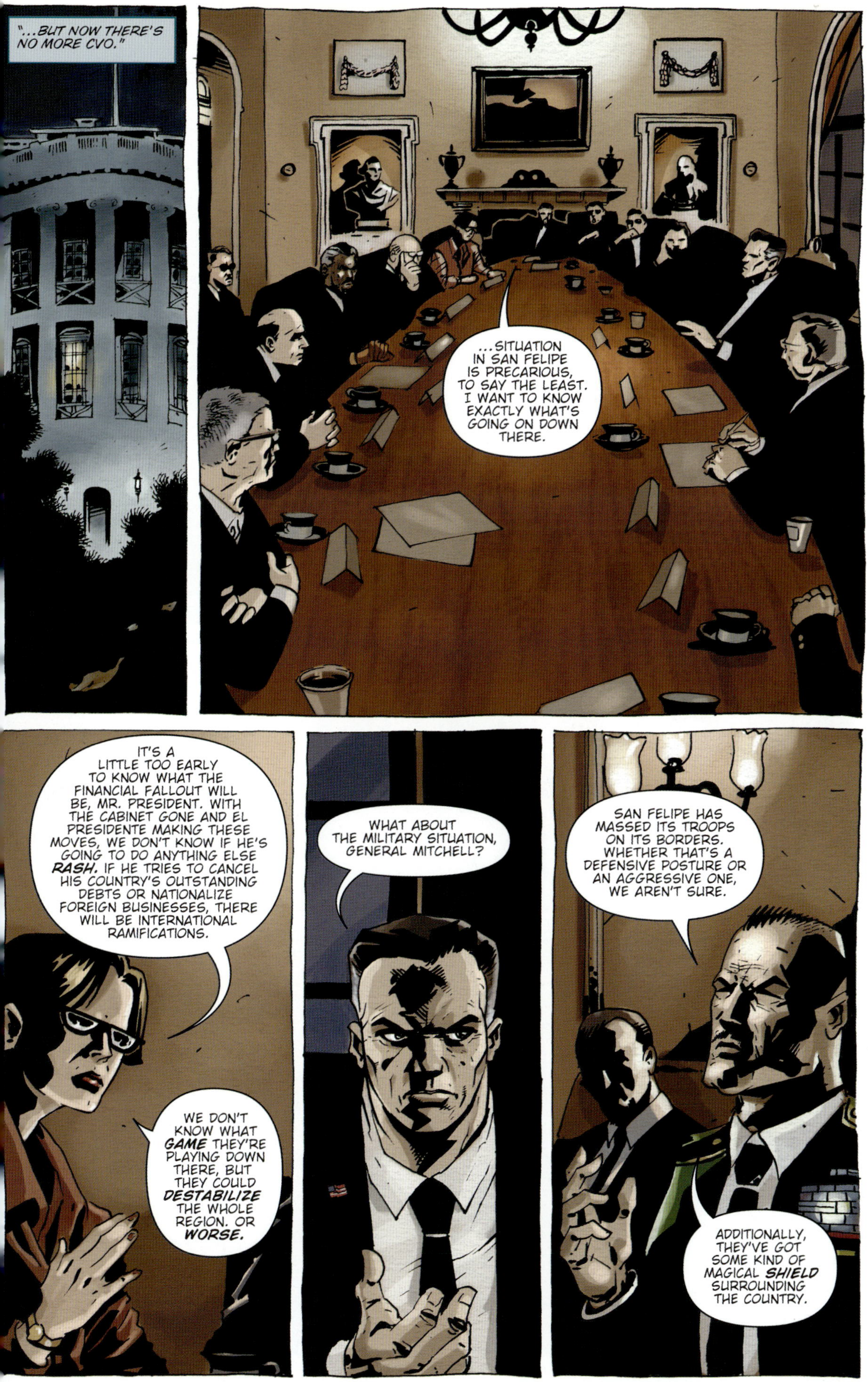
"...BUT NOW THERE'S NO MORE CVO."
...SITUATION IN SAN FELIPE IS PRECARIOUS, TO SAY THE LEAST. I WANT TO KNOW EXACTLY WHAT'S GOING ON DOWN THERE.
IT'S A LITTLE TOO EARLY TO KNOW WHAT THE FINANCIAL FALLOUT WILL BE, MR. PRESIDENT. WITH THE CABINET GONE AND EL PRESIDENTE MAKING THESE MOVES, WE DON'T KNOW IF HE'S GOING TO DO ANYTHING ELSE RASH. IF HE TRIES TO CANCEL HIS COUNTRY'S OUTSTANDING DEBTS OR NATIONALIZE FOREIGN BUSINESSES, THERE WILL BE INTERNATIONAL RAMIFICATIONS.
WE DON'T KNOW WHAT GAME THEY'RE PLAYING DOWN THERE, BUT THEY COULD DESTABILIZE THE WHOLE REGION. OR WORSE.
WHAT ABOUT THE MILITARY SITUATION, GENERAL MITCHELL?
SAN FELIPE HAS MASSED ITS TROOPS ON ITS BORDERS. WHETHER THAT'S A DEFENSIVE POSTURE OR AN AGGRESSIVE ONE, WE AREN'T SURE.
ADDITIONALLY, THEY'VE GOT SOME KIND OF MAGICAL SHIELD SURROUNDING THE COUNTRY.

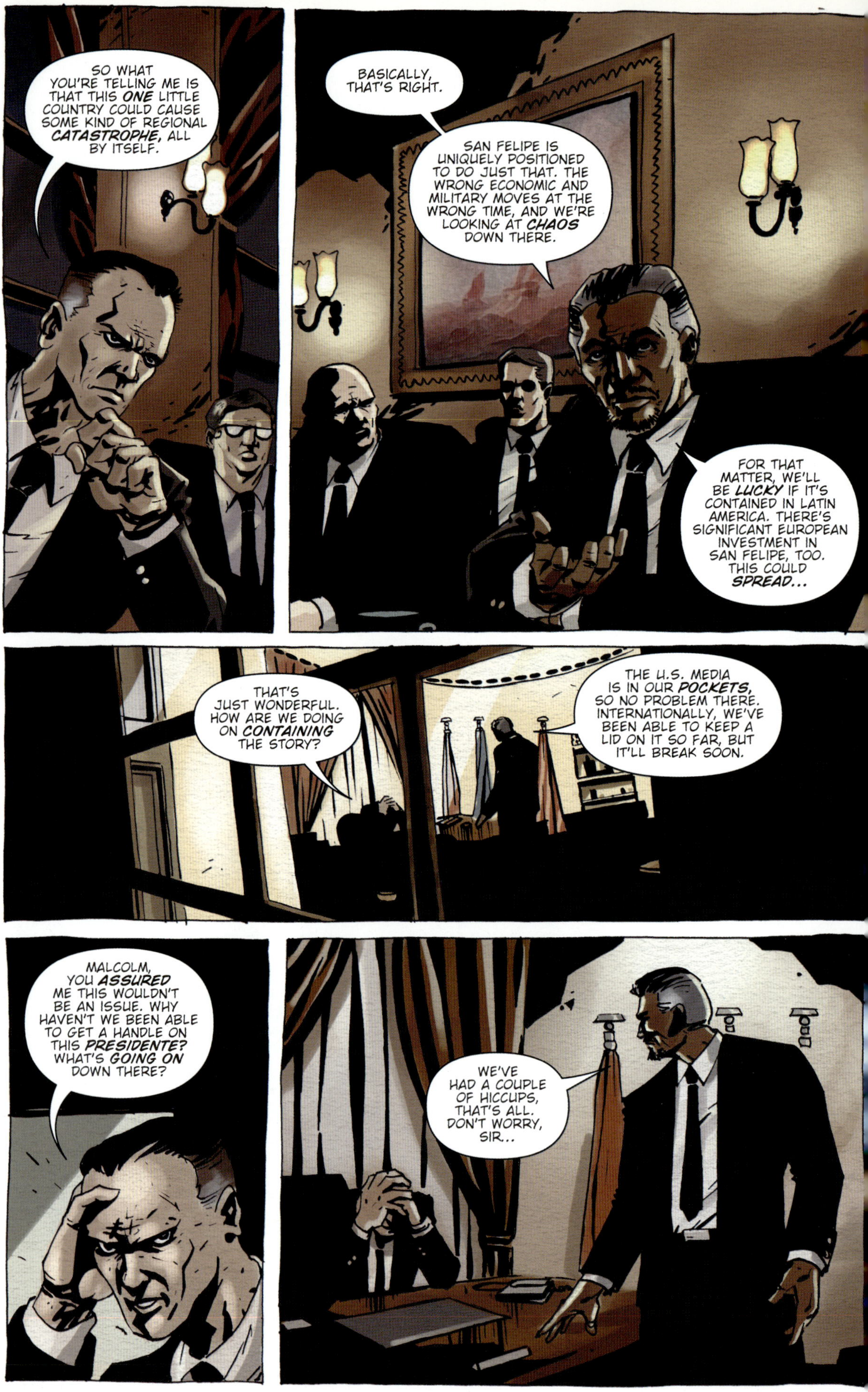
SO WHAT YOU'RE TELLING ME IS THAT THIS ONE LITTLE COUNTRY COULD CAUSE SOME KIND OF REGIONAL CATASTROPHE, ALL BY ITSELF.
BASICALLY, THAT'S RIGHT.
SAN FELIPE IS UNIQUELY POSITIONED TO DO JUST THAT. THE WRONG ECONOMIC AND MILITARY MOVES AT THE WRONG TIME, AND WE'RE LOOKING AT CHAOS DOWN THERE.
FOR THAT MATTER, WE'LL BE LUCKY IF IT'S CONTAINED IN LATIN AMERICA. THERE'S SIGNIFICANT EUROPEAN INVESTMENT IN SAN FELIPE, TOO. THIS COULD SPREAD...
THAT'S JUST WONDERFUL. HOW ARE WE DOING ON CONTAINING THE STORY?
THE U.S. MEDIA IS IN OUR POCKETS, SO NO PROBLEM THERE. INTERNATIONALLY, WE'VE BEEN ABLE TO KEEP A LID ON IT SO FAR, BUT IT'LL BREAK SOON.
MALCOLM, YOU ASSURED ME THIS WOULDN'T BE AN ISSUE. WHY HAVEN'T WE BEEN ABLE TO GET A HANDLE ON THIS PRESIDENTE? WHAT'S GOING ON DOWN THERE?
WE'VE HAD A COUPLE OF HICCUPS, THAT'S ALL. DON'T WORRY, SIR...

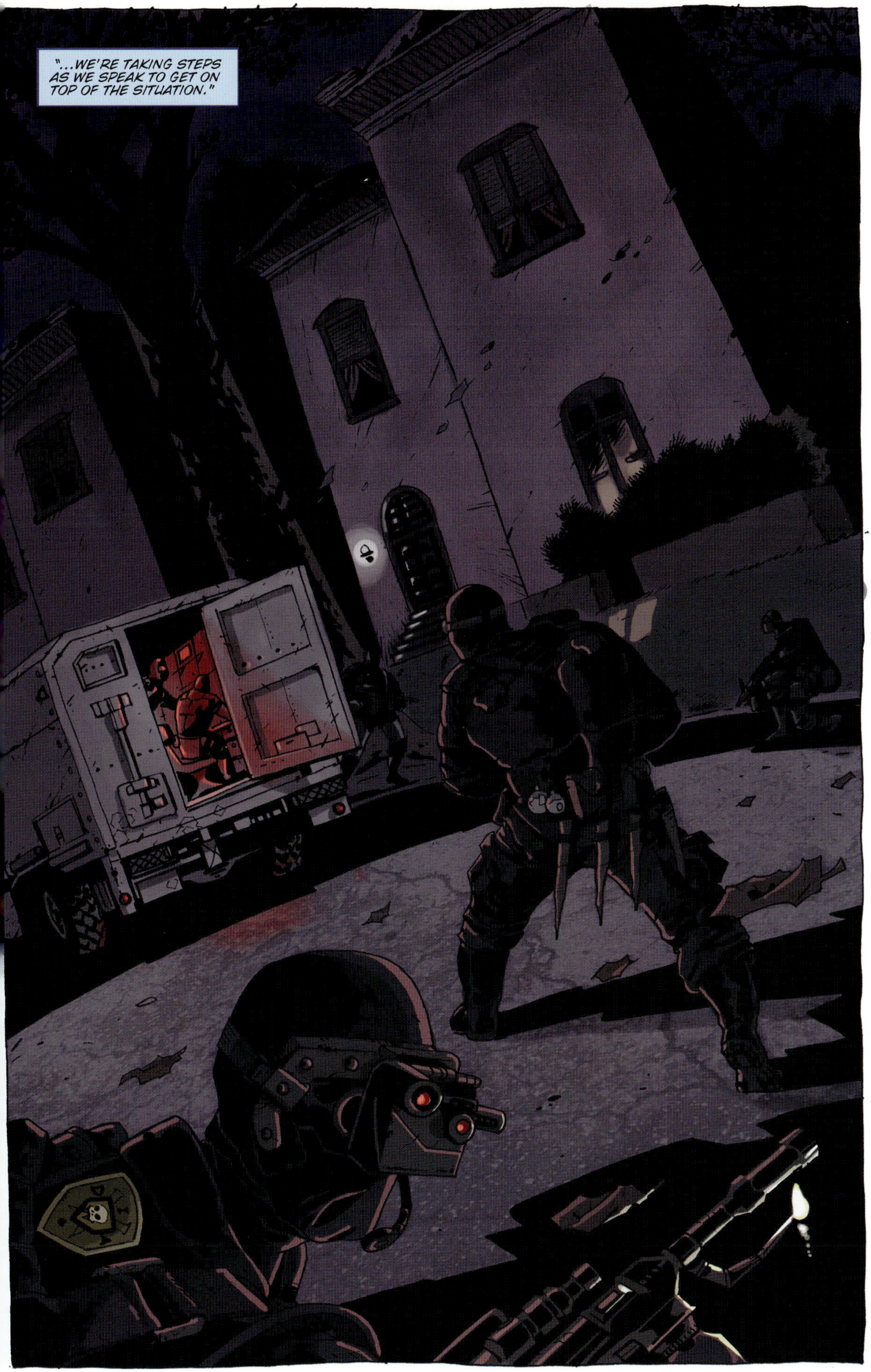
"...WE'RE TAKING STEPS AS WE SPEAK TO GET ON TOP OF THE SITUATION."

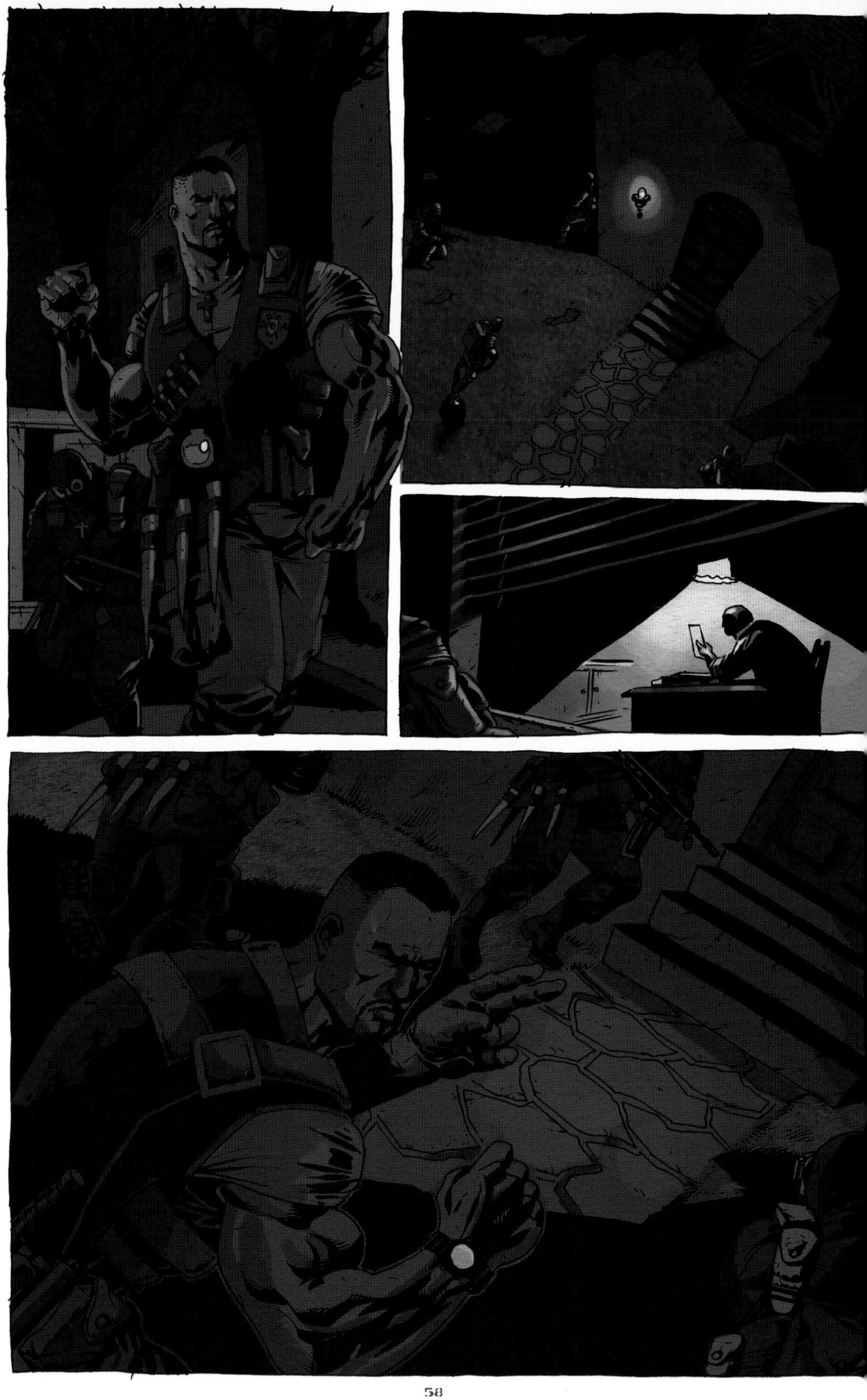

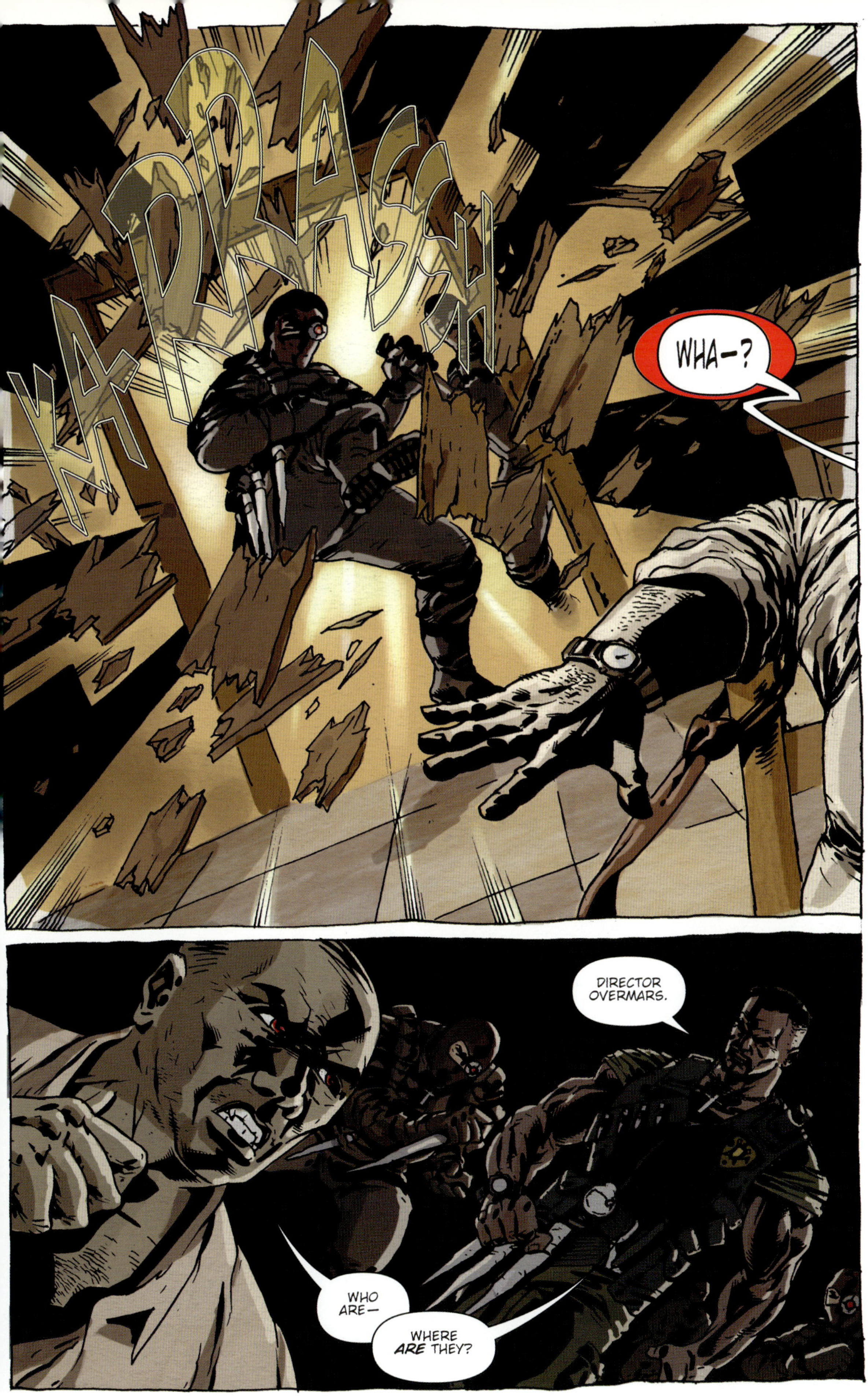
WHA–?
DIRECTOR OVERMARS.
WHO ARE–
WHERE *ARE* THEY?

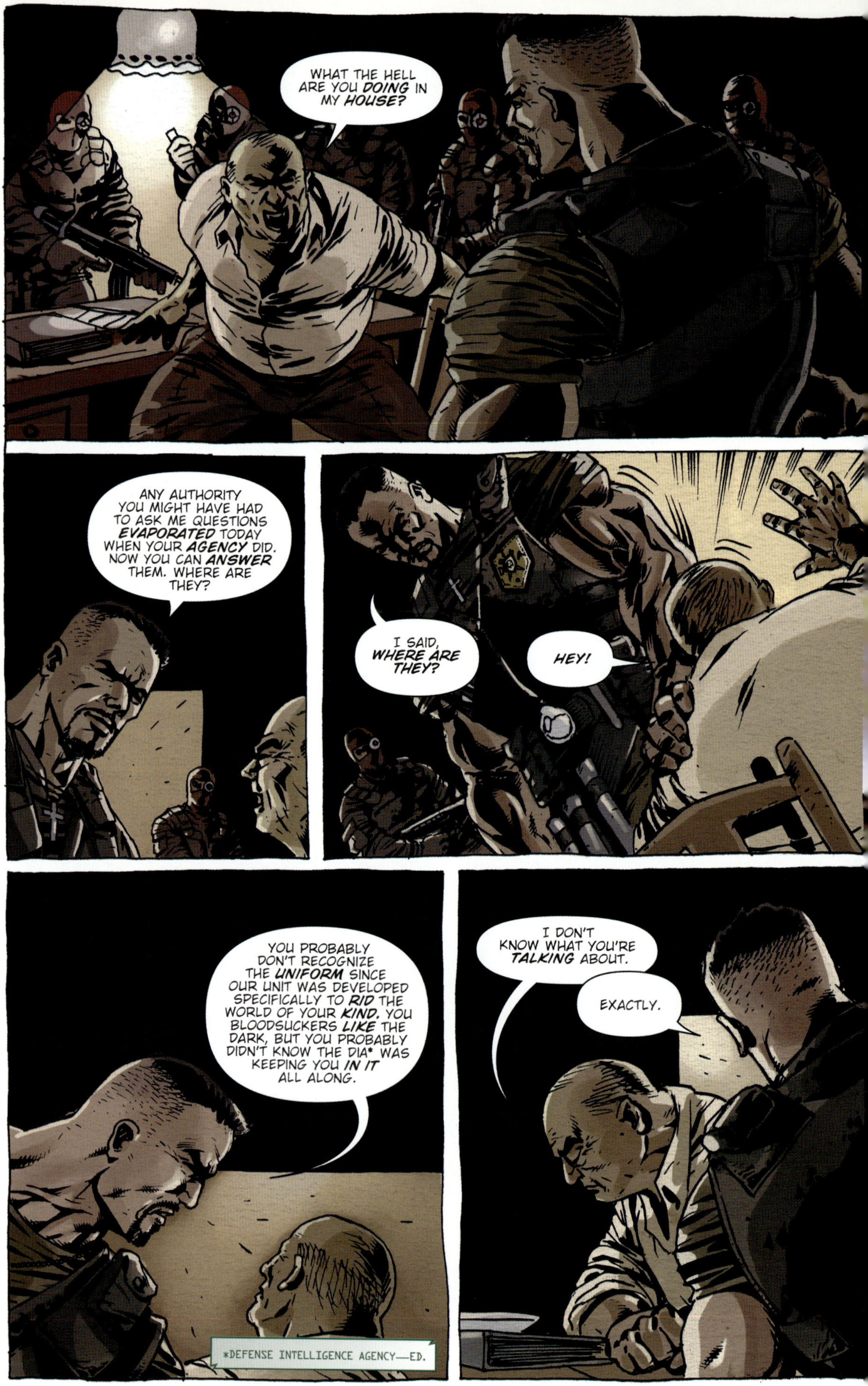
WHAT THE HELL ARE YOU DOING IN MY HOUSE?
ANY AUTHORITY YOU MIGHT HAVE HAD TO ASK ME QUESTIONS EVAPORATED TODAY WHEN YOUR AGENCY DID. NOW YOU CAN ANSWER THEM. WHERE ARE THEY?
I SAID, WHERE ARE THEY?
HEY!
YOU PROBABLY DON'T RECOGNIZE THE UNIFORM SINCE OUR UNIT WAS DEVELOPED SPECIFICALLY TO RID THE WORLD OF YOUR KIND. YOU BLOODSUCKERS LIKE THE DARK, BUT YOU PROBABLY DIDN'T KNOW THE DIA* WAS KEEPING YOU IN IT ALL ALONG.
*DEFENSE INTELLIGENCE AGENCY—ED.
I DON'T KNOW WHAT YOU'RE TALKING ABOUT.
EXACTLY.

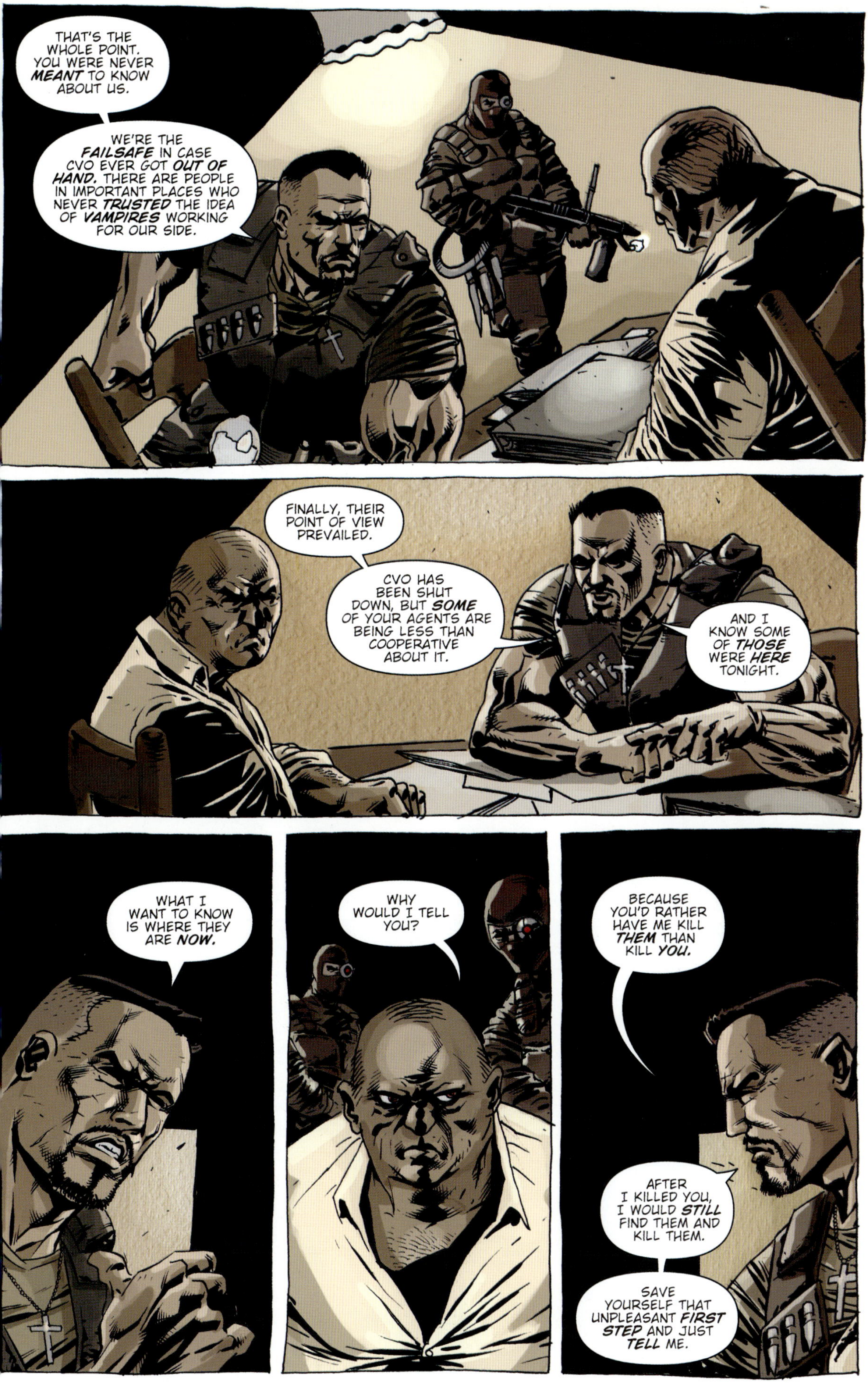
THAT'S THE WHOLE POINT. YOU WERE NEVER MEANT TO KNOW ABOUT US.
WE'RE THE FAILSAFE IN CASE CVO EVER GOT OUT OF HAND. THERE ARE PEOPLE IN IMPORTANT PLACES WHO NEVER TRUSTED THE IDEA OF VAMPIRES WORKING FOR OUR SIDE.
FINALLY, THEIR POINT OF VIEW PREVAILED.
CVO HAS BEEN SHUT DOWN, BUT SOME OF YOUR AGENTS ARE BEING LESS THAN COOPERATIVE ABOUT IT.
AND I KNOW SOME OF THOSE WERE HERE TONIGHT.
WHAT I WANT TO KNOW IS WHERE THEY ARE NOW.
WHY WOULD I TELL YOU?
BECAUSE YOU'D RATHER HAVE ME KILL THEM THAN KILL YOU.
AFTER I KILLED YOU, I WOULD STILL FIND THEM AND KILL THEM.
SAVE YOURSELF THAT UNPLEASANT FIRST STEP AND JUST TELL ME.

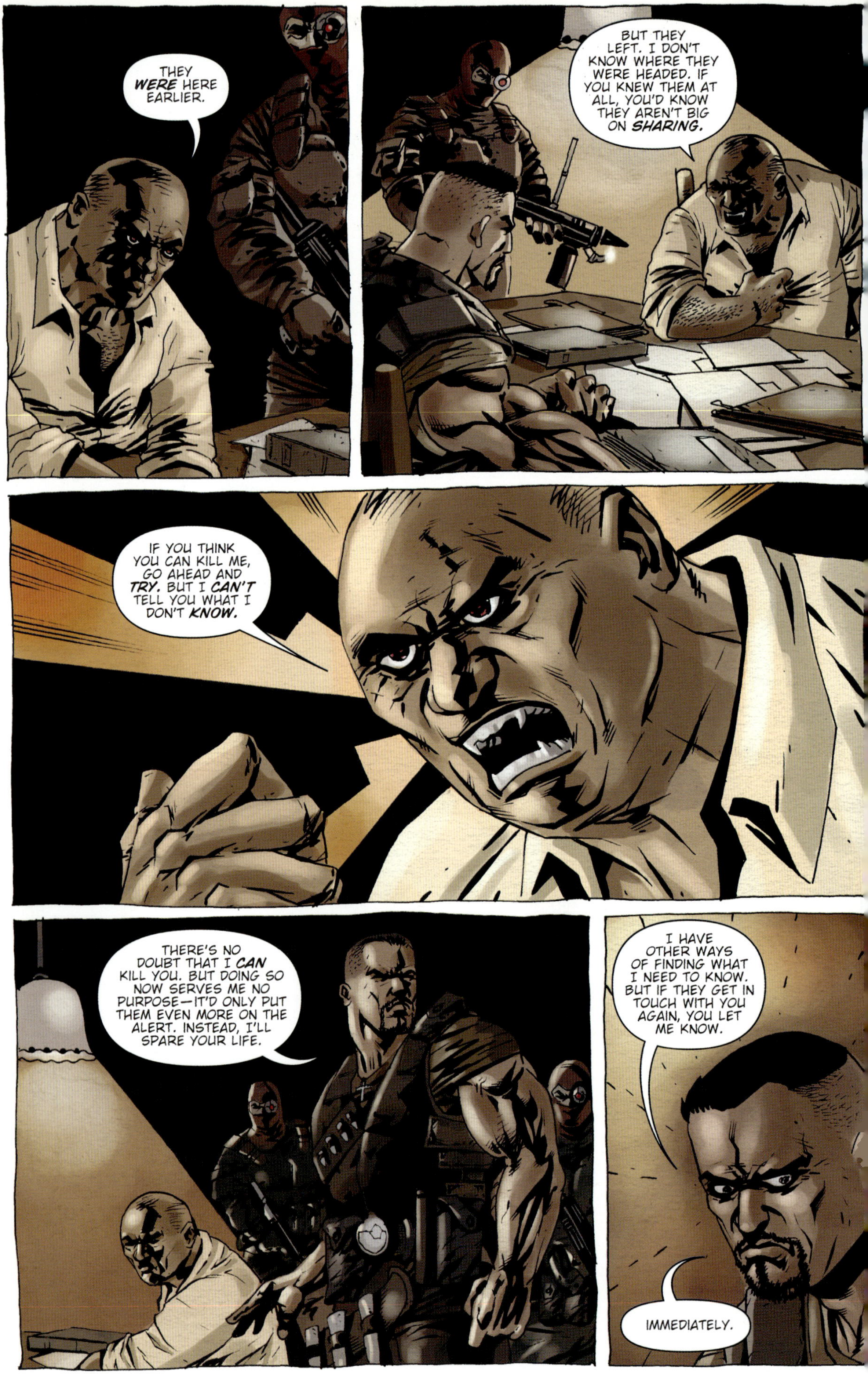
THEY WERE HERE EARLIER.
BUT THEY LEFT. I DON'T KNOW WHERE THEY WERE HEADED. IF YOU KNEW THEM AT ALL, YOU'D KNOW THEY AREN'T BIG ON SHARING.
IF YOU THINK YOU CAN KILL ME, GO AHEAD AND TRY. BUT I CAN'T TELL YOU WHAT I DON'T KNOW.
THERE'S NO DOUBT THAT I CAN KILL YOU. BUT DOING SO NOW SERVES ME NO PURPOSE—IT'D ONLY PUT THEM EVEN MORE ON THE ALERT. INSTEAD, I'LL SPARE YOUR LIFE.
I HAVE OTHER WAYS OF FINDING WHAT I NEED TO KNOW. BUT IF THEY GET IN TOUCH WITH YOU AGAIN, YOU LET ME KNOW.
IMMEDIATELY.

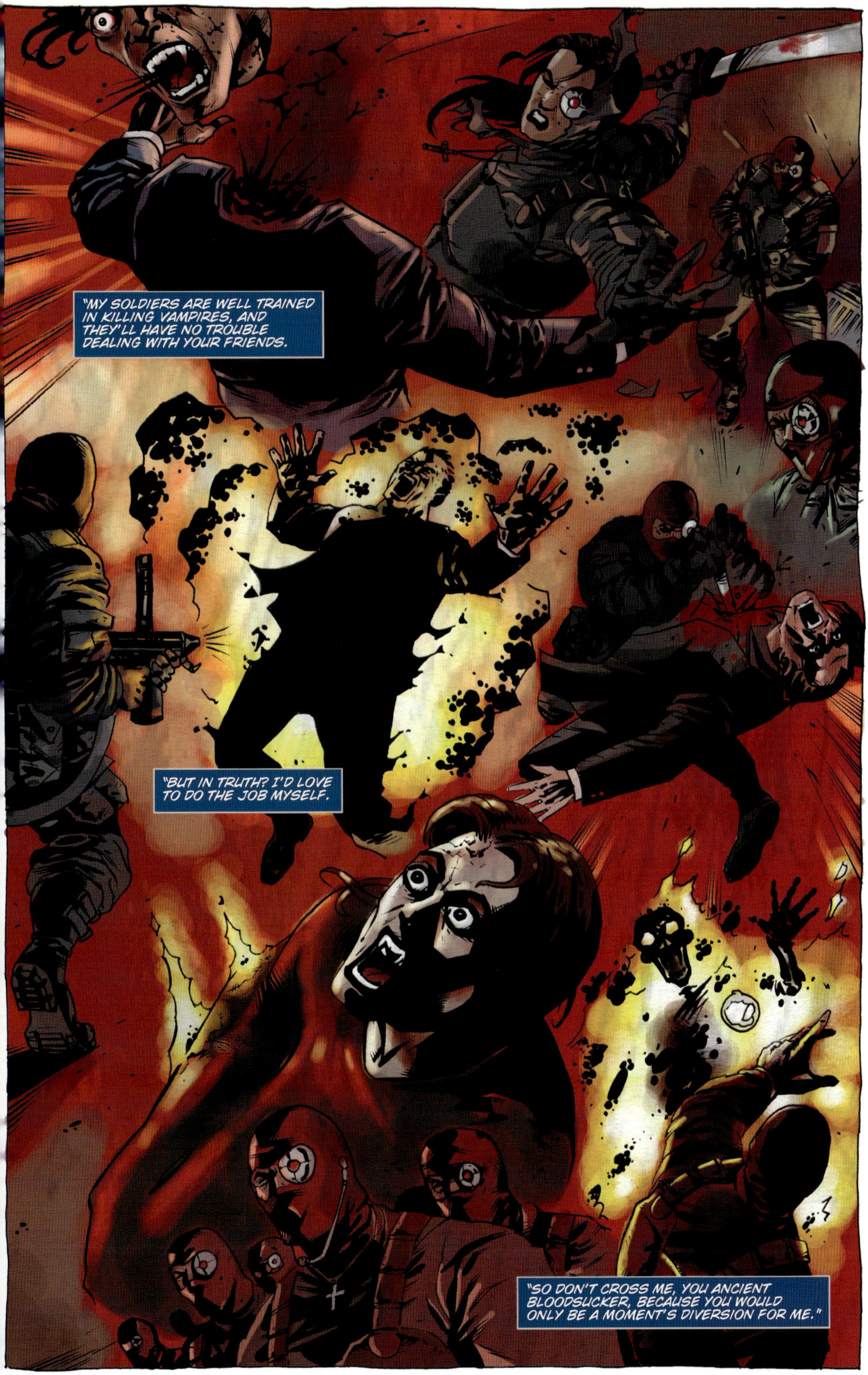
"MY SOLDIERS ARE WELL TRAINED IN KILLING VAMPIRES, AND THEY'LL HAVE NO TROUBLE DEALING WITH YOUR FRIENDS.
"BUT IN TRUTH? I'D LOVE TO DO THE JOB MYSELF.
"SO DON'T CROSS ME, YOU ANCIENT BLOODSUCKER, BECAUSE YOU WOULD ONLY BE A MOMENT'S DIVERSION FOR ME."

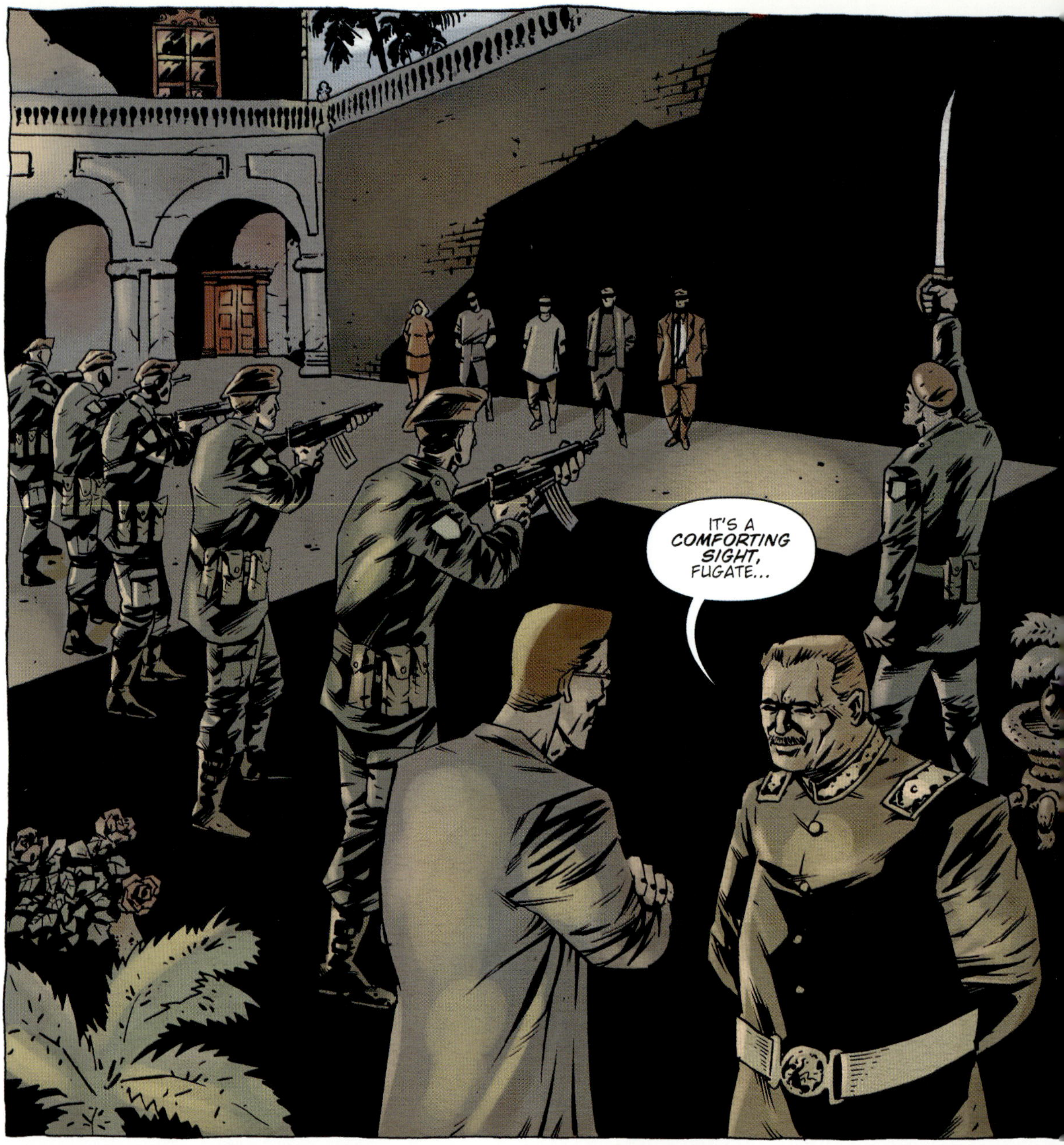
IT'S A COMFORTING SIGHT, FUGATE...

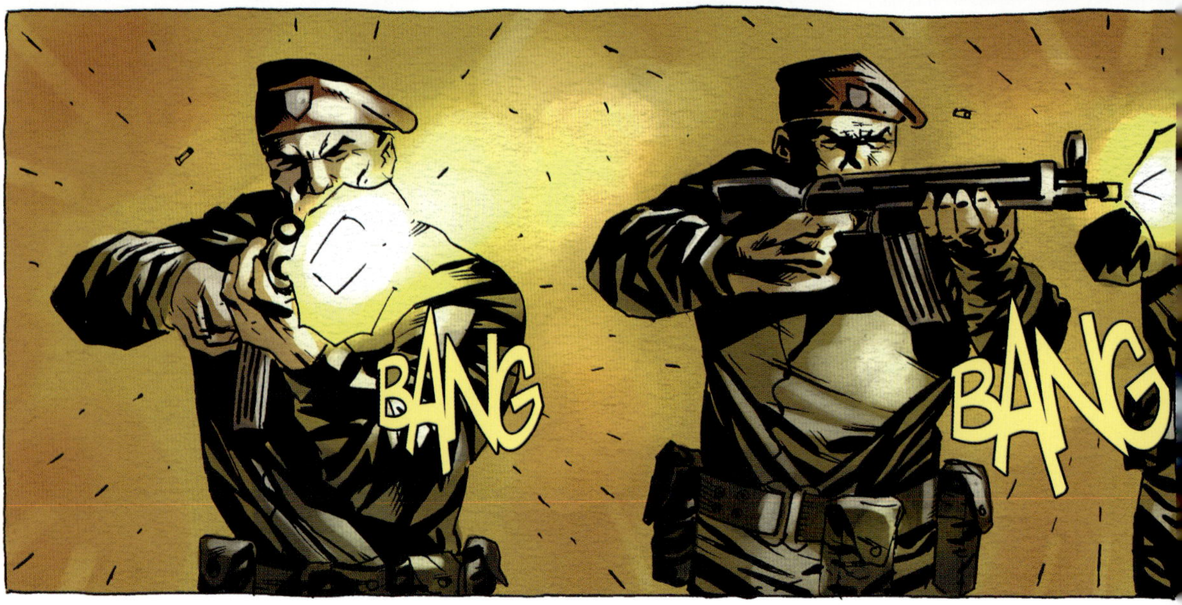
BANG
BANG

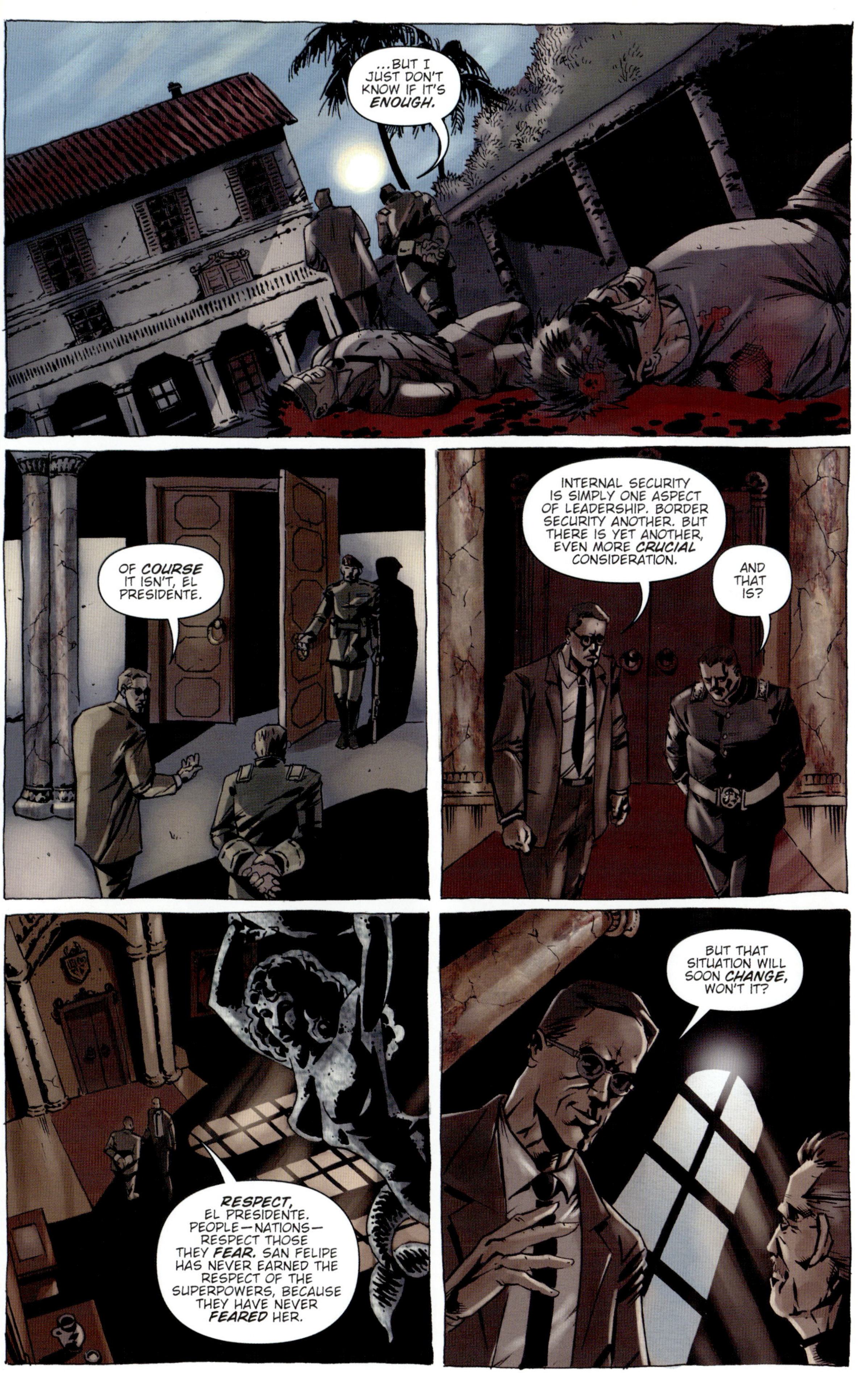
...BUT I JUST DON'T KNOW IF IT'S ENOUGH.
OF COURSE IT ISN'T, EL PRESIDENTE.
INTERNAL SECURITY IS SIMPLY ONE ASPECT OF LEADERSHIP. BORDER SECURITY ANOTHER. BUT THERE IS YET ANOTHER, EVEN MORE CRUCIAL CONSIDERATION.
AND THAT IS?
RESPECT, EL PRESIDENTE. PEOPLE—NATIONS—RESPECT THOSE THEY FEAR. SAN FELIPE HAS NEVER EARNED THE RESPECT OF THE SUPERPOWERS, BECAUSE THEY HAVE NEVER FEARED HER.
BUT THAT SITUATION WILL SOON CHANGE, WON'T IT?

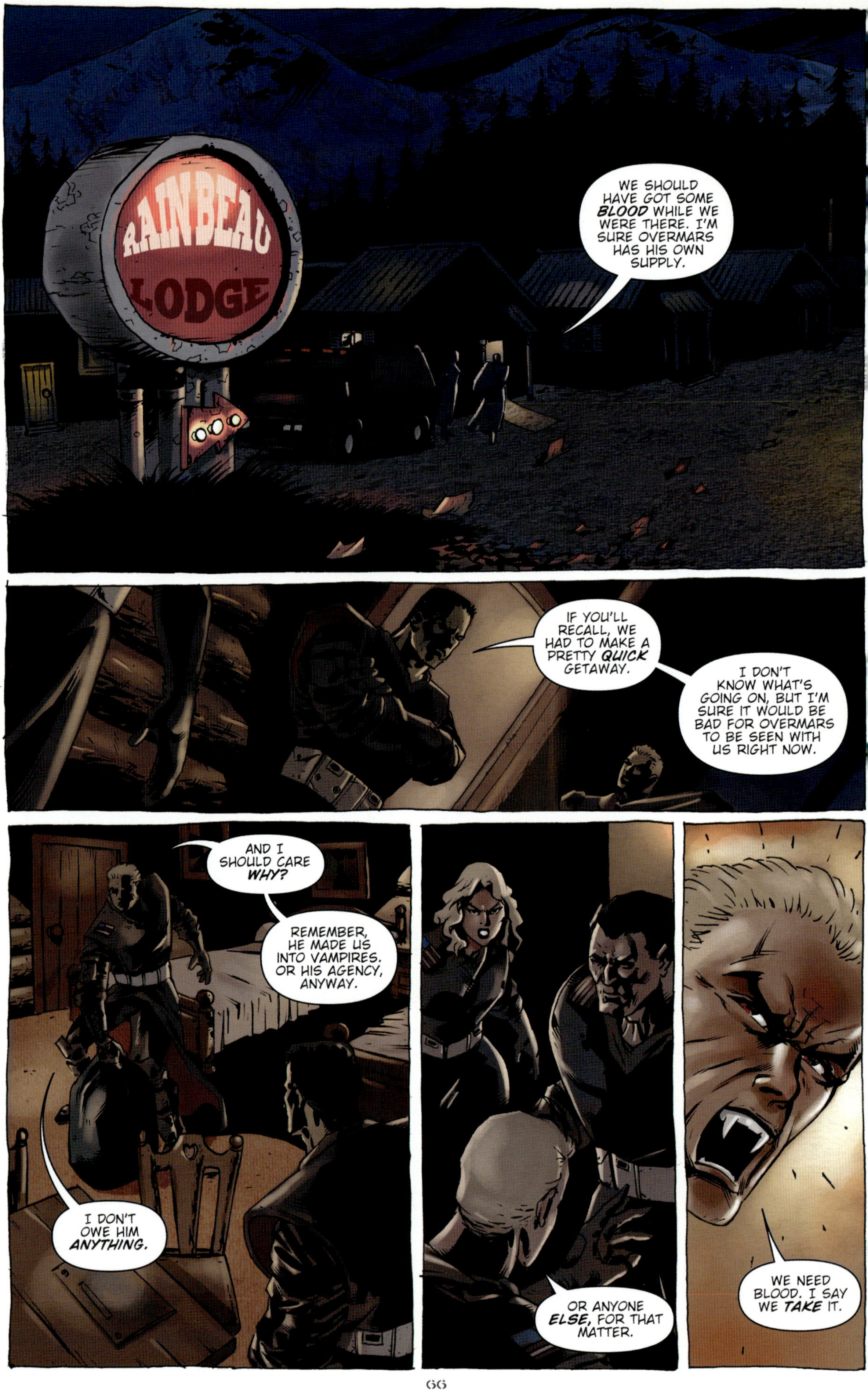
RAINBEAU LODGE
WE SHOULD HAVE GOT SOME BLOOD WHILE WE WERE THERE. I'M SURE OVERMARS HAS HIS OWN SUPPLY.
IF YOU'LL RECALL, WE HAD TO MAKE A PRETTY QUICK GETAWAY.
I DON'T KNOW WHAT'S GOING ON, BUT I'M SURE IT WOULD BE BAD FOR OVERMARS TO BE SEEN WITH US RIGHT NOW.
AND I SHOULD CARE WHY?
REMEMBER, HE MADE US INTO VAMPIRES. OR HIS AGENCY, ANYWAY.
I DON'T OWE HIM ANYTHING.
OR ANYONE ELSE, FOR THAT MATTER.
WE NEED BLOOD. I SAY WE TAKE IT.

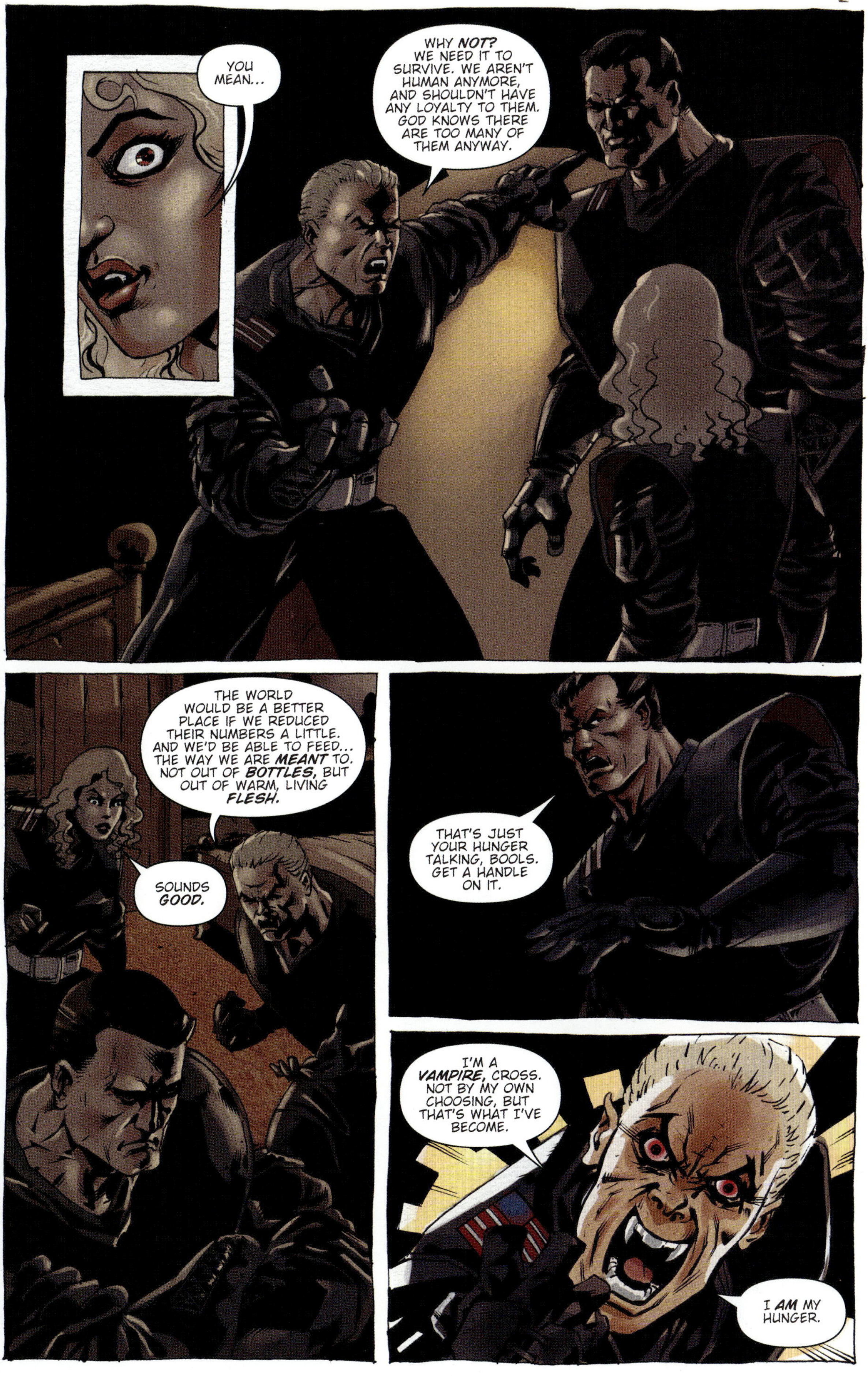
YOU MEAN...
WHY NOT? WE NEED IT TO SURVIVE. WE AREN'T HUMAN ANYMORE, AND SHOULDN'T HAVE ANY LOYALTY TO THEM. GOD KNOWS THERE ARE TOO MANY OF THEM ANYWAY.
THE WORLD WOULD BE A BETTER PLACE IF WE REDUCED THEIR NUMBERS A LITTLE. AND WE'D BE ABLE TO FEED... THE WAY WE ARE MEANT TO. NOT OUT OF BOTTLES, BUT OUT OF WARM, LIVING FLESH.
SOUNDS GOOD.
THAT'S JUST YOUR HUNGER TALKING, BOOLS. GET A HANDLE ON IT.
I'M A VAMPIRE, CROSS. NOT BY MY OWN CHOOSING, BUT THAT'S WHAT I'VE BECOME.
I AM MY HUNGER.

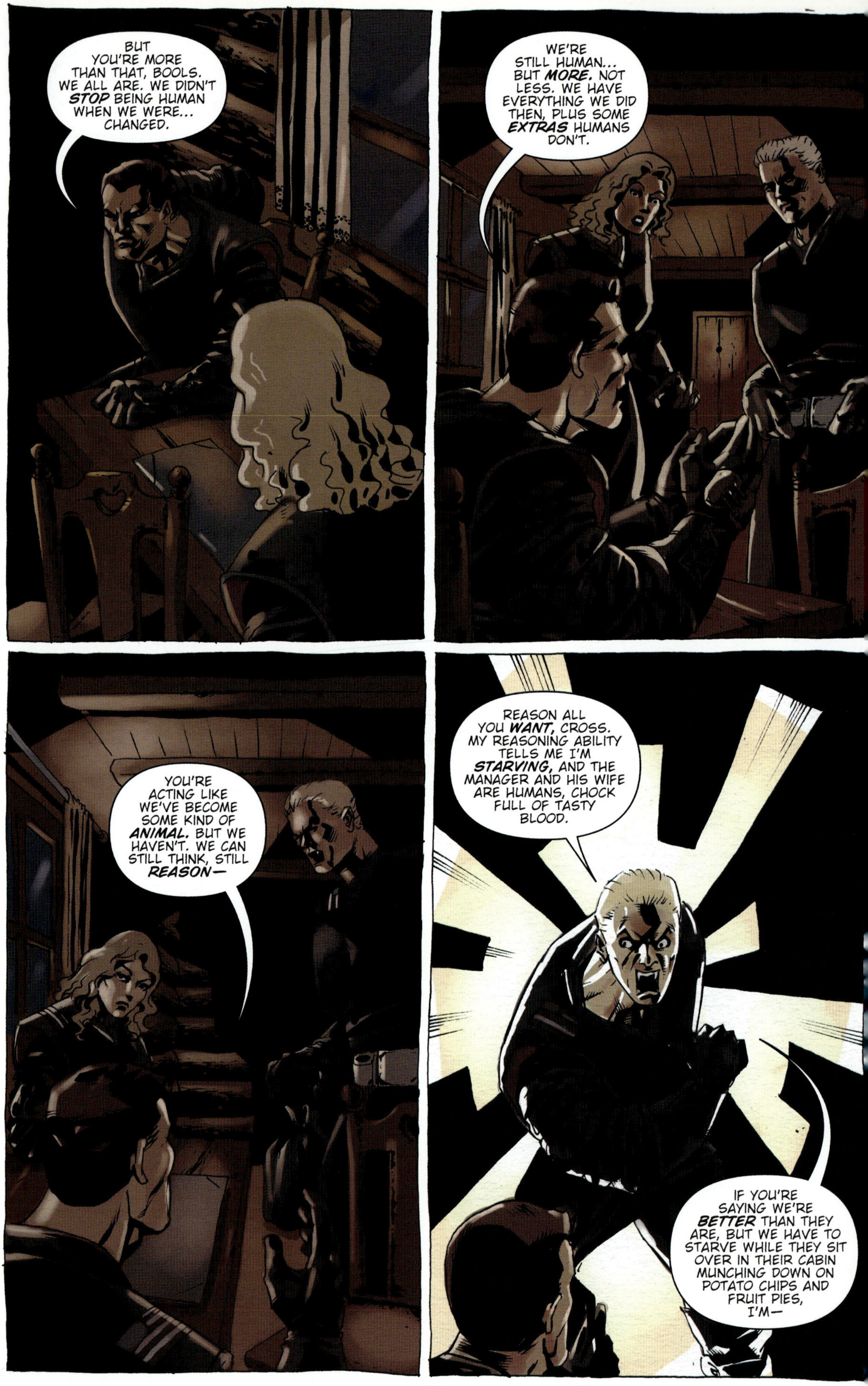
BUT YOU'RE MORE THAN THAT, BOOLS. WE ALL ARE. WE DIDN'T STOP BEING HUMAN WHEN WE WERE... CHANGED.
WE'RE STILL HUMAN... BUT MORE. NOT LESS. WE HAVE EVERYTHING WE DID THEN, PLUS SOME EXTRAS HUMANS DON'T.
YOU'RE ACTING LIKE WE'VE BECOME SOME KIND OF ANIMAL. BUT WE HAVEN'T. WE CAN STILL THINK, STILL REASON—
REASON ALL YOU WANT, CROSS. MY REASONING ABILITY TELLS ME I'M STARVING, AND THE MANAGER AND HIS WIFE ARE HUMANS, CHOCK FULL OF TASTY BLOOD.
IF YOU'RE SAYING WE'RE BETTER THAN THEY ARE, BUT WE HAVE TO STARVE WHILE THEY SIT OVER IN THEIR CABIN MUNCHING DOWN ON POTATO CHIPS AND FRUIT PIES, I'M—

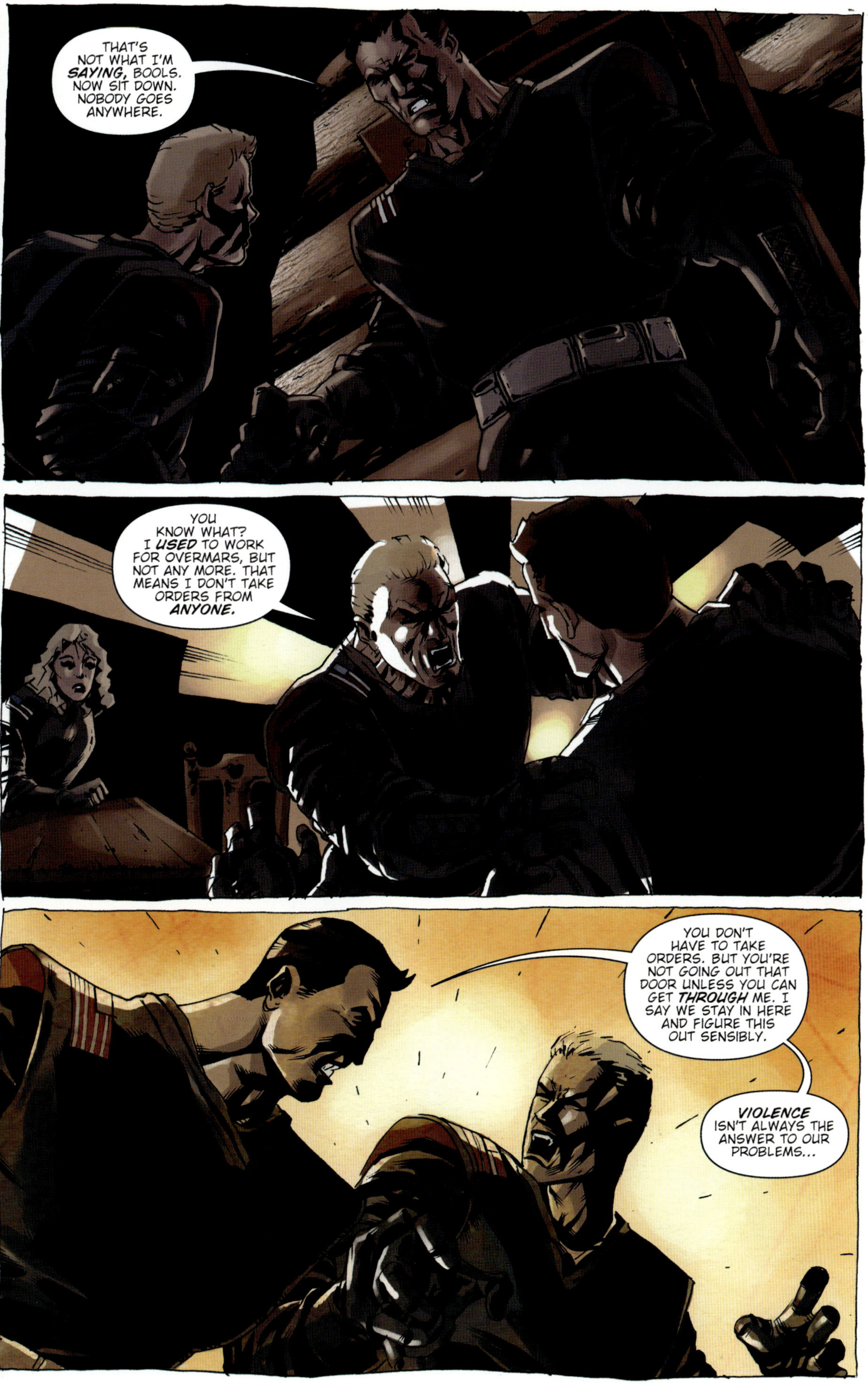
THAT'S NOT WHAT I'M **SAYING,** BOOLS. NOW SIT DOWN. NOBODY GOES ANYWHERE.
YOU KNOW WHAT? I **USED** TO WORK FOR OVERMARS, BUT NOT ANY MORE. THAT MEANS I DON'T TAKE ORDERS FROM **ANYONE.**
YOU DON'T HAVE TO TAKE ORDERS. BUT YOU'RE NOT GOING OUT THAT DOOR UNLESS YOU CAN GET **THROUGH** ME. I SAY WE STAY IN HERE AND FIGURE THIS OUT SENSIBLY.
VIOLENCE ISN'T ALWAYS THE ANSWER TO OUR PROBLEMS...

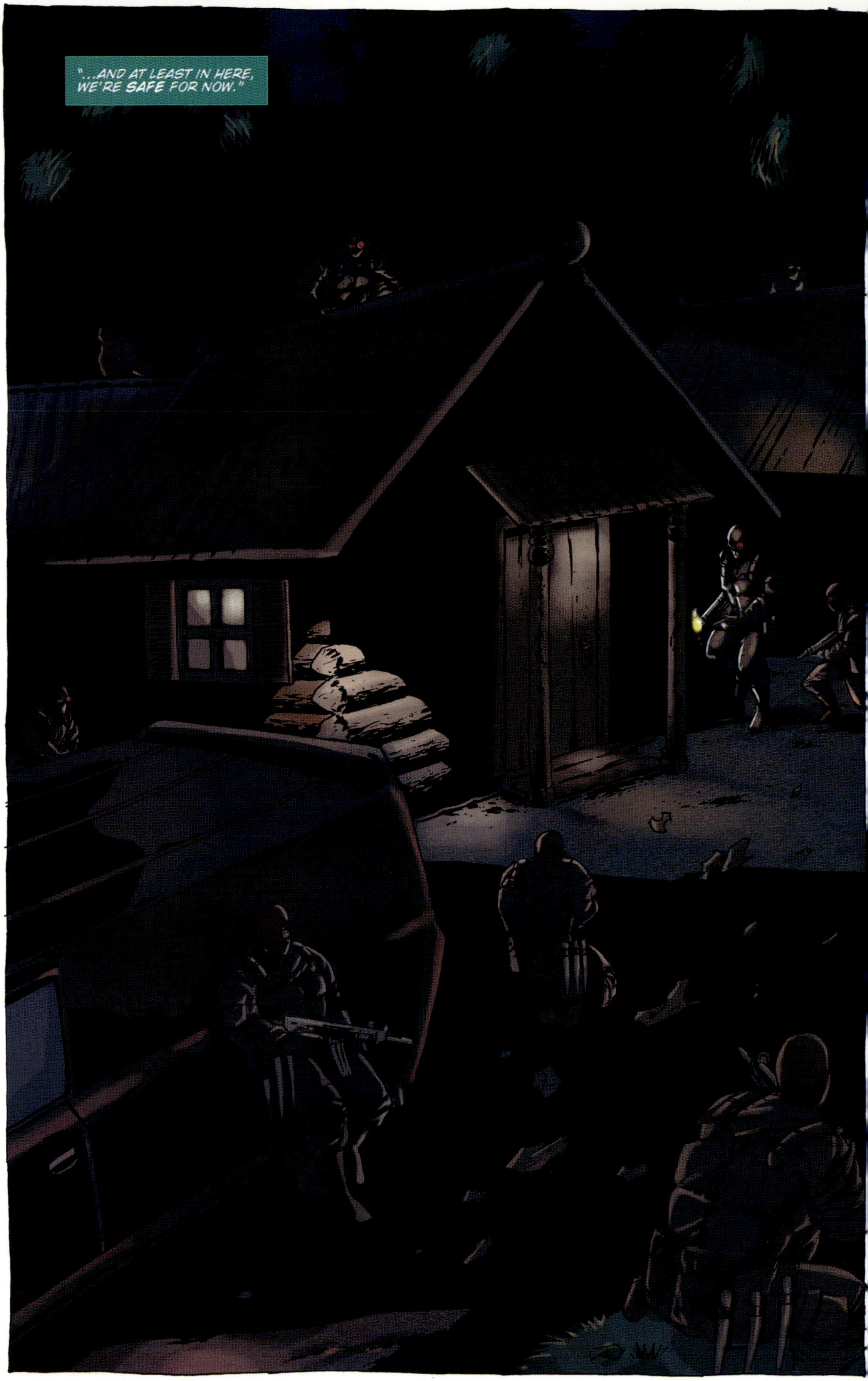
"...AND AT LEAST IN HERE, WE'RE SAFE FOR NOW."

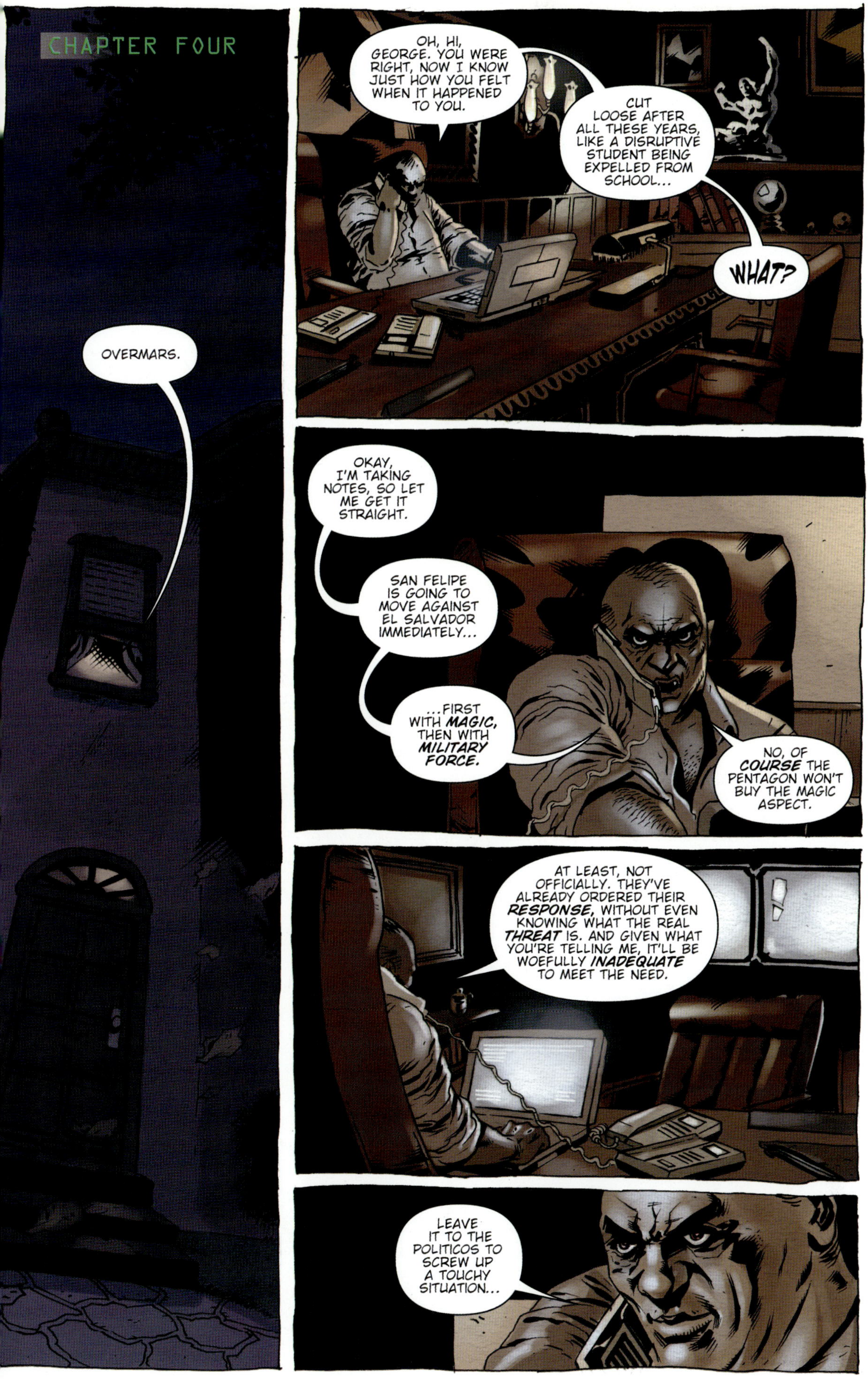
CHAPTER FOUR
OVERMARS.
OH, HI, GEORGE. YOU WERE RIGHT, NOW I KNOW JUST HOW YOU FELT WHEN IT HAPPENED TO YOU.
CUT LOOSE AFTER ALL THESE YEARS, LIKE A DISRUPTIVE STUDENT BEING EXPELLED FROM SCHOOL...
WHAT?
OKAY, I'M TAKING NOTES, SO LET ME GET IT STRAIGHT.
SAN FELIPE IS GOING TO MOVE AGAINST EL SALVADOR IMMEDIATELY...
...FIRST WITH MAGIC, THEN WITH MILITARY FORCE.
NO, OF COURSE THE PENTAGON WON'T BUY THE MAGIC ASPECT.
AT LEAST, NOT OFFICIALLY. THEY'VE ALREADY ORDERED THEIR RESPONSE, WITHOUT EVEN KNOWING WHAT THE REAL THREAT IS. AND GIVEN WHAT YOU'RE TELLING ME, IT'LL BE WOEFULLY INADEQUATE TO MEET THE NEED.
LEAVE IT TO THE POLITICOS TO SCREW UP A TOUCHY SITUATION...

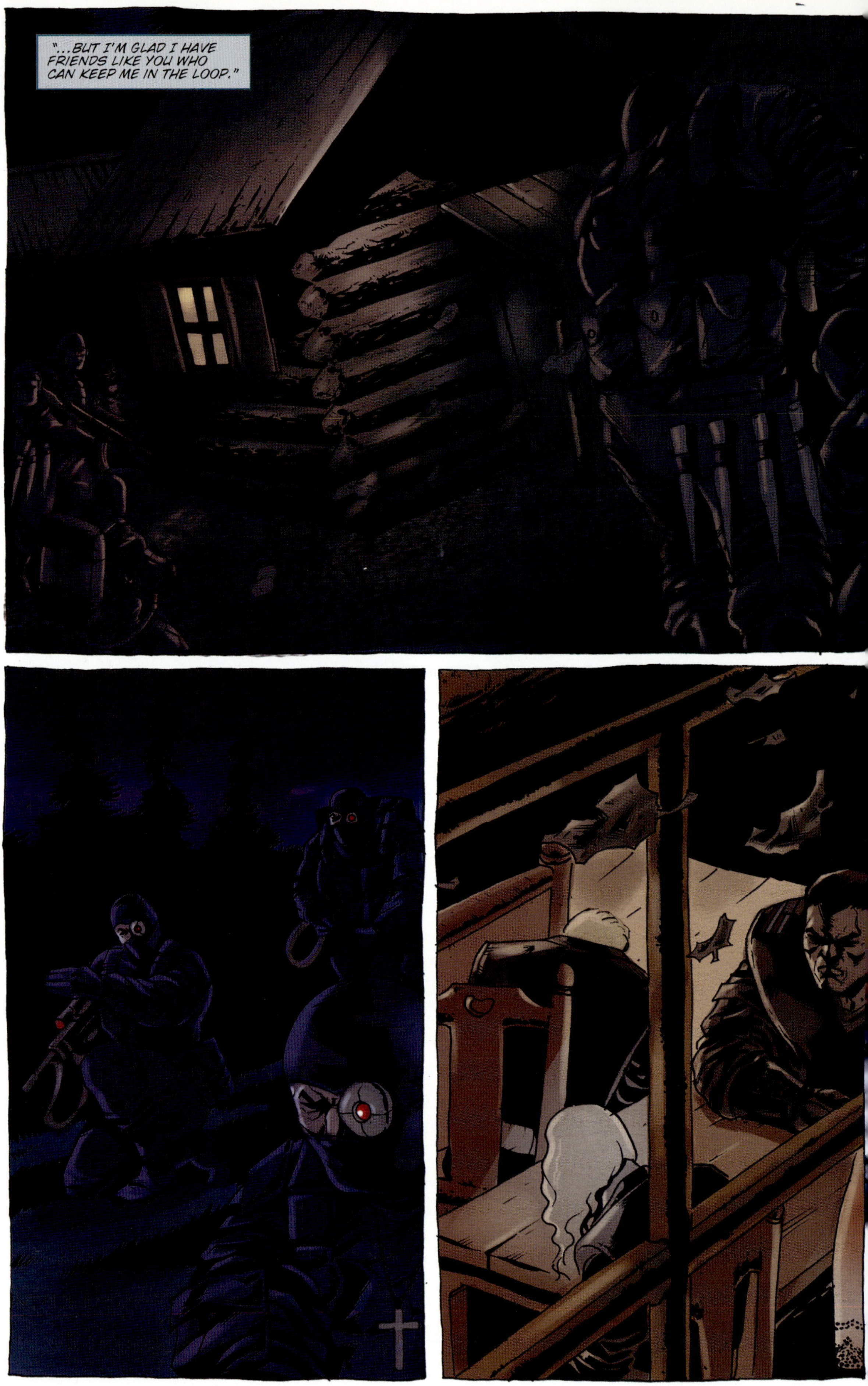
"...BUT I'M GLAD I HAVE FRIENDS LIKE YOU WHO CAN KEEP ME IN THE LOOP."

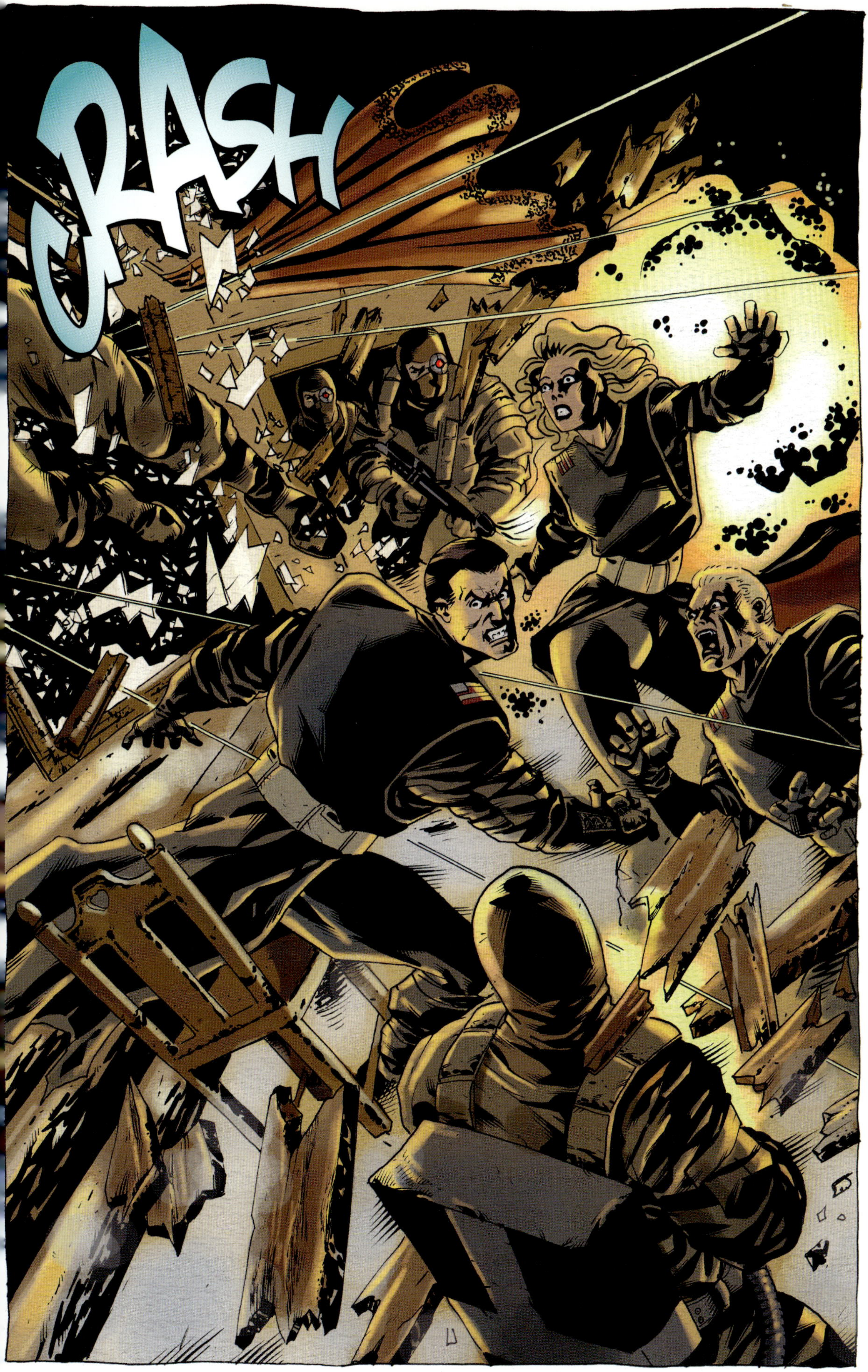
CRASH

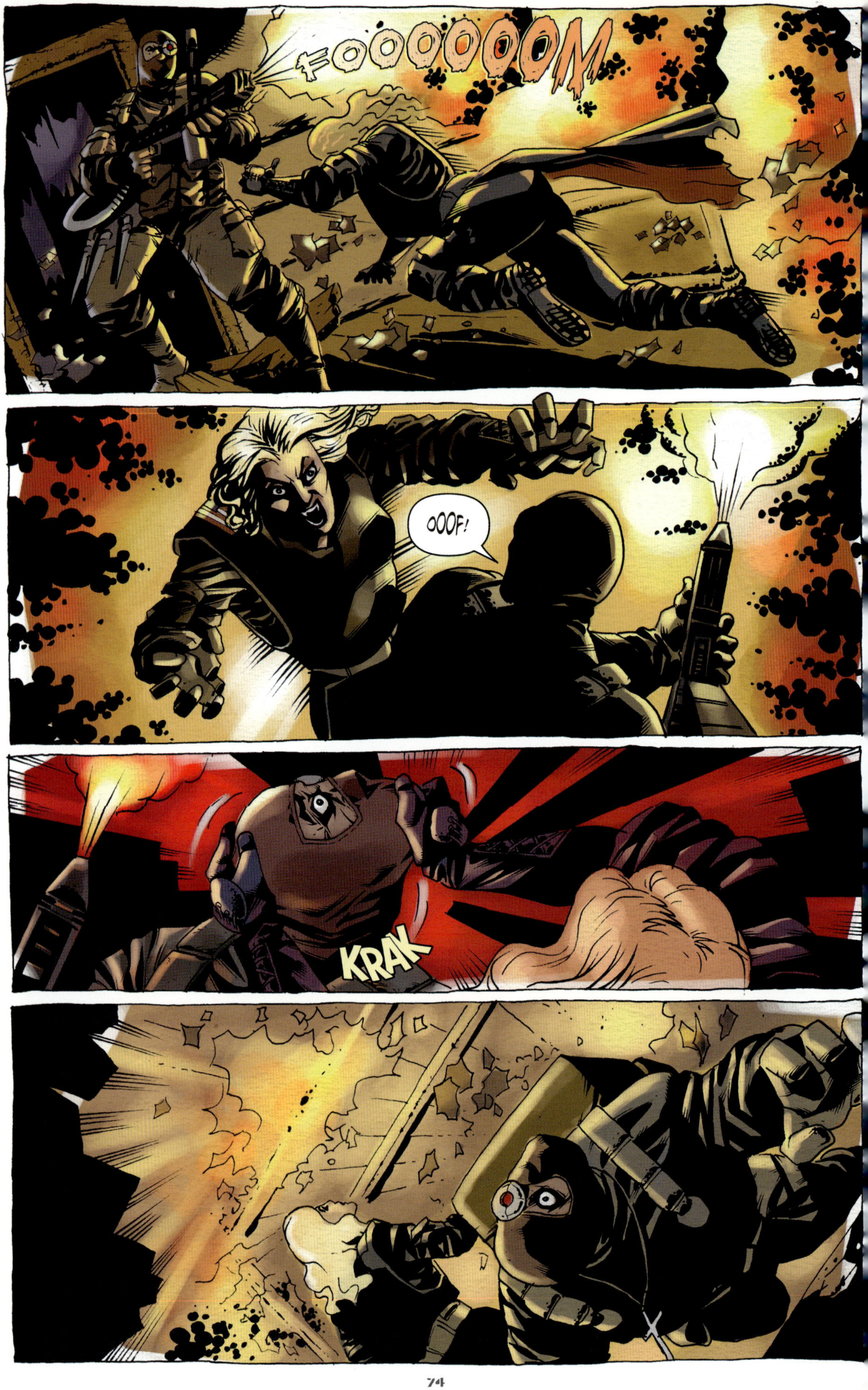
FOOOOOOM
OOOF!
KRAK

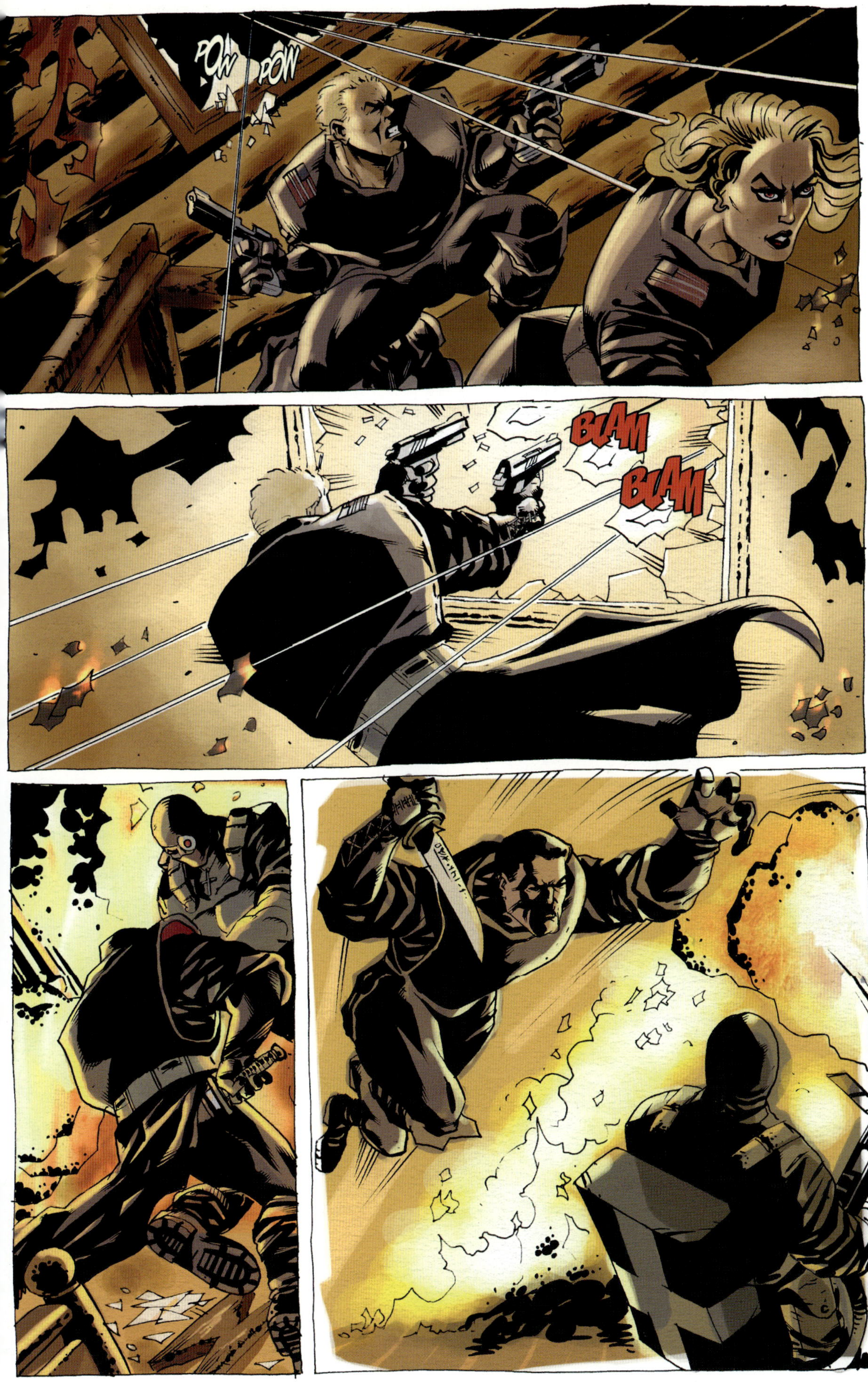
POW
POW
BLAM
BLAM

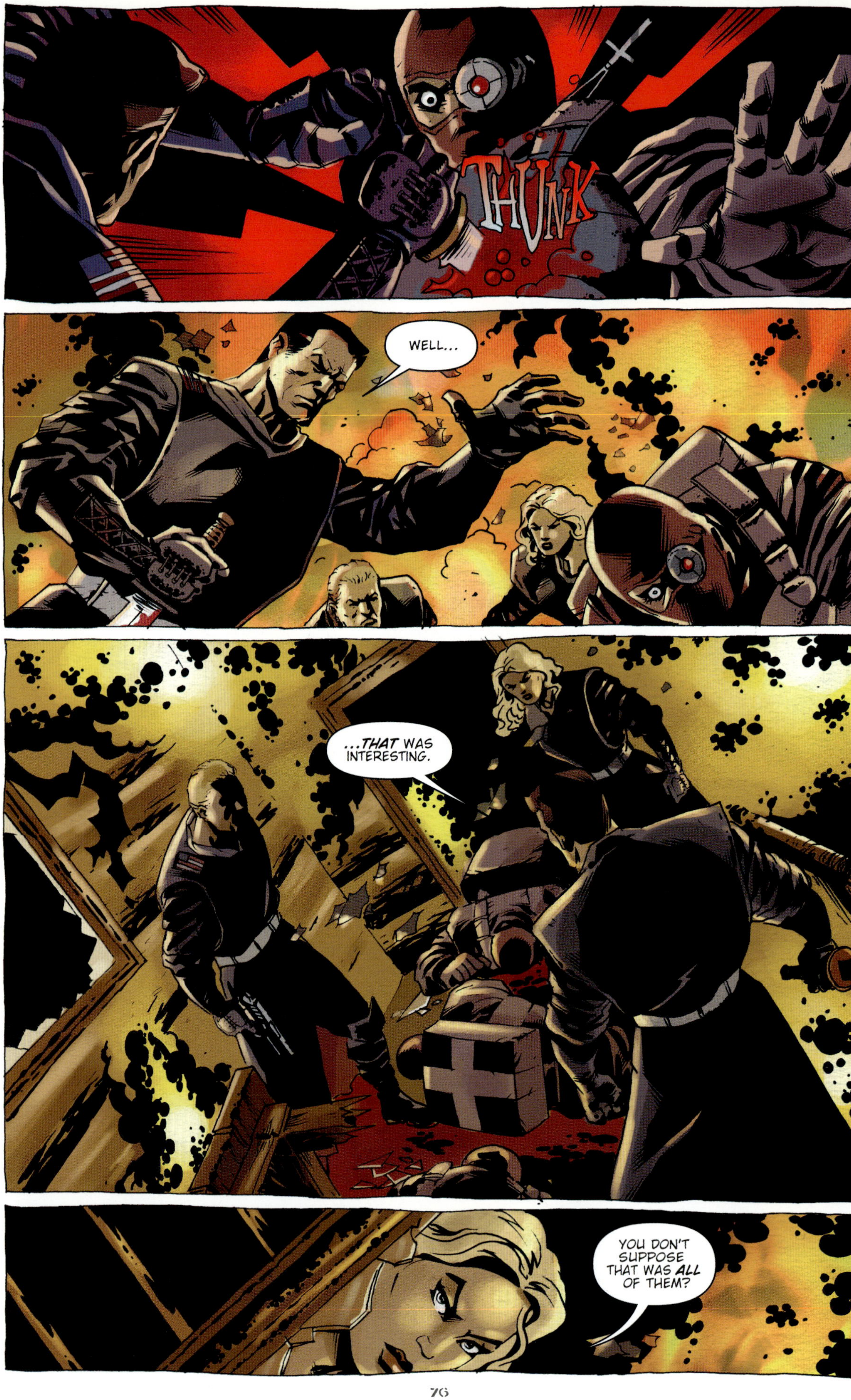
THUNK
WELL...
...THAT WAS INTERESTING.
YOU DON'T SUPPOSE THAT WAS ALL OF THEM?

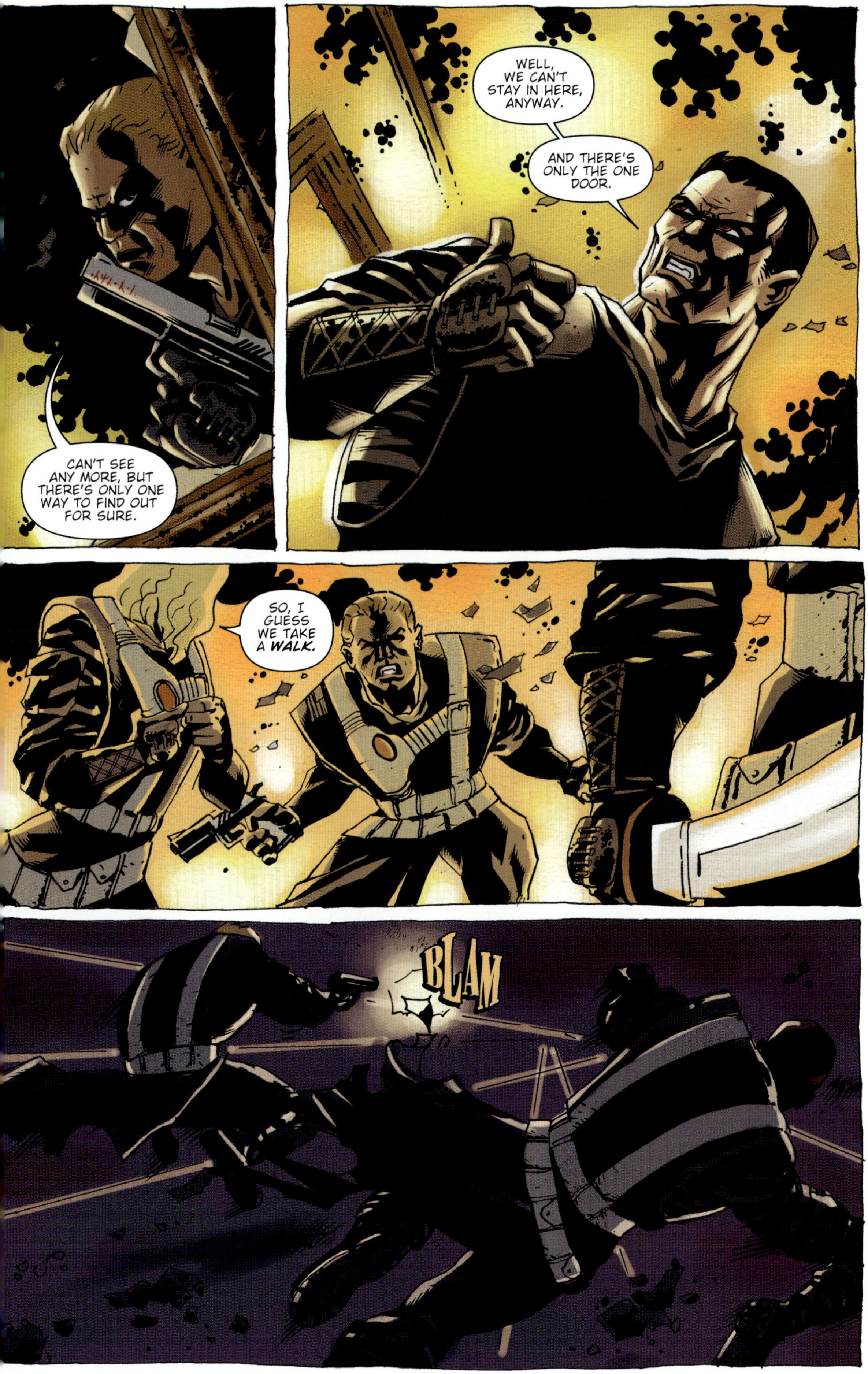
WELL, WE CAN'T STAY IN HERE, ANYWAY.
AND THERE'S ONLY THE ONE DOOR.
CAN'T SEE ANY MORE, BUT THERE'S ONLY ONE WAY TO FIND OUT FOR SURE.
SO, I GUESS WE TAKE A **WALK.**
BLAM

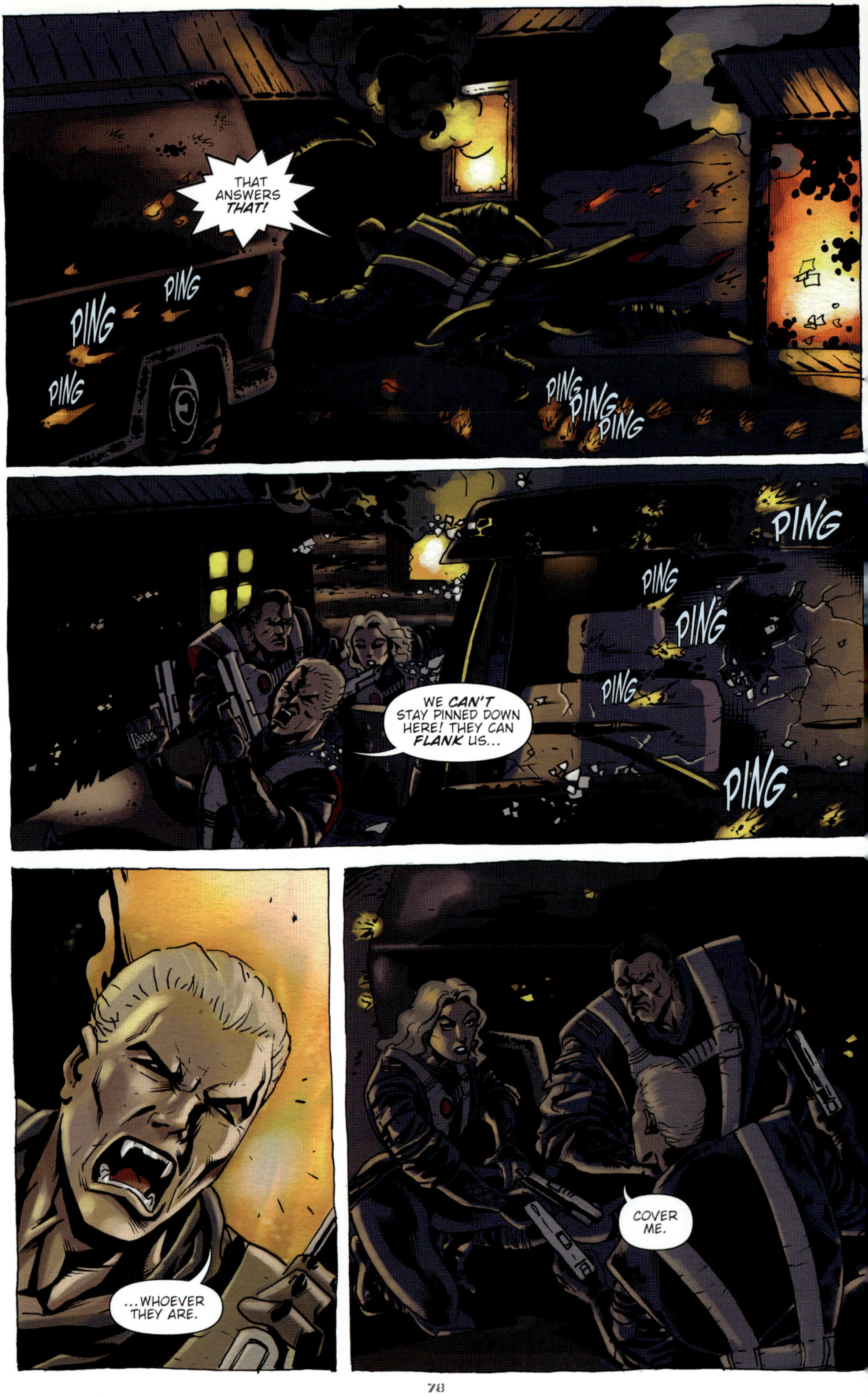
THAT ANSWERS THAT!
PING
PING
PING
PING PING PING
PING
PING
PING
PING
PING
WE CAN'T STAY PINNED DOWN HERE! THEY CAN FLANK US...
...WHOEVER THEY ARE.
COVER ME.

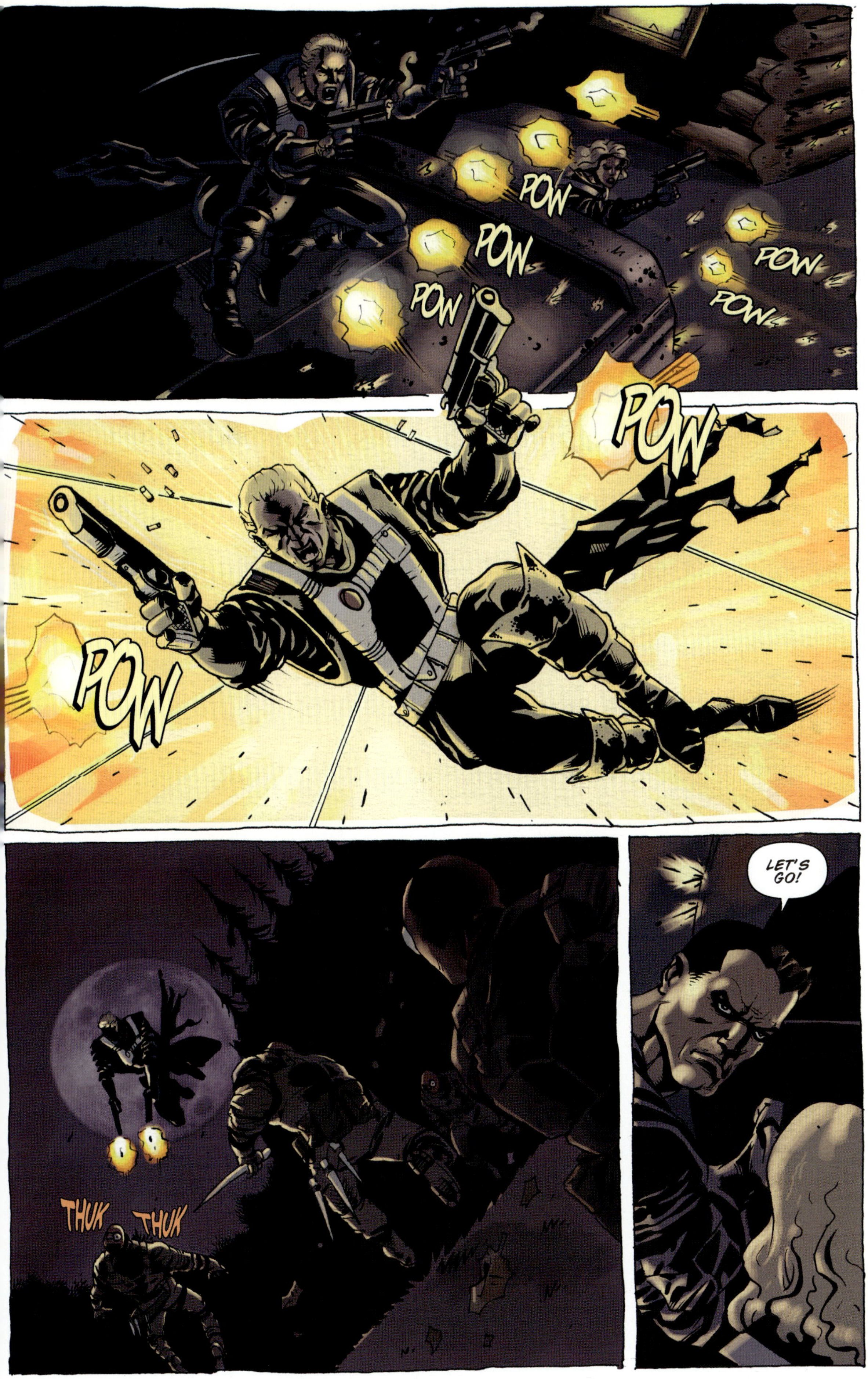
POW
POW
POW
POW
POW
POW
POW
THUK
THUK
LET'S GO!

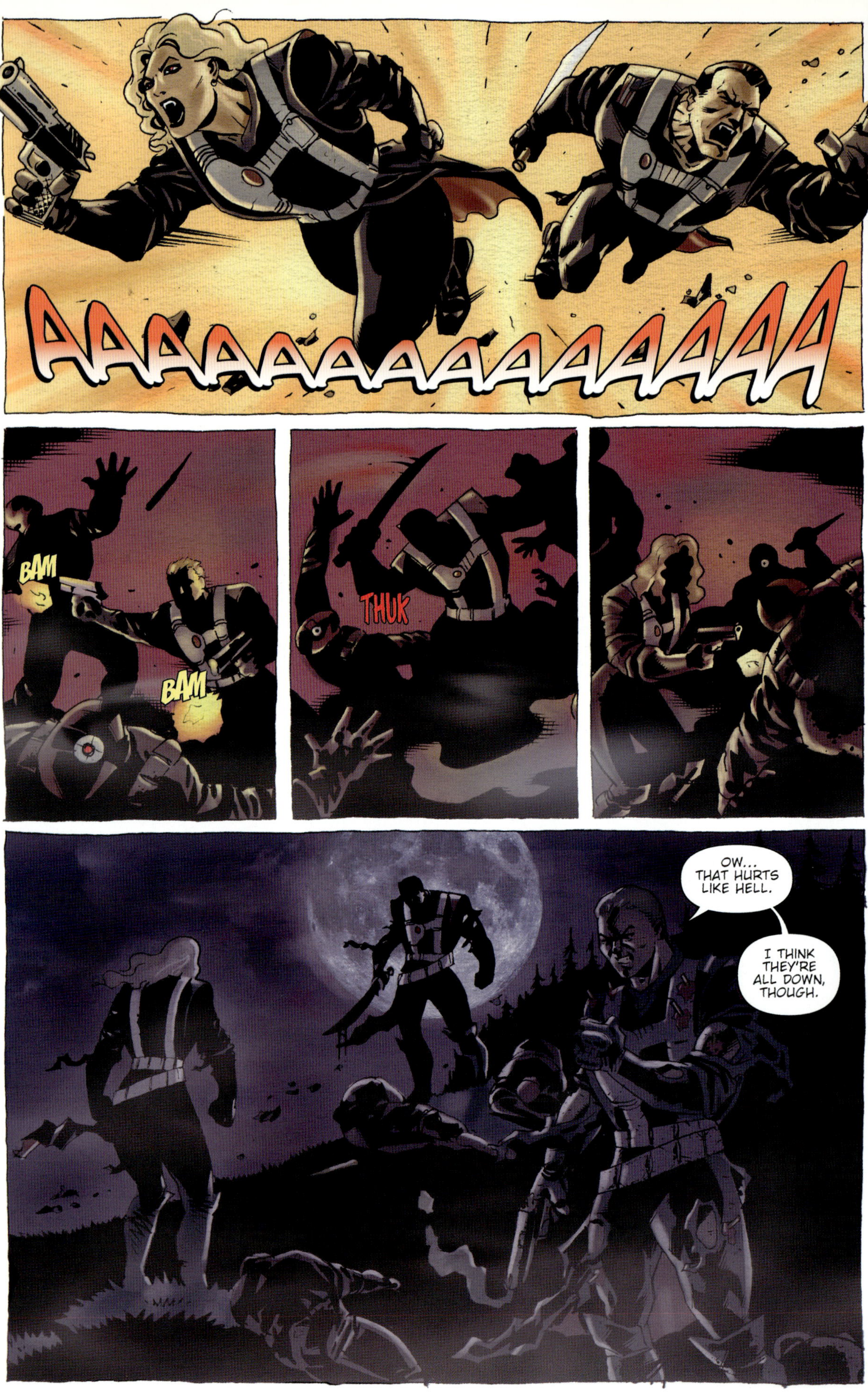
AAAAAAAAAAAAA
BAM
BAM
THUK
OW... THAT HURTS LIKE HELL.
I THINK THEY'RE ALL DOWN, THOUGH.

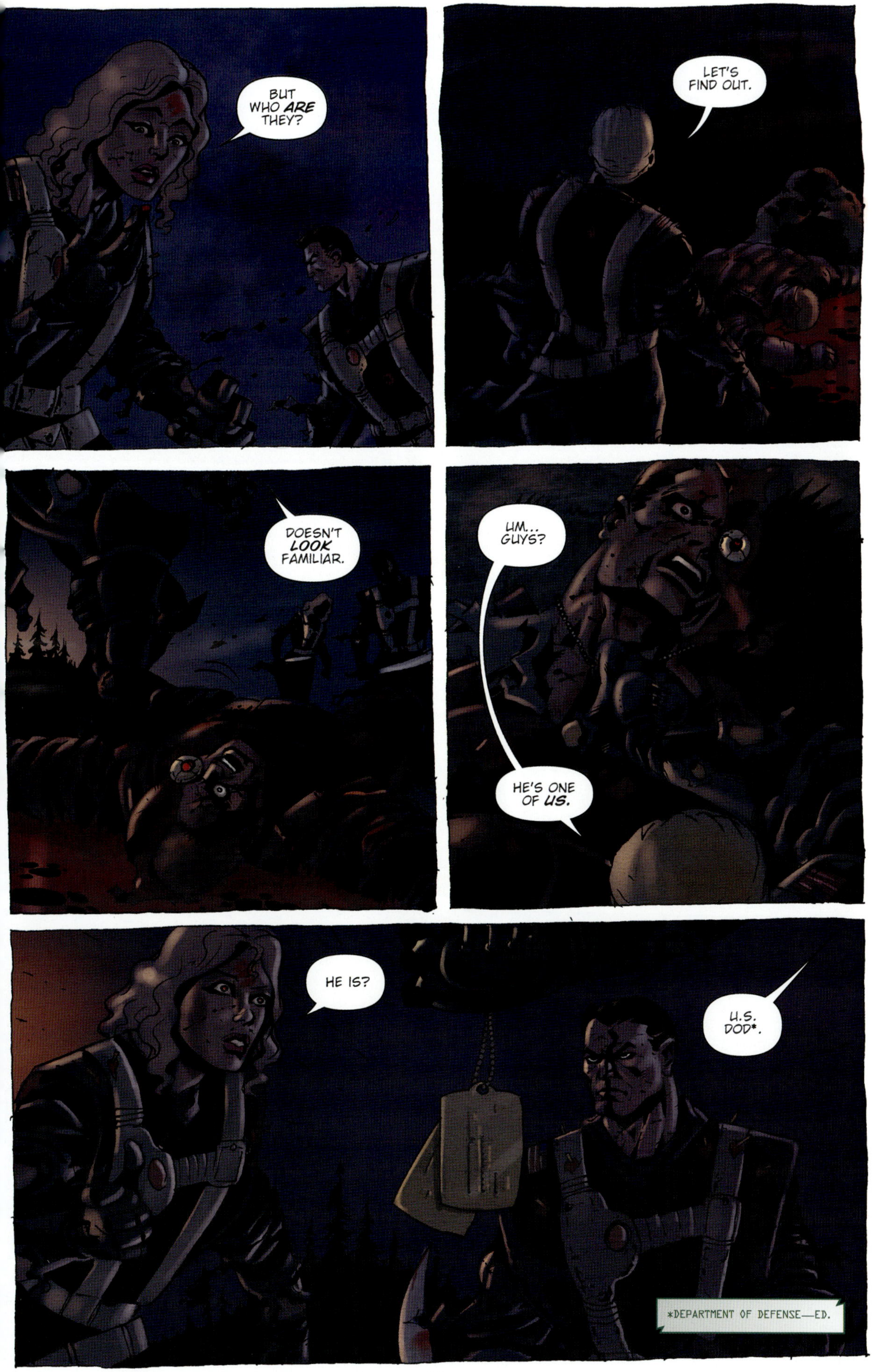
BUT WHO ARE THEY?
LET'S FIND OUT.
DOESN'T LOOK FAMILIAR.
UM... GUYS?
HE'S ONE OF US.
HE IS?
U.S. DOD*.
*DEPARTMENT OF DEFENSE—ED.

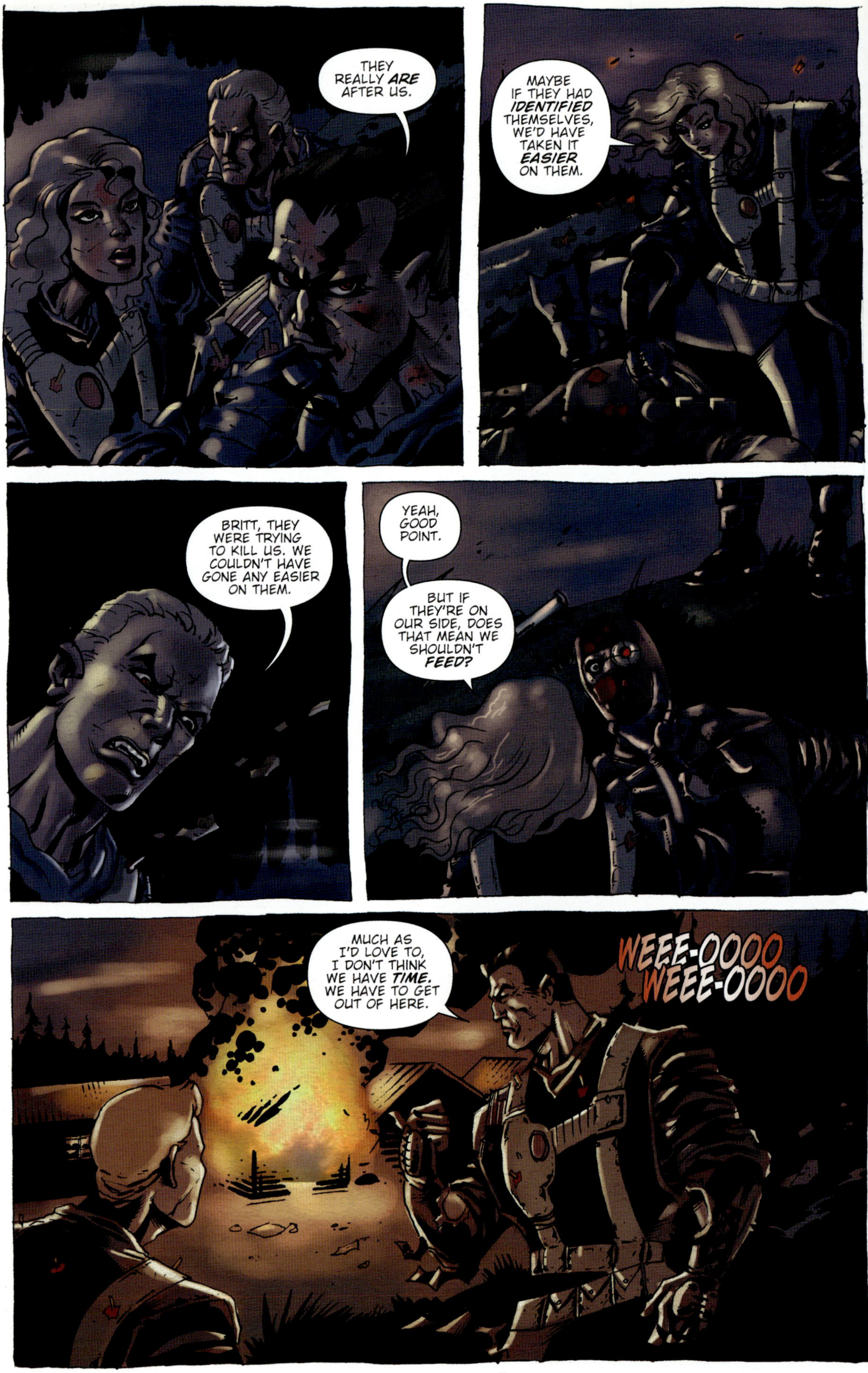
THEY REALLY ARE AFTER US.
MAYBE IF THEY HAD IDENTIFIED THEMSELVES, WE'D HAVE TAKEN IT EASIER ON THEM.
BRITT, THEY WERE TRYING TO KILL US. WE COULDN'T HAVE GONE ANY EASIER ON THEM.
YEAH, GOOD POINT.
BUT IF THEY'RE ON OUR SIDE, DOES THAT MEAN WE SHOULDN'T FEED?
MUCH AS I'D LOVE TO, I DON'T THINK WE HAVE TIME. WE HAVE TO GET OUT OF HERE.
WEEE-OOOO
WEEE-OOOO

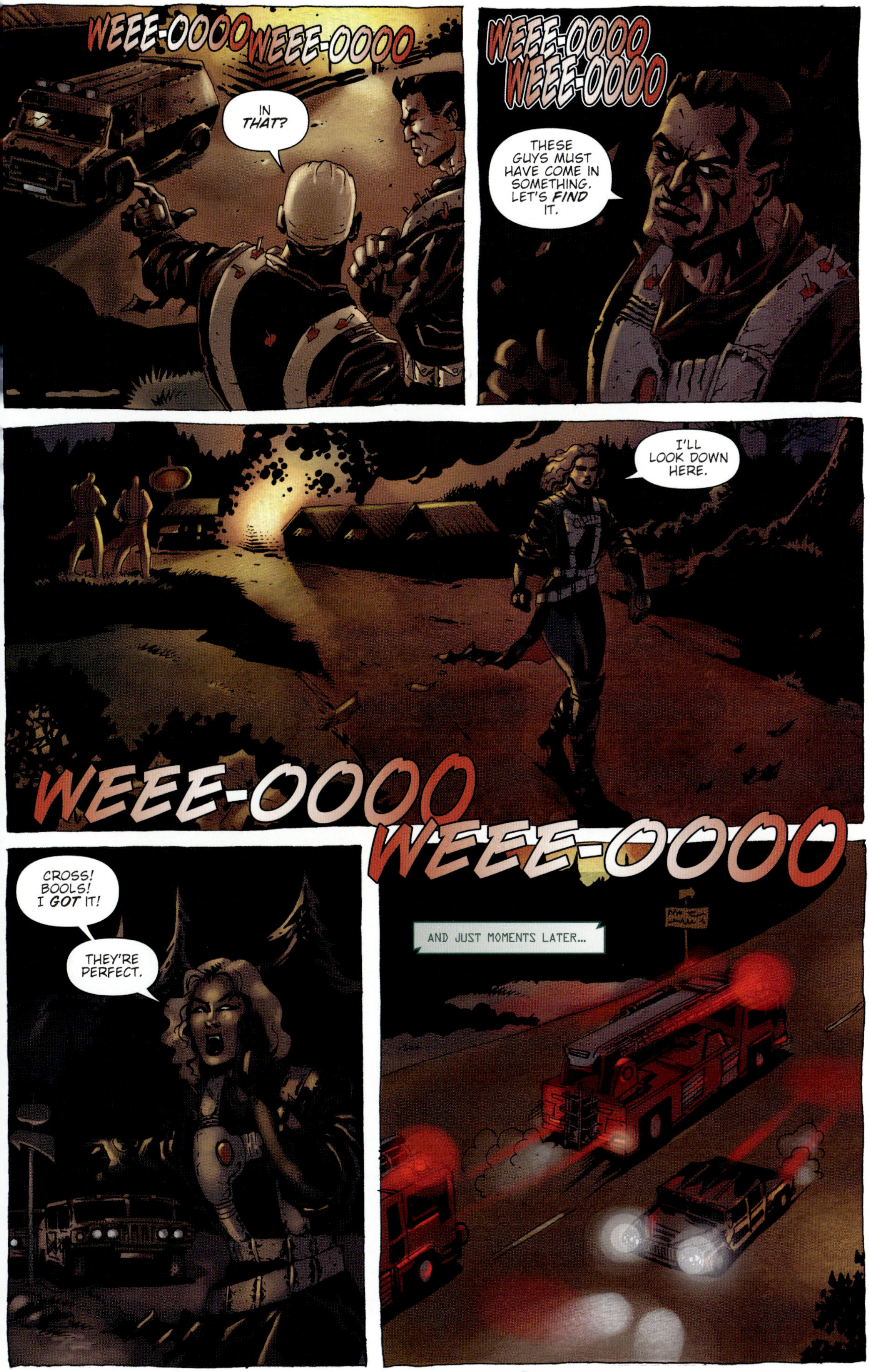

WEEE-OOOO WEEE-OOOO
IN THAT?
WEEE-OOOO WEEE-OOOO
THESE GUYS MUST HAVE COME IN SOMETHING. LET'S FIND IT.
I'LL LOOK DOWN HERE.
WEEE-OOOO WEEE-OOOO
CROSS! BOOLS! I GOT IT!
THEY'RE PERFECT.
AND JUST MOMENTS LATER...

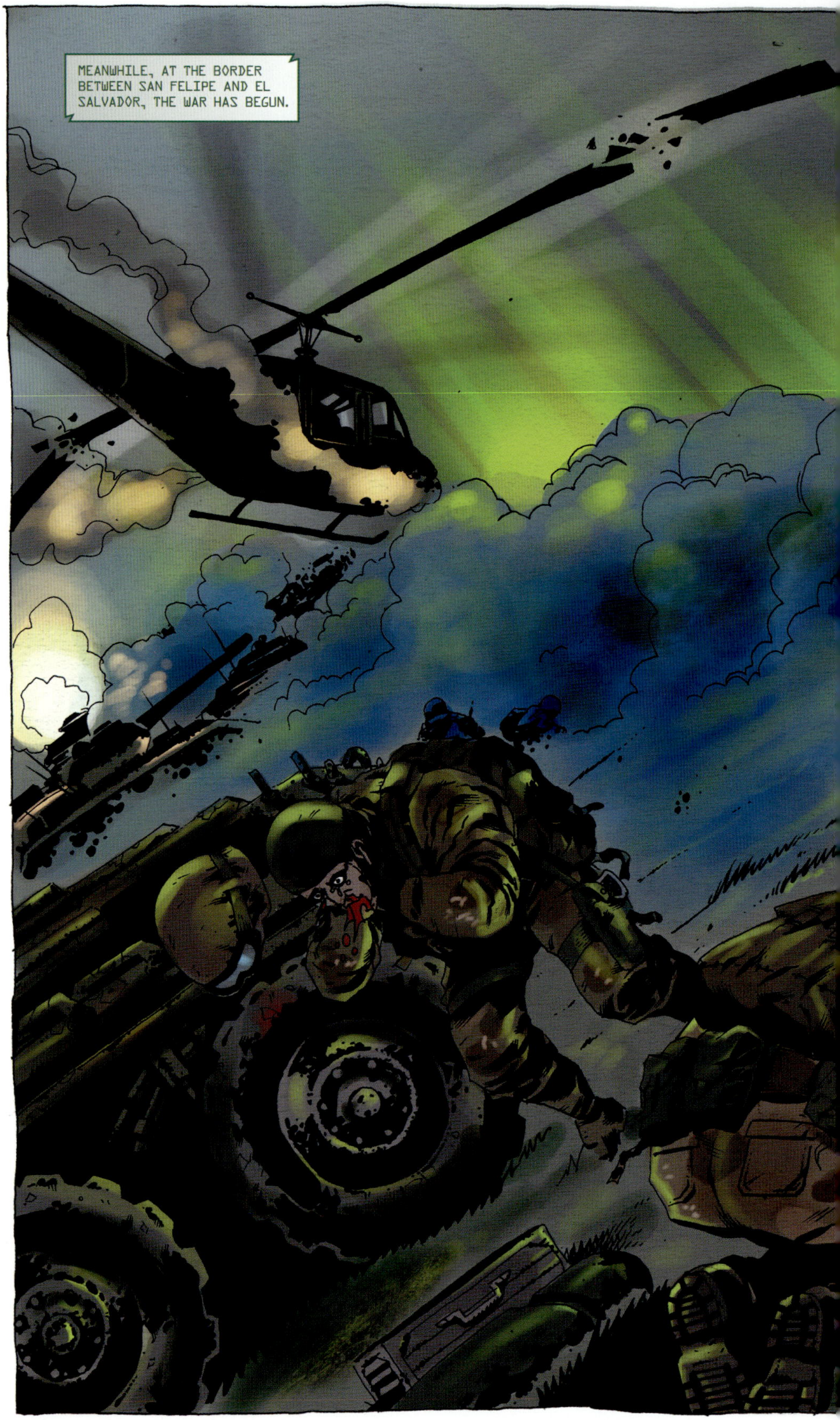
MEANWHILE, AT THE BORDER BETWEEN SAN FELIPE AND EL SALVADOR, THE WAR HAS BEGUN.

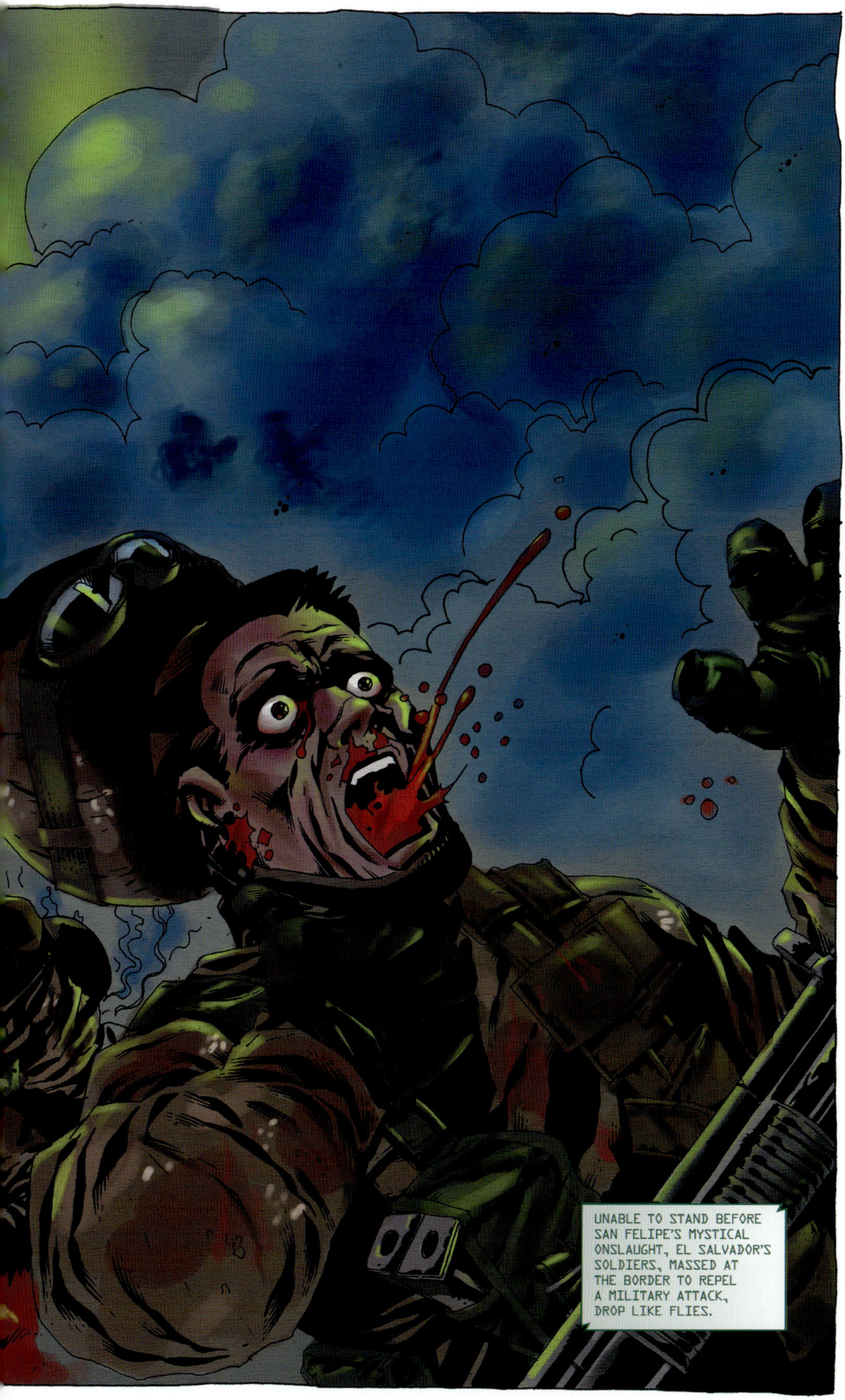
UNABLE TO STAND BEFORE SAN FELIPE'S MYSTICAL ONSLAUGHT, EL SALVADOR'S SOLDIERS, MASSED AT THE BORDER TO REPEL A MILITARY ATTACK, DROP LIKE FLIES.

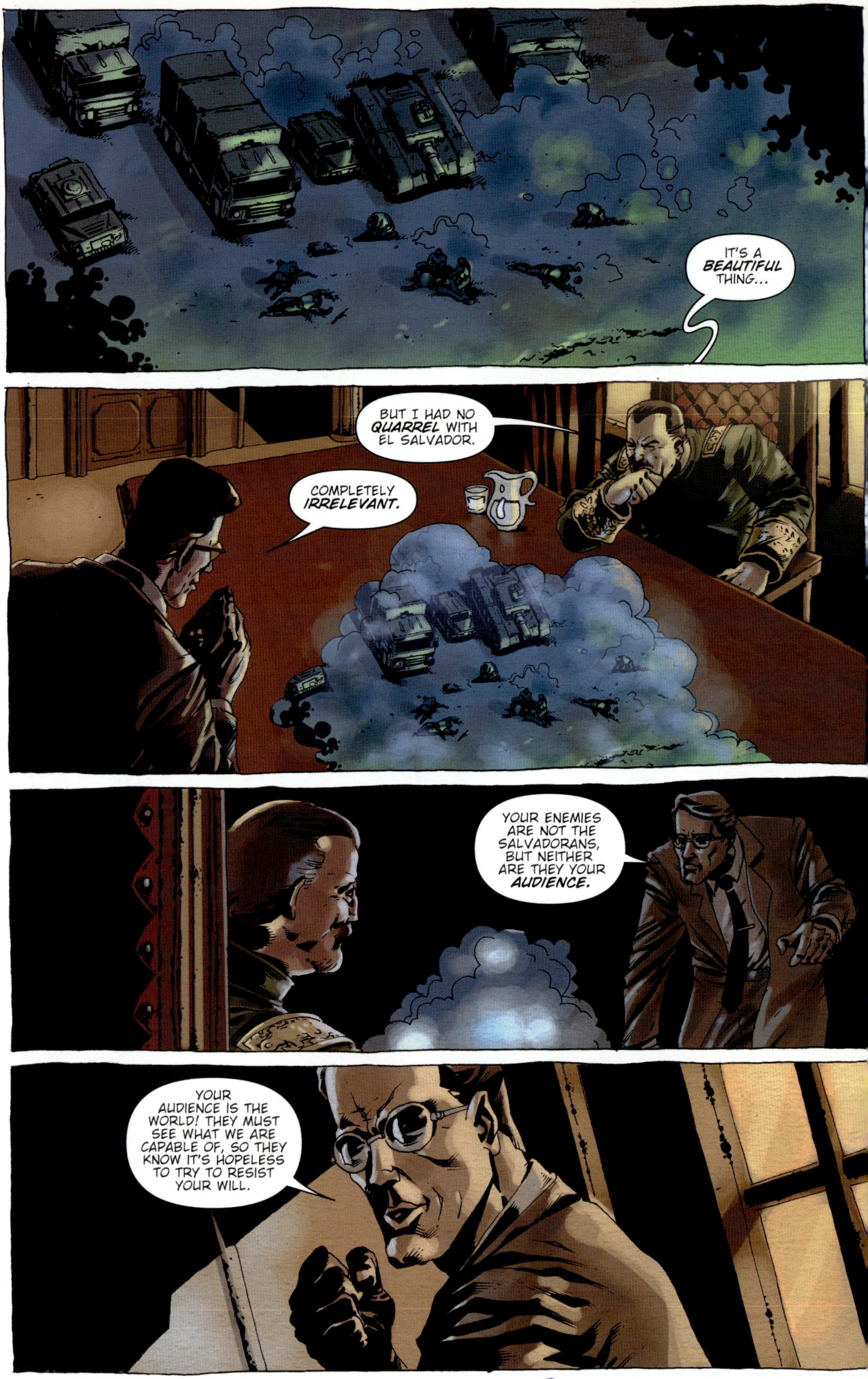
IT'S A BEAUTIFUL THING...
BUT I HAD NO QUARREL WITH EL SALVADOR.
COMPLETELY IRRELEVANT.
YOUR ENEMIES ARE NOT THE SALVADORANS, BUT NEITHER ARE THEY YOUR AUDIENCE.
YOUR AUDIENCE IS THE WORLD! THEY MUST SEE WHAT WE ARE CAPABLE OF, SO THEY KNOW IT'S HOPELESS TO TRY TO RESIST YOUR WILL.

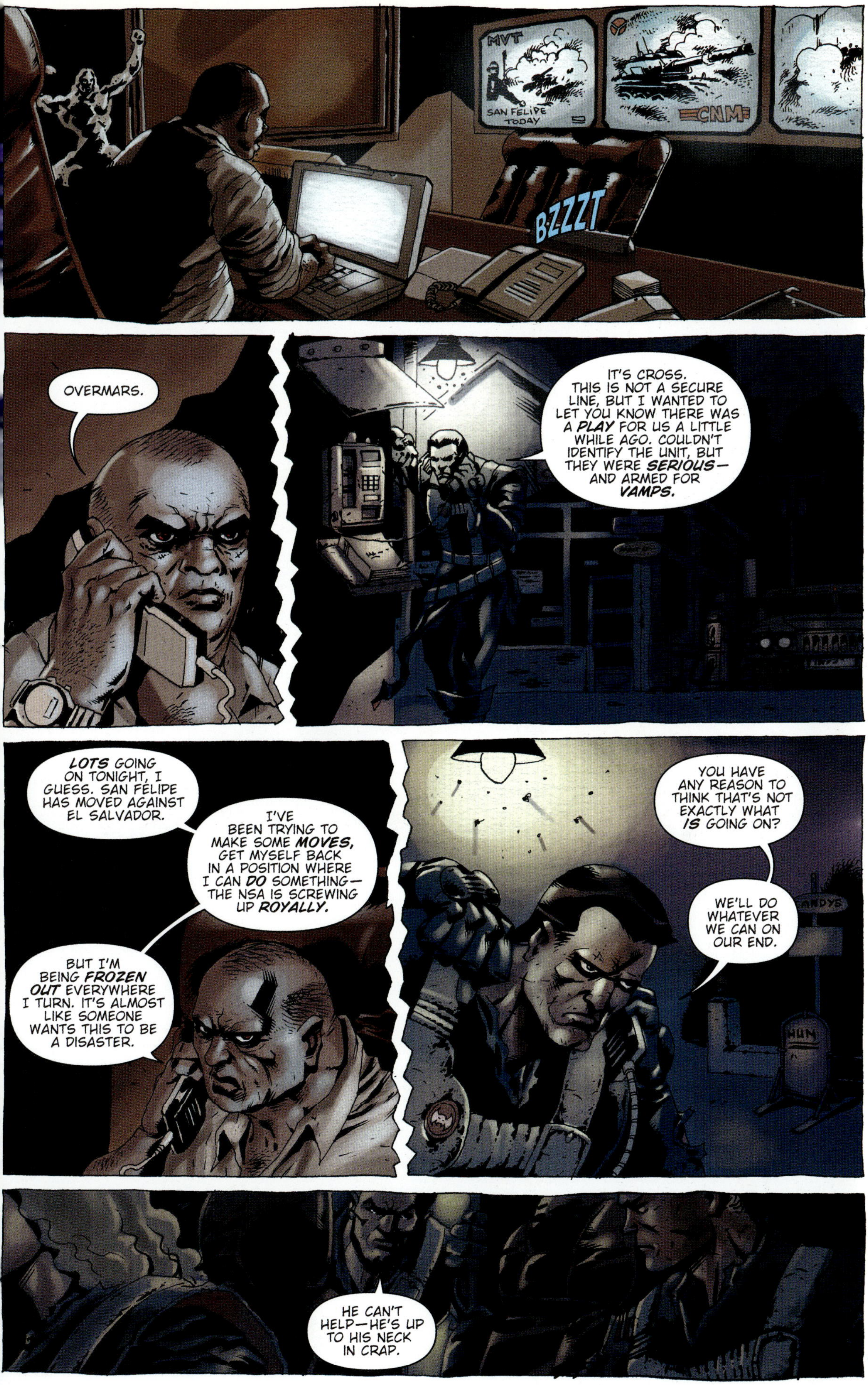
MVT
SAN FELIPE TODAY
CNM
BZZZT
OVERMARS.
IT'S CROSS. THIS IS NOT A SECURE LINE, BUT I WANTED TO LET YOU KNOW THERE WAS A PLAY FOR US A LITTLE WHILE AGO. COULDN'T IDENTIFY THE UNIT, BUT THEY WERE SERIOUS—AND ARMED FOR VAMPS.
LOTS GOING ON TONIGHT, I GUESS. SAN FELIPE HAS MOVED AGAINST EL SALVADOR.
I'VE BEEN TRYING TO MAKE SOME MOVES, GET MYSELF BACK IN A POSITION WHERE I CAN DO SOMETHING—THE NSA IS SCREWING UP ROYALLY.
BUT I'M BEING FROZEN OUT EVERYWHERE I TURN. IT'S ALMOST LIKE SOMEONE WANTS THIS TO BE A DISASTER.
YOU HAVE ANY REASON TO THINK THAT'S NOT EXACTLY WHAT IS GOING ON?
WE'LL DO WHATEVER WE CAN ON OUR END.
HE CAN'T HELP—HE'S UP TO HIS NECK IN CRAP.

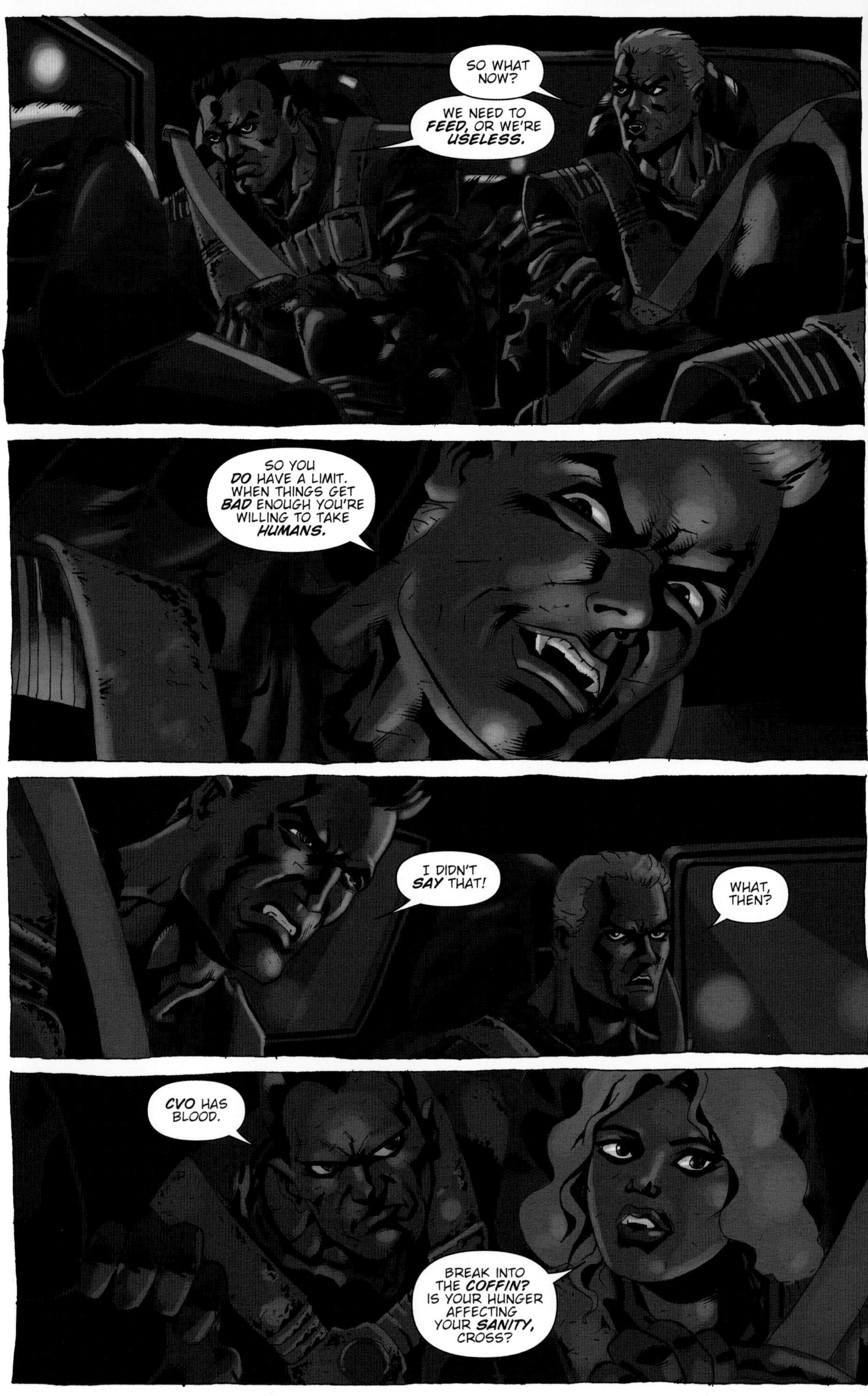
SO WHAT NOW?
WE NEED TO FEED, OR WE'RE USELESS.
SO YOU DO HAVE A LIMIT. WHEN THINGS GET BAD ENOUGH YOU'RE WILLING TO TAKE HUMANS.
I DIDN'T SAY THAT!
WHAT, THEN?
CVO HAS BLOOD.
BREAK INTO THE COFFIN? IS YOUR HUNGER AFFECTING YOUR SANITY, CROSS?

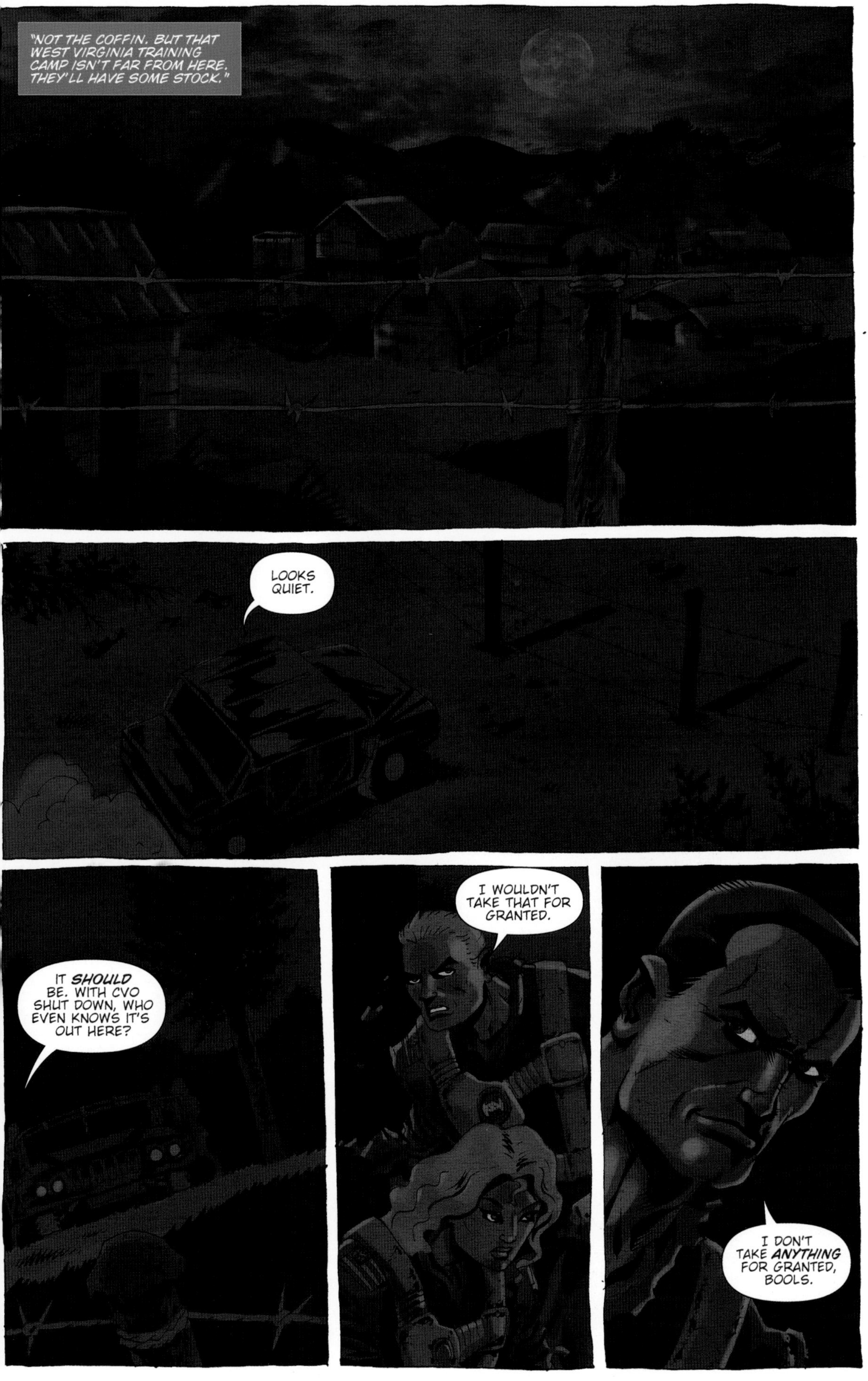
"NOT THE COFFIN. BUT THAT WEST VIRGINIA TRAINING CAMP ISN'T FAR FROM HERE. THEY'LL HAVE SOME STOCK."
LOOKS QUIET.
IT *SHOULD* BE. WITH CVO SHUT DOWN, WHO EVEN KNOWS IT'S OUT HERE?
I WOULDN'T TAKE THAT FOR GRANTED.
I DON'T TAKE *ANYTHING* FOR GRANTED, BOOLS.

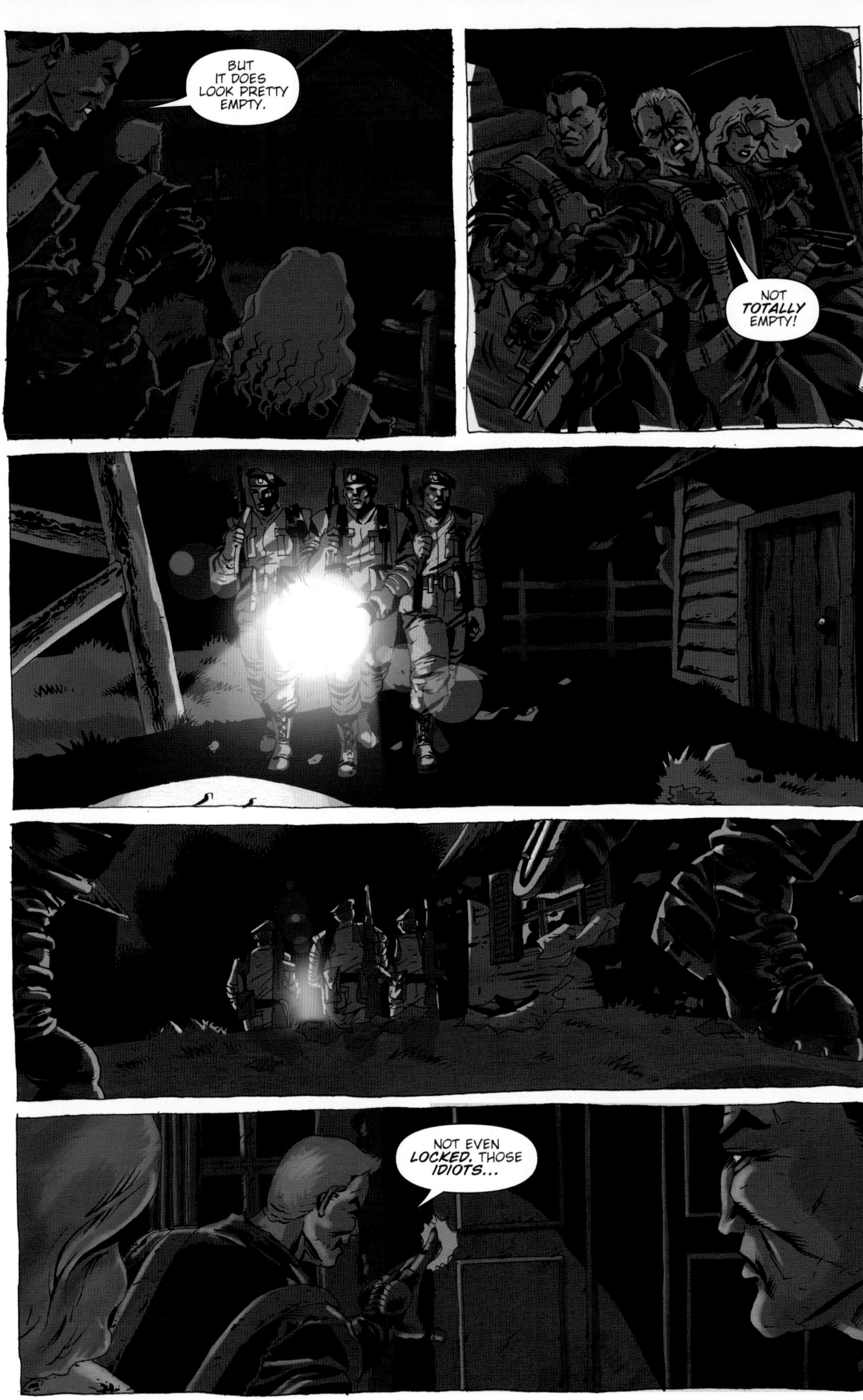
BUT IT DOES LOOK PRETTY EMPTY.
NOT *TOTALLY* EMPTY!
NOT EVEN *LOCKED.* THOSE *IDIOTS...*

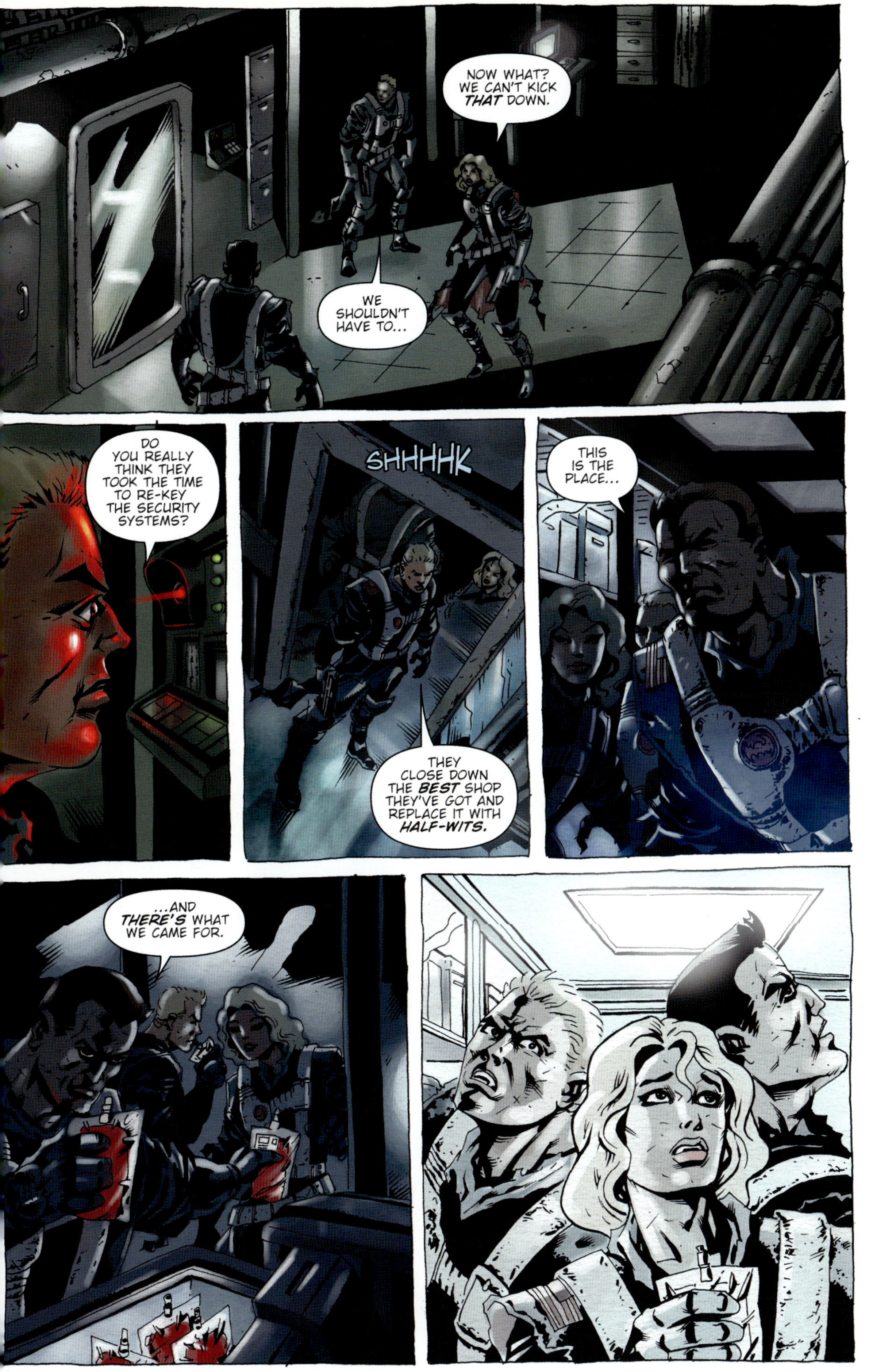
NOW WHAT? WE CAN'T KICK THAT DOWN.
WE SHOULDN'T HAVE TO...
DO YOU REALLY THINK THEY TOOK THE TIME TO RE-KEY THE SECURITY SYSTEMS?
SHHHHK
THEY CLOSE DOWN THE BEST SHOP THEY'VE GOT AND REPLACE IT WITH HALF-WITS.
THIS IS THE PLACE...
...AND THERE'S WHAT WE CAME FOR.

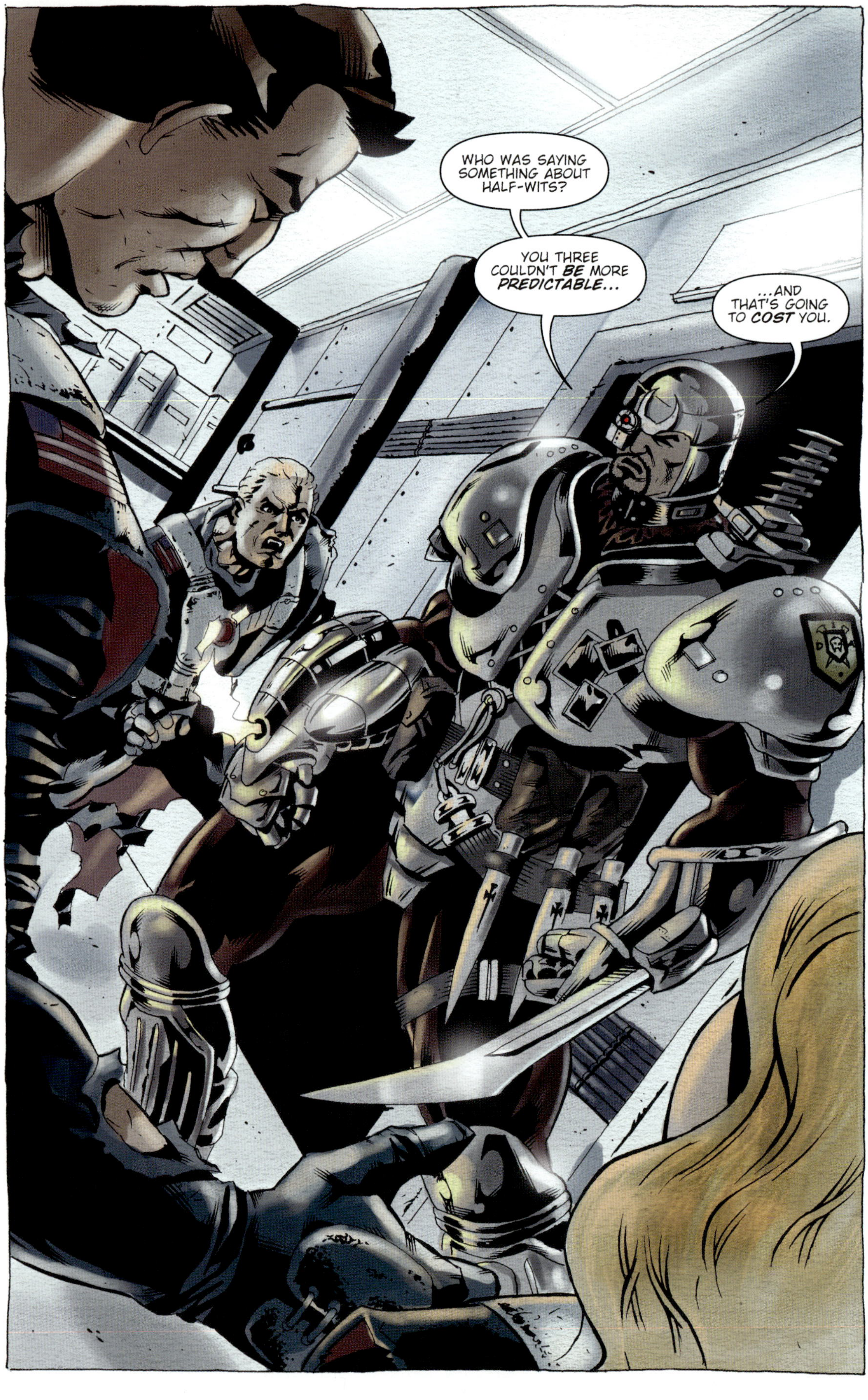
WHO WAS SAYING SOMETHING ABOUT HALF-WITS?
YOU THREE COULDN'T BE MORE PREDICTABLE...
...AND THAT'S GOING TO COST YOU.

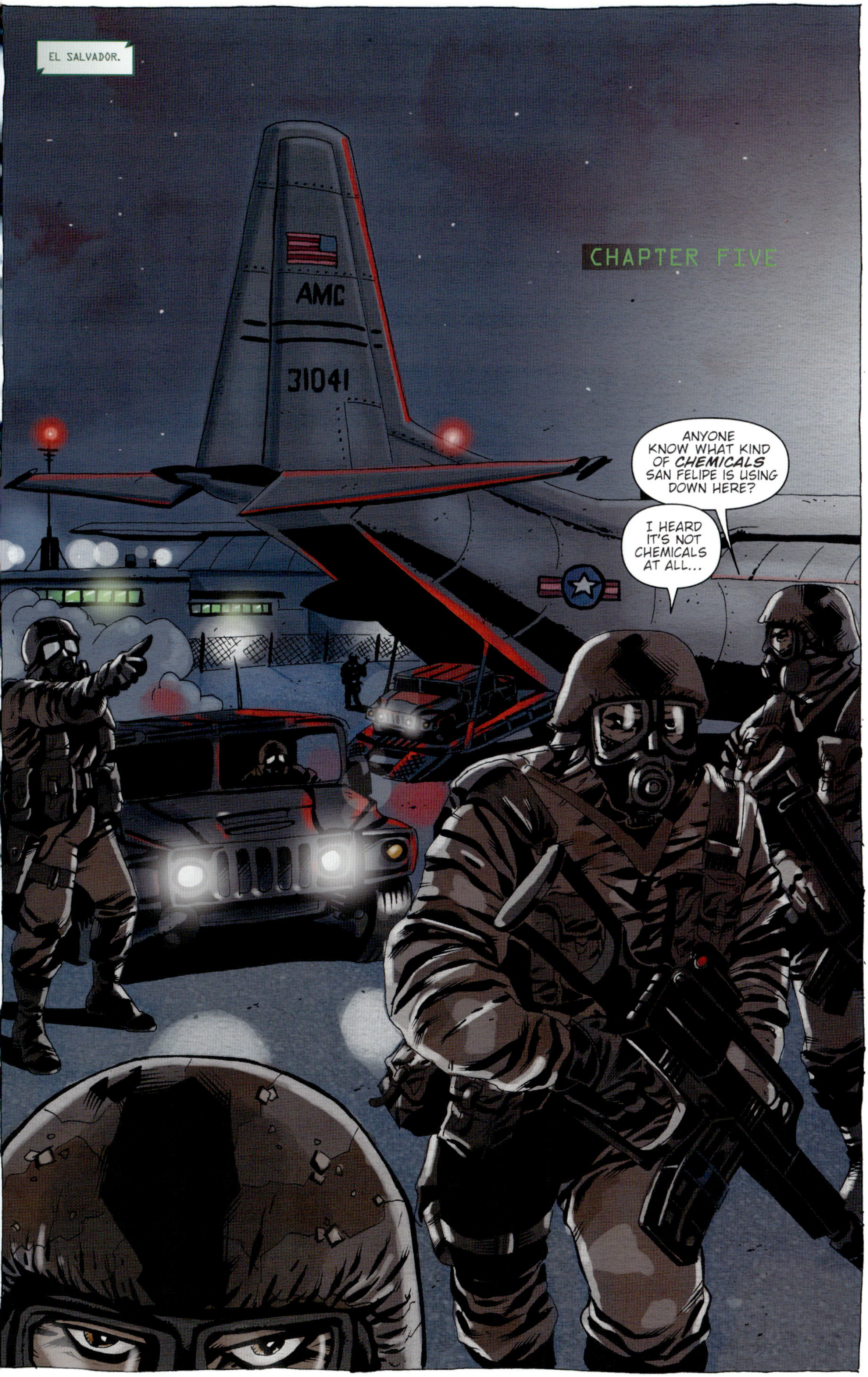
EL SALVADOR.
AMC
31041
CHAPTER FIVE
ANYONE KNOW WHAT KIND OF CHEMICALS SAN FELIPE IS USING DOWN HERE?
I HEARD IT'S NOT CHEMICALS AT ALL...

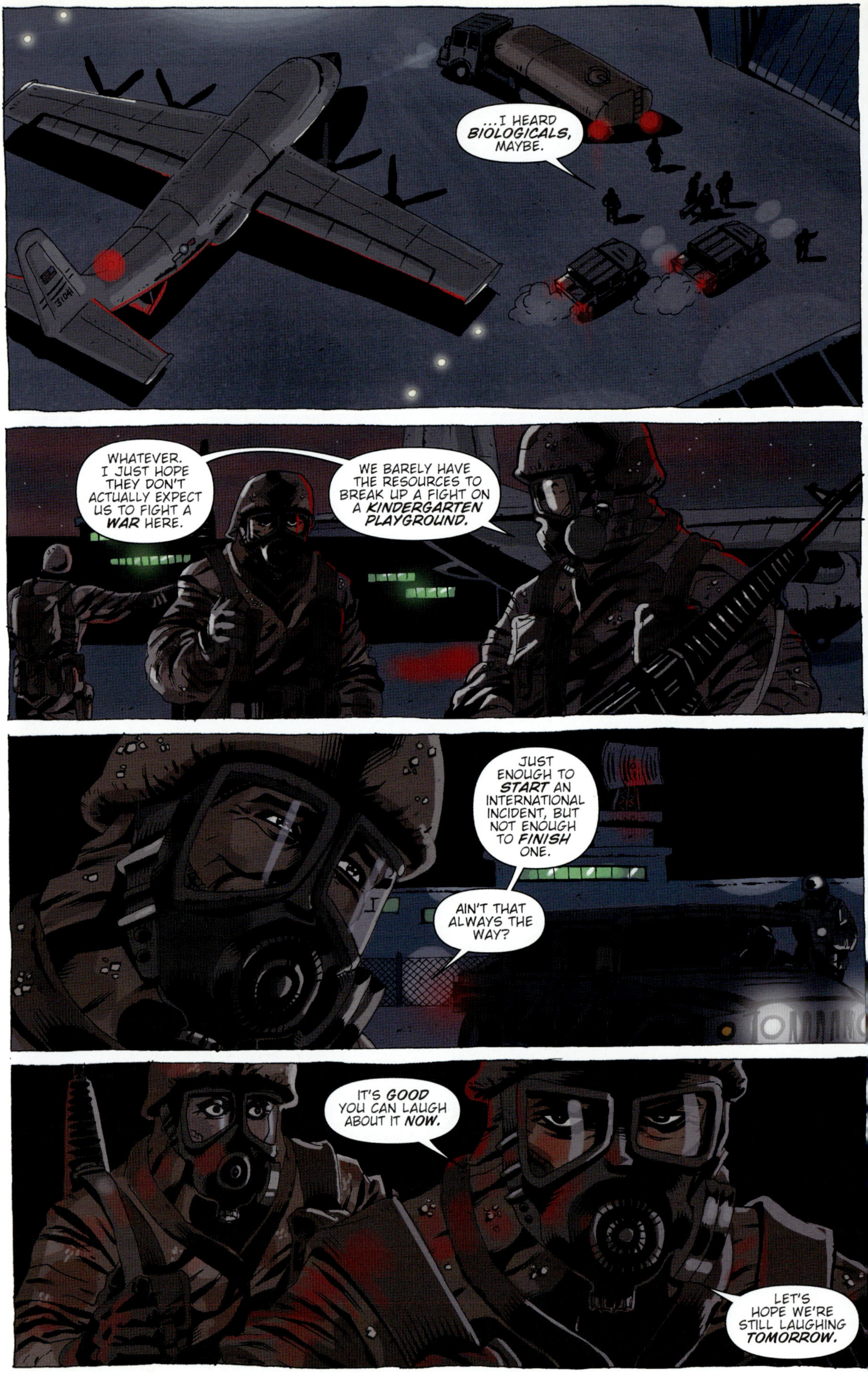

...I HEARD BIOLOGICALS, MAYBE.
WHATEVER. I JUST HOPE THEY DON'T ACTUALLY EXPECT US TO FIGHT A WAR HERE.
WE BARELY HAVE THE RESOURCES TO BREAK UP A FIGHT ON A KINDERGARTEN PLAYGROUND.
JUST ENOUGH TO START AN INTERNATIONAL INCIDENT, BUT NOT ENOUGH TO FINISH ONE.
AIN'T THAT ALWAYS THE WAY?
IT'S GOOD YOU CAN LAUGH ABOUT IT NOW.
LET'S HOPE WE'RE STILL LAUGHING TOMORROW.

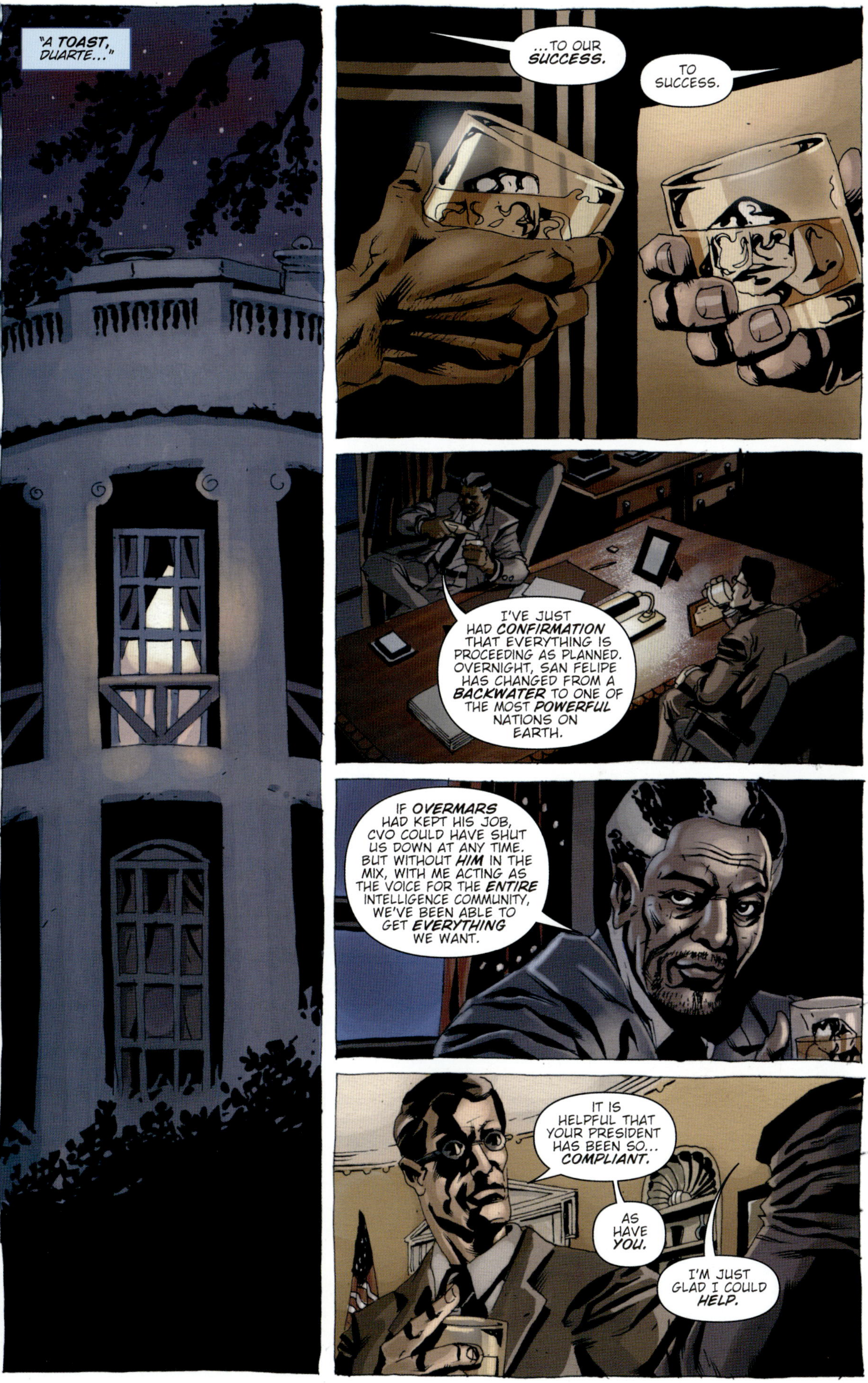
"A TOAST, DUARTE..."
...TO OUR SUCCESS.
TO SUCCESS.
I'VE JUST HAD CONFIRMATION THAT EVERYTHING IS PROCEEDING AS PLANNED. OVERNIGHT, SAN FELIPE HAS CHANGED FROM A BACKWATER TO ONE OF THE MOST POWERFUL NATIONS ON EARTH.
IF OVERMARS HAD KEPT HIS JOB, CVO COULD HAVE SHUT US DOWN AT ANY TIME. BUT WITHOUT HIM IN THE MIX, WITH ME ACTING AS THE VOICE FOR THE ENTIRE INTELLIGENCE COMMUNITY, WE'VE BEEN ABLE TO GET EVERYTHING WE WANT.
IT IS HELPFUL THAT YOUR PRESIDENT HAS BEEN SO... COMPLIANT.
AS HAVE YOU.
I'M JUST GLAD I COULD HELP.

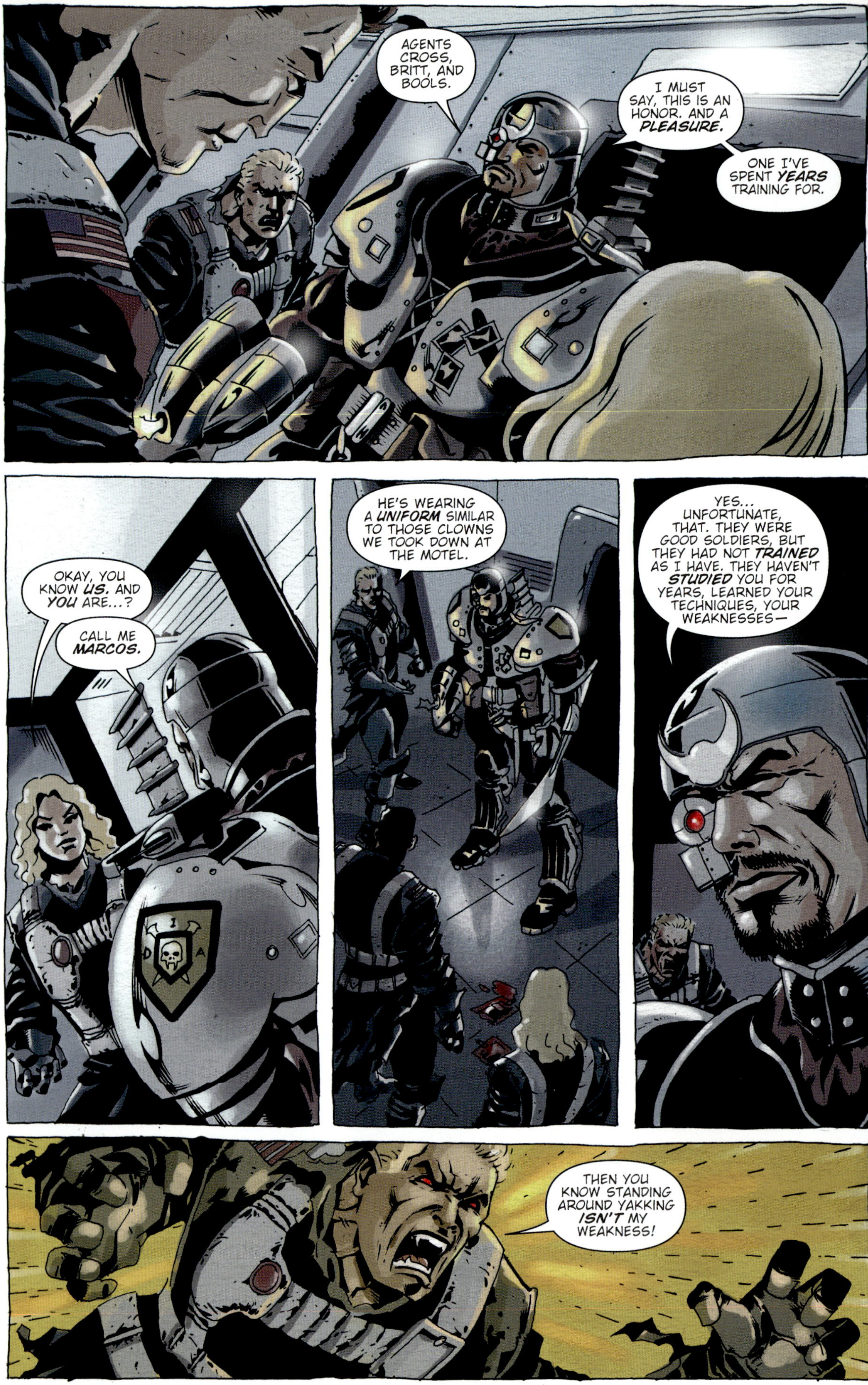
AGENTS CROSS, BRITT, AND BOOLS.
I MUST SAY, THIS IS AN HONOR. AND A PLEASURE.
ONE I'VE SPENT YEARS TRAINING FOR.
OKAY, YOU KNOW US. AND YOU ARE...?
CALL ME MARCOS.
HE'S WEARING A UNIFORM SIMILAR TO THOSE CLOWNS WE TOOK DOWN AT THE MOTEL.
YES... UNFORTUNATE, THAT. THEY WERE GOOD SOLDIERS, BUT THEY HAD NOT TRAINED AS I HAVE. THEY HAVEN'T STUDIED YOU FOR YEARS, LEARNED YOUR TECHNIQUES, YOUR WEAKNESSES—
THEN YOU KNOW STANDING AROUND YAKKING ISN'T MY WEAKNESS!

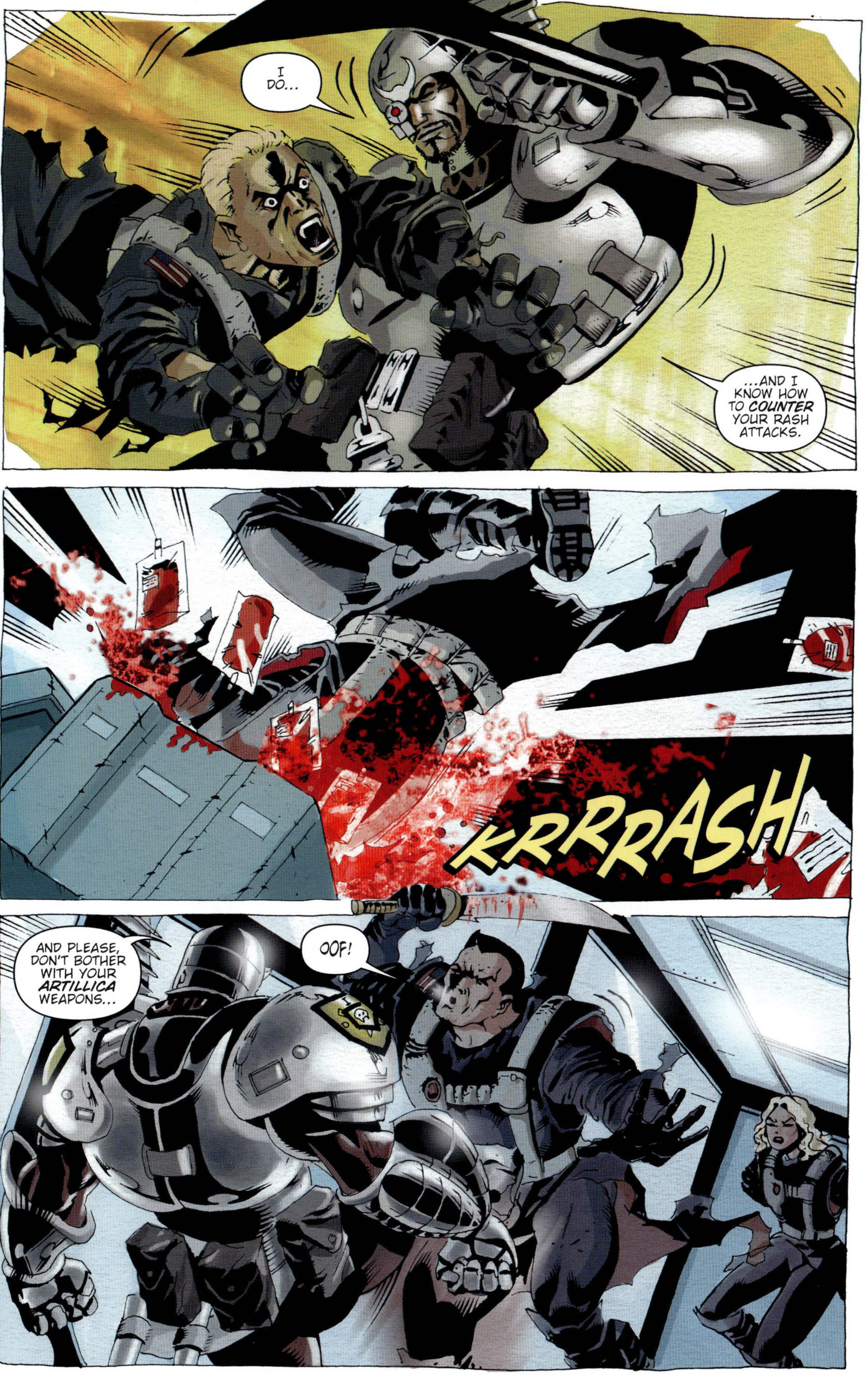
I DO...
...AND I KNOW HOW TO COUNTER YOUR RASH ATTACKS.
KRRRASH
AND PLEASE, DON'T BOTHER WITH YOUR ARTILLICA WEAPONS...
OOF!

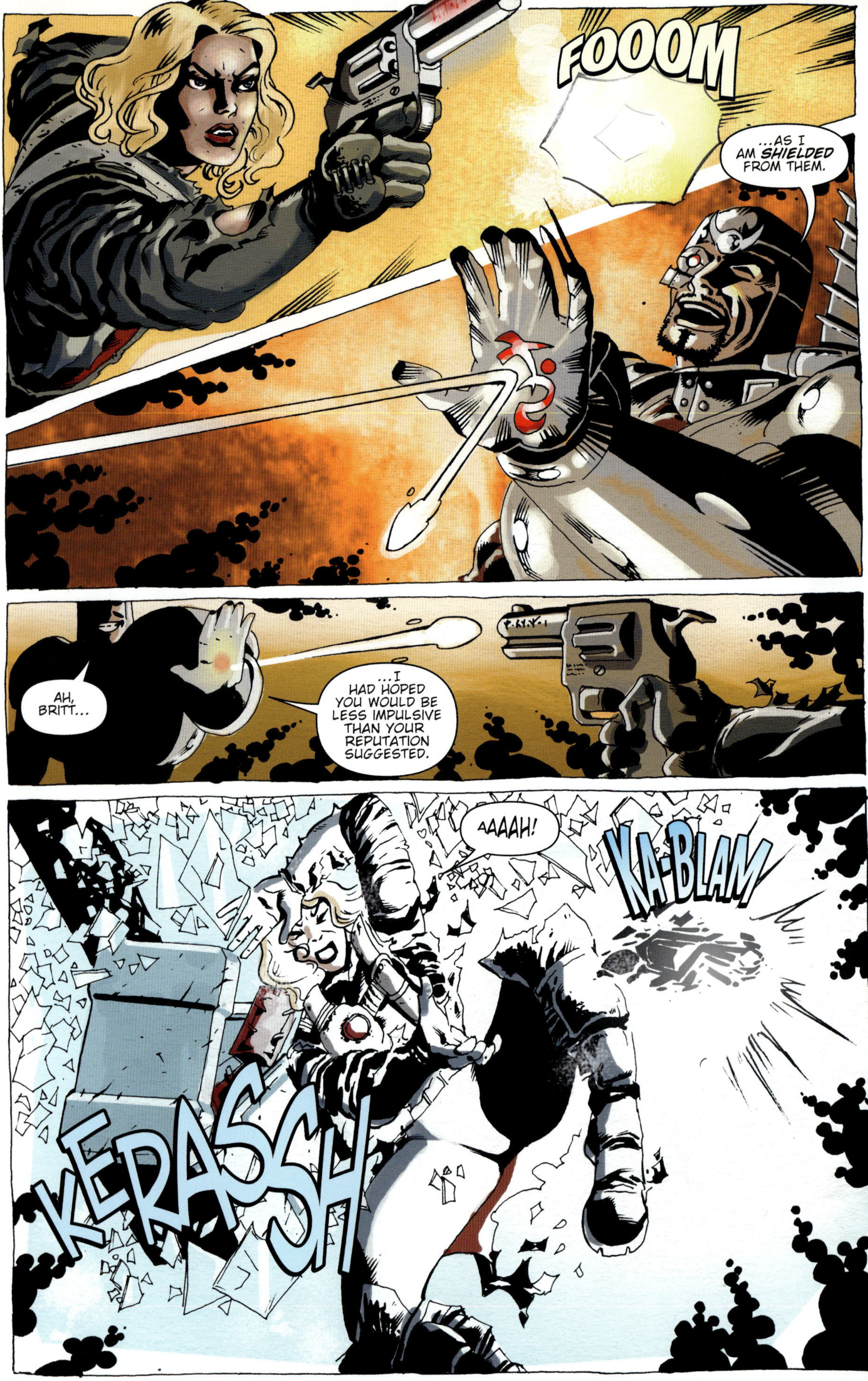
FOOOM
...AS I AM SHIELDED FROM THEM.
AH, BRITT...
...I HAD HOPED YOU WOULD BE LESS IMPULSIVE THAN YOUR REPUTATION SUGGESTED.
AAAAH!
KA-BLAM
KERASSH

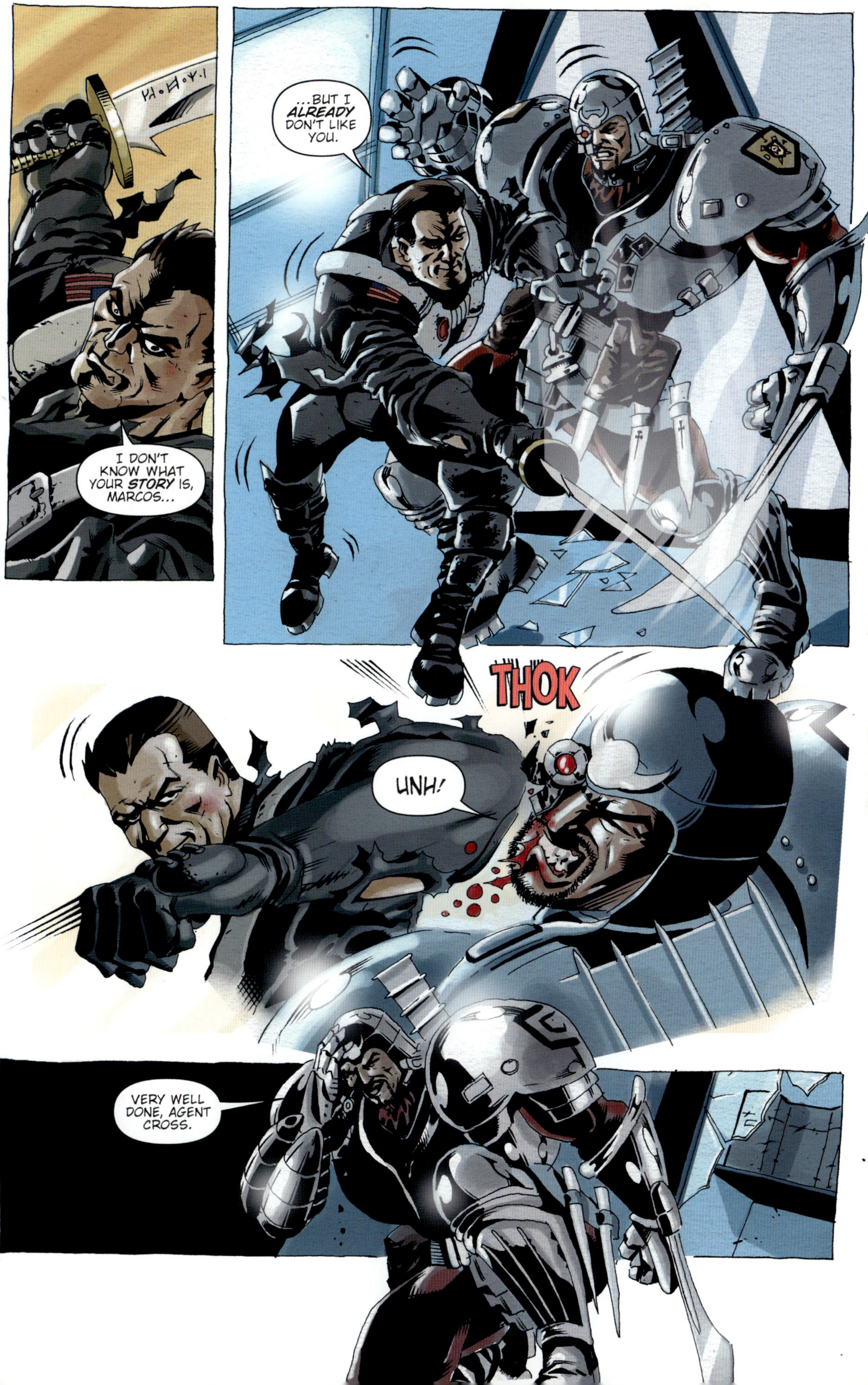

I DON'T KNOW WHAT YOUR STORY IS, MARCOS...
...BUT I ALREADY DON'T LIKE YOU.
THOK
UNH!
VERY WELL DONE, AGENT CROSS.

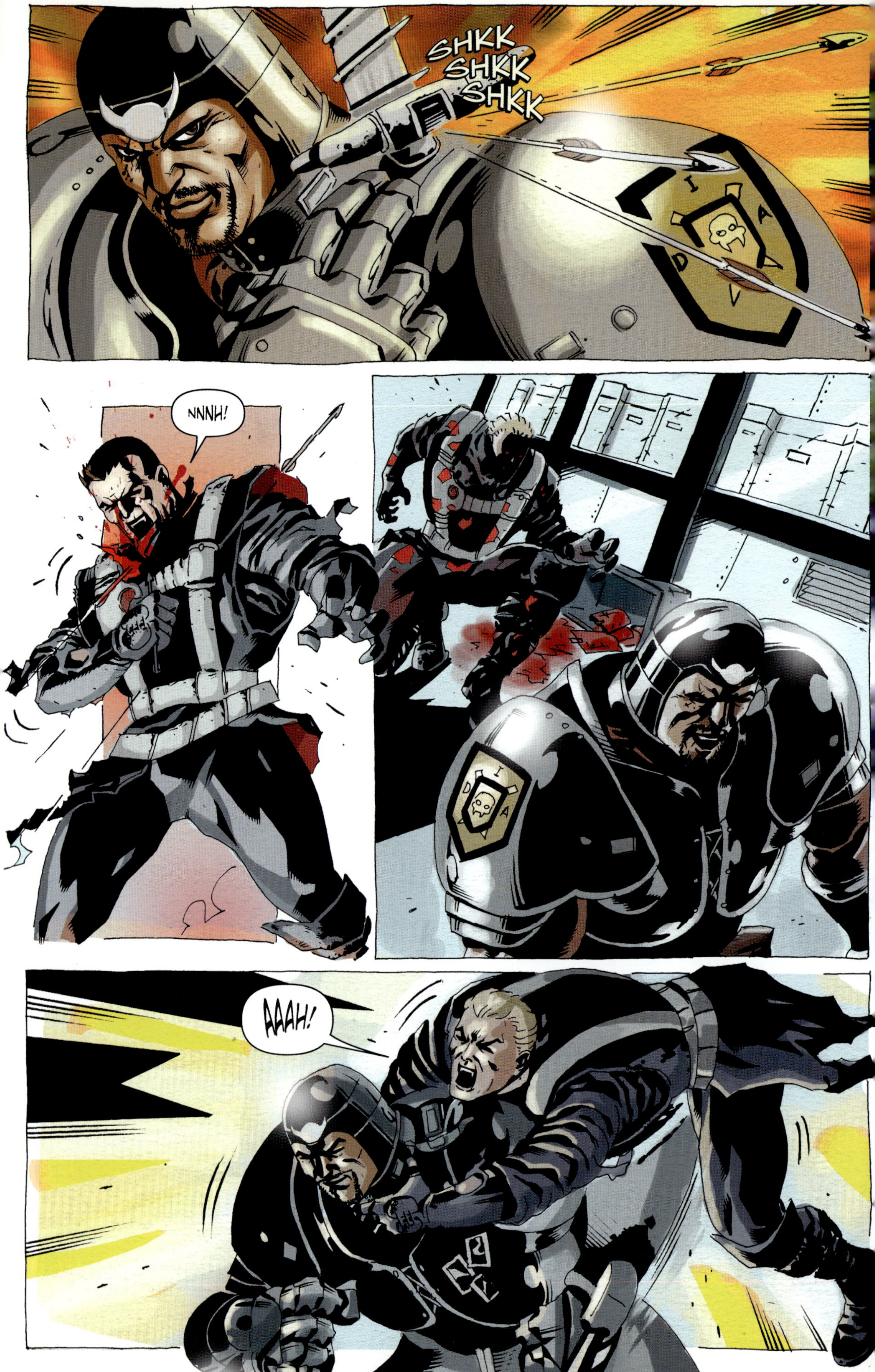
SHKK
SHKK
SHKK
I A D V
NNNH!
I D A
AAAH!

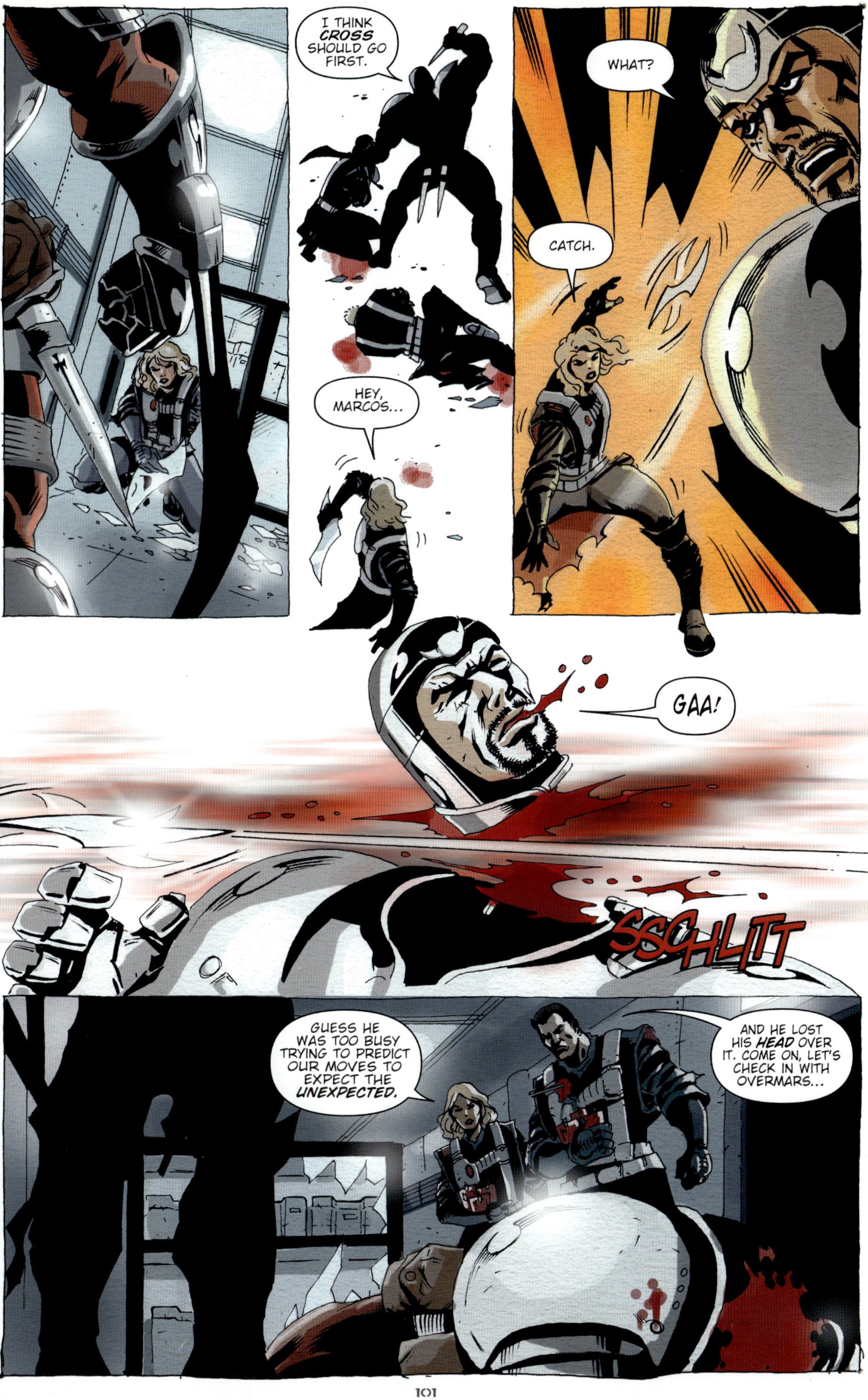
I THINK CROSS SHOULD GO FIRST.
WHAT?
CATCH.
HEY, MARCOS...
GAA!
SSCHLITT
GUESS HE WAS TOO BUSY TRYING TO PREDICT OUR MOVES TO EXPECT THE UNEXPECTED.
AND HE LOST HIS HEAD OVER IT. COME ON, LET'S CHECK IN WITH OVERMARS...

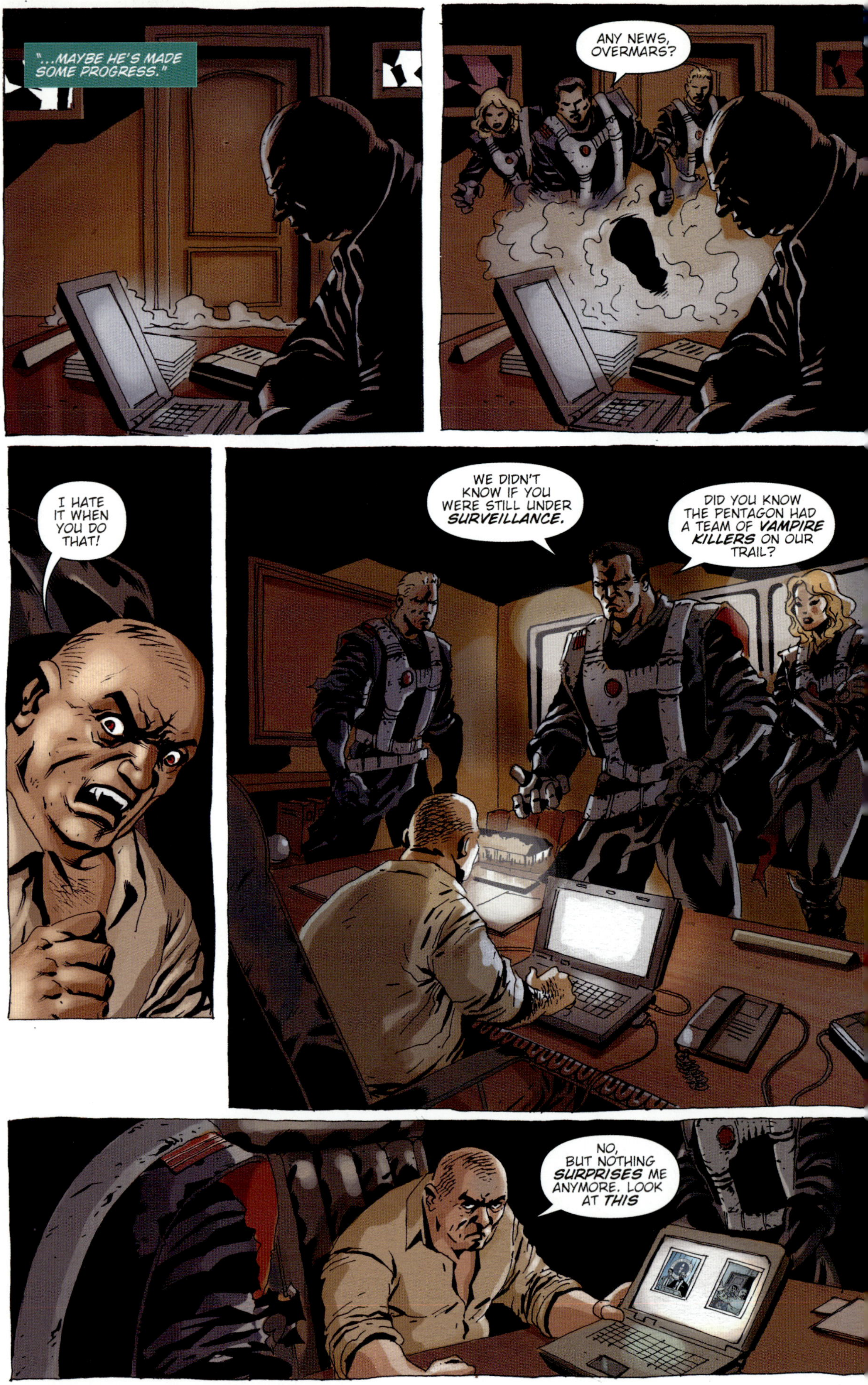
"...MAYBE HE'S MADE SOME PROGRESS."
ANY NEWS, OVERMARS?
I HATE IT WHEN YOU DO THAT!
WE DIDN'T KNOW IF YOU WERE STILL UNDER SURVEILLANCE.
DID YOU KNOW THE PENTAGON HAD A TEAM OF VAMPIRE KILLERS ON OUR TRAIL?
NO, BUT NOTHING SURPRISES ME ANYMORE. LOOK AT THIS

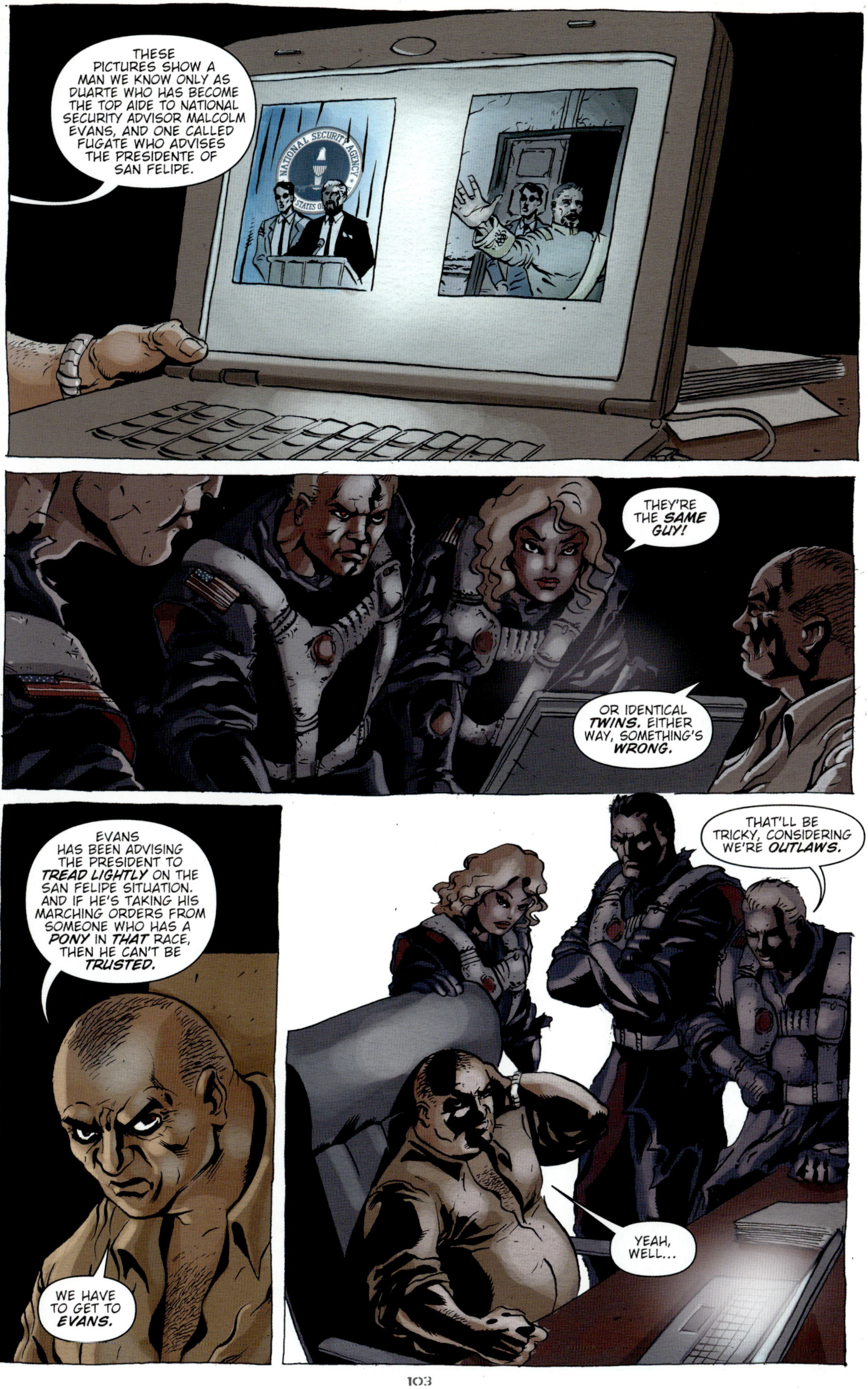
THESE PICTURES SHOW A MAN WE KNOW ONLY AS DUARTE WHO HAS BECOME THE TOP AIDE TO NATIONAL SECURITY ADVISOR MALCOLM EVANS, AND ONE CALLED FUGATE WHO ADVISES THE PRESIDENTE OF SAN FELIPE.
NATIONAL SECURITY AGENCY
THEY'RE THE SAME GUY!
OR IDENTICAL TWINS. EITHER WAY, SOMETHING'S WRONG.
EVANS HAS BEEN ADVISING THE PRESIDENT TO TREAD LIGHTLY ON THE SAN FELIPE SITUATION. AND IF HE'S TAKING HIS MARCHING ORDERS FROM SOMEONE WHO HAS A PONY IN THAT RACE, THEN HE CAN'T BE TRUSTED.
WE HAVE TO GET TO EVANS.
THAT'LL BE TRICKY, CONSIDERING WE'RE OUTLAWS.
YEAH, WELL...

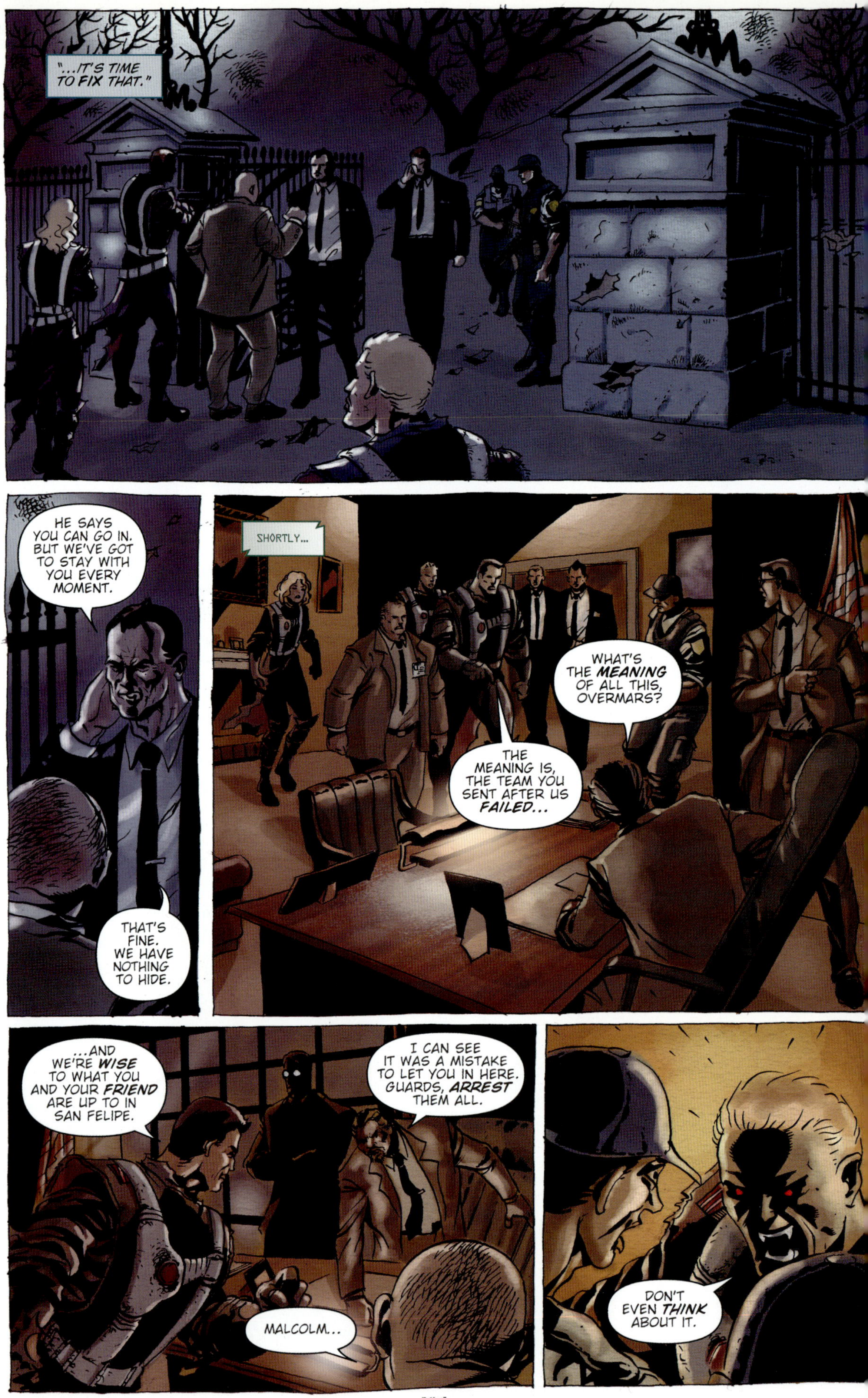
"...IT'S TIME TO FIX THAT."
HE SAYS YOU CAN GO IN. BUT WE'VE GOT TO STAY WITH YOU EVERY MOMENT.
THAT'S FINE. WE HAVE NOTHING TO HIDE.
SHORTLY...
WHAT'S THE MEANING OF ALL THIS, OVERMARS?
THE MEANING IS, THE TEAM YOU SENT AFTER US FAILED...
...AND WE'RE WISE TO WHAT YOU AND YOUR FRIEND ARE UP TO IN SAN FELIPE.
I CAN SEE IT WAS A MISTAKE TO LET YOU IN HERE. GUARDS, ARREST THEM ALL.
MALCOLM...
DON'T EVEN THINK ABOUT IT.

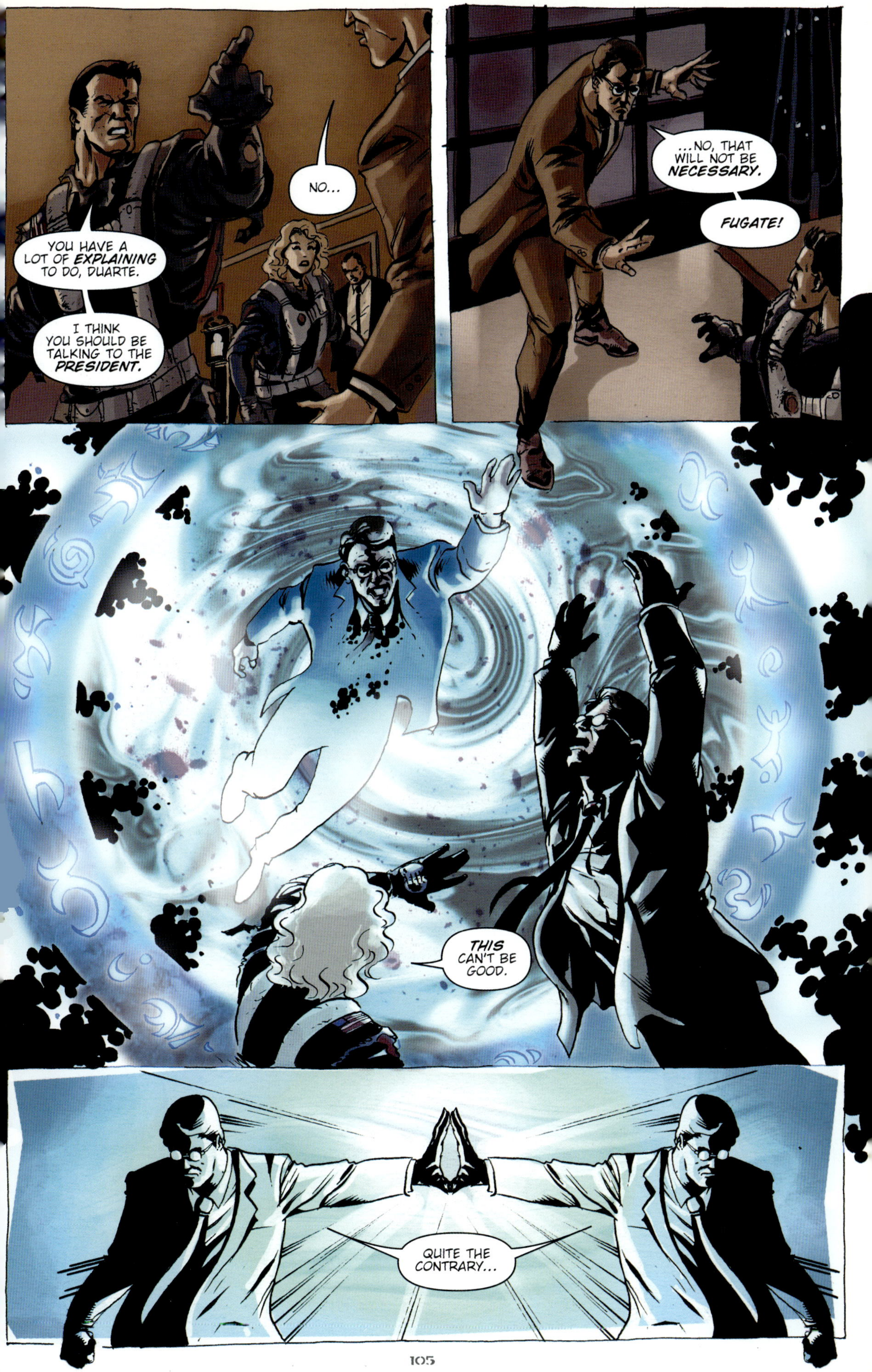
YOU HAVE A LOT OF EXPLAINING TO DO, DUARTE.
I THINK YOU SHOULD BE TALKING TO THE PRESIDENT.
NO...
...NO, THAT WILL NOT BE NECESSARY.
FUGATE!
THIS CAN'T BE GOOD.
QUITE THE CONTRARY...

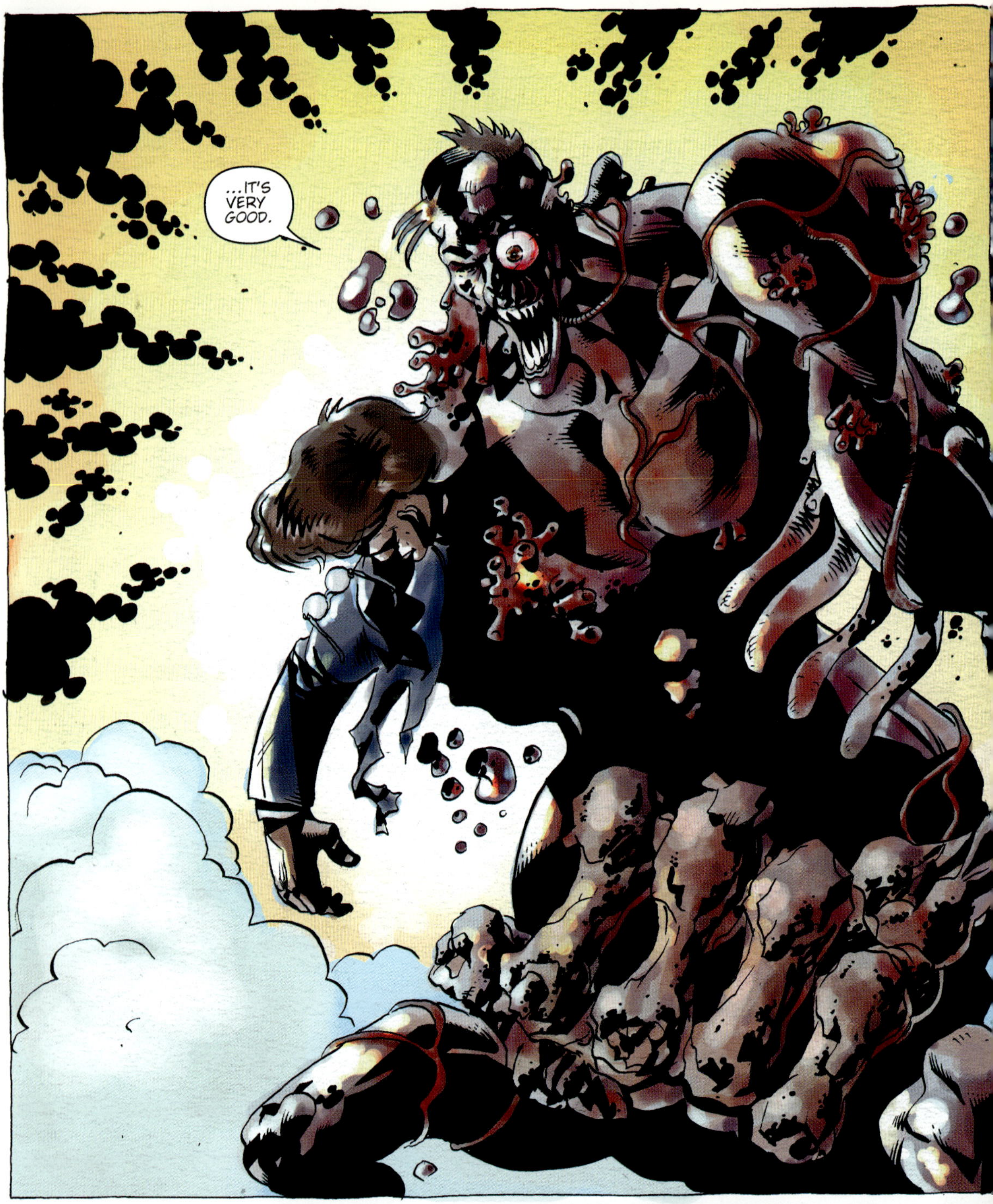
...IT'S VERY GOOD.

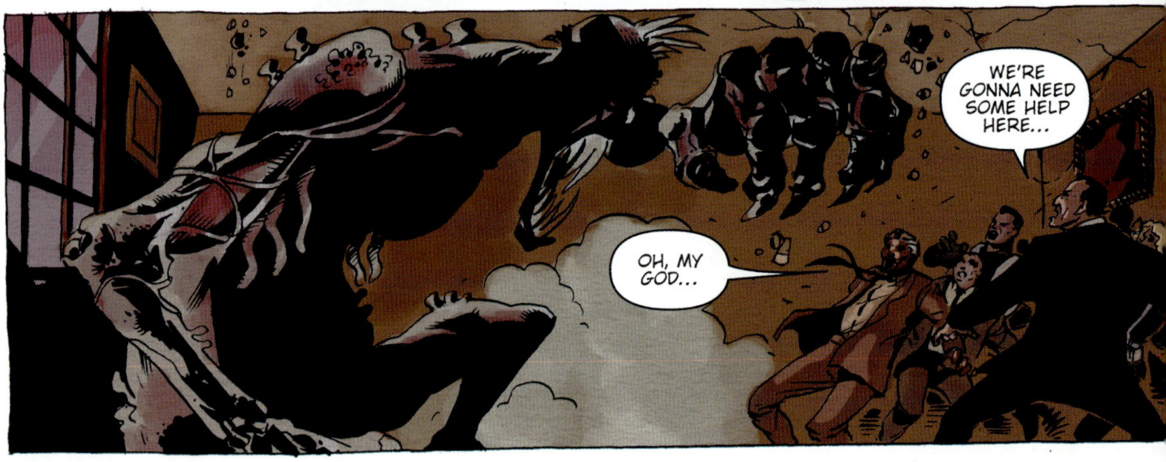
WE'RE GONNA NEED SOME HELP HERE...
OH, MY GOD...

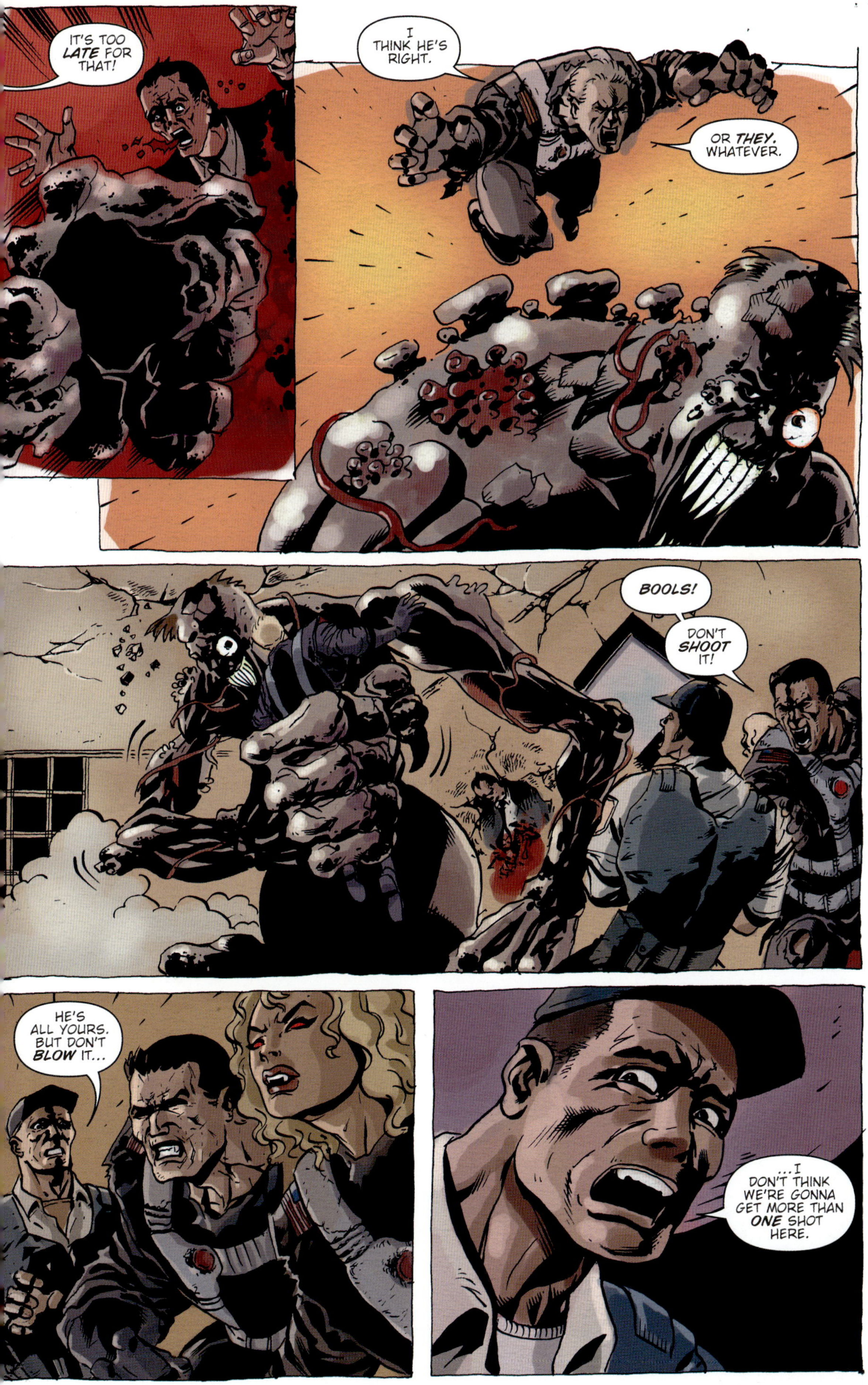
IT'S TOO LATE FOR THAT!
I THINK HE'S RIGHT.
OR THEY. WHATEVER.
BOOLS!
DON'T SHOOT IT!
HE'S ALL YOURS. BUT DON'T BLOW IT...
...I DON'T THINK WE'RE GONNA GET MORE THAN ONE SHOT HERE.

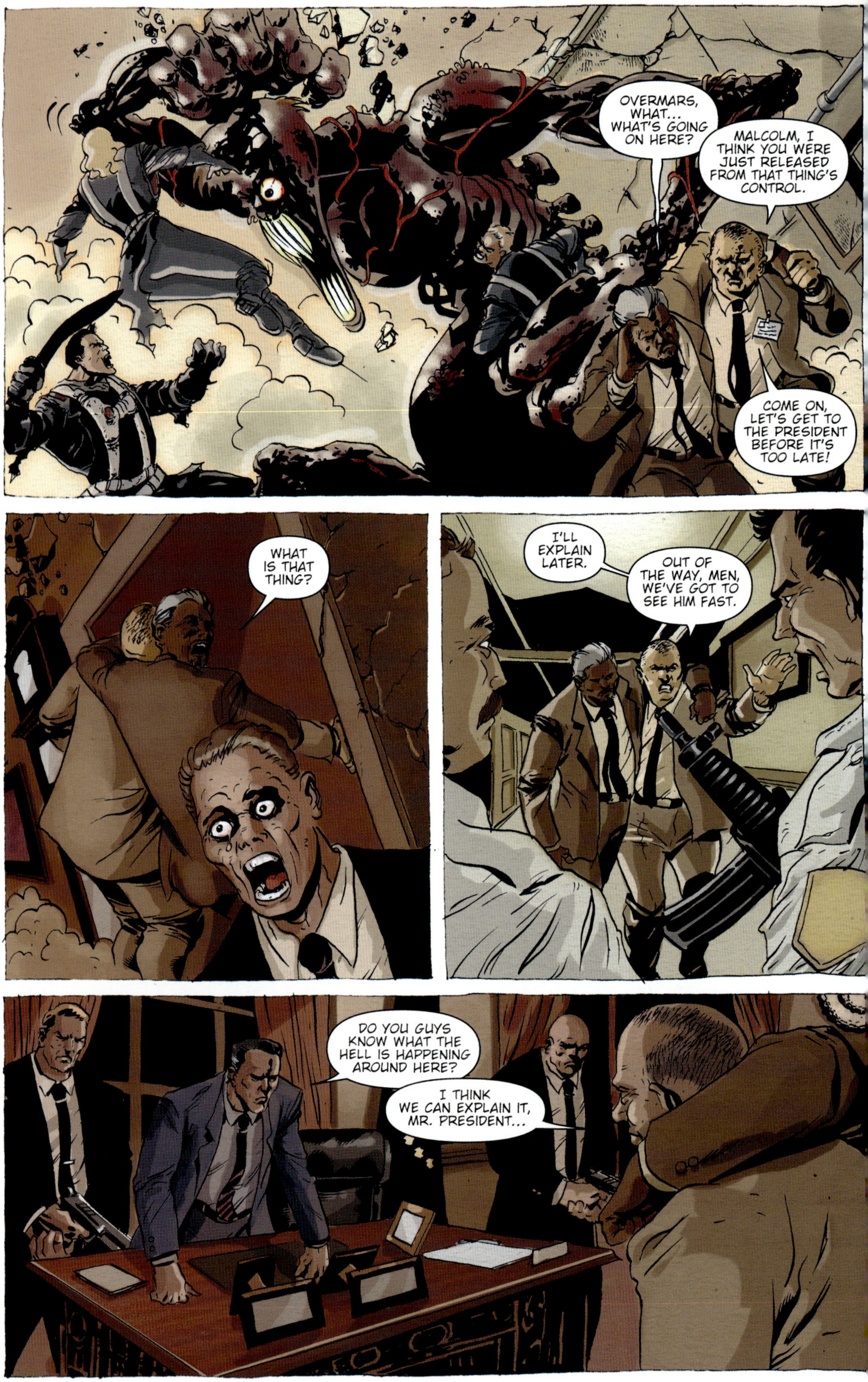

OVERMARS, WHAT... WHAT'S GOING ON HERE?
MALCOLM, I THINK YOU WERE JUST RELEASED FROM THAT THING'S CONTROL.
COME ON, LET'S GET TO THE PRESIDENT BEFORE IT'S TOO LATE!
WHAT IS THAT THING?
I'LL EXPLAIN LATER.
OUT OF THE WAY, MEN, WE'VE GOT TO SEE HIM FAST.
DO YOU GUYS KNOW WHAT THE HELL IS HAPPENING AROUND HERE?
I THINK WE CAN EXPLAIN IT, MR. PRESIDENT...

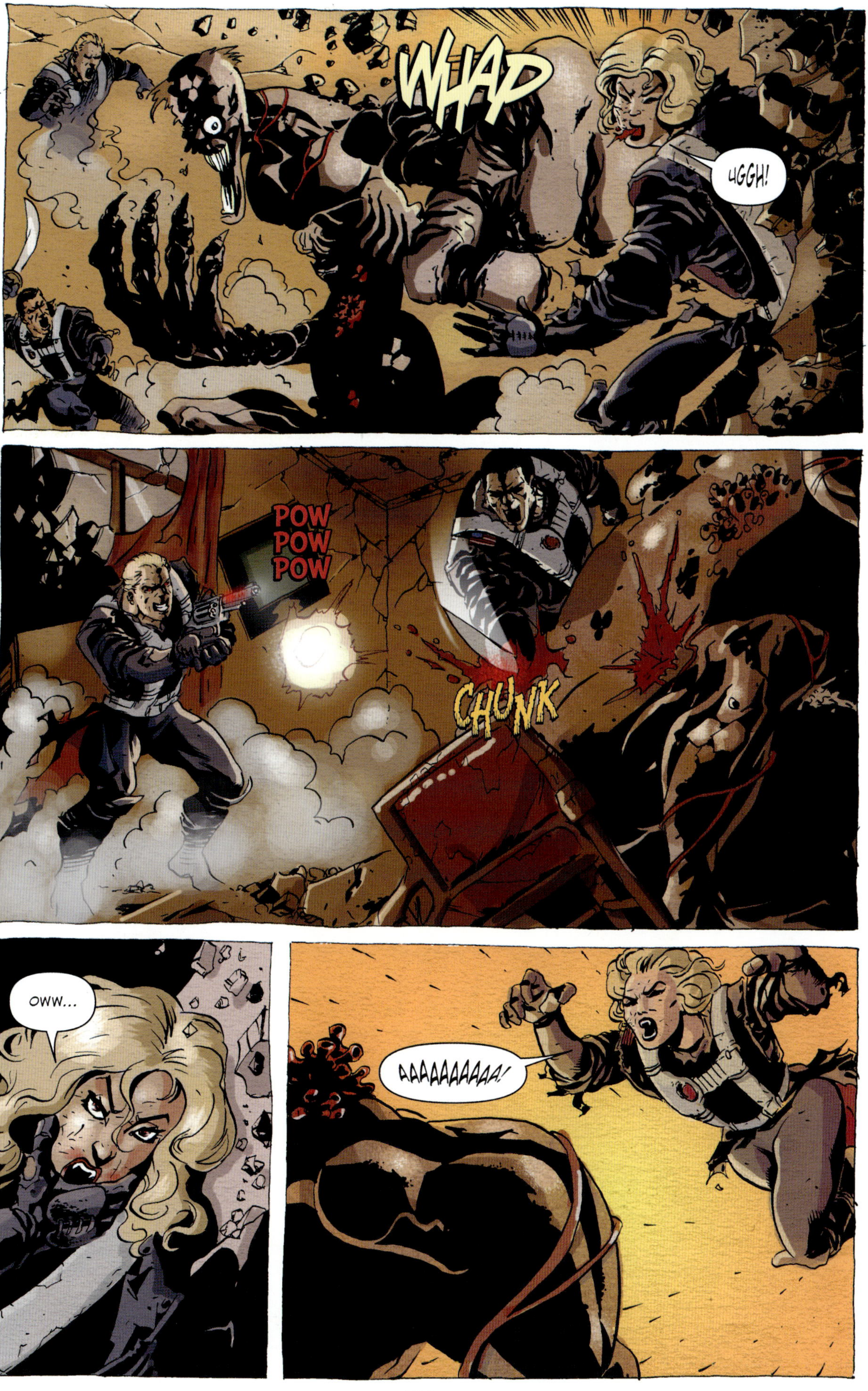
WHAP
UGGH!
POW
POW
POW
CHUNK
OWW...
AAAAAAAAAA!

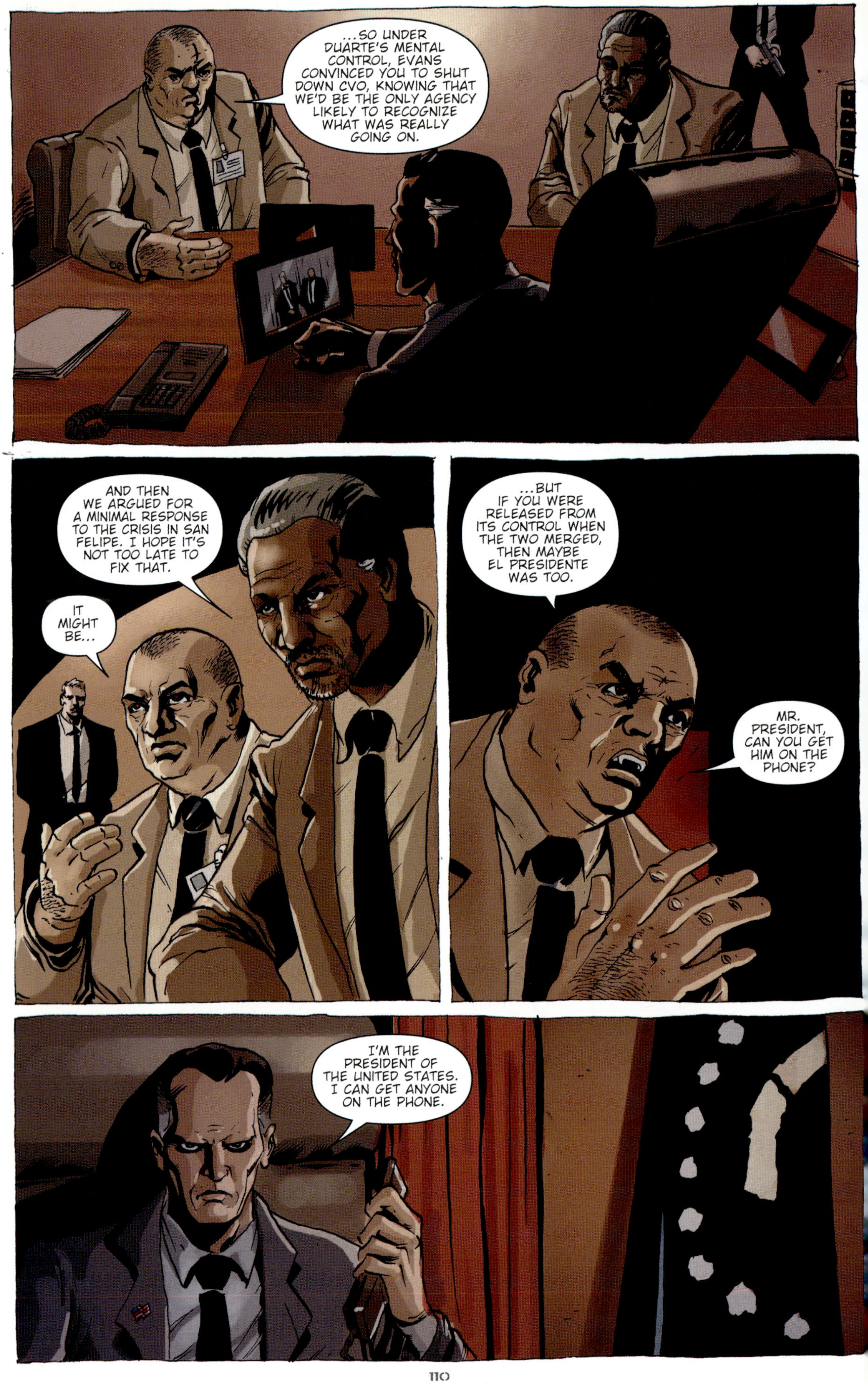
...SO UNDER DUARTE'S MENTAL CONTROL, EVANS CONVINCED YOU TO SHUT DOWN CVO, KNOWING THAT WE'D BE THE ONLY AGENCY LIKELY TO RECOGNIZE WHAT WAS REALLY GOING ON.
AND THEN WE ARGUED FOR A MINIMAL RESPONSE TO THE CRISIS IN SAN FELIPE. I HOPE IT'S NOT TOO LATE TO FIX THAT.
IT MIGHT BE...
...BUT IF YOU WERE RELEASED FROM ITS CONTROL WHEN THE TWO MERGED, THEN MAYBE EL PRESIDENTE WAS TOO.
MR. PRESIDENT, CAN YOU GET HIM ON THE PHONE?
I'M THE PRESIDENT OF THE UNITED STATES. I CAN GET ANYONE ON THE PHONE.

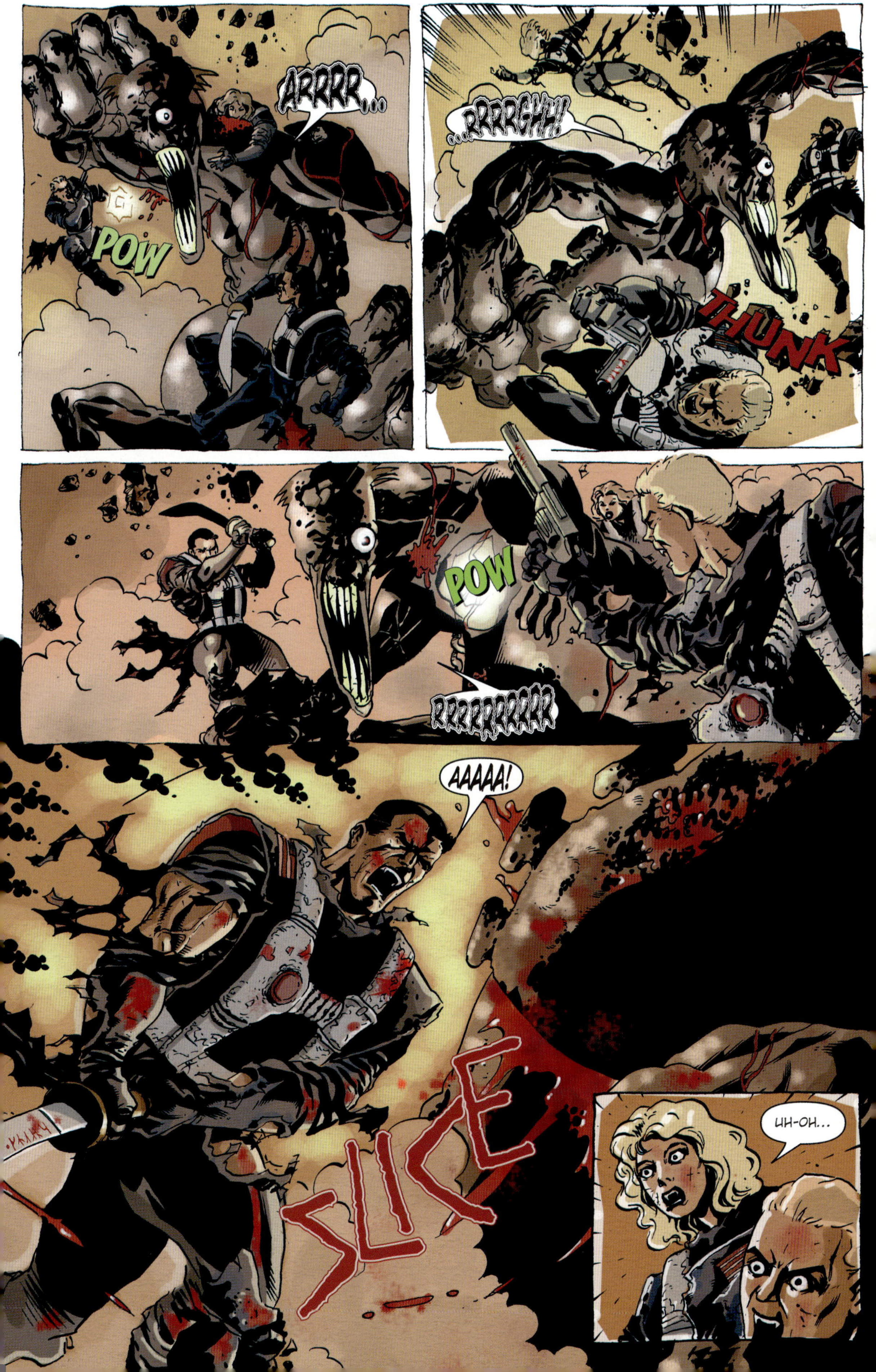

ARRRR...
POW
...RRRRGHH!
THUNK
POW
RRRRRRRRRR
AAAAA!
SLICE
UH-OH...

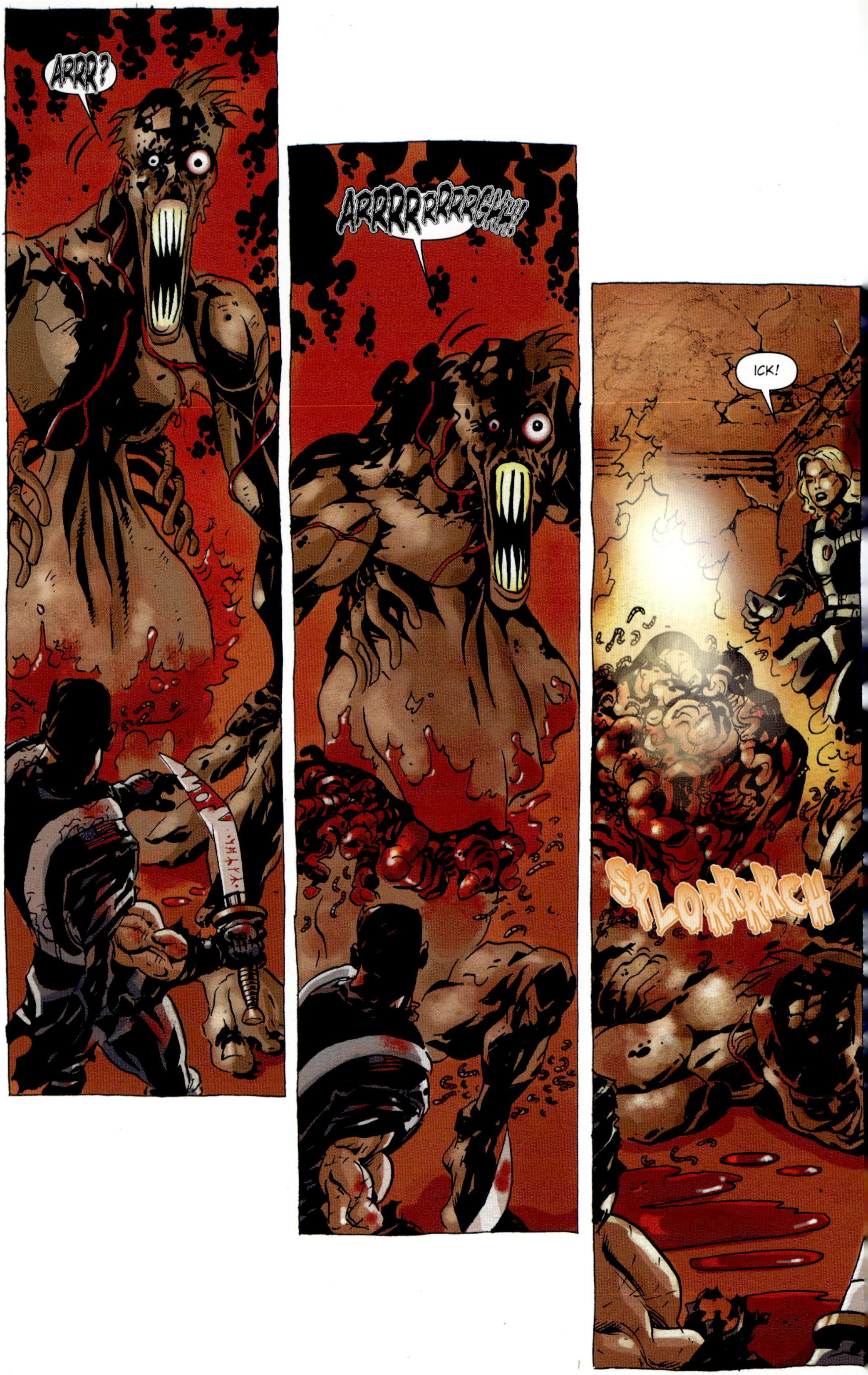
ARRR?
ARRRRRRRRGH!!
ICK!
SPLORRRRCH

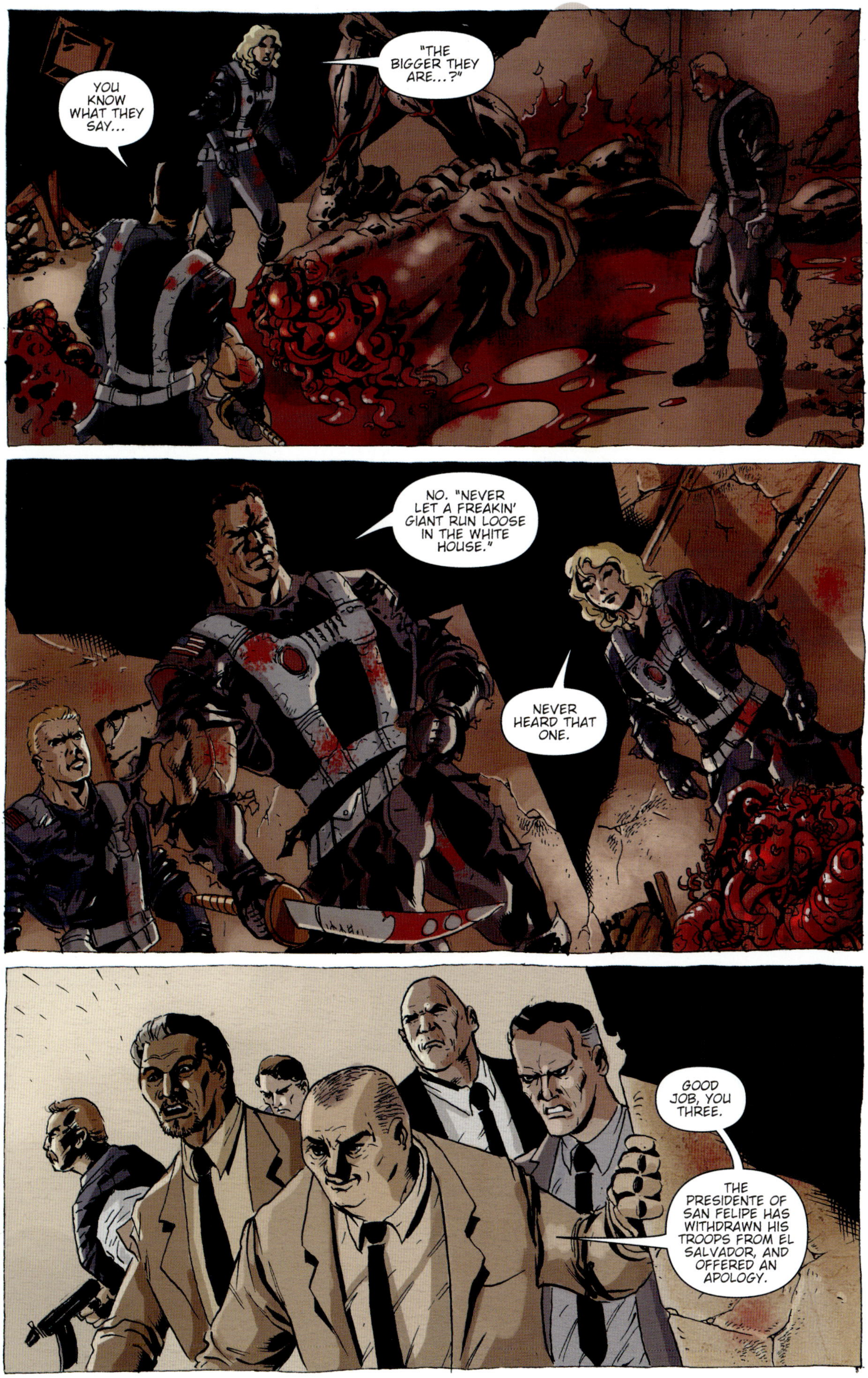
YOU KNOW WHAT THEY SAY...
"THE BIGGER THEY ARE...?"
NO. "NEVER LET A FREAKIN' GIANT RUN LOOSE IN THE WHITE HOUSE."
NEVER HEARD THAT ONE.
GOOD JOB, YOU THREE.
THE PRESIDENTE OF SAN FELIPE HAS WITHDRAWN HIS TROOPS FROM EL SALVADOR, AND OFFERED AN APOLOGY.

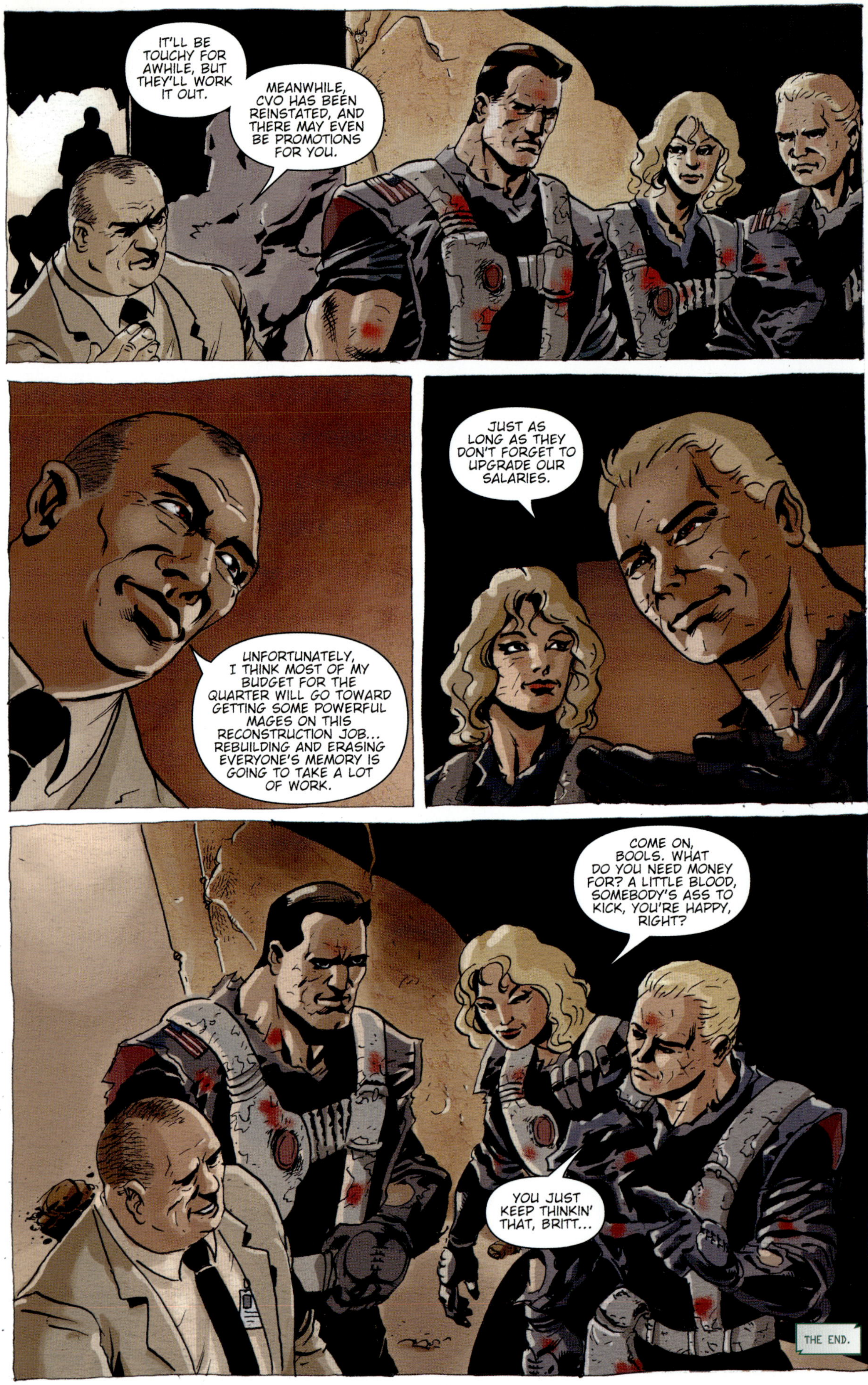
IT'LL BE TOUCHY FOR AWHILE, BUT THEY'LL WORK IT OUT.
MEANWHILE, CVO HAS BEEN REINSTATED, AND THERE MAY EVEN BE PROMOTIONS FOR YOU.
UNFORTUNATELY, I THINK MOST OF MY BUDGET FOR THE QUARTER WILL GO TOWARD GETTING SOME POWERFUL MAGES ON THIS RECONSTRUCTION JOB... REBUILDING AND ERASING EVERYONE'S MEMORY IS GOING TO TAKE A LOT OF WORK.
JUST AS LONG AS THEY DON'T FORGET TO UPGRADE OUR SALARIES.
COME ON, BOOLS. WHAT DO YOU NEED MONEY FOR? A LITTLE BLOOD, SOMEBODY'S ASS TO KICK, YOU'RE HAPPY, RIGHT?
YOU JUST KEEP THINKIN' THAT, BRITT...
THE END.

CVO
covert vampiric operations™

ROGUE STATE

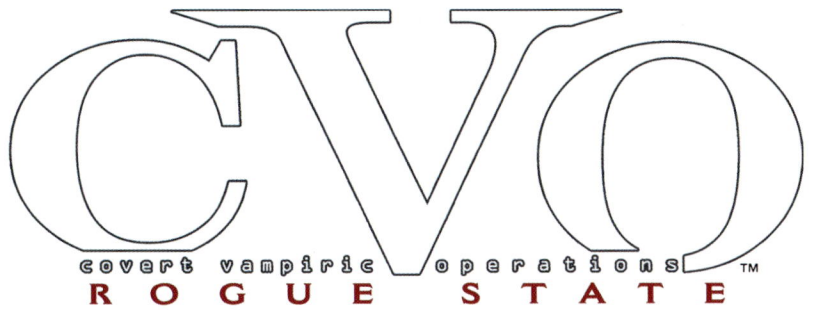

Art Gallery by

Antonio Vazquez
& Fran Gamboa,
Sulaco Studios

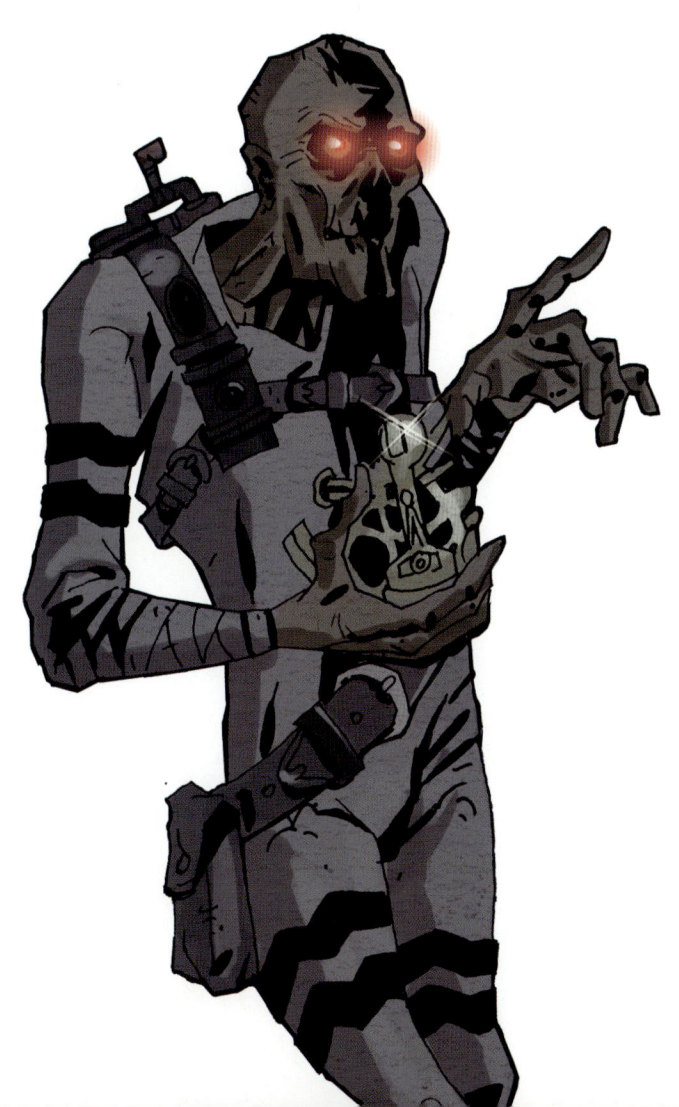

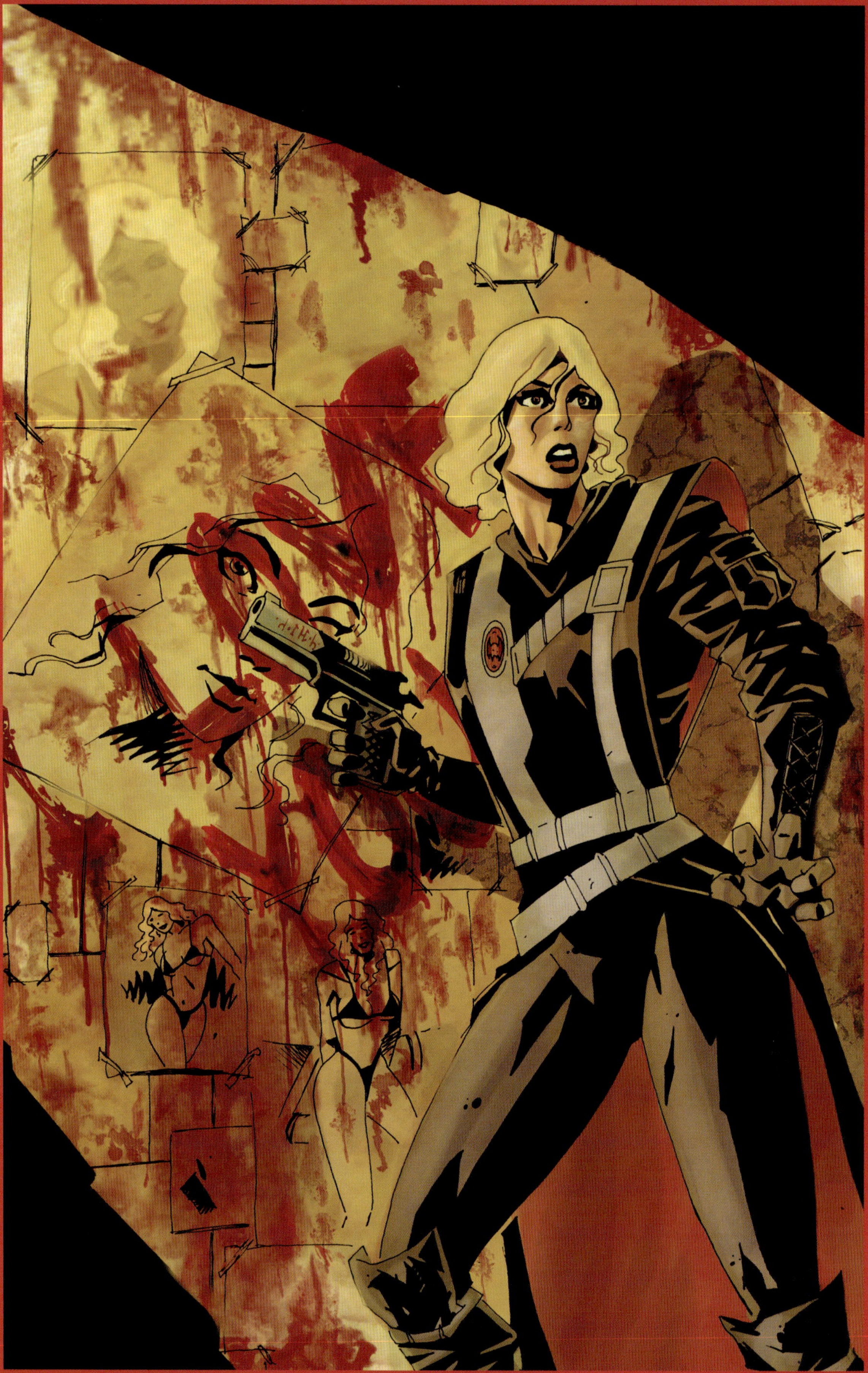

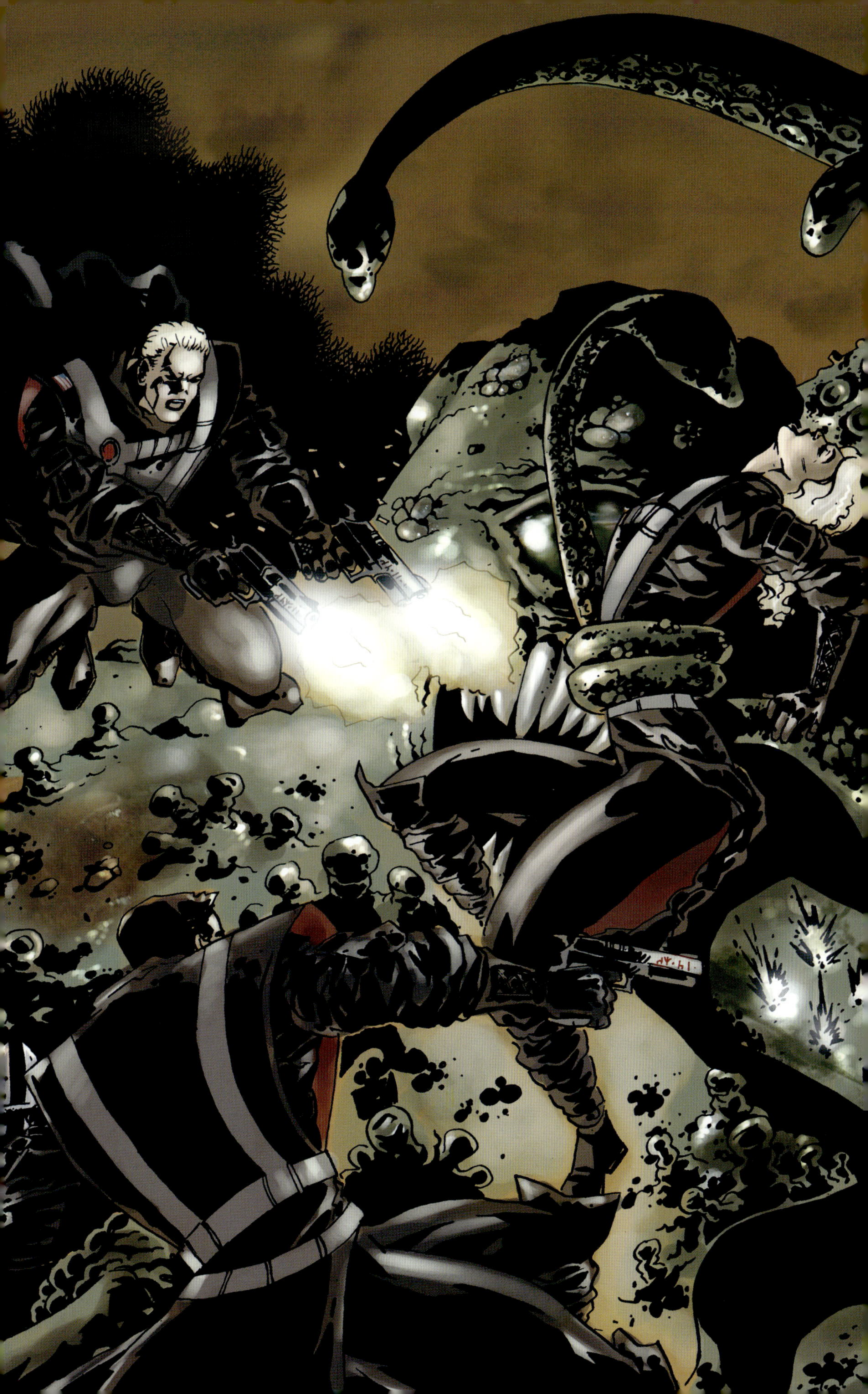

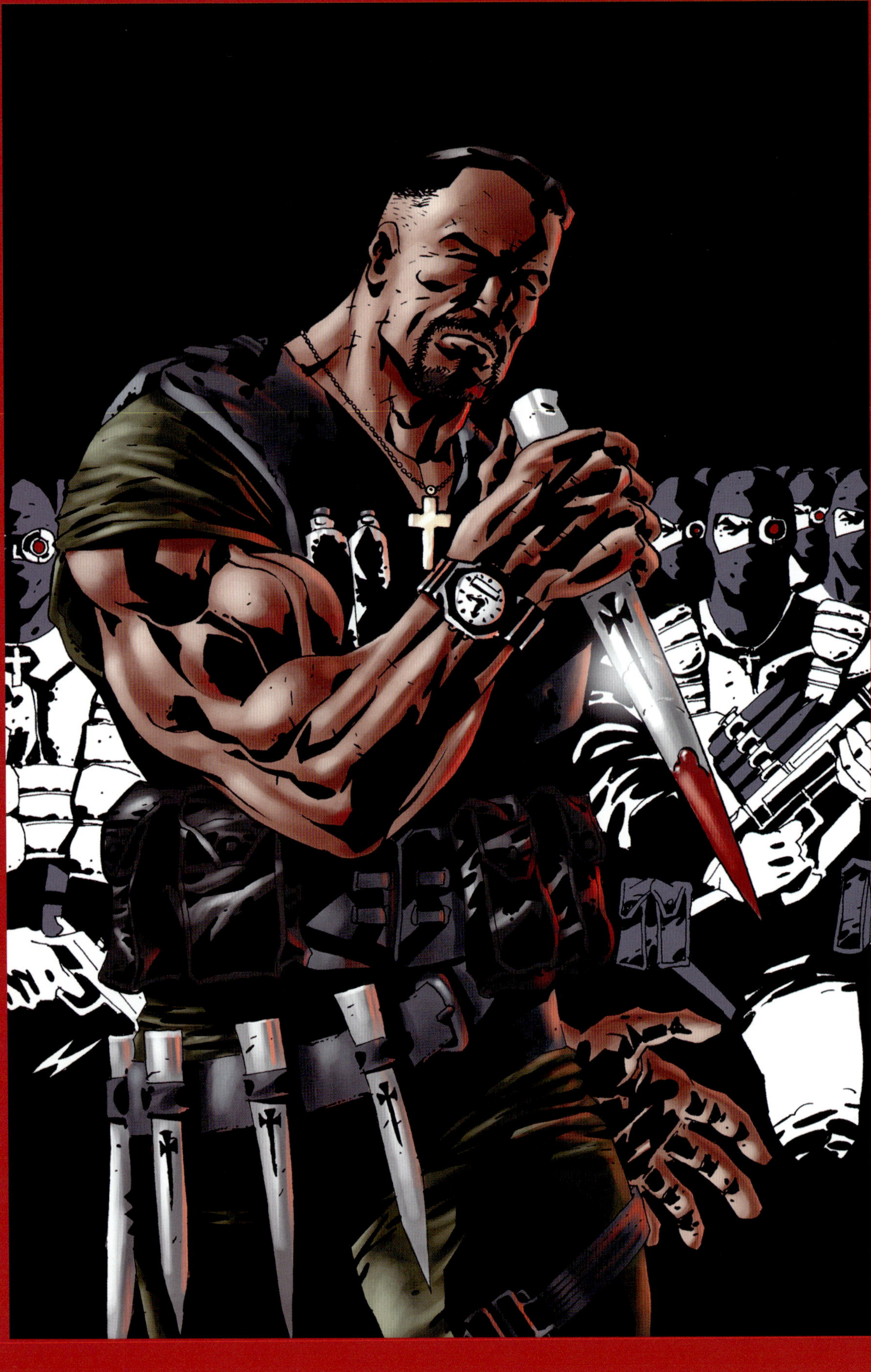

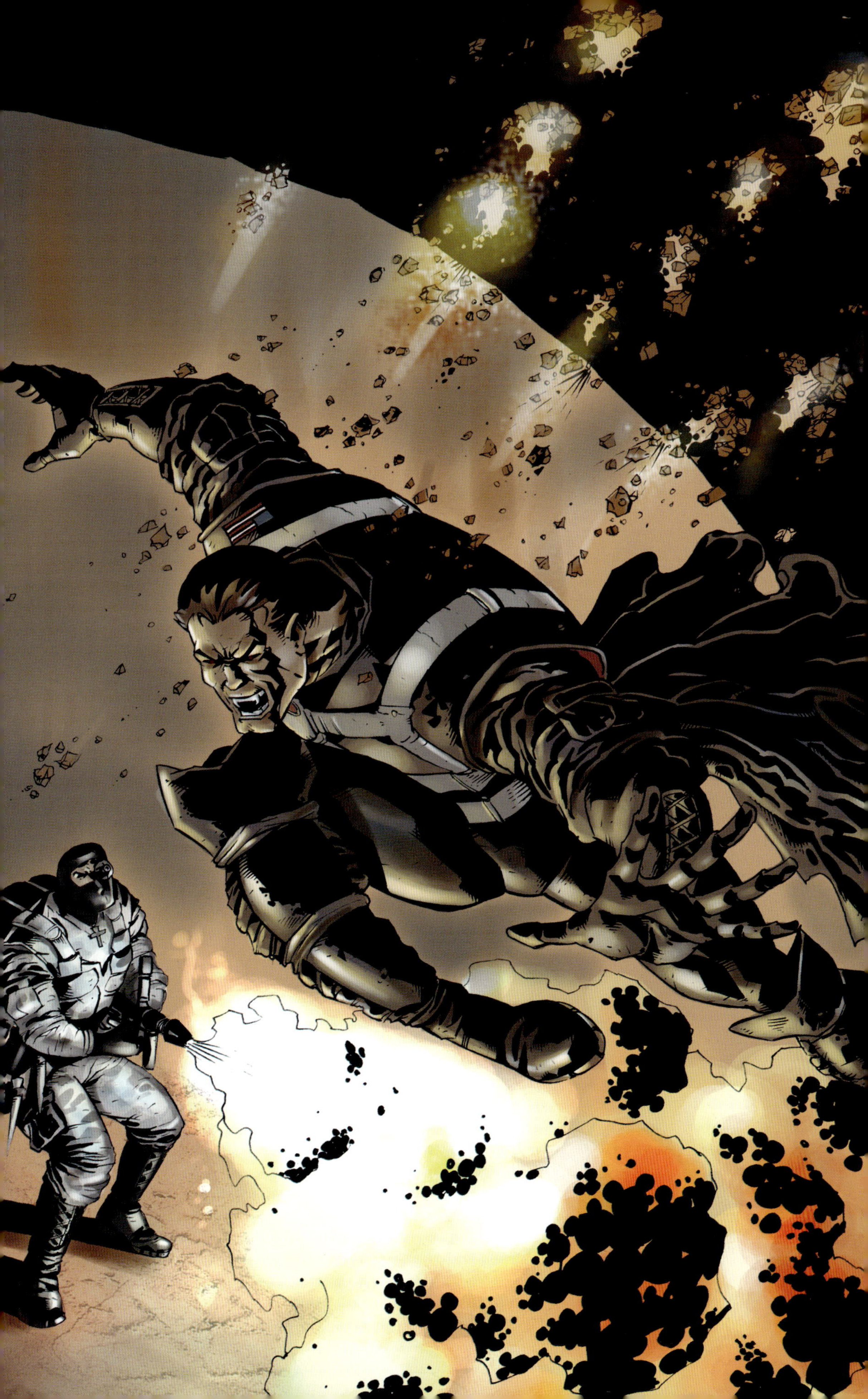

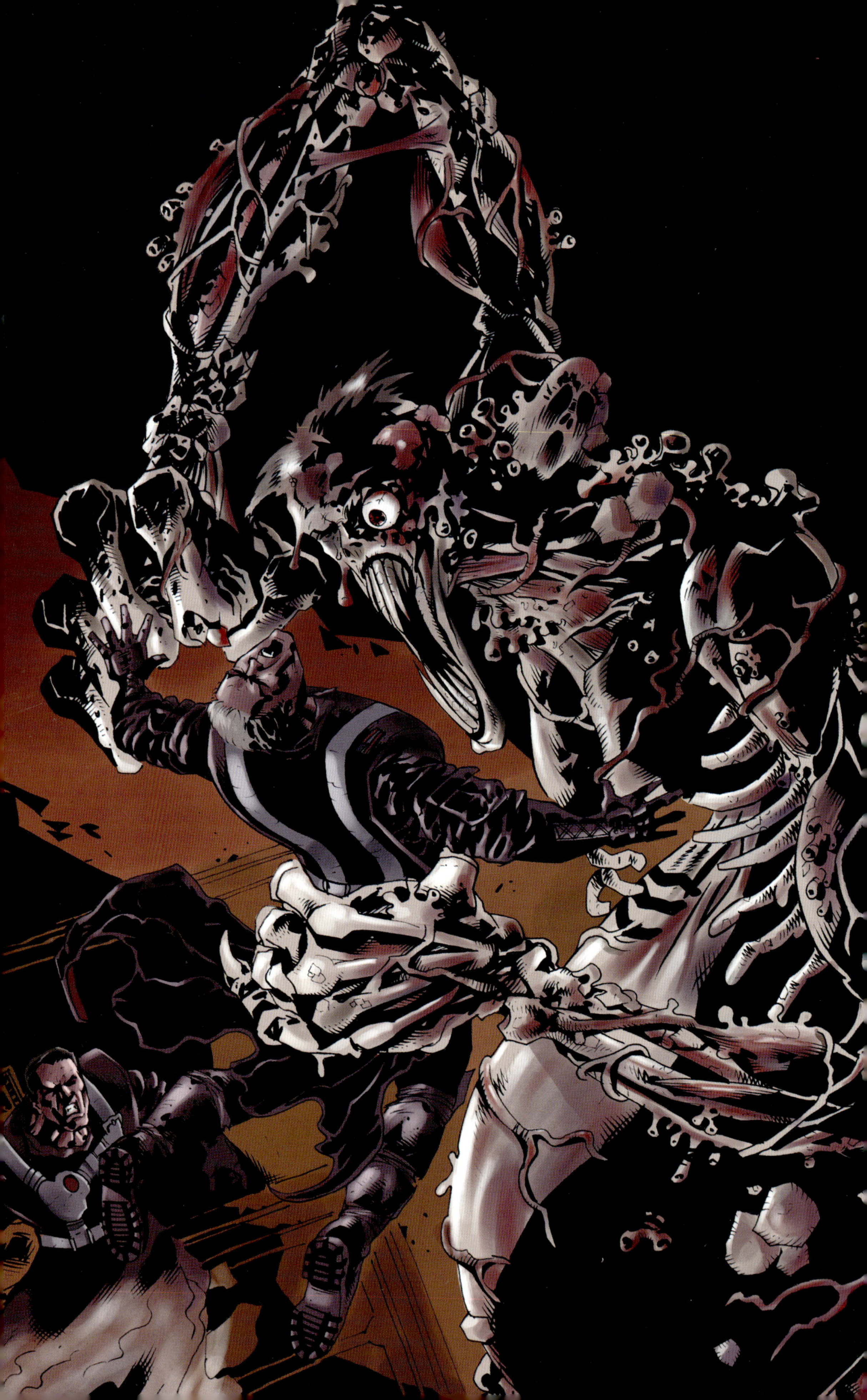